LADY OF BRASS

METHOD OF THE KILL
BOOK TWO

JONATHAN MALONEY

SKYNATION PUBLISHING

Lady of Brass

(Method of the Kill #2)

Edited by Paris Thompson

Cover design by Dayna Watson

ISBN 978-1-7640541-0-2 (paperback)

ISBN 978-1-7640541-1-9 (hardcover)

ISBN 978-1-7640541-2-6 (digital online)

www.skynation.info

For Blue, who taught me to finish what I started.
For Pop Jack, who showed me the majesty of patience.
Tis the Legend, and Himself.

Russell Square
British Museum
Lincoln's Inn Fields
Waterloo Bridge
Trafalgar Square
Charing Cross Rail
And Foot Bridge
300
3000
5700

THE WARDS

CRIPPLEGATE
Finsbury Circus
St Paul's Cathedral
Southwark Bridge
London Bridge
300
3000
5700

OF LONDON

Prelude

An Open Grave, Unanswered

It could be said that a funeral is a place of silence lacking in resolutions.

Confronted with a grave, a coffin, and the presence of the one who is, in fact, no longer *present*, there are always questions to be asked. Some are simple and cold, prying and blunt, that speak loudly of the one who asks. Others are complicated, and bear with them a pain that comes from never knowing the answer. It is a time of doubt and wondering, where no revelations are forthcoming.

Not merely for the fact that the one who has such truths can in no way bring them forth, but because it *does not do* to ask questions in a time of grief. No matter how many of them there might be, it would not be right to ask the why, the where, the how. Under the weight of that oppressive atmosphere, the staunchest would bite their tongue, bury their words, and offer only condolences instead.

Especially now, at this particular grave. So many curiosities sang in the hearts of those that bore stoic witness. Even the ignorant could observe the discordance, and fill their mind with thoughts of the who, and why, and how—who the coffin was for, a coffin that was so small and light, so richly lacquered and gilded. Why there were not tears, but instead shattered quiet, a place where realisation had not yet fully come to recompense, and the stunned state of grief drowned out all else. And how, how it had all come to be. The air was heavier than most, the shadow of a life lived to less than its full potential, nor to the cusp of it.

And yet for all that weight, there were no questions asked. It was dangerous to ask them here... for far more reasons than simply manners. There were names at this funeral, names belonging to individuals who had borne them in their bloodline for centuries, and they did not tolerate curiosity, idle or otherwise. They did not entertain even the *idea* of inquiry—at least, when they were the ones being asked.

In the midst of that grey misery of mourning, one individual however *was* asking them, and with ferocity. Asking, but of themselves. Asking and creating answers—forcing those responses to be reality would be a problem for another person, but not for this one. This individual had the means, and the power, and the will. But that was nothing compared to the force of their *right*.

This individual understood that there were rules, and laws. There always was, but the truth was they were for everyone else. Those who made the laws did not obey them. They made them so that *others* would be forced to live under them, and thus preserve things as they should be—power in the hands of those who wield it, and never in the hands of those who must work under them. So it had been for centuries. So it would always be.

This situation then, was simple. There were rules. And they

would be ignored, for only a fool allowed things meant for lesser folk to interfere with what they willed to be so.

They had already begun to that very effect. The coffin held what it needed to and nothing more. No one saw anything they were not supposed to. No one dared voice their questions, knowing that they would not be answered. The will of that which wished the thing done was absolute.

And so, a new story began where one had ended.

Chapter 1

A Nail in a Broken Heart

The sun was setting.

Over a city made into a smear, a horizon of haze and foul smells were rendered visible. Smoke stacks belched out coal smog, which hung in the air before drifting down to drown the unfortunate in filth. Split by a river and spreading like an open wound, oozing and suppurating, London city snarled and spat, coughing its tar-filled lungs into the face of the cloudy, mourning sky.

Even at its best, London city in the last years of the nineteenth century was always lacking. The finest architecture, or most well tended parks would always have something that lingered in the corners; the presence of an unfortunate reminder that this, the oldest and grandest city in England, had spent the better part of nearly two thousand years accumulating a layer of grime and corruption that could not be pried out of it with any amount of effort. And though there surely had been such an effort made in the past, a concerted desire to try and conceal the centuries old foulness here and there, in some places such effort had been forgotten. And in some, it had never been tried at all.

Bugsby's Marshes were located on a curled crone's finger of land thrust into the path of the river Thames, bearing the brunt on both sides of muck brought in and out with the tide. The upper, and oft ignored, corner of Greenwich, whichever way the wind blew, it brought with it the soot and stink of different industry, all mixed in with the perpetual reek of the turbid river.

It was here that people eked out a life which was disregarded by those around them. Clinging to the riverbank and awash in the stench of it, buildings huddled amidst the ruin. Some were old, wrought of stone and of such foundations that they had been reused and refitted and given new purpose for centuries. Some were nothing more than shacks, cobbled together out of refuse and rubbish.

Most were something in between. Decrepit buildings, origins lost to time, gradually sinking into the muck that they were set upon, being consumed by the passage of years into the soft, water-laden mud. They were endlessly crumbling, repaired in only the loosest fashion by the flotsam that swept up on the tide. Bits of broken ships that had sunk any number of years ago were prominent in the creation of walls, or roofs—sun bleached timbers with only the faintest echoes of the desperate prayers and screams of the men who had drowned trying to cling to them. The ghosts of the dead were thick in that stinking marsh, silent but knowing, witnessing the slow demise of all that dwelt in the wretched swamp's embrace.

Nestled in the depths of this stench and morass, jutting against the water and crowded on both sides by buildings that were in equal measure ruins, was a waterfront dive. Presumably at some point in the past, some enterprising soul had decided that what people really needed in the Bugsby's Marshes was a convenient spot for them to drink and forget that they were actually *in* the Bugsby's Marshes. It was a rundown building made of weatherworn timbers, run through with dry rot and held together only by the rust clinging to the nails that would likely shatter under the most weightless of pressures.

Nevertheless, someone dwelt there. The latest in a line of proprietors that held onto the place because no one would ever buy it from them; a burly man, with scars and burns up his bared forearms, and a protruding lower jaw that thrust out pugnaciously at the whole world. He stood behind his bar, bereft of patrons and drinks both, and was seemingly satisfied with it. The common room was small, with a staircase leading to the gloomy rooms above that seemed to have been never used, lit by a couple of lanterns that were fitful even in the sunset light. The fireplace was full of dried firewood but unused—kept and ready for a particularly cold night, but in this early summer those were a far off future, even in infamously unseasonable London.

So when the scrape of the door, leading out to the river of mud that was the exterior street, was heard, the air of the place turned hard, wary, and unsure, full of suspicion and caged paranoia. A young man in a coat a size too large for him slipped inside, closing the door behind him before approaching the bar. He walked with a peculiar nervousness in his step that he was trying to overcome by being overtly bold, but instead, it served to make him appear even more out of place by his uncomfortable energy. He was young, handsome in an ordinary sort of way, with a shock of mousey blonde hair and a smile that radiated terror as he approached the barman, whose battered face twisted yet further in a sign of silent displeasure. The approaching youth seemed to have that effect on people.

"Good evening, sir!" he said with only a *trace* of a squeak in his tone. "Might I trouble you for a dram of warming spirit? I fear I have a bit of a thirst." A few small coins were laid on the bar, to counter the spectacularly awkward exchange.

The barman flicked his gaze down to them without uncrossing his arms, and the request hung in the air long after its echoes faded. One could not help but consider that this scenario was something unheard of in this nameless bar, and as such the dulled universe needed a moment to filter this occurrence into the mind of the silent barman. The overlarge jaw worked, grinding on blackened teeth. A syllable was grunted in response, before the scarred arms unfolded. The figure started to move, with a slowness that creaked as badly as the stool upon which the newcomer sat himself, gingerly testing the weight to see if it was about to collapse and, unable to reach a satisfactory conclusion, chose instead to stand.

The newcomer looked around. His gaze lingering briefly on the upstairs rooms, before drifting over the rest of the establishment. Customarily, this was the moment where one made a polite mention of the place they were in, finding some words to try and compliment the surroundings. This was not possible, and such words were choked out of the lungs instead, blasted out by the sheer magnitude of such an insurmountable lie to overcome. A darkened glass with an even darker, unknown rotgut sloshing around in it was thrust towards him and the coins snatched up, as the young man offered a hand, finally introducing himself and, in so doing, setting the stage for the act to come.

"How do you do, sir? My name is Bartholomew Bartleby, but you may call me Mister Barty."

A cheerful tone, and a hopeful one, as that hand remained out, trembling with nervous energy. The barman stared at it, then at the face it belonged to with its terrified, anxious grin and, in defiance to all evidence to the contrary, reached out with one large and sweating hand more akin to a paw, and shook Barty's own once with polite camaraderie.

"S'Bob," he mumbled out, and that seemed to be it. There may have been any number of nicknames given to the fellow, but they were not to be shared, it appeared.

Barty nodded in acceptance, wiping his hand as surreptitiously as he could on his coat. Introductions were aside and yet for all the humble simplicity of the barman's moniker, Barty remained quite fearful. He had come to this nameless bar with a purpose, and it was time to make that apparent.

"You will have to forgive me, Goodman Bob," Barty started apologetically, granting a title to the man before him that was in defiance of all evidence. "But it would appear that you are not having much business as of late." He glanced around the common room, as though in the time since he had arrived, affirmation to the alternative might have appeared. It had not. "A slow season, I take it?"

A grunted reply, as a cloth that *might* have been clean once was produced to wipe ineffectually at a bar top that refused such petty advances.

"S'right. And the one before that. One before that, too. Far back as I can remember." Bob's voice had more gravel in it than a mine pit, rasping and sour. He hawked and spat into his tin, a faint *ting* of a marksman at work clanging off the side. There was a pause, but no conversation followed. The barman kept his secrets and instead chewed on whatever horrible thing was lodged in his cheek, squinting at the youth in front of him, who had sniffed at his drink before hurriedly putting it down as it set his eyes to watering.

Barty, meanwhile, was struggling somewhat. Not simply because the man before him was not exactly talkative, but for other reasons that he knew would become apparent the longer he took. He coughed into his fist and tried a different tactic. "Good sir. I was wondering if you could help me with something?" He kept his tone polite, but there was an edge of strain to it. "I was wondering if—"

The barman cut him short. "Ye aren't from around here, are ye?" he grunted, turning to spit once again. Barty hesitated, then shook his head. The barman made a bestial sound in the affirmative, and resumed his endless and futile task of cleaning the counter. "Iff'n ye were, ye would be knowin' ye don't ask for help around here. Folks are clear out of it. So why don't ye finish that drink and head on out, Mister? Let's forget you wandered in here." The last words came out in a growl and, to emphasise his point, the barman reached beneath the countertop and pulled out a long, weathered billy club, wrapped with lead at the end. Setting it on the bar between himself and Barty, he spread his hands to the sides and leaned forward, his eyes narrowing even more so. He let the moment hang. The sight of the weapon made his argument for him.

This, typically, was where conversation ended. In normal circumstances, a person as skinny and as small as Bartholomew Bartleby would cower and shrink, slipping away while mumbling apologies and perhaps leaving the tell-tale scent of an open privy in their wake. If they were suicidal, they would react with offense and try to impose some sort of non-existent authority. But Bartholomew Bartleby reacted in neither of those ways, because he was Bartholomew Bartleby. Or, as he was known to a community far more terrifying than the man before him, he was Mister Barty.

Barty took a deep breath and leaned back, giving the man before him a hard look. He reached for the drink before him, and knowing he would regret it later, swallowed it with the air of one resigned to his fate, before setting the glass down with a *clink*. After swallowing the foul fire, he counted to three, and exhaled. He spoke then in a quiet voice, softened to a whisper, as though he was afraid of being overheard.

"Two days ago, a young woman went missing from her family estate," Barty said, holding eye contact as the barman froze in place, his chewing ceasing immediately. "She is being searched for throughout the city, and talked about on every corner. Her father is very upset."

There was nothing but silence, the pressure of held breath tightening the air. The building creaked again, wood shifting and groaning as the dying place settled a little more. Barty held the stare of the man before him, who was the first to look away with a shrug, taking the glass that his lonely patron had emptied.

"Whats'it matter to me, then?" he grunted defensively. He put the glass away without cleaning it and did not refill it, setting his hands on the bar once more, closer to the billy club. "That's a toff's problem, not got nothing to do with me."

The threat of violence still hung in the air. As before, that would normally be enough for most people. But Barty had been in the presence of far greater violence for months already. It held less terror for him now, as much as that fact disturbed him. He sighed, and shook his head. "You may say so, sir. But I am afraid to say it is about to *very much* become your problem."

Barty leaned forward. "The young woman is named Lady Catherine. She is beautiful, vivacious, and in love with someone whom, according to her family, and perhaps more than just them, she should not be. Lady Catherine and her lover are, from all accounts, on their way to travel far, far away where her family cannot find her." He took a deep breath. "There are some very, very cruel people coming after her and her lover, sir. I am hoping that by finding them first, any unnecessary bloodshed can be avoided."

The barman froze. His tightened jaw wavered. His chewing remained stilled. And as Barty watched, his gaze flicked up and to the left, to the rooms above. But Barty had known that from the moment the man had first gone still; as soon as he had mentioned the missing girl, the air had been thickening, and the creaking of the building had gone quiet. He let out a breath and pressed onwards.

"I would very much like to avoid violence, Goodman... Bob," Barty said quietly. Seeing a hand reach for the billy club, he held up both of his own. "Not from me," he said hurriedly. "I am talking about other people who will come after me. People who will not take no for an answer." A bead of sweat dripped down the barman's temple. The room darkened as the sun slipped lower. "He is a friend of yours. I know he is. This is for his sake, too." Barty's tone was hushed, but fraught with a growing urgency. Time was running out.

The bulky man's expression twitched once again, something wavering around the edges of it this time—a mixture of anger and anxiousness. The squinted eyes looked hesitant for a moment, and Barty tried again.

"They are going to try and run out the window escape, out to the boat on the docks," he said in a tone that was unhappy, watching the barman steadily. "But it is too late for that. It is too late to run." He reached out slowly, and placed a hand on the billy club, even though if the man opposite him made even a slight effort, he could yank it clear. "The best thing that can happen right now is that you call your friend and Lady Catherine down, so he and I can talk. Please. Call them down." The moment hung in the air. The ruined bar held its stale breath.

The barman twitched again. And this time his features *shift-ed*. Rippling like water on a pond, they warped and ran, his eyes changing to all manner of colours. They let go of the club and spun to the upstairs, while Barty remained where he was, his expression falling, as the moment snapped and fell to ruin. "Miska! Catherine! RUN!" The rasping, gravelly voice had changed, becoming something altogether younger, clearer, and desperate.

Barty's shoulders slumped as there was a sudden eruption

of commotion upstairs; the sound of running feet, stomping, and frantic movement. "I am sorry," he said, and he meant it, his expression one of misery. "But I did tell you it was too late." There was a scream—a woman's scream, high-pitched and frightened—and then the scene exploded into a flurry of wrath and fury.

The walls of the rooms were made of wood so ancient it had turned brittle and fragile with rot, serving as nothing more than a vague sense of privacy rather than any sort of protection. So when the two figures grappling with each other crashed into it, they simply continued on, through the flimsy railing of the upper balcony, then crashing down through a table below, sending splinters and shards in every direction, along with familiar, vitriolic cursing.

Jean Reynard rolled clear of the wreck, swearing the air around him black as he staggered to his feet. The figure with whom he had come flying was writhing, but in a strange way that spoke not of pain but of something else, of change and transformation, all the while growing larger. Jean did not give them a chance. He snatched up a chair from beside him and started to beat the shapeshifting figure, each blow shattering the chair further as he continued to curse, furious and loud.

"Jean! Stop!" Barty shouted from where he huddled against the bar, shielding his head with both hands. "You'll kill him!"

Jean halted, holding the broken remnants of the chair in both hands. "Haven't damn well shot him yet, have I?" He was bloodied on his brow and mouth, his expression one of wrath. Turning back to the recumbent figure, he raised the fragments of the chair again to continue the beating, but instead was flung away, landing heavily against the bar next to the cowering Barty with a grunt of irritation and pain merging together.

"And I bloody well still should," Jean snarled as he pushed himself up. The figure he had come through the wall with warped like a horizon on a hot summer's day, and became a great, hulking shape—a simulacrum of one of the many who worked the docks and darker streets of London, their clothes straining as they grew bigger. Whatever they had been when they went through the wall, they were now a scarred, brawny veteran of bar brawls and other viciousness. Barty, who had seen quite enough of that sort of thing to last him a lifetime, scrambled to the side.

The barman, still standing behind the bar, grabbed the billy club and finally roused into action. He swung, but Jean was faster. With the awareness of all too many battles, he caught the blow and wrenched the club out of the air with one hand. In the same movement he reached forward, grabbed the barman who called himself Bob by the back of his head, and brought him to kiss the counter in a way that left him both breathless and bereft of his front teeth. Deciding then and there that such was enough, even as their features twisted and rippled, they slumped back with a groan behind the bar.

Jean turned on the spot to the figure behind him, which had now pulled itself to its full height. While Jean was hardly a short man by any means, this new form of whoever it was he had been grappling with now was a good hands length taller than he was. Their features were twisted, mottled, near unrecognisable as human. It was a face of rage and desperation and terror, but there was also a youthful look to the eyes, an almost innocent inexperience and confusion that simply did not fit the face at all. They raised both fists in readiness, and Jean straightened. Holding the club he had wrenched free a moment ago, he seemed to think better of it and tossed it to the ground. Leaning back and arching his spine, he reached behind the bar and plucked up the same bottle of whatever horrible booze that Barty had forced himself to drink. Standing there, Jean yanked the cork out with his teeth, and guzzled from the bottle, all the while locking eyes on the figure opposite him. He raised his free hand and beckoned, before tossing the bottle to the corner and stood there, grinning.

There was something in that grin that made people pause. It was wide, sharp, and hateful, edged in razors and malice. Jean's eyes lit up, burning with the fire of rage within them that made them bright, cold, and painful. No sane man would step to a smile like that—it would be akin to walking into the path of a falling axe without flinching. But Jean's target was, while not driven from sanity, absolutely at the cusp of their desperation. They charged. Jean moved in to meet them.

Barty ducked for cover as the bar became a place of war. A chair flew over his head and smashed a row of empty bottles as he cowered. He felt the weight of the revolver in his coat and forced himself not to grab for it. This was not the right time, even now. This was not that sort of story, even if he already hated how it was going.

A table flew through the air, barely missing him. There were sounds like a rack of meat being hit with an iron bar and grunts of pain. A rib snapped somewhere, with the familiar muffled *thwap-crack* sound that Barty had, to his displeasure, become familiar with. And then a woman screamed, as Barty turned to look.

"MISKA! STOP!"

The scene was a tableau. A beautiful young woman, with simple clothes and stunningly bright, long blonde hair, was standing at the top of the stairs, her face streaked with tears and terror. Jean and the figure he was fighting were frozen in the moment, both about to swing on the other, but the cry of the young woman had slammed down on them both and held them in place, as surely as manacles and chains. Barty watched the figure whom Jean was fighting staring at the young woman—Lady Catherine, of course—and then shuddered as he changed, shrinking, his features distorting, as his eyes turned a shade of bright, shining yellow and his skin became a smooth grey. He subsided, and Barty saw defeat and shame on his face.

Jean Reynard, however, proceeded to be Jean Reynard about the whole matter. If nothing else, he never believed in giving his enemies a second chance.

He reached out like a striking serpent to grab a miraculously unbroken lantern, and flung it underarm across the room to the open, unlit fireplace. It exploded in a shower of glass and flame, the ancient, dried wood laid in the grate catching and flaring upwards, casting the room in shadows. The man with yellow eyes and grey skin flinched and raised his hands to ward off a blow, as Jean reached into his coat—but he spun not towards the figure, but away, towards the large dark shadow that the fire behind them cast against the wall.

Pulling a long, black nail from the depths of his coat, Jean slammed it into the shadow with one hand and hammered it home with his open palm, even as Miska shrieked impossibly high and shrill before he collapsed in pain and went down on both knees, writhing and whimpering.

Catherine screamed and ran down the stairs, as Barty pushed himself out of the corner, but he was too late to intercept her. Sobbing, she ran to the stricken figure, calling out his name. "Miska! Oh, Miska, what has he done to you?"

It was Jean who answered her, even as he pulled a cigarette from the interior of his coat alongside a match, looking down at the pair of them dispassionately. "Black iron. He cannot take the touch of it. Not to any part of him." He said it with dispassionate cruelty, while behind him, the shadow of the supine, writhing Miska remained where it was. Pinned to the wall by the nail at its heart, flailing and soundlessly screaming, it struggled to free itself, clutching at the nail and unable to pull it out. Barty shuddered at the awful sight. Jean, who had seen more awful sights than he cared to bother recalling, did not look at it as he lit his match upon the bar and set the end of his cigarette alight, flaring smoke soon after out his nostrils. "Works wonders upon changelings."

Miska, the changeling in question, wrenched his head towards Jean. His face was lined now with feathers, his nose more akin to a beak. The eyes were yellow all through with no iris, the black pupils huge as tears flowed from them in his agony. "Don't hurt her. I'll kill you if you hurt her."

"We are not here to hurt her!" Barty blurted out. "We are here to take her home." He stepped forward. This was all wrong. The Lady Catherine was distraught, but her touch on the monstrous looking Miska was nothing short of loving. She knelt at his side with his head in her lap, cradling him, one hand holding both of his while she ran her fingers through his hair, which was also woven through with feathers. While still in pain, he looked up at her with an expression that was agonised for more reasons than just physical trauma.

"You are... you are not frightened of him? You know what he is?" Barty could not keep the surprise out of his voice. Both of the stricken lovers looked at him with equal parts helpless frustration and defiance, as Jean barked a harsh laugh to one side.

"Of course she does." His tone was scathing in its contempt as he stalked away from the spot. He kicked a chair with a boot to set it back upright, taking a seat upon it and looking down at the captured duo. "She knows full well just what he is. And I would wager she did from the start." His harsher tone faded as the pair cowered, leaning forward and holding his cigarette in one hand. He blew harsh smoke to one side, staring down at the broken couple while he spoke to Barty without looking at him. "What then, did you think would happen? That by word alone you would break the back of true love, cut a single heart back into two with just some magic words? Love is a stronger thing than that, and much more poisonous, too." He sounded, despite all his violence and the blood that ran down his scalp from a wound that had not yet clot, strangely melancholic. There was no reading his expression.

"It was a damn sight better than what *you* wanted to do, Jean," Barty snapped back. He had come here hoping to speak to both of them, to reveal the truth of Lady Catherine's lover—a shapeshifting changeling, born of the world of secrets and hidden mysteries, who could take on other forms at will. He had believed as much as Catherine's father, the Lord Beauchamp, that she had been bewitched and deceived into loving a man who was merely pretending to be something he was not. He had hoped to reveal the truth and end the matter peacefully, with her willingly returning home to her father. A misadventure brought to a peaceful end, and with lessons learned amongst hearts broken.

Jean had first been called upon by the police, then the Beauchamp household, in order to return their errant daughter. And he had done so, when every other effort to follow a man who could change his face had turned up blank. But Jean had questions others did not know to ask, along with a blunt and violent approach to getting answers, until Barty finally pleaded for the chance to do things his way. Jean had told him he had until they tried to run. And from the way he had positioned himself, taking advantage of Barty's distraction due to his conversation with the barman as he had tried to negotiate, he had known all along that this was where things would end. Barty hated it.

He moved to the wall and wrenched the nail out of it, unable to watch the shadow screaming silently any longer. The shade shuddered and slithered to the floor. There was a strange feeling of relief, amidst aching hurt, that passed through Barty as it flowed away, and the nail in his hand felt strangely hot and heavier than he expected. He shoved it in his pocket and moved to stand beside Jean, holding up both his hands in useless apology while the two errant lovers, one human and one something else, huddled together in defeat.

"I truly did not wish for things to come to this," Barty said, after a moment of awkward hesitation. "I had hoped—"

"If you did not want for violence, then perhaps you would have been better served keeping elsewhere, and *letting us go*," Lady Catherine snapped with tear-streaked defiance. "As for my father, I will *not* be going back to him. Why could you not leave us alone?"

Barty opened his mouth, but it was Jean who leaned forward, his expression hardening as he spoke in his harsh, growling voice. "Six o'clock, on the Victoria dock. Passage on the *Diligence*, correct?" The pair froze once again, staring at him, as Jean continued, "There are already men on the ship and on the docks, waiting for you. They might not know you, changeling, but you cannot hide that face of yours enough so that they would not know you, Lady Catherine." Jean shook his head. "They were going to drag you back to your father in a sack, while cutting his throat and leaving him to sink on the tide." He raised one hand and pointed to the door to which Barty had first crossed through. "There was one watching the door to this place. I did not even bother looking for you, I looked for them. And they had you in their hand well before I arrived on the scene."

"Before *we* arrived," Barty interjected, but Jean simply grunted dismissively. The changeling Miska groaned and pushed himself upright, despite the efforts of his lover to keep him close to her.

"Where? Where is he?" His features were inhuman, but Barty was struck that despite all that, his voice was melodious, even beautiful, wrought through with the emotions he was struggling with.

Jean waved a hand in irritated dismissal. "Asleep and trussed up in the alleyway opposite. He will not be going anywhere to report on what is happening here. And just as well."

The changeling shivered, and then his features wavered once more before settling. They were similar to his inhuman, true form, but lacking the monstrous traits, his eyes taking on an entirely normal brown, his features fine and slender. He was, at least in that form, a terribly handsome young man, and Barty could not help but feel a fresh surge of sympathy.

"We have done nothing wrong, sir," Miska said quietly, his tone firm. "We love one another." He looked to the Lady Catherine then, his expression melting into adoration. "She knew me from the moment she saw me, even when my face was not mine."

The young woman, even in the midst of her heartbreak, smiled at him, touching his cheek with a gentle hand. It was a sweet, loving moment and thus Jean shattered it with a grunted snort of annoyance.

"That is all well and good, but I was not conscripted to hear a story of adolescent romance. I was told to bring a young woman back home, by any means possible. And I will do so."

They both bristled at that, but Jean levelled an accusing finger into the face of Miska and spoke harshly. "You know who and what I am, boy. You know full well I could have had you face down in the dirt to never rise again, and the lady trussed up in a sack if I so chose. So do not seek to test me further." The finger remained pointed, rigid and unmoving in the air, as the changeling opened his mouth, and then slowly closed it again. Jean nodded, and moved the hand away. "You can thank my ever inconvenient and perpetually useless assistant for the fact that I have, for the time being, tried a more diplomatic approach than what I am normally known for." His tone was dry, and he let the statement linger as he inhaled on the cigarette, his lip curling as he set the end of it into an inferno, before exhaling the smoke out his nostrils.

Barty stood smarting and red-faced to one side after Jean's less-than-kind description, as the man went on, "You will be going back to your father this evening, girl. And you, feyblood, will be allowed to leave here. With your fellow from behind the bar." He glanced over his shoulder to where the forgotten former barman still lay in silence, before resuming addressing the pair. "He will wake in a little while. Get him out of here, and get him rested. But you want to be well gone before dawn, before the others come looking for you." His jaw worked. "Having familiarity with your other pursuers, and how fervently they desire to be paid for their efforts, they will be most forthcoming in violence should they find you."

"I would fight one or a thousand of them if I had to, to protect my love," Miska responded with fierce determination, but Jean laughed at him derisively.

"You could not best me and there was but one of me, boy," he spat scornfully, pulling the cigarette out of his mouth and flicking it to the fire. "You amused me up until now, and I let you get your frustrations out, but I will give you this single warning. You know my name, and what I have done. *Do not test me further.*" His voice dropped to a stern growl, and his eyes narrowed. In the depths of his coat were visible various holsters and other means of holding weaponry, but they were less threatening than the look on his face.

Barty knew that look. Jean gave no second chances. "I am afraid he means it," Barty said quietly. "Please." He did not try to argue out of it. He did not try to stop the coiled threat of violence at his side. He had tried and failed too many times before now to know the futility of it.

Something about the look on his face reached through to the shapeshifting youth before them. His face twisted as he buckled, crumbling as his bravery quailed. *You are not a killer. But he is*, Barty thought to himself. *And you know it, all too well. They all do.*

Jean grunted, nodding as though an agreement had been reached, but the young Lady Catherine, unheeded and ignored up until this point, was herself not yet done. She pushed herself to her feet with an attitude of bridled fury borne of heartbreak and glared down at Jean, her eyes full of tears and helpless rage.

"And I get no say in this? I am as much able to decide my fate as a lamb led to slaughter?" She looked down at Miska, her expression torn and hurt to see him so cowed, before snapping a glare back to Jean and Barty. "I have had my life decided for me by men, who have claimed to know better than I do, who believe that my own decisions are nothing but mistakes. And now that I make a choice of my own, fully aware and knowing, I am told I cannot? Who are you to do so? How *dare* you? How dare you both!"

Barty squirmed under the weight of her wrath. Jean, however, simply leaned back in his seat and gave her a long, silent look before replying. "I was not aware I was here to educate someone on *how the world is*." His tone was flatly incredulous. "You are the daughter of a peer. Your life is not yours. It belongs to those of your name and you cannot change it. None of us can." He pushed himself to his feet, hand moving to the holstered gun at his side. "The world now is thus. You are going home. If you do not, one way or another, your lover dies." His hand remained on the grip, but he did not draw it. Whatever message he wished to relay was clearly made.

The silence lingered, but Catherine did not falter. She stood in stark, stilled defiance, a woman with no power left to her, standing against a man armed and fiercely dangerous, she did not blink and she did not cower. For all her stillness, even against the wrathful entity that was Jean Reynard, her silent rage was the greater.

Barty was watching Miska's face in that exchange, and in the threatening stillness afterwards. He saw the changeling's naked emotions play over their features in a rippling wave, before realisation came crashing down at the end. Jean was implacable, as Barty well knew. Though his time with him had been both brief and fraught with violence, it was clear that the changeling knew it too. Barty watched him crumble, and sink inwards as the weight of the matter broke him down. When he spoke, his voice was hoarse, forced through the throat as though choked by the agony each word was costing him, far greater than his physical injuries.

"Go with him, Catherine. While there is time." He did not look up, staring at the ground with the posture of a broken man.

The young woman looked shocked, taking a step back.

"You... you cannot mean that, Miska. You said—"

Her shaking voice was cut off by Miska, his voice rising in volume, in a sharp, black, and bitter tone. "I said a great many things, Lady Catherine. And I wish that they were all to come true." He looked over at Jean then, his expression a mixture of despair and hopeless hatred. His expression melted and changed once more, back into the feathered, inhuman features that were his true shape—a reality painfully revealed, and confronted as he went on, "But he is right. It... it was naught but a dream. We have to wake up and face the reality." He shook his head, which once again lowered. "Go home, Catherine. We cannot stop him, let alone the rest."

The young noblewoman's face was a moving picture of overwhelming emotion, twisting from disbelief to anger and other feelings so deep and potent that they stole all her words from her. Before Barty's eyes she seemed to wilt, the fierce desperation and defiance melting out of her and leaving a dulled, lifeless visage where she took all that feeling, and locked it behind a masked expression; one that Barty could not help but think she had too many years already to practise. Even so, she struggled visibly, before turning abruptly on one heel and marching towards the exit.

Barty finally found his voice. "I can fetch your things for you, Lady—"

"No." Her tone was cold. "There is nothing here that I wish to take with me." She did not slow her pace. Jean watched her a moment, then followed after her without a word or backwards glance to the crestfallen Miska, who seemed only more crushed. So broken was he that Barty could not help but crouch beside him, tentatively reaching out to put a hand to his shoulder—the young changeling flinched and struck Barty's hand away before he could speak.

"Leave me alone. Just go away." His voice was thick with his loss.

Barty, by now, could recognise a lost cause when he saw it. He backed away, but had only taken a couple of steps before Miska spoke, his voice breaking as it did so.

"Wait... can you... can you give her this?"

Barty turned as the changeling reached up and, with a pained grimace, grasped a single black feather growing suddenly from his brow and wrenched it clear, holding it out with blood still upon the quill. Barty blinked at it for a long moment as the seated youth held it, his bright yellow eyes pleading. Without knowing why—but the burden of guilt upon him was no small part—Barty reached out and took it wordlessly. The feather was sharp-edged and dark, the threads glittering an odd shade of blue. With care, Barty placed it in his pocket and nodded, before leaving the desolate youth to his solitude.

Once outside in the street, he took a deep breath. Sucking in even the fetid air of Greenwich, laden with the reek of the Thames, was preferable to the miasma of despair that he had left behind in that nameless bar. Upon letting out the thickened air, the remnants sticking in his throat and stinging, he looked around.

The coach was there, of course. That strange and spectacular coach with its even stranger master, the unknowable entity of silver and shadow that was called Puck. Lanky and tall, crooked at odd angles and spindly, his silver hair gleamed as bright as the polished enamel of the coach which he had, he claimed, sung into existence. Lady Catherine was being helped into it by Puck, who stood wordlessly to one side with the door opened, his head lowered—something that Barty had never seen him do before. Indeed, the coachman was bereft of his terrifying smiles and knife-edged laughter in this moment, and was as sombre as Barty had ever seen him. His head lifted to Barty then, sensing that gaze upon him, and those gleaming eyes without expression held young Bartholomew Bartleby a moment before the faintest flicker of a smile appeared, edged in regrets. He slithered away then, flowing up the side of the coach in a liquid movement that was more suggestive of a serpent, and was in his seat in the space of a wink. Once more Barty shivered. Once more he wondered just what Crook, or Puck, or whatever he was truly called actually *was*. But this was not the time for knowing.

Jean was not waiting for him, clambering up into the coach with a roughness that made the structure wobble, and Barty was clumsily behind him, sitting down opposite their charge—it was hard to think of her as someone they had res-cued—and Lady Catherine stared out of a window with the distant, lifeless gaze of someone whose dreams had died. Jean said nothing. Crushed down by their shared silence, Barty's tongue was cloven to the top of his mouth as the coach slid away and along the road, with even the strange, unnatural horses that Puck was able to guide with nothing but seemingly a thought contriving to keep their clopping canter to a low, muted volume. And so the journey continued as they left the marshlands of Greenwich behind, and pressed onwards into the burrows and journeys of London itself.

It was some distance from Greenwich to Kensington, but it passed by with a surprising lack of eventfulness. The difference between the districts could not be more pronounced; the marshlands had been a stinking ruin, compared to the relatively clean streets of Kensington, one of the more well-to-do suburbs of London. Barty would seldom have imagined himself ever having business in such a place. But being in the company of Jean Reynard opened more doors than one might otherwise have either imagined, or liked.

This one had been forced open. Lord Howard Montague, who also happened to be the Chief Inspector, had sent his long suffering underling Inspector Creek to knock upon Jean's door until it buckled, and entreat him to find the young woman who now sat opposite them, pale and still as a porcelain doll. A personal favour to her father, as it were, a favour that had been called in, and to avoid trouble of Jean's own from previous misadventures—the near destruction of much of Old Bedlam being key amongst such things—he had been forced to meet with Lady Catherine Beauchamp's father. The man had spared no expense, nor had he spared any scruples either. Lord Dean Arthur Beauchamp had made it quite clear what he expected of Jean to do to young Miska for taking his daughter from him—much as he had expected the shadow lurking thugs that planned to murder him for a few blood soaked pounds sterling. Jean had made no indication one way or the other, but when the time had come, he had not done so.

As they crossed over Westminster bridge, Barty's nerve was finally gathered enough. He reached into his pocket and pulled forth the black feather that had been given to him, holding it out and speaking in an awkward, stuttering tone. "Your young man wanted for you to have this."

Lady Catherine blinked, seemingly startled out of her thoughts, pulled back from whatever lonely abyss she had placed herself. She stared blankly at the feather, and her lower lip trembled a moment before she clamped it tight and looked away once more. "I would rather not. I would sooner try and forget him entirely." Her voice was cracked, her anger searing, but it was an anger Barty recognised. A righteous fury to keep her grief at bay. "I do not wish to remember his false claims of affection," she finished bitterly, turning in her seat.

A moment of silence fell, leaving Barty awkward, but it was Jean who responded, surprising the other two occupants. "There was nothing false in what he felt. Whatever else you may be angry at him for, that should not be one of them." He was looking out the window, but turned to stare at Lady Catherine, slumped in the coach seat with his arms folded across his chest. "Hate him for his foolish dreams. Hate him for pulling you along into this mess. But love will make fools of all. Most especially men, I tend to find," he added, his tone turning sour as he looked away once more.

Lady Catherine's hands clenched into pale fists. "I would ask how you are so sure of such a thing, if you are so knowing?" Her tone was tight, controlling her storm of emotions, and the anger that her captor was now ruthlessly rousing further.

The hunter sighed, irritably, and then gave a brief, dismissive shrug. "He knew who I was the moment he laid his eyes upon me. He knew what trying to fight me would mean. And yet he did not hesitate. He stepped between you and I, and cast himself at me."

Lady Catherine gave a small sniff, turning her head away again. "I do not need protecting," she stated stiffly.

Jean's response was a hard, dismissive chuckle that had all the warmth of an icicle, and just as sharp. "We all do, at one point or another. But that is not the point I am making. A man that would spit in the face of death to protect another? That is one who would do anything for love."

She quivered. "Then why did he give up, and place me into your charge, if that is true?" There was still anger there, but now there was an undercurrent, a note of pleading. Of wanting to understand—and wanting it to be true.

But Barty had figured it out by now, the pieces clicking into place. "Because it is also love to let someone go, if the alternative is something worse. Now you do not have to grieve for him."

"Nor have his death on your conscience," Jean finished. "In the end, that was all he could give you, and all he could spare you from." He fell silent then, but there was a brooding about him, his focus turned inwards. Barty could guess where but did not dare even think it.

The young noblewoman paled yet further, if such a thing were possible. "You would have killed him then, if he had not bid me to leave?" she asked in a mixture of accusation and horror.

Jean did not look at her, staring instead out over the grey streets, the darkened corners, the world outside the window and all its secrets. "Yes, Lady Catherine. I would have. Though I would have regretted it." His tone was expressionless. He might as well have been speaking of the weather.

Lady Catherine's mask was crumbling. She cracked at her edges, her face shifting as her eyes turned watery. Wordlessly, she reached out with a pleading hand towards Barty, her palm outwards. He placed the black feather into her hand, which she clutched swiftly to herself, her straightened posture sinking as the sounds of quiet, whimpered tears filled the small space of the coach.

They rumbled on, and Barty could not help but miss the silence as he wondered if they had done the right thing this day. But as he looked upon the crying young woman before him, he had his answer.

Chapter 2

By Such Sins, Forgiveness Undone

The Beauchamp estate in Kensington was, Barty could not help but notice, a rather dour sort of place. It was walled and secluded from the main street, with iron spikes set atop the granite barrier that, while stylish, were nevertheless as spiky as they were forbidding. The rust that had formed on them ran down the blackened walls, giving the uncomfortable impression that the very stones were bleeding.

There was little ceremony as they took the gravel carriage road into the estate, passing by the rough men who opened the gate for them. Groundskeepers, they were called colloquially. But, like most of their kind, they had a jagged and hard look to them, shadowed beneath shallow brim caps and wearing tweed; they were faceless men who did the jobs around the estate, stoked the boilers, cleaned the stables, and, when the occasion called for it, broke the bones of those that needed breaking. They were men who had come up from the street and brought it with them—into the houses of the high and mighty. Because the noble born often had the need to inflict harm upon those that were beneath them, but dignity demanded they did not dirty their own knuckles while doing so. Instead the powerful paid other people for that pleasure, and it took a certain type of fellow to not only do so, but also draw great satisfaction from it.

From the looks of it, as Barty took in the figures lurking in whatever gloom they could find themselves in, Lord Beauchamp's groundskeepers, hired thugs, or whatever you wanted to call them, were the sort that drew entirely too much satisfaction indeed. They were sizing up the coach and those within it with the air of highwaymen in hope of a score, and Barty felt his anxiety rise. This was not helped in the least by Jean, who had also caught the air and tasted it. He was coiling in on himself, gathering up whatever dread violence that stirred in his soul as he sensed the promise of further blood on the air.

As the coach rolled to a halt with a trill of a whistle from Puck, Jean was already jumping out of the coach and onto the gravel below. The cluster of shadowy figures drew closer as the doors of the estate manor—a darkened building of high, barred windows and gothic architecture—opened wide, and the Lord Beauchamp stepped out.

He was, as Barty had felt on their first meeting, a thoroughly unimpressive looking man. He wore expensive clothes in the latest fashions, but did not have the form to fit them, as though his manner of dress would make up for the fact that in no way did he match up to his name nor his title. He was short and round, with too many chins and an overbite coupled with large front teeth that gave the impression of a rabbit. His daughter, in comparison, was a figure that exemplified everything that he was not, but Lord Beauchamp made up for his woeful lack of physical character in the worst and laziest way possible—by being a small-minded bully with a penchant for abuse of his power. Barty did not like him. Jean gave no indication whatsoever of how he felt about them, which to Barty's mind indicated that he loathed the man, but was doing his practised best to conceal it.

"*Finally*," the man barked. He stood at the top of the stairs leading to the door to remain physically aloof from those who would otherwise tower above him. With his hands on his hips, the rotund lordling lifted his nose. "I see you have found my misbegotten daughter at last. Hopefully not too spoiled by her adventures." Even in his spitting bile, there was a twist of a spiteful smile on his face, a triumphant one. There was a snigger from the shadowy figures around them as Barty stepped out to help Lady Catherine alight from the coach.

She ignored his hand and stepped out on her own. Though her features were marred by her grief, in this moment her expression was carved of stone. She looked up at her father with an unafraid, defiant, and cold-eyed stare that, compared to his watery gaze, far outdid his own in authority. Without a word, she strode up the steps, and past him towards the open doors. Barty could see a woman there in the shadows. A tall, middle-aged woman with the features of one beaten down by the unfortunate truth of being married to the man who continued to rant at his daughter, as she steadfastly ignored him.

"We shall be having words, Catherine! You *will* learn your place in this house!" He shook a pudgy fist at her back as she passed, then sneered and looked back to Jean and Barty, his piggish eyes turning to a squint. "Do tell me, are you so cursed as to have a rebellious upstart of a daughter, Mister Reynard?"

he asked in a lofty tone. Perhaps seeking common ground, even as his daughter and who Barty presumed to be her mother retreated into the cold, dark depths of the home that now struck Barty as being closer to a prison.

"Rebellious, yes. She learned from her mother," Jean said slowly, standing with arms folded across his chest. "She is, after all, a better teacher than I am."

The statement was ambiguous enough. Barty understood full well what Jean meant, but it flew over the short head of the Lord Beauchamp, where his extra height afforded by the front door steps availed him not. He laughed the short, confused laugh of someone who thinks they have been told a joke but did not understand, and nodded.

"Quite so, quite so! Daughters learn all their worst habits from their mothers. The weakness of the heart, the soft-minded inclination towards emotional outburst. She has learned *none* of the virtues I have tried to teach her, and has ever been defiant, disobedient, and disrespectful to her betters. Shameful, really. As a fellow father, you have my sympathies!" There was a smug, self-congratulatory tone to his voice, the tone of a man who never imagined that those in his company would disagree with him.

Jean raised a single eyebrow, the temperature around him dropping several degrees with the frostiness of his response. "If it is all the same, I would rather have my payment instead, that I might be done with our arrangement." His tone was dismissive, but his gaze flinty, no longer hiding his disgust. Whatever common ground the man before him thought they could reach was well gone, and Barty could understand why.

While Jean's relationship with his surviving child was a tempestuous one, there was no part of the statement made by the Lord Beauchamp that Barty could ever see Jean agreeing with.

Beauchamp seemed to have understood it also. He took a step back, retreating as men without spines tend to do when confronted with even the hint of a threat. Looking furtively around to the gathered men hovering about the coach—a half dozen of them now, lurking at the edges—Beauchamp gathered himself and lifted the chin that he did not have to speak down to Jean. "And what of the... miscreant that stole away my daughter? Have you *dealt* with them, then, as I requested?"

Jean squared his shoulders, as Barty nervously looked left and right between the figures standing to each side, not so close as to be deliberately dis, but not nearly so far away as to *not* be a threat. They bore unsmiling faces and many scars along with them, and Barty could make out the shapes of clubs at belts, with hands close by.

Jean did not even bother to look at them. He simply hawked and spat to one side. "He learned his place in the world, as it were. He will not trouble you again," he said shortly. "Now, as much as this was a favour for Montague, I believe this is where you pay me for my trouble."

"That does not answer my question!" Beauchamp barked. "I wanted that wretch *disposed* of, permanently. Is that what you did? Speak plainly!" He was sweating now, his nose turning purple as his eyes bulged, an ugly man made even more so, becoming ever more repulsive with each word.

Jean sighed. "Well, if we are speaking 'plainly' and 'clearly' about matters, Lord Beauchamp, then allow me to be earnest.

No, I did not indulge your spiteful little demand to kill your daughter's lover... Nor did I allow him to be murdered by the scum in your employ, either. Since you were not 'clear' in your request, I left it up to my own discretion." He gave a mirthless smile that showed too many teeth. "And if we are to continue this path of honesty, I would like to freely admit that I find your company repugnant, your favour worthless, and that I wish most earnestly that we had never crossed paths. And though your money might well carry the stink of your person upon it, it nevertheless shall spend just as well. Now avail it to me, and we can quit each other's company as we so richly desire to."

For the first time since Jean had taken Lady Catherine into his custody, he seemed pleased—refreshed, even. Lord Beauchamp on the other hand, had gone pale in his shock, and then fury. His mouth worked as his tongue twisted over itself, unable to find the words before he finally snapped, spitting wildly as he shrieked in response. "How *dare* you speak to me like that! Men! Get this filth off my property immediately!" He gestured sharply, waving the gathered groundskeepers to move in—and, with the sauntering, confident step of men used to such things, they strode forward.

Barty quailed and shrank back. Jean, on the other hand, had an immediate solution to the problem, in that he smoothly drew his pistol from his coat and shot the closest man in the knee in one clean, practised gesture. Even as the fellow went down howling, the gunshot echoing around the estate, the rest of the groundskeepers evaluating their heavy wooden clubs against the steady hand and smoking revolver that held it, and coming up short in comparison. They reconsidered their choices and scrambled back from the scene, while the Lord Beauchamp stood bug-eyed in the realisation of his underestimation of Jean Reynard.

When the screaming had died down to jaw-clenched whimpering, as the floored man held onto his shattered leg with both hands, Jean kept his eye on Lord Beauchamp and spoke flatly. "Two minutes, I would wager."

The stunned Beauchamp blinked in wide eyed bewilderment. "For... for what?"

Jean kept the revolver out, reaching into his coat to pull out a second firearm with his left hand, a twin-barrelled pistol of an older style and much heavier calibre. Whereas the revolver would punch a bloody hole through someone, this heavy contraption was designed to remove limbs in the ugliest way possible. "Two minutes until the police arrive to investigate the gunshot. Two minutes until you'll have to explain to Lord Montague how things got so *twisted* around. Two minutes until your daughter fleeing your house and bringing it into disrepute becomes common knowledge, Lord Beauchamp... unless you bring me what I am owed." He let the knowledge hang in the air for a moment. A distant whistle was heard, maybe that of the police; this was Kensington after all. There were always police nearby to keep the riff raff out, to where they could commit crimes out of sight of the rich. "The clock is ticking, Lord Beauchamp," Jean emphasised. He pulled the hammer back on the second, heavier pistol. "You best hurry while you can."

The seconds ticked by. Lord Beauchamp was confronted with the inexorable reality of a man who turned to violence without fear of consequence, with an ease that left all in his company distinctly uncomfortable. Lord Beauchamp was, while more foolish than most and more stupid than many, not so much of either as to not realise that the one before him meant every word. Beyond that, the reality of being alone save for the armed, cold blooded madman before him was a pressing fact that readily presented that he was not, in fact, equipped to deal with the matter. Lord Beauchamp hired other men to do work for him. He was a man who made decisions—small-minded, mean and cruel decisions that were born out of the petty malice that made up his persona, and Barty watched all of this be written upon his pathetic features before he came to the inevitable decision, which was to make this all go away as quickly as possible.

It took but moments after that. Money changed hands swiftly. Jean holstered his firearms and departed as the Lord Beauchamp scurried back into his manor, while his whimpering, crippled groundskeeper was dragged away to whatever poor care he might be afforded. The carriage departed just before any police arrived and embarrassing questions were asked about an accidental gunshot. Barty was struck into silence, sat opposite Jean, while above, Puck whistled cheerfully at some private, terrible amusement. The last thing Barty saw before they turned out of the yard, was a pale, indistinct figure standing forlorn and alone at an upstairs window, caged behind glass and caught in a world not of her choosing. Guilt crashed over him in a wave.

Jean had shoved his payment into his coat as they went, but he was staring at Barty now, who was doing everything he could to avoid his gaze. It availed him not, however, as Jean finally spoke. "You think we did the wrong thing today, don't you?"

Barty squirmed, his heart still racing from the entire affair, the screams of the shot man still ringing in his ears, the stink of gunpowder burning his nostrils. He took a moment to gather his thoughts before taking a deep breath. "I do, and I doubt you could persuade me otherwise."

"I have no intention to," Jean said sourly. "I have no desire to waste my time arguing against the truth."

The admission rattled Barty somewhat, halting his reply momentarily. "You agree then? You believe we were mistaken to do this?" He could not conceal his surprise.

Jean gave a faint shrug, slouched in his seat and glaring with unseeing eyes into the distance. "I do. I despised that toad from the first moment I laid eyes upon him, and, though it will warrant a tirade from Montague when next we cross paths, I shall have one in kind." He grimaced, working his jaw in his perpetual anger, grinding his teeth against one another. "Out of all alternatives, this was the least miserable."

"There had to be a better solution. We could have found a way to help them, to perhaps protect them. There had to be a *right* way about things in all this, Reynard." Barty's voice was pleading, quietly wishing.

Jean's head turned on a tilt as a small, mirthless smile formed, his gaze almost pitying while his tone turned merciless. "It is an amusing conceit amongst those who have not been shown otherwise, I suppose, that there is somehow a great cosmic divide of purely right and wrong, of correct and incorrect, of justice and injustice, all warping together to create a sense of righteousness." He shook his head. "It is something gathered from faery tale, Bartleby, and most of *those* have as much accuracy as there is gold in seawater. The world does not care about such things. It will grind to dust those who put their faith in righteousness prevailing inevitably as it turns, spinning ever onwards and ignoring all pleas to the contrary." He sighed then, settling from his bitter admonition. "They both get to live. They live in sorrow, and they live with regret, but they are different regrets than the ones they would have chosen for themselves. The result was always going to be the same... except they both live instead. I will take what meagre victories I can muster. As miserable as they might be, they are better than the alternatives. There is no victory in death. I have seen far too much of it to know the truth cannot be otherwise."

Barty went quiet, biting back his thoughts. Jean kept those grey eyes on his assistant, knowing far too much in that harsh stare. "You have been listening to my daughter too much, Bartleby. Her hopes were noble, but our hands, in this matter, were tied. At least this way, they both get to survive."

Barty was stung by that, wincing as he remembered something he was trying to forget. "Elanor is going to be furious when she finds out what we have done."

Jean settled further into his seat, leaning his head back as he closed his eyes. "I am sure it will be fine," he said without a trace of irony. Barty had to wonder as they travelled onwards.

IT WAS NOT, IN FACT, FINE.

This was made abundantly, and rapidly, clear as they entered the Lodge of the Society of the Hound, the erstwhile home of the monster hunters of London, and where Barty had found himself calling home for some months now. The unobtrusive building was as ambiguous as ever from the exterior as they approached—a deceit Barty had learned was a common theme in nearly all their continued dealings, and his new life in the strange, wild world he had found himself a part of, in his search for truth and the answers to questions he had never known existed.

Puck was already departing around a corner, making his way to the place between places where he kept himself out of sight, but not so far away that he could not be called, his last whistle hanging upon the air in silver motes.

Those pleasant tones were cast to the winds of pandemonium the moment they passed the threshold.

Elanor Reynard was in many ways her father's daughter, but normally far better tempered, far more even headed. A thoughtful counterpart to her parent's aggression, she was of a mind that leaned towards understanding and coexistence with the many and varied beings that hid in the shadows, towards protecting them from a world that did not want them or understand them. After a period of estrangement from her father, she had returned to once more take up residence in the Lodge alongside the other remarkable inhabitants. She'd taken up many duties and roles, but mostly argued with her father—particularly about his methods.

Her opinion on the matter of Lady Catherine and her changeling lover was, as noted, made apparent when, not two steps through the front door, she hurled a long dagger with ferocious force from the stairs where she stood. It hissed through the air as though tearing it before impacting with a meaty, wooden *thunk* into the door frame past Jean's head, the blade sinking a good two inches into the solid oak.

Her father seemed to take this in stride. "Lovely to see you, daughter," he said dryly, holding where he was.

Barty, on the other hand, was emphatically less composed. The dagger was vibrating in the frame a scant few inches from his head, and he stared at it with a stunned gaze that was mirrored back at him, trembling as the blade itself did from the force with which it had struck. He was only dimly aware for the moment of the rich argument going on near to him.

"You rotten sneak thief," Elanor spat. Her pretty features, marred by the scarring upon her cheek and brow, were twisted in fury. "You hurry out and leave this? A *note?*" She waved the offending piece of paper in Jean's face fiercely as she strode up to him. Shorter than her father, her dark hair unbound and wild, she bristled like a badger in her affront. "You said you were going to try and help them! What did you *do?* "

"We helped them," Jean answered flatly, "and I did not write that note. My assistant did, and you can thus take it up with him." He gestured vaguely to Barty, while side-stepping his furious daughter and marching down the hall.

Elanor glared at the shrinking Barty, who inwardly groaned at being dropped headlong into the wrath of the younger Reynard, and wished fervently to become invisible. Elanor skewered him for a moment longer, before speaking sharply after her departing parent. "We will be talking about this later, Father."

"Capital," Jean remarked over one shoulder, as he continued to the kitchens. And possibly the wine cellar thereafter, leaving Elanor and Barty alone.

Neither one appeared entirely pleased about this matter. Glaring at the young man for a moment longer, she marched past him, muttering to herself, before yanking the dagger out of the doorframe. She spun back to Barty, gesturing with the knife as she began to berate him.

"Start speaking, and spare nothing. Explain to me what was so important that you both scurried out of here without so much of a word, skulking out into the wilderness. You *both* knew my feelings on the matter of Lady Catherine. What tran-spired?"

Barty was forced to stare, however unwilling, at the point of the blade waving scant inches from his face, the second time in mere minutes that it was altogether too close to his head. Watching it in the manner of one holding eye contact with a swaying serpent, he relayed the tale—how they had acted on a tip from a member of one of the many street gangs that Jean had contact with, how they had tracked down Lady Catherine and interrogated the watching thug to find out the details of what was to come, and then the sorry story of how the matter had ended; with both brokenhearted, but alive. And throughout it all, Elanor listened with increasing coldness.

"Your father chose what he believed was for the best, with what choices were available," Barty concluded, pleading despite his own feelings, perhaps to justify it to himself. "He did not want you with us, because he knew that you would have preferred to help them rather than return her to her family. You said as much yourself when you first learned what was going on." He took a deep breath. "I am sorry for leaving just a note. I did not feel I could find the words to properly convince you otherwise, so I did not even think it worth it to try."

Elanor listened in ever more sour silence. When Barty finished, she turned and placed the dagger on a side table before she spoke in a controlled, cold voice.

"My father I can understand, even if I do not agree with him," she said evenly, more like Jean now with every tightly measured syllable. "He has his way of doing things, and I have to acknowledge that. But I felt that you agreed with me when we spoke of the situation. You even supported my points to my father when I pushed to smuggle the pair away and refuse the payment, if it was what they both wanted, and if her choice was truly informed. You tell me now she knew exactly what he was, and yet chose him anyway, and then you separated them by force? Why?" She sounded upset, betrayed. "Because he told you to? Is that all? I know you have more spine than that."

Barty was stung. "Your father is my employer, Elanor, I cannot—"

But she was having none of it, cutting him off. "He is your *master*, you mean, and if he bid you bark you would wag your tail if you could." Her tone was scathing, but she looked away as she said it, as though she knew she had gone too far, but was too angry to stop herself. Barty stiffened, and straightened.

"It is not so easy for me to deny his wishes," he replied with as much of a level tone as he could manage. "You have the ability of doing so... I do not. So I did what I could, under the circumstances." He grimaced then, shaking his head. "Your father felt that this was the most positive result. They at least both get to live."

"He *would* think that preferable," she muttered darkly, but with begrudging recognition. The look she cast him, however, had more than a measure of spite to it, before she narrowed her eyes, something ticking away behind them. She spun on her foot. "We will talk about this later. Right now I am too disappointed in both of you. Now come on." She was striding to the stairs leading to the basement, and the elevator within. "Adam wishes to talk to you."

Barty hesitated. In the few short months since Elanor had returned home, there had been tears, difficult conversations, and often shouting. The shouting had continued as time had gone on, as both father and daughter struggled to reconcile their fractured relationship. Barty had kept out of it, and this unfortunately had the byproduct of both of them venting their frustration upon him, as he was cursed by birth and demeanour to be easily shouted at. Now things had instead turned quieter, sharper... the words had daggers within them and icy anger. This was not in any way better, however. In many ways, it was far worse.

He hesitated too long. Elanor snapped up as she descended,

"Hurry up!"

Without thinking, he was taking steps after her, and resenting it. While he would always be glad to respond to Adam's requests, Elanor was much too like her father while in his company, in that requests instead became commands. He had once tried to point this out to both of them. He was lucky to get out of the room alive before an argument on some other subject once more dragged father and daughter into war with one another.

Elanor remained stubbornly wordless as they descended in the elevator. Barty, still feeling guilty and exhausted of being the one to bear the brunt of the anger of the warring pair, kept his tongue and near held his breath. The elevator rattled and clanked as it went and announced their coming, and so it was that as they stepped into the long, cavernous hall that made up the armoury, with benches and racks of armaments, lab equipment and other wondrous things, they were greeted with a friendly wave from a rather incongruous duo.

One was tall, and one was short, but only so far as one was obscenely tall and the other of a slightly less than average height. The shorter one, seated cross-legged on a table, was called Benji, a young man of werewolf descent, which was marked by his strange, lupine ears and clawed fingers, at odds with his demeanour which was as kind as any that Barty had ever known. He ceased waving from his spot atop the wide, heavy table, upon which was a scattered myriad of various tools and devices that Barty himself could not quite name.

Benji was a young man, only a few months younger than Barty himself, and now resided in the cellar of the Lodge. He was an outcast amongst outcasts, thrown out by his fellows who themselves had to hide their mixed, accursed heritage from the wider world by dwelling beneath the city of London and in its shadows. His reason for exile was that he had dared to give information about a murderer to one Jean Reynard—a man because of whom the werewolf population of Europe was now substantially smaller than it had ever been before. Now, few of the pure strains remained, if there were any left at all. But if there were, none of them had anything but hatred for Jean Reynard—a tragedy two fold for how it had come to be, a hatred that endured, and would ever endure, for how deep its wounds ran. But that was a tale for another time.

Elanor had argued for Benji being kept at the Lodge. After all, it was their shared fault that he had been caught in the situation, and without his help they would never have solved the case of the Bedlam murders at all. By his extraordinary sense of smell he had uncovered crucial evidence that had laid a trail directly to Bethlehem asylum and the murderer hiding within it, and it was now that sense of smell that was being put to good use by the other inhabitant of the cellar, who turned with careful, deliberate movements to the newcomers.

The terribly tall person was Adam. They were, as had been noted, enormous, of a size and height that baffled observation. Hands the size of dinner plates, clad in a leather coat made of half a dozen other coats all stitched together crudely. That vastness was coupled with a face that was a patchwork horror of corpse flesh, an inhuman figure in every way, until they smiled, and spoke.

"Barty, Elanor. How lovely to see you both." Adam's voice

was as beautiful as their visage was terrible. Though they smiled with a ruined mouth, there was no malice in it, no rancour. They spoke with a warmth that was utterly, entirely without guile and perfectly genuine. They moved with care; not because they were clumsy or awkward, but because they were considerate of their surroundings and others nearby, making sure with each and every gesture that they did not accidentally break something, or someone, by swinging an arm too swiftly.

Barty knew precisely why. Adam could have picked up the twenty foot long table that their comparatively diminutive companion was seated upon with one hand. He had watched Adam straighten a steel bar with their hands once without seemingly any effort, and they were able to carefully twist and reshape metal to create tools that they needed with but a simple touch. Iron gave up under their expert care, moulded as easily as a child might shape clay. It was extraordinary to watch, and yet for all that strength, and all that power, Adam was by far the gentlest being that Barty had ever met.

They and Benji made an excellent pairing. Benji's sense of smell was so incredibly precise that he could participate in Adam's scientific undertakings and accurately relay information that Adam would otherwise have missed. He was able to assist in investigations as well—a bit of mud scraped from a floor could be brought to him, and he would be able to correctly identify the street it came from with a bit of precise scenting. But more than that, they both recognised the outcast in one another and the need for friends. Not for the first time, Barty felt a twinge of regret that neither of them felt that they could go out into the world to make such companions. They were both better people than he deserved to be in the company of.

Especially after today.

"As requested, my father's erstwhile lapdog, and ever helpful assistant in ruining peoples lives," Elanor said with bitter grandiosity, reminding Barty of his crimes and making him wince.

Benji and Adam exchanged a look at that, before the giant gently pressed on. "Well, be that as it may... I have made some arrangements for you, Bartholomew." One of the very few to use his full name, this was Adam through and through; the very notion of doing otherwise would be considered unconscionable.

"Please, you should just call me Barty, Adam," he replied gently, with a rueful smile, trying to push past the awkward introduction as he stepped forward. There was a black cloth laid out beside Benji, under which some indistinct shapes could be seen. "If Puck heard you calling me that, he might be inclined to admonish me in some fashion."

"The Prince of Midsummer would have to find his way down to my domain, and that is highly unlikely. He has an aversion to being indoors, let alone underground," Adam said dryly, with a faint twist of a smile on their misshapen lips. "Thus, I think I shall be quite all right for the time being, and so shall you—particularly in light of the following." They reached down—Benji casually rolled backwards off the table out of the way to land on both feet—and pulled the cloth away, revealing what was beneath.

"Reynard requested that you expand your arsenal, Barty," Adam said lightly, as they gestured to the glittering accoutrement before them. "You still have that revolver that was given to you, and that you appear to have grown quite attached to... but it is not appropriate for every situation. As it is, I have deployed my own discretion while taking into account your nature and stature, and come up with the following solutions."

Benji was grinning, bouncing on the heels of his feet, his sharp teeth showing in his good cheer. "You can give someone a right stitch-up with this lot, Barty," he said happily. As Barty looked down, he swallowed, and could not help but agree as Adam went on to casually explain.

"The blackjack is a simple solution to difficult problems," Adam said, gesturing to an object of leather and stitches, shaped rather like a basic club. "Filled with lead shot, it can bring an excessive amount of weight down when applied smartly to the back of the head. Not too hard of course, as otherwise they might never wake up." Adam picked it up with two fingers and brought it down carefully on the table. It made a satisfying and solid *thump* despite that care, before the giant gently placed it back down as they moved on.

"Secondly, for a more direct confrontation, a set of brass knuckles." The heavy metal had loops for fingers, and a leather wrapped grip in the middle for wrapping the hand around. "I added a little extra comfort, but do be aware that these are designed for a single punch to take an opponent by surprise and put an end to conflict as quickly as possible. Extended use is neither practical, nor safe for the hands." They lifted them between thumb and forefinger, then set them down again. "I fear I cannot demonstrate these, as it is... not entirely practical," they explained delicately, as though they needed to when their fingers, the thickness and size of a generous bratwurst sausage, could never fit into the loops provided.

"I admit I am more than a little perturbed to think what I could be using these for, truth told," Barty replied with awkward hesitancy. "They look like they could hurt someone." He eyed the last two objects on the cloth, which seemed even more worrying. Adam began to answer, but was cut short by a ridiculing snort from Elanor behind them.

"I would dearly love to have someone explain how a firearm is less about hurting people than these," she said, drawing closer.

Barty rolled his eyes, then thought for a moment before answering. "I only used it once, really, and I did not enjoy it. But I did not need to hurt anyone with it. I just had to... point it at them." He still remembered the look he had gotten down the other end of the barrel while he held the damn thing in his sweating hand. He woke up at night remembering it. "These are not for the threat of force... they are for *using* force. For hiding away until the right time, and then hurting someone."

Adam gave a gentle cough, before speaking. "I understand your dislike of violent action, despite the company you keep, Bartholomew," they explained. "But it is by such company that you will inevitably find yourself in a position where you will likely need something along these lines to protect yourself. Not everyone shares your proclivities."

Barty remained unconvinced, especially in the sight of the two remaining weapons on offer. He reached out to take the smaller, and lifted an evil little thing of razor edges and glittering metal, holding it up to the dim, dusty light of the armoury.

The switchblade was small and compact, easy to hide in a pocket to bring out at the right time... a time when someone would not expect it. Barty pressed the release and flicked his wrist—the first time it did not fully extend, but on the second attempt he managed it.

"Always handy to have a good knife on hand," Adam said cheerfully, "and that one is a little more special than most."

Benji hummed, a little unhappily, from the side. "S'got silver on it. Gilded onto it, just a bit really, but s'more than enough to make it sting if you touch it." He grimaced. "At least if you're like me an' some others."

He was eyeing the blade warily, and Barty eventually did him a service by retracting the blade and putting it down. But truth told, he was glad to have it out of his hand. It reminded him of another time, long ago, when such things as a knife in one's hand were the difference between safety and absolute horror—a door he wanted closed forever.

The final addition to Barty's growing arsenal was something that was, unlike the rest of his equipment, far more difficult to conceal. It was a sword with a one-handed grip, set beside a scabbard to be attached to a belt. It was around two feet long if Barty was any judge, with a single edge akin to a cavalry sabre, despite having a straight blade, which itself was around an inch wide. He picked it up, finding it lighter than he expected.

Barty held it with his hand protected by the hilt that curved down to the pommel. He turned it in his grip, twisting it, gauging the weight. It had a strange ease of movement to it, a fluidity of motion that he did not fully understand, but then, he had never held a sword before.

"This is beautiful," he said aloud without meaning to. And it was; the blade gleamed bright and polished, oiled and smooth. The metal was faintly rippled as though with a pattern, but the surface bore a perfect sheen.

"Why, thank you," Adam said, a faint smile on their features. "I shall take that as a compliment, and most gratefully."

Barty put the meaning behind the statement together. "You made this then?"

The giant nodded a couple of times, the smile flickering a little wider. "I did indeed. I based it upon your measurements, and ran some calculations upon the weight. I think it will suit you very well."

Barty was abashed, and felt a glow of appreciation building as his tongue tripped over itself. He struggled to find the words to express his sudden overwhelming gratitude, even as a well of shame threatened to swallow it up. But it was cut entirely short by a disdainful sniff from Elanor.

"Before he is given such a thing, do you not think he should know how it works? A sword is not a pistol, after all. Though I am surprised you know how to even use that at times." Her tone was scathing, contemptuously dismissive, and Barty knew she was still furious at him, having no means to take her anger out on her true target. It rankled him, his temper flaring a moment.

"I am sure that I can figure out how to stick the pointy end into someone, if it ever came to that," he said acidly, picking up the scabbard and, after missing the first time, managing to get the blade home within it with a satisfying *click* that nevertheless did not quite make up for the failed first attempt.

Elanor, watching with her arms folded over her chest, did not appear terribly impressed.

"I am sure you will prove an absolute terror," she said, conveying utterly that she did not find him so. "With all your aptitude and skill, I am sure all my father has to do is to tell you to become a master swordsman and you shall, by your sheer unthinking loyalty, become so in an instant."

Benji could not help but snigger at this, but soon cut it off at a warning look from Adam, who seldom needed to give them. Barty, wounded by such statements and with his temper drawing to its limits, finally snapped back in reply.

"If you could do any better, perhaps you should show me, rather than mock me incessantly."

The air of the room cooled then, as Adam and Benji both took an inward breath. Elanor's expression followed a habit of her father's, the lines around her mouth hardening as her eyes flashed and she fell into absolute silence. Barty found himself holding his breath—just as the pair behind him were doing—as his heart thundered in his ears, before Elanor closed her eyes and turned away.

Barty breathed out in relief, glad for but a moment before he heard movement. Elanor was pulling off her coat, revealing a long-sleeved white blouse and a scarlet vest. Discarding the coat to the floor with a careless toss, she took her long, loose hair and tied it in a quick but firm knot at the back of her head to keep it from her eyes. She moved to a nearby rack and selected from the axes, swords, maces and other variants of archaic and more modern weaponry, a sword that was similar to Barty's own, though perhaps a touch longer. She tested the point with one leather-clad hand, speculatively, and then nodded to herself before giving it a few experimental swings to get the weight of it.

"Well, if it is instruction you seek, it would be my *sincerest* pleasure to teach you."

Her tone was sharper than the steel blade she carried, as she turned herself to face him side on. Her left hand went to her waist, narrowing her profile as much as possible. Her right hand held the blade, the grip low with the point raised. Barty felt trapped, not least by the look in her eyes, which were as cold as he had ever seen from her.

But he was also angry, and tired, and had once more had a long day where he had tried to do his best, and failed to measure up. Elanor was standing a few yards away, so he looked around a moment, trying to find a good place for the pair of them to practise. He drew the sword and started to speak, gesturing vaguely with the blade as he looked about. "So should we find a spot—"

Elanor moved faster than Barty could have believed. Either the distance was deceptive, or she was just that quick on the dash, because suddenly she was right *there* in front of him, catching his vaguely waved blade and turning it. He scrambled back with a sharp grunt of shock, as Benji and Adam moved smartly away.

"Wait! I am not ready!" he squeaked in a most embarrassing tone, as he tried to backstep, frantically flailing his own blade utterly ineffectually before him. It did him no good.

"Ready? Do you think your enemies will be waiting for you to be *ready*, Barty?" Elanor mocked scathingly. She moved like a dancer, her steps dashing her forward as she struck controlled, swift blows that caught Barty's useless flailing and shifted them away, turning him this way and that. As she went she would catch him repeatedly with stinging slaps from the blunt side of her sword to his arms and shoulders, mercilessly whipping him with it. It was a searing, embarrassing pain as Barty rapidly realised he was not simply outmatched, he was being punished.

"You run after my father in his shadow, obeying his every command, too afraid to think for yourself, and you insist that you can do so while doing no harm?" she pressed, stalking after him as Barty scrambled around a rack. "Do you think that being helpless will somehow protect you?" She sidestepped, darted back as he desperately tried to follow her movements, lunged and struck a scalding blow to the inside of his thigh. It made him stumble forward as she slipped around behind him. "My brother was a pacifist, but at least he knew how to *fight*," she spat. "All you seem to know how to do is follow, and let other people do your fighting for you. How long do you think that is going to last?"

Barty had no answer for her. He was stinging all over from where she had hit him and struggling to get so much as a breath. But Elanor was relentless in her pursuit and savage in her anger as she vented her frustration. Whatever lesson that was to be learned in how to defend himself or use a sword was utterly cast aside. All she was teaching him was new ways to hurt, in whatever way she could.

"I am not your brother!" he grunted out, wincing as she scored his ribs. "Stop comparing me to him!" He slashed ineffectively, desperately, the pain and desperation overriding his reluctance to attack back at her.

She weaved back from the swipe and countered with a series of whiplash strikes with the flat edge that drew yelps of pain from him as she growled her response. "Oh that I know *full* well. At least he had courage, and yet here you are, trying to *replace* him!" She pressed on in a furious assault now, the sharp sound of steel on steel ringing louder and louder as she forced Barty back. "You cut me out of your work, you go off without me instead of listening to me, you do whatever he says! You think he will not kill you like he killed him, if it came to it?" Her voice rose in volume, becoming a furious shout. "You will never be James, because he was not *pathetic*!"

Her twin brother, slain to save her life when a werewolf curse had overcome him. Shot by his own father in the midst of the change. The departed genius son of Jean Reynard, who had helped solved the Ripper case as an adolescent, who had worked to create agreements and treaties between monstrous communities before his death, after which Jean had begun a brutal campaign of bloody destruction in retribution, that left him the most feared monster of all—a blood soaked legacy that Barty, in all his inexperience, had walked right into and become utterly bound to. That direct accusation made him hesitate at precisely the wrong moment.

He saw it coming, the first time he'd recognised what was about to happen in the whole affray. Her anger caused her to overextend herself; she put too much force into the thrust, and he tried to throw himself backwards, throwing up his left hand to defend, but it was not enough. He felt the razor-sharp edge of the blade slice through the skin of his palm, parting muscle, and about to push entirely through his hand to his eye beyond it when things very, very abruptly stopped, and a vast presence made itself felt through sudden stony silence.

Adam was there. Their enormous hand had caught the blade in the air, wrapped around it, and held it. Elanor still holding her sword, blinking in shock, her cheeks flushed and expression startled. With no effort, Adam reached down and removed her hand from the hilt, and then gently extracted the blade from Barty's palm, who dropped his own sword to press his thumb from his right hand into his palm to stop the blood. In truth, it had sunk only a fraction before Adam had caught the blade, but it still was one more pain amongst all the others, the many welts and bruises that she had given him in her wrathful admonition. But Barty had had quite enough of it, and the pain fuelled a furious rebellion.

"I am not trying to be your brother!" he snapped. "I am just trying to be Bartholomew Bartleby. Whatever you are angry about, it is very clearly not me, so *stop* using me as your whipping boy, Elanor. Take your problems to your father, but do not bring them or anything else to my door again. I am tired of being the easier target."

The look on her face paled, but not with anger. If anything she looked like she had been slapped, so shocked she was.

"Enough." The word was rumbled with enough deep, rolling force to it that it set the air to vibrating. An overwhelmingly powerful, contained force kept in mere words, it stole the breath from Barty and made him tremble, his anger draining from him. It took a moment to realise who had spoken as he looked up into Adam's face.

Up until this moment, Barty realised he had been startled or shocked by the look of Adam. Afraid, perhaps at times, until he had learned how foolish it was. But in this moment, there was fear. Absolute, complete fear, the sort that crawled down the spine on frozen claws, making him lock up in place. Adam's expression had no gentleness to it. There was no humour either. The stone-cold stare of the dead and death itself looked down at him, reminding Barty fully just what Adam actually was.

"I-I'm sorry," Barty stammered. "I-I did not mean to... to..." Words failed him. In this startling moment of realisation, his speech crumbled, scattering into echoes and dust, as a fear he could not control—a primal, ancient fear he could not name—stopped him cold.

Adam stared down at him for a long moment, before Benji appeared alongside them, one clawed hand coming to rest on Adam's vast forearm. "Easy there, big one. Just a little out of hand, that's all."

The giant blinked once, a slow and stony gesture. Then their expression shifted, taking on life once more in a pained grimace and then they were Adam, looking miserably apologetic. They gently lifted the blade they held clear, stepping away in the gulf of guilty silence with that heavy tread, to carefully place it back down with deliberate slowness upon the table. No one said a word. Barty had, for a moment, quite forgotten about the pain in his hand and the many bruising strikes of steel he had taken all over. He was not the only one subdued.

Elanor herself wore an expression of clear shame, looking furtively to Barty before taking a step towards Adam and speaking. "Adam, I am sorry—" She halted as one huge hand was raised to stop her.

"My temper is shorter than usual, Elanor, but allow me to make it my excuse to be emphatic. You will, both of you, never behave like that in my presence again, is that understood?" Adam's voice was low and firm. "You will also resolve any difficulty you have with each other before you venture down here again. Are we clear?" They turned then, their massive brows drawn downwards, and set that unblinking stare on them both.

Barty ducked his head rather than meet that gaze. He could have argued that this was not entirely his fault, but it did not matter. Adam had been nothing but kind to him, had presented him with a gift, and the immediate thing he had done in the aftermath was get into an argument. It may have been a long time coming between him and Elanor, but it did not change the fact that none of that was Adam's fault, and they deserved better respect. He felt ashamed.

"Completely clear, Adam," Elanor said meekly.

Barty nodded along with her words, hurriedly adding his own affirmation. "Entirely so, Adam."

"Excellent," the giant rumbled, then sighed. "For the time being, perhaps you should head upstairs, Elanor. Bartholomew, take a seat so that I might see to that hand."

Barty lifted his head, about to protest, but Elanor was already hurrying away to the elevator with a quickened step. Benji, giving the remaining pair a worried look, scooped up her coat and hurried after her. He did not have to explain; Benji owed his position in the house to Elanor and had been her friend well before that.

But that left Barty alone with Adam. The giant pointed to a seat without looking. "Sit yourself down, Barty." There was no arguing with their tone, and so Barty sat down by the table, huddled in his chair like an admonished schoolboy. It reminded him rather strongly of his days in the orphanage—too much so, with the aches and bruises forming all over his body.

But Adam was there to cure ills, not to create them. They returned shortly, bearing a wooden box that they opened and placed on the table before, with careful deliberation, they came down on one knee before Barty. Barty saw that the box was carefully lined with a few bottles, needles, thread, and other various implements.

"Your injury, Bartholomew," Adam said gently, beckoning, and Barty presented it after a brief hesitation. Adam took Barty's entire forearm in the grip of a gloved hand, and inspected the wound with a careful squint. Barty winced and looked away from it, catching sight of the various weapons still on the cloth that Adam had produced for him before things had gotten out of hand.

"I did not thank you, Adam," Barty said regretfully, his tone ashamed and subdued. "I did not mean to make you angry. I was foolish."

There was a moment of silence, then a sigh. "I am fully aware that this is an extremely foolish household, Bartholomew," Adam said, their tone gently rueful. "I am normally quite at peace with it. After all, I have made far worse messes in my time here. Though I am far more at ease when it is my own safety upon the line, than those I care about."

As they spoke, Adam plucked a single bottle of clear liquid from the opened box, delicately removing a stopper before dripping a measure of the substance onto Barty's palm. He felt fresh fire in his hand as it made contact—whatever the stuff was, it burned hellishly and made him yelp. His instinctive response was to pull away, but Adam's grip would have held back a rolling boulder—Barty did not manage to move away as much as a millimetre.

"Apologies," Adam said wryly. "I probably should have warned you."

Barty hissed between his teeth, stamping his feet a little, but shook his head. "No, no I had that coming."

Adam gave a soft chuckle, and shook their head as they carefully extracted a deeply curved needle and thin thread, holding them in massive fingers awkwardly a moment, before trying to thread the needle. It did not go well, until Barty wordlessly reached out and took the obstinate strand with his free hand. "Hold it steady, could you?"

Adam nodded and held the needle between thumb and forefinger as Barty squinted. "You said your temper was short today, Adam," Barty said as he carefully made an attempt with the thread. "You will have to forgive me, but I do not think I have ever known your temper to be anything more than placid. Is something the matter? Beyond two reckless people making a mess of your home?"

The giant being did not smile at that, their features turning to a slight frown instead. They took the needle once Barty had threaded it, and carefully took aim.

"There is a storm coming... a rather potent one, if I am to be any judge," Adam said slowly as they dug the needle into Barty's palm with a smooth, quick movement. It made Barty jump, but once again, there was no budging that incredibly strong grip. "I fear I am quite sensitive to them, rather more so than most people. I fear that they tend to play upon my sensibilities."

Barty was caught between confusion and pain, but the curiosity, ever his most present trait, won out in the end. In between biting his tongue as Adam completed the first stitch and then moved to the second, he pressed further. "Is there a particular reason for that?"

Adam nodded as they set the second stitch, made a simple loop to secure it on itself, then passed Barty a pair of small scissors. "I fear that they rather remind me of my creation, you see. It was, shall we say, a rather traumatic event, after all."

Barty took the scissors with a blink, snipping the excess thread. "I am afraid I do not know the circumstances of your... uh, how did you put it?" He set the scissors away, as Adam lifted out a simple bandage, wordlessly wrapping it around the palm. The whole thing was itching already, but he was grateful for it. In a day or two, it would be entirely fine. He resisted the urge to pick at the bandage as Adam let him go, settling for rubbing his wrist instead as he leaned back.

Adam remained where they were for a long moment, before they started to speak without looking at Barty. "When I first opened my eyes, I had no idea where I was. This was, however, only a brief terror compared to the realisation that I did not know *who* I was. My first waking moments of existence—as I knew them to be, anyway—were ones of fear. I remember the smell of burning metal, the taste of it in the air, and the rumble of thunder. I was awake and I was knowing, but in a world that I did not understand. Even thought was difficult, and then..." They trailed off slowly, thinking for a moment, then pushed themselves to their feet.

"Look upon your hand a moment, Bartholomew, if you could be so kind. Tell me what you see," Adam said quietly, fidgeting with their massive gloves. Barty was confused, but looked down to the bound appendage.

"... A bandage? Fingers?" he responded in conclusion, to which Adam gave a low and sad chuckle.

"Think as Jean would have you think, my friend. In the simplest terms, what is it that you see?"

Barty was still befuddled, but he looked again to his appendage, opening and closing it. "My hand," he said with faint confusion, looking up to see that the vast figure of Adam nodding gently.

"Indeed so. When you see your hands, any part of yourself, you know full well what it is... it is yours, it is a part of you, and it belongs to you." Adam began to carefully peel off the glove they wore on their right hand as they went on, "The first thing I recognised of myself were the hands I bore. But unlike yourself, Bartholomew, I had an entirely different realisation." The glove was removed, to reveal for the first time what lay beneath.

It was difficult to describe. Barty could see each articulated joint of the fingers, which appeared to be a mixture of flesh, bone, and steel. He could see the glint of copper wiring, running along each digit like sinew, partially encased by stitched together flesh. As he stared, a spark of energy arched from one fingertip to the next, before Adam closed that enormous hand with a grimace.

"The first thing I realised about myself was that my hands were not mine, Bartholomew. Nor then, is any part of me. I am, in all ways, not myself. Not my own. Not even this is allowed to me." A deep gulf of sorrow lay in their words, a vast and abiding regret, an ocean of tears unwept by eyes that could not spring them forth. "The storms remind me of that moment. They remind me that my body is not mine, and that I am, by extension, no one at all."

Barty wanted to say something. He wanted to protest that statement, but his tongue was cleaved to his mouth even as he felt himself blinking back tears he did not fully understand. The sorrowful Adam saw his distress, and carefully pulled back on their glove, giving a kind smile on their ruined features.

"Ah, do not concern yourself with it, Bartholomew. Run along now, could you? I will send your things up after you when time allows. You have had a long day." They turned away, heading deeper into the armoury.

Barty knew a dismissal when he heard one, however polite. He nodded and hurried along. By the time he dared to look back as he waited for the elevator to return, Adam was out of sight, leaving him alone with a guilt he did not understand.

Chapter 3

Carnivale

Living in the Lodge of the Society of the Hound had its downsides, being caught in the war between father and daughter. Yet, there was one facet of it that made the entire thing bearable for Barty, and that was having his own room.

In this room he had peace, quiet, and isolation. A bed large enough to stretch out in, a fireplace to keep him warm, and his very own brass bathtub as well. There were other things that he had added in his time there—a simple wood-and-canvas screen to conceal his bathing area, in case Jean or any other member of the household entered in their customary fash-ion—abruptly, and without knocking. This method had led to some embarrassing interludes that Barty did not wish to ever repeat. On an old oak desk sat his phonograph with its growing collection of wax recording cylinders unto which he would, when privacy allowed, record his thoughts and findings. More conventional pen, ink, and paper allowed for simpler methods of note taking, alongside some basic pieces of machinery that Barty took upon himself to try and repair. At present, it was a telescopic eye piece—Barty had taken it apart in an effort to clean the lenses, but was having a little trouble getting the alignment correct in putting it back together. It gave him something to do in the quiet hours.

Barty had never slept well until the haphazard events of his life brought him to this room. It provided safety, warmth, and comfort; things he had always been without. In the orphanage, it had been far different—there had been all the others around him, and the monsters in the shadows that hunted for the children who were most vulnerable. Sleep had been difficult to find, knowing how close *they* were. Outside of that, he had been living in share houses that had their own problems, or a room that was barely bigger than the bed he now slept in. Here? Here was paradise in comparison. Even if his dreams were troubled, they were at least deep, protected in that isolation that brought with it security.

Perched on the windowsill he kept a small mirror and razor, which he used to shave when the rare occasion called for it, for Barty regrettably lacked the ability to grow a decent beard. The window was small and opened onto the narrow alley beside the building, only a few feet wide, but in the early morning the sun shone down its narrow length so that if one angled the mirror *just* right, it would catch the light and, if they so desired, aim its bright, searing beam at a sleeping Barty until it forced him awake... which someone had indeed just gone and done.

Barty squinted, rolled, then thrashed about blindly while covering his eyes. He was never a graceful waker even at the best of times, and he had lingered awake long into the previous evening, staring at the ceiling until he had finally drifted off, consumed with the thoughts of Adam and their predicament, and the wider, ongoing household conflict. But that lengthy deliberation was now being rewarded with an early rousing, as startling as it was uncomfortable. He sat up in bed, blinking and disorientated, as a familiar voice spoke nonchalantly from the window.

"You know, you're terribly skinny. No one is going to shout at you for eating a little more, Barty."

Elanor cast a critical gaze over him as he rubbed at his eyes with one hand. She was dressed in a fine riding coat of dark red, fitted trousers, and high boots. A rather flamboyant hat with a wide brim and a large, white feather stuck into its band, sat atop her head. She was carefully putting the mirror down, having used it to jolt the sleeping Barty out of whatever forgotten dream had held him. Her expression was enigmatic as Barty first wondered what she was doing there. But the next, and far more overwhelming realisation, came when awareness bloomed that he was, in fact, mostly naked, save for his bed drawers and the sheets that had, until his frenzied thrashing, covered him. He seized them up to his neck, blushed bright crimson, and manfully managed a very informative sound of "*whzzp?*"

It was the best he could manage for the time being, circumstances being what they were.

"Yes, quite," Elanor said with amusement. She seemed in a far better mood than the last time he had seen her, or perhaps she simply enjoyed seeing him in distress, the latter being the more likely. She chuckled, shaking her head, and strode out of the room. "Breakfast downstairs, and get yourself dressed. We are going out today."

Barty grimaced. The twinges of his bruising and his bandaged hand came back to remind him of yesterday. "And if I am not inclined to?" he grumbled as she reached the door.

"Too bad," she shot back with heightened cheer, and kept on going without closing the door behind her. Barty found use for some of Jean's more creative curse words under his breath as he heard her descending the stairs, taking them three at a time from the sound of it. "Hurry up now, Bartholomew Bartleby! The day is not going to wait, nor will these scones!"

That made him perk up. Scones meant jam. Scones meant cream. There had never been a more finer union. He gave in and roused himself. A man does not argue when there are scones involved, especially not fresh-baked ones, unless they are a very foolish fellow indeed. Ignoring the stiffness in his bones and bruises on his body, he put himself into motion, still grumbling, but mostly for the look of the thing. Scones undid all ills.

The kitchen was a little more alive than usual. Benji was cleaning dishes, humming as his long ears flicked at the sides of his head, upright and swivelling. Elanor was sitting in an open window that overlooked the meagre backyard of the Lodge, looking rather more pensive, and of course, there was Jean.

He was in his customary chair with his familiar pose; sunk deep with his elbows on the arms of his throne, reading a newspaper that concealed all but his hands that held it. He did not bother to lower it as Barty entered and sat down at the table.

Throughout his time in the Lodge, Barty continually endeavoured to learn more about Jean by observing his behaviour. He struggled to get answers out of him otherwise, as Jean was naturally recalcitrant and refused to respond to questions—direct or indirect—at the best of times, and such times were few and far between. While he had spoken about his son at length, even if it was with difficulty, he despised explaining himself. So, Barty had been forced to rely on other, more exotic methods. The first of those was what he called the 'newspaper measure'.

As far as gauges went, it was extremely reliable and entirely simple. When Jean held a newspaper, his grip would tell an observer a great deal. If his hold was loose and light, his mood was likely neutral. But if the paper was crushed under a grip that was fighting the urge to turn into a fist, then it was poor. With careful understanding, the *amount* of pressure could be more accurately gauged, with 'higher' being an indicator of a poorer state of temperament.

Today, Barty could immediately see, was not the best of days. Any more pressure and the paper was going to rip under the sheer force of whatever fresh fury was powering Jean's blazing spirit.

"Good of you to join us, Barty," Jean said sourly from the depths of the newspaper. He flicked the sheet down to bring his bloodshot glare to his assistant, brows furrowed. "I thought for a while there you were going to sleep all day."

Barty did not answer. He instead dedicated this time to the important business of scone acquisition, for it would wait no longer. There they were, upon the table alongside the ever present and ever steaming pot of tea—the surest proof of an English household as there could ever be—with a bowl of strawberry jam and another of cream that had already seen a great deal of damage done in the assuaging of other morning hungers. But some scones still remained, freshly cooked with the dawn. He collected a number of them on his plate—and remembering the admonition of Elanor, which still embarrassed him, he took one extra to be sure—before pouring himself a cup of tea.

"Those bruises looked mostly healed already," Elanor said pleasantly then, still looking out the window she was propped up in. She was holding something in her hand on the outside, something thin and long that she spun about between her thumb and forefinger—Barty saw it was a feather of some kind.

He had a mouthful of scone at this point, and for the second time that morning he answered her question as best he could, with a muffled sound that soon gave way to slight choking.

Jean's eyes narrowed. "Bruises, you say." He was staring hard at Barty now. "I do not recall granting you any yesterday, by action or direct cause."

"Oh, Elanor did that," Benji said cheerfully from the sink as he finished drying a plate.

Jean skewered him with a stare that made the wolfish youth pause a moment, then set it upon Barty once more. "Is that so? And how did she manage that?"

"I was teaching him how to use the sword that Adam made for him," Elanor said airily as she pried herself out of the window frame, letting the feather fall from her fingers to tumble outside, before pulling the window closed. "He was not very good at it."

"You are hardly a good gauge to judge skill against, Elanor," Jean said dryly, turning a page of the paper. "You're the best swordsman *or* woman I've ever come across. Near anyone would be inept against you, let alone a beginner." He said it plainly, without pride or flattery—he was simply stating a fact. But Elanor nevertheless seemed taken off guard by what was clearly a rare compliment. Jean did not seem to notice. He was glaring at the paper again.

"Well, never mind that," Elanor finally said, regathering her poise. "Come on Barty." She slipped around the table, and clapped him on the shoulder. "Time for us to be off."

He choked momentarily, still with a mouthful of scone that he had stuffed himself with rather than embarrass himself by answering questions. This unfortunately had the opposite effect when it rendered him unable to speak.

"Off? Off to where?" Jean growled. He looked outright suspicious now, trying to figure out what was going on and what his daughter was not telling him.

She remained cheerful, wielding Barty like a shield to deflect questions as she gave him a little shake. "Oh, nowhere important. Barty promised to take me to the park, by way of apology. I thought it very gracious of him. Don't you think so, Father?"

"Quite," Jean said in a flat tone which indicated he felt entirely otherwise. He closed the newspaper with deliberate slowness—Barty could not help but notice that there were indeed tears where his hands had been holding it—and leaned forward as his gaze bore into Barty. "What an *excellent* idea you had there, Mister Barty." That was what Jean said, but what Barty understood was what was written large on Jean's features. *We will speak of this later. You shall not enjoy the conversation. But I just might.*

It was the exact opposite of reassuring.

He swallowed, his mouth dry, and covered up his sudden panic by taking a sip of his tea. Elanor was already setting off.

"Make sure to get your coat, Barty. We'll be back before dinner, Father. I promise." She said in the light and airy tone of an outright lie as she stepped out.

Barty, sweating profusely, was looking back at Jean in a state of panic. He swore he could see his own gravestone reflected in Jean's eyes, down to what was written upon it; *Here lies Bartholomew Bartleby, who spent time alone with the daughter of the worst man in the world, and suffered for it. May his tomb serve as a warning to other fools.*

It was rather too close to reality for him to feel comfortable, and so, taking his last scone with him, he scurried after Elanor, Jean boring a hole between his shoulders as he went. His fate was, for the time being, forestalled.

Powered by his desire to escape, Barty nearly scuttled head-long into Elanor at the exit, where she was waiting with an amused look on her face that had just a trace of smugness to it. She was holding out his coat and hat, which he took without thinking, and then bumbled past her and out onto the street, rounding on her when she closed the door.

"Why in God's name did you make it sound like it was *my* idea?" he asked, exasperated.

Elanor shrugged and lightly made her way down the steps. "What difference does that make?" she asked, as she set her hands into the pockets of her coat and sauntered along.

Barty stuffed his scone to his mouth, and flung on his coat and hat before rushing off after her. "The *difference* it makes, is that it is just not done to take a young lady somewhere without the permission of their guardian." Elanor stopped so abruptly at the term that Barty nearly stumbled, as she spun and gave him a thoroughly unimpressed look. "... Parent," Barty finally corrected himself. The notion that Elanor, who had operated independently in the hidden Under of London with all its monsters and strange beings, would need a guardian was clearly something that offended her.

She sniffed and continued on, and Barty once more fell into pursuit as they travelled south. He wondered if he should whistle for Puck, but Elanor's quick and determined step made him think otherwise.

"Look at me, Barty," Elanor said dryly, turning in place and now walking backwards as she spread her hands to each side with nonchalance. "Do I appear like I am one for wearing concealing dresses, suffering through agonising corsetry, and lowering my eyes in the presence of a man?" She halted, mockingly raising the back of her hand to her brow and went on in a faux weakened voice. "But now that you mention it, I fear I am too overwhelmed by my choices. Oh, my dearest Barty, I am quite overcome by emotion and simply must faint!" She tilted backwards, as though she actually meant what she said, but as Barty jumped forward to catch her, she corrected herself and swung back up, laughing as he was left feeling as silly as he looked.

"Please, Barty. I am not that sort of person, and have no intention of being so. I have far more important things to worry about than that sort of nonsense." She spun once more away from him and quickened her step, and Barty had to do the same to keep up.

"But still, surely—" he tried lamely, but she was having none of it.

"I think you also have far more important things to worry about, truth told," she interrupted, "for example, my father wondering how I saw you naked." She smirked back at him, her eyes sparkling with mirth, the smirk splitting into a grin as she saw her companion turn white with horror.

The bruises. Of course, how could she have seen them otherwise? Barty felt his cheeks grow hot as he stumbled over his response. "N-nonsense! I was not naked!" His voice grew shrill in the doing, and a little too loud for comfort. Passersby were looking at them now. This did not help matters.

Elanor squinted at him speculatively, still grinning. "You looked *rather* naked to me, Barty. Fret not though." She patted his shoulder and increased her pace yet again. "I am sure he will kill you quickly... he likes you, after all. Now hurry! We have not got all day."

God save me from this family, Barty thought, as he swallowed his dread and followed after her. *They will be the death of me yet.*

The spectre of Jean loomed large in his consciousness, reminding him that such a death might be entirely direct in its coming. Checking over his shoulder briefly in a panic, and finding the street far too full of shadows even in the bright mid-morning sun to be comfortable, he put his head down and hurried after Elanor.

Early summer in London was best described as a begrudging affair. The sun shone bright when it could slice through the smoke and low clouds, or when the wind was high enough to keep the skies clear. There was greenery in the gardens and parks, and warmth aplenty. But the weather could be unpredictable and swiftly so, and rain, the ever present entity, came quickly and without mercy, cruelly denying the masses of warmth. But this day, the foul weather had, for the time being, given up the fight—if however reluctantly. The clouds were high and fast, blowing ahead of the storm that Adam predicted was approaching. It left the air charged and full, the tension it brought measured by the welcome warmth of the sun.

Elanor flagged a carriage down to shorten the journey. The trip to Southwark Park was a few miles, and even the swiftest pace on foot would have taken much of the day to get there.

"Why not have Puck take us? He seems to enjoy that sort of thing," Barty finally asked, his curiosity overwhelming him. They rode in a humble open buggy, their elderly driver hunched over his single heavy draft horse that was pulling them along at an adequate but wobbly pace. Elanor was looking pensively out over the street without seeing anything. Something appeared to have drowned her earlier amusement, but Barty knew enough to know she would respond when ready.

With a faint huff of a sigh, she appeared to dismiss whatever occupied her thoughts, and then looked at him with a shrug and a grimace. "He would enjoy it entirely too much. Puck's motivations are beyond me." She tilted her head, giving him a speculative look. "You know, you place a great lack of caution in Puck's character. Are you quite aware of their nature?"

With her words, Barty had a memory flung back at him; a vast shadow edged in silver, swimming with eyes and teeth, a smile that was too large and would devour him whole and into nightmares, a horror that had become the crooked form of Puck once more. A name stolen and given back to him. He shivered, and shrugged. "Somewhat." He glanced to the carriage driver, and kept his words careful. "They are certainly a... unique individual."

Her gaze remained on him a moment, before she nodded and leaned back. "Puck is someone I do not take lightly, Barty. I certainly would not have them running unimportant tasks for me. It might offend him, and it does not do to offend one such as he. Not ever. I'll not take that chance."

The vision of what Puck was hiding remained lodged at the back of Barty's skull, worming around the base of it and his spine. "That is quite understandable." He let the matter drop, save for taking the moment to rearticulate his own thoughts on how to treat Puck moving forward.

They rolled on, until Elanor leaned over and tapped the driver, and the buggy pulled to a halt. A few coins were granted, a tip of the hat in gratitude, and Barty and Elanor stepped off at their destination.

Southwark Park was a little pocket of green and pleasantry.

At its border were workhouses, and the Surrey Commercial Docks just beyond that, a noisy place at all hours, and a hellish cacophony at its busiest height. But Southwark Park was a garden of Eden hedged in by the world around it, with well tended paths and an ornamental lake and cricket ground on the southern end.

It was in this direction that Elanor guided them, and it did not take much effort to spot what she had brought him to; the ornamental lake was girded by a recognisable sight on one side—a collection of red painted, highly decorated enclosed wagons, strung up pavilions and tents, and a large, low burning fire around which were clusters of people. A caravan circus of travelling entertainers. And from the look of it, a Romani one, with each of the caravan vardo being so magnificently detailed. Barty paused without quite knowing why, but Elanor was cheerfully making her way towards them.

"Are you sure this is where you wanted to come?" Barty asked, a little perturbed. Like most English folk, he was wary around the Romani people, by way of superstition. That, and the ever present fear of the misunderstood that was as much English nature as it was to enjoy a cup of tea.

Elanor gave him a pitying look, understanding what he was getting at, and rolled her eyes before giving him a shove forward. "*Yes*, Barty, I am quite sure. Now come on." There was no arguing with her.

A man with a moustache almost as wide as his golden speckled smile welcomed them in at the simple ticket gate, bowing as he guided them in. He spoke in a language that Barty did not recognise, but to his surprise, Elanor replied in the same tongue. Whatever she said made him chortle, but before Barty could ask what was so amusing, he was being swept along and into an entirely new world.

The carnival circus was a wild affair, kept compact in its grounds but no less entertaining for that. The food was simple but hot, roasted chestnuts and partridges cooked over a low banked fire. There were people watching in amazement as grinning Romani danced here and there, with music played from guitar, violin, and pipes pushing the beautiful frenzy onwards. There were fire swallowers, a contortionist who could touch her toes to her forehead over her back, and a bulky fellow with bare knuckle scars and a barrel-sized torso, who bent an iron bar into a circle. It was during this performance, as both of them sat eating roasted chestnuts amongst the grass, amidst the happy sounds of the meagre but appreciative crowd, that Elanor finally got to the point of the whole matter.

"I have not apologised properly," she said pensively, watching with unseeing eyes as a man abused an innocent piece of metal. "For the other evening, I mean."

Barty glanced down at his hand. He had removed the bandage in the morning, but the stitches remained. It itched still, to remind him of its presence, but the bruises had already faded in their ache, the warmth of the sun having done wonders. She had been less fierce on him, in her unorthodox teachings of swordplay, than he had feared.

He took a deep breath, closing his fist. "You were upset. But I meant what I said, Elanor. I am not your father, and I am not going to be held responsible for his actions, either. I beg you, do not make me a substitute for anger directed at him."

She grimaced, exhaling. "You are right. It was not fair of me... I was frustrated, but it was no excuse." She looked over at his closed fist. "How is it?"

Barty tried to wave it off. "Fine... it is fine. Adam stitched it back up in moments. It is just an unpleasant itch now." He tried to give a smile, but it was a lopsided affair. "I mostly feel the bruise upon my ego. Jean said you were the best sword fighter he had ever seen, and I certainly got to feel *that* well enough."

Elanor snorted, perhaps with embarrassment and amusement both. "He's being generous, and overly so."

Barty, however, would have none of it, shaking his head. "Have you ever known your father to be generous? He has only ever stated facts as he sees them. If he said it, he meant it."

Elanor seemed to accept this, however reluctantly, picking at the grass before her with her free hand. Then she sighed, and gave Barty a meaningful look. "You know, traditionally, this is where *you* are supposed to apologise, as well," she said dryly, and perhaps a little disappointed. Barty blinked, confused, but then remembered what had started the fight in the first place.

"Ah," he said, going silent as he gathered his thoughts. He spoke just as Elanor opened her mouth. "You were right, you know. Your father admitted as such, at the end of it all."

"I beg your pardon?" She sounded faintly astonished. Both her brows lifted and her eyes went wide with uncharacteristic surprise.

Barty, with his gaze downcast, continued on, "You told us you believed that the Lady Catherine was fully aware of the nature of her lover, and was willingly complicit. I thought she did not know, and Jean believed that she was being led astray by malicious intentions on Miska's part. Jean and I believed that if there was a *chance* that she was ignorant in either instance, we had to act upon it. We worked on that basis, and on the knowledge that if we did not resolve matters immediately, one or maybe both would die at the hands of Beauchamp's thugs." He scowled. "We were wrong. She knew exactly what he was, and he truly did love her. Jean admitted that to her at the end, when she was despairing in believing that his affections were false." He took a deep breath. "You were correct. We were both wrong, and I am sorry that we did not heed you."

Elanor was silent for a long moment. She eventually picked another roasted chestnut out of the small bag, eyeing it for a time in contemplation. "My father believes the worst in people. He cannot help it. It is what he is." She frowned as she went on, "But you are not him, Barty. You are your own person—and as much as it might seem otherwise, my father does not need people who agree with him. He needs those who do not."

To cover his confusion, he retrieved his own chestnut. They no longer burned his fingers, but he held it with care regardless. "I thought he had that, in you."

Elanor gave a small chuckle at his response, but it was regretful as she went on, shaking her head, "No, no. I argue with my father, because that is what I cannot help but do. He makes me angry, and I do not know why." She shrugged. "You are the one he chose for that role. It is what he needs you for... what he picked you for. Not to follow him blindly, but to challenge him."

Barty blinked, thinking back. "I have not been doing a good job of that as of late," he admitted to himself. "He has been sharper with me in recent weeks, I've noticed."

Elanor was nodding. "He's frustrated too. We all are," she confessed. "Not just with you, but in general, Barty. There is a great deal to learn in this world, to understand—and that includes knowing the hearts of our peculiar family, which is not the easiest thing to manage."

He ruminated on it, even as the small crowd broke into applause. The massive man on the crude stage, bearing a smile that was practised enough to almost appear genuine, waved and bowed, and then strode off, bearing his pretzel-shaped bar as a trophy of his deeds. Elanor pushed herself to her feet, and held out her hand to Barty to help him stand. The extended sitting had made the bruises ache a little more than he expected, and he was stiff as he stood, needing a moment to stretch. Elanor was peering about as though looking for something, her expression distant. She nodded to herself and then pointed with her thumb into the deeper mess of tents away from the fairground of the entertainment.

"This way. I want to show you something."

She beckoned him on. Without knowing what else to do, he followed her. But there was a part of him that was puzzled. There was a firmness to Elanor that had not been present for the whole day, until now. He followed her as they moved into pavilions, towards the vardo caravans arrayed protectively together.

There was a simple rope fence bordering the grounds between the caravan cluster, separating the crowd from wandering into what was clearly an area not meant for them. This fact was not lost on Barty as Elanor lightly hopped over the barrier. He tried to get her attention by hissing her name, but she pushed on. After a moment of panic, he looked around to see if they were being observed, but all eyes were on a fire dancer on stage, spinning while twirling smoking flames on sticks faster and faster. Not far from them, a knife thrower was hurling blades through the spinning arms and fire, without looking at their target. Absolutely no one was watching the anxious young man and his overly bold companion, enraptured by the show. He swore, and hopped over the railing as well.

The atmosphere changed with uncanny swiftness. He crept after Elanor into the shade of one of the caravans, feeling the air turn close and oppressive. The vardo caravans were decorated with exquisite relief carvings, painted in bright colours, closer to works of art than means of transport. Each was sturdily built, on four strong wheels, with windows and drawn curtains that concealed whatever secret worlds were within. Odd shaped wind chimes, more akin to secret symbols, were clustered together on beams, and above the door that led into the rear of each caravan was nailed an iron horseshoe, wrapped with some sprig of a plant that Barty did not recognise, nor understand the significance of. The horses that pulled them were absent. And though they were but a few steps from the fairground and all the people within it, the place was worryingly, eerily quiet. It made him lock in place, blood turning colder as he looked around, noting far more shadows than before. The clouds of the coming storm had drawn in, the bright day turning overcast and oppressive, as the sun was swallowed up by the murk.

A harsh croaking cry came from above. His gaze shot up to

bear witness to an enormous raven, perched on the eaves of one of the caravans. It was looking down at him with a beady black eye, soulless and wrathful. Something about it made him tilt his head in a moment of vague, inexplicable recognition. The bird noticed him looking and screeched once more at him, a rebuke for his staring.

"Here, Barty." Elanor pulled his attention away from the errant corvid. Her voice was soft, showing she, too, was feeling the change in pressure in the air. She offered a sense of safety, however, that Barty felt he desperately needed. He had never felt so *watched* before, the hairs on his neck sticking up like the worst of nights in the orphanage. He stepped over to her, as she stood before a large caravan that looked older than the others. Flower pots holding roses hung from hooks at its windows, ringing them in thorns and blood red blooms. The silent, ominous structure looked like it was waiting for him. He recognised the feeling all too well.

"Elanor, we should *not* be here," Barty hissed. "This is clearly a private place, and this is not—"

But she held up a hand, placing one finger to her lips, shaking her head. Her face, shadowed by her wide brimmed hat, suddenly held a troubled look. She looked like she was having doubts about something, but Barty could not understand what.

"We are exactly where we need to be, Barty. *You* are exactly where you need to be right now." She said it in a subdued whisper, and Barty wondered if she was persuading herself. She reached up, and opened the dark door to the caravan—it creaked so loud and sharp that it tore the air itself—and gestured for him to climb the steps, to ascend into what was, to

Barty's eyes, a living, breathing void of inescapable darkness. He could make out absolutely nothing within whatsoever. No night sky could ever be so lightless, nor the deepest pit.

"Go in, Barty," Elanor said softly, but her command was inexorable. He opened and closed his mouth, confused, and more than a little intimidated. "It will be fine. But someone is waiting for you." She gestured with her chin up at the interior.

Barty hesitated, then took a couple of steps forward, unsure of himself as he ascended one creaking step, then another, before he stopped at the threshold, gripping the door frame with one hand. Even at this distance, he could see nothing, just empty darkness, and perhaps some vague shapes which could have been old ghosts he had long wished forgotten and unmade. His spine quivered. His blood cooled and his nerve failed, as he turned on the spot to look at Elanor, still standing on the step.

"Elanor"—his whisper firm but his knuckles white as he gripped the door frame—"I do not know what is going on here, but I can tell you I am *not* going in there without a proper—"

He never got to finish. There was a croaking cry and the raven launched itself off its perch and flew at him, black wings outstretched, screaming as it went with the call of the grave. In a panic, he sprawled backwards, falling into the depths of the caravan with a thud onto a heavily carpeted floor. The raven flew over his head and into the darkness, and he sat up in time to see Elanor, her expression unhappy but her jaw set, close the door in his face with a loud thump, leaving him in absolute blackness.

Barty's tongue cleaved to the roof of his mouth, as his blood turned to ice and a cacophony of terrified thoughts ran wild as panicked horses through his skull. The shock of the whole thing had taken him entirely off guard, and he scrambled about on the floor, thrashing and waving his arms around to ward off blows that were not coming. The void had devoured him.

A strike of a match in the recesses of the caravan flared bright as a supernova in his vision, banishing the darkness. Though the light was still dim, Barty was at least able to see his hand in front of his face, as the rich, warm accented voice of a woman, husky from smoke and stern with authority, spoke from the depths of shadow.

"Do not crawl on the floor, my dear. That is the province of rats."

Barty rolled over onto his stomach, with the cautious, careful slowness of one feeling as though to move too fast would result in violence. As he did so, he took in his surroundings.

The interior of the vardo was a cramped affair. When one lives their entire life within such a small space, clutter inevitably follows, but the arithmetic of necessity ruled that none of it was unimportant. There were herbs and flowers hanging from the ceiling, clustered and tied together, and as Barty took a deep breath he felt almost dizzy from the potency. Sage and lavender, rosemary and mint were pungent and soothing, alongside cloves, aniseed, and other mixed scents that Barty could not identify. There were shelves and cupboards, and furniture that had been bolted down. A small cast iron stove with a chimney was tucked away to one side, with closed curtains beyond.

A table, small and round with a patterned table cloth, was

firmly attached to the wall, a closed and curtained window above it. There was a stool there, on his side, and on the opposite a woman was holding aloft the lit match.

He could make out few attributes of her. She was mostly in shadow, but the flickering flame gave details upon which his eye lingered. She wore a tasselled shawl of deep and dark red, and much of her face was obscured by darkness. Her hand was dusky, and marked with an intricate array of what Barty thought were tattoos, spiralling in patterns along the back of her hand and up her forearm, which was lined with bangles. Rings adorned her fingers—on the thumb was a most curious one, large and silver with a curved blade that extended past the end of the thumb, like the talon of a bird.

The woman, whoever she was, lit a candle that was set into a holder, bolted onto the wall. As the room flared brighter, she gestured with an open hand to the stool. "Sit." Her voice was firm, the accent musical.

But as the light illuminated the interior, Barty finally saw what was above her. Two deer antlers hung sidelong from a roofbeam and, perched upon them in silence, was not one raven, but four, all of them staring at him down the length of their beaks, as though sizing up a day old lamb that had wandered just a little too far from the flock. They looked familiar.

To say it was unnerving was a severe understatement. But Barty was Barty, and under that core of befuddlement, curiosity, and occasional maddened desperation was also a temper, and it flared up now.

"Madam, I am not sure what sort of game this is, but I am *not* inclined to play it without a further explanation—"

"*Sit.*"

The word travelled into his ears, took control of his muscles, and wrestled him into place before he could protest. Barty blinked, his tongue tangled in his mouth, looking around himself in confusion before focusing on the concealed woman before him. Above him, a raven cawed mockingly.

"How did you do that?" he asked numbly, feeling a chill pass through his body. The woman before him sighed, then lifted her shawl clear and leaned forward, interlacing her fingers together as she fixed him with piercing, midnight eyes, shadowed with kohl.

She was a beautiful woman, her complexion olive, and dark curls, save for a few strands of silver that streaked sharp and bright through her long hair, cascaded unbound over her shoulders. She had to be in her early forties if Barty was to guess, but it was hard to tell; she seemed somewhat ageless. Her impassive expression spoke to her being unimpressed with his appearance, but the intense stare was otherwise impossible to read. She hardly seemed to blink as she watched Barty carefully.

"By the power of suggestion, young man," she said with a hint of dry irony in her tone. "But before you open your mouth to ask another question, I will instead ask you one first—what are you doing, uninvited, in my home?" The burr of her accent turned stern, and those midnight eyes hardened.

Barty swallowed, as the reality of the situation manifested fully. He was lucky the woman had not screamed for help. He did not want to imagine what his fate would be if he was caught trespassing by the rest of the wagons' inhabitants. What had

Elanor done to him? And why?

"My companion, she"—he gripped his knees tightly, feeling a wave of disappointment and anger pass over him—"she tricked me into being here. It was not my idea."

A throaty chuckle was her reply, the woman leaning back and covering her mouth. "You have strange friends, boy, if they would leave you in the vardo of a Romanichal witch." She lowered her hand, a smirk on her full lips and her eyes flashing. "Entire bloodlines have been cursed to hell for far, far less."

Barty felt his heart jump, and he swallowed his growing terror. He started to babble an apology, but the four ravens above him chose that moment to caw as one, and flap their wide wings, so loud as to rattle the vardo, and cowed him into admonished silence. The woman before him—or witch, as she called herself—was unbothered by their outcry. She simply waited, and her eyes never left Barty as he floundered, his words robbed from him. When the outrage of the corvids had come to an end—though they remained ruffled, offended by the existence of this uninvited interloper—she sighed, and then gestured to her side, revealing a fancifully decorated teapot and two exquisitely formed teacups, of purest white porcelain, thin as paper and edged with gold.

"It just so happens that I was about to take tea. It would be unspeakably rude of me not to offer you some." Her tone turned dry at this, the implication that intrusion into her home was somehow less rude. "You can tell me your name, and of your friend, yes? And then I will decide what to do with you."

He sat awkwardly, fidgeting, as she poured two cups from the teapot. It was warm, not hot, not freshly made. But Barty held the cup he was given as a lifeline as panic continued its attempts to drown him. A naturally nervous young man—even when he was not in the caravan of a witch—this was altogether too mysterious for his sensibilities.

"My name is—" He held himself, having learned lessons of giving names too freely. "My name is Barty. Mister Barty to some."

The woman raised one eyebrow, a faint smirk curling her lips. "Is that so, 'Mister' Barty?" Her tone was faintly mocking, as she took a sip of her tea. "Well then. You may call me Madam." She gestured with one of those richly ringed hands, setting the bangles on her forearm to clanging. "Go on now. Take a sip, before it grows cold. It would be... bad manners, otherwise." There was a warning note to her voice, as she took another sip of her tea, her stare remaining intent. Barty swallowed, and obliged her, taking a mouthful. The tea was bitter, steeped too long, but he swallowed stoutly as she observed him, taking another sip to be sure. It gave him time to think, at least.

"So," the Madam intoned then, "Tell me of why you came to my door, of all doors, Mister Barty. Few come here without good reason." She leaned forward.

He laughed nervously, holding the tea cup with both hands in an awful attempt to hide his anxiety. "I do not have a reason, as I said—someone tricked me into coming here. And when I leave here, I will ask her *emphatically* what she was thinking." He turned to the door, unable to keep a touch of anger out of his voice. Right now it was very difficult for him not to be frustrated at Elanor. He was lucky this woman, for all of her talk of being a witch, was so polite.

"She, you say?" she asked over his shoulder. He blinked, and took a moment, before coughing and turning back around to face the woman who was watching him patiently.

"Ah—yes. She." He took another sip of the bitter tea.

She watched him with a raised brow. "And what is her name?"

Deception stirred, albeit too late. "Er... Elizabeth." It was as good a name as any. "Elizabeth Smith," he finished in a manner that was as helpful as the deception was useless, as though the falsehood was not written bright in the very stars as being an outright lie. The raised brow remained so. She did not appear to be impressed by his efforts of dissemination, and truth told, Barty himself was not either. He was out of practise with his lying, and it showed.

The Madam sighed, and set down her tea. "Very well then." She held her hand out, palm up. She was looking at him intently as she did so, a stare that went into him, but did not dive deeper. But Barty felt uncomfortably *seen* in the moment, as his tongue twisted in his mouth, the bitterness of the tea seemingly intensifying as his heart raced.

"You come into my home, without knowing the reason why, with no will of your own?" She shook her head, curling her fingers and then opening them once more, the dotted tattoo pattern extending to her palm and along her thumb, as hypnotic as a serpent. "You are one in need of answers, clearly, because you are distinctly lacking in them for *my* satisfaction, at least." She sniffed disdainfully.

He shrank, feeling his muscles tighten slowly, an ache forming as the strange tension grew. "What do you want of me?" he asked worriedly, as she continued that all too sharp stare.

"Give me your hand, young man." Her voice was quiet, but commanding. Barty hesitated, still at a loss for what was going on.

"Whatever for?"

She did not blink. "Because you are trespassing, a crime you must yet earn forgiveness for. If you are to be forgiven, you will give me your hand, so that I might read your fate."

Barty was unsure, but nevertheless set down his teacup. "Why would you want to know my fate?"

The woman sighed, exasperated. "Because when you have crossed it as many times as I have, lost child, you learn to respect it, and to act in accordance to its whims. You might be here by accident. Or there might be a purpose. I will find out which."

She snapped her fingers. Once more Barty felt his actions were not quite his own. He leaned forward and presented his hand, as though his arm was pulled along by a string, the muscles responding to orders that did not come from his own will. Strong fingers wrapped around his wrist and eased him closer. The woman hummed a moment, looking down to the stitches in the palm.

"Well then. This shall make things a little easier." Without warning, she pressed the point of the blade on her thumb into the stitches, slicing through them and into the healing wound, tearing it open. Pain bloomed like a flower, far sharper than the first injuring, when his blood had been pumping and adrenaline had dulled it. This felt like a hot sawblade digging into his flesh, and he cried out in surprise and tried to pull his hand away, but his limb would not move.

The woman, her expression impassive, held the thumb blade in the wound as blood flowed out, watching Barty's expression, before pulling the blade free and—to Barty's absolute horror—putting it in her mouth. She grimaced as she sucked it clean, and spoke in a surprisingly matter of fact tone. "You really do need to eat more, dear. This is far too thin to be good for you." For Barty, who had expected a simple and trite palm reading, this was entirely too much.

Never mind that was the second time someone had said matters regarding his fortitude to him that day, and he did not even register that even the tone sounded familiar. He was too busy trapped in the realisation that he simply could not move. His muscles were locked in place, so tightly that it felt like he was cramping all over. "What... did you... do to me?" Barty managed to force the words out, but with difficulty, choking over every syllable.

The woman sighed, a bored sound, then—after dumping its contents back into the teapot—she placed her empty cup beneath Barty's hand, twisting his wrist so his blood dripped into the porcelain. "A mild poison. It reacts to tension in the body and heart rate, to put the muscles into a state of spasm and paralysis," she answered brusquely, studying the rate of his blood flow into the cup, frowning as she did so.

He struggled with the sensation, and as his body stiffened he realised something. "You... you drank it... too."

She was nodding, still assessing the dripping blood. "Yes. But my heart beats as I tell it to. It has no effect on me."

This answer made no sense, but it was now so difficult to speak that Barty felt it was pressing to ask more pertinent questions. "Wh-why?" Barty choked out, feeling his eyes bulge as his body remained stubbornly out of his control. The woman calling herself Madam snorted with genteel grace and turned his hand palm up once more.

"Well, I had hoped you might tell me what brought you here and more besides, but since you wished to play the game of Silly Buggers, Mister Bartholomew Bartleby"—and he flinched spasmodically as she said his full name—"then I shall oblige you by playing it *better*."

She pulled a box from the floor at her feet and opened it, revealing a collection of darkened bottles as Barty stared in a panic. She was working fast and without ceremony; a woman intent on her task, and one she had clearly practised. And all the while Barty could but sit there, able to breathe and nothing more, as ache set into his knees, his elbows and shoulders. The sensation of trying to move and being unable to do so was painful, making his eyes water and face redden—yet his arm remained extended, the fingers locked. Madam, the witch or whoever she was, poured a selection of powders into the cup with the blood she had taken from Barty's burning hand, and then lit a match and tossed it into the mix.

There was a small flash of flame that turned into a cloud of smoke, tinged with strange colours and sparks. It flared, and the strange witch-woman breathed it in with her eyes closed, drawing in a great draught of the weird vapours; she held it, and opened her eyes wide, taking his bleeding hand in hers and exhaling, blowing the smoke directly into his face as she held his gaze.

He tried to hold his breath, but she pressed on the cut in his palm with her forefinger to make him gasp and suck in the smoke. It tasted strange, like metal and flowers and other herbal scents, sweet and bitter, sour and soft. He coughed, blinking, as the world began to change.

It was rapid, his perception turning in ways he had never known before. New colours entered his vision, and a strange ringing began in his ears. There were ripples in the air and sparkles of light at the edges of things, the room suddenly growing brighter. He stared enraptured, blinking at the teapot which had candle light shining off it in streams and stars. It was the most beautiful thing he had ever seen before.

"Look at me, Mister Barty." The voice was soft, but commanding. When he fought to turn his head, it was like it was stuck in thick treacle. He was acutely aware of every muscle in his neck and head, each one activating and pulling and shifting his vision around, with such slowness that he felt the world had itself ceased its spin, and now he, Barty, was pushing all of creation with his movement.

After an eternity in the stars, where worlds lived and died and were reborn, he finally made eye contact with the witch. She was looking at him with dark, dark eyes that turned darker still, darker and darker until she blinked and then they were inky black; eyes the colour of a raven's wing without light, and as he heard their cry above him and yet so far away, he fell into the void of her gaze and reality tilted into that darkness. The last thing he heard, as the world ended, was her voice from far, far away.

"Let us look back... and see where you began."

CHAPTER 4

BLACK FEATHER PROMISES

It was always cold in Saint Mary's at night. In summer it was merely chilly, but in winter you froze. You huddled and shivered and only fell asleep because you were unable to fight the exhaustion any more, all while never knowing if your eyes would ever open again.

Nevertheless, it was a comfort in that such nights were safer. The orphanage creaked less as the predators, the false guardians who did not seek to protect but instead looked for victims, were too cold themselves; lurking around their fires while their charges shivered in frostbitten iciness, protected by meagre, threadbare blankets and nothing more. More frequently than any sort of decency would allow, they would remove the body of some child who froze to death, with their fingers chewed by rats who scented a meal that would not struggle. Sometimes they would remove the body of one the monsters had hurt too much, the bruises and blood covered by cloth that did not hide the extent of the sin. No one asked why, no one asked how, and no one cared who. Orphans were the forgotten children, with no one to love them, the cast aside and the offspring of the dead or damned. The burden that only existed until it could be shifted to the workhouses, to toil until death there instead. But some learned. Some were different; more clever than the rest. Barty had been one of those.

He had learned how to survive early. To keep himself apart. To hide under the bed when necessary, and to stuff his bed sheets to make it look like he was there, when in fact he had found somewhere else to conceal himself. He had slept in cupboards, in iron bathtubs, anywhere he could keep out of sight and out of mind. He had trained to hide himself from notice, to pretend to be sick, so when the work crews came looking for new people to grind under the wheels of relentless industry, they would not choose him. And then he had managed to conceal a knife that he had stolen, and keep it in his hands as he was sleeping, until he grew old enough that he no longer drew the eye of the creatures in the dark—but he kept the knife anyway, because he learned not to be stupid either.

And he had survived. But not without cost. The price had been invisibility, and few friends, until a voice had spoken through a crack in a wall, and that voice had saved his life. A voice, and two blue eyes, all that he could ever see of his friend, and it was enough.

In a corner, huddled against the mouldering bricks, where no one could have guessed that a friendship was blossoming, they had come to know one another. Meagre cracks in the wall, affording but slight glimpses of the other. Charlotte was her name, an orphan next door where the girls survived, segregated from the boys for the sake of decency, in a place that made a brutal mockery of such a notion by the blood it shed and the lives it ruined. Through the wall that kept them from each other, they had shared their stories, and had invented a place for no one but themselves. Barty had imagined what she looked like, beyond those scarce glimpses, as she made jokes about the world they did not get to see, the life they did not get to live, and the hope they did not have. She had sung songs that she had composed, just for him to hear, and they had been the shield against despair that kept him going. She had laughed as he tried to sing them himself—as poorly as possible—just to hear her happiness, even at his expense, because that was a price he would gladly pay.

He remembered this night. This was the night after Charlotte had quit the place at last; been sent on her way to the world they had learned about but not seen. The world they both longed for but feared, because when all you knew was fear, it was a natural thing to pass that dread onwards. But he had burned for it, and that night he burned all the hotter in his bed as that longing consumed him. Holding the knife under his pillow, he struggled between waking and dreaming, fraught with an imagining of the world that Charlotte had found, that she had promised to make her own and sing her songs to prove herself; to show that she mattered, that she existed, and that she was worth the love she had been so cruelly denied. And Barty had cried that night, because he had not told her he loved her, because he had not said that she had saved him, even after promising once the doors opened for him—to escape that awful place—he would find her, and she had promised she would wait for him. He had not said it to his only friend for fear of what he might hear in reply, and he had been left instead with regret. Barty resolved to correct that, in his heartbroken sorrow, the first chance he would get. But it was six years from that night, and he had never seen her again.

You hide it well, this part of yourself. Or are just very good at forgetting.

The voice was familiar. It was close, bouncing around in his ears. And it was not his own. He sat up his skinny, starved frame in the meagre bed, with rows of the same stretching out to either side of him. Vague, formless lumps lay still and silent in each, huddled in on themselves—their only protection a flimsy sheet and a prayer to a God that did not hear them. Barty held the crude knife in one hand, pointed out in the gloom, as he blinked at the speaker; a great black raven sat at the end of the bed, staring down at him with one altogether human looking eye.

He felt his world tilt. Had this happened? Was this happening? Had he dreamed the life after this moment, or was this the dream? The raven cocked its head, and its beak moved.

Slow down, child. We are learning together today. I said I would find your fortune, and I keep my word. The raven hopped along the sheets to land on his knee, an inch from his held shiv. It spoke with a woman's voice, but the words were ones he only heard in his head.

"I..." He opened and closed his mouth, stammering in a whisper. "I-I thought that meant... reading palms. Crystal balls."

The raven cocked its head again, in a manner expressing incredulity. *If I wanted nonsense, perhaps. But I have no time for nonsense, and nor do you. Now get up. We cannot linger here.* She hopped off his knee, spreading her wings as she did and flying off into the gloom.

The situation had a deeper level of unreality to it now, as he slowly pushed himself out of bed. He looked down at himself, realising that he was dressed as he had been when he stepped out with Elanor that morning, a time that felt years and years ago, but, if his surroundings were any indication, simply had not happened yet. It was, to say the least, disorientating. He felt disjointed, like he was not quite himself, and as he looked around at the endless rows of beds surrounding him, stretching off endlessly into the encroaching dark, the misshapen lumps of sleeping figures slid into focus, and he had the uncanny awareness that underneath each blanket was nothing but stuffed bedclothes and other things to conceal the fact there was no one there. He was alone.

A door opened somewhere. In the shadows beyond his vision, a floorboard creaked; the agonising cry that gave warning of a dreadfully deliberate step, of a heavy figure that was seeking a living body, and he was the only one present. His heart pounded. He had lived this nightmare before. He froze in place, knowing he could not run fast enough, or far enough, to get away, and that *thing* in the shadows, that pretended to have a soul, was going to come for him, and catch him, and that would be the end of him, except for the screams.

The raven landed abruptly on his shoulder, its talons digging through his coat as the pitch black beak clicked its warnings into his mind. *We have no time for this nightmare, Mister Bartleby. This is not your place any more. Now take the door, and leave.*

He needed no encouragement, even if he felt it was hopeless. He turned and ran as the shadows rolled behind him, tasting blood and wanting more. There was crimson dripping from his palm and the shadows licked it up as they came after him, clawing at the floors and flowing over the beds as they panted and hissed with stinking breath that smelled of rotting teeth and alcohol. The door was before him and coming closer, the raven on his shoulder flapping her wings to push him faster, and as he felt that foul breath on his neck, he turned the handle and stepped out through the frame, and felt a familiar, soft crunch underfoot.

Snow was falling, the ice in the air forming in his lungs, and faceless people walked the street, paying him no heed. He was outside. Past the walls that had held him, dirtier on this side than within, and yet far more beautiful. This was the day he had left the orphanage to find his own path; this was the day he was free.

The raven left his shoulder and landed on the ground before him, preening her feathers with a disdainful sniff. *Not so good at forgetting as I thought.* She turned her beady eye up to him, and though her expression was unreadable, the vaguely familiar voice of the raven turned unexpectedly sympathetic. *But I do not think anyone could blame you for that.*

Barty did not notice. He was looking around. There were people, but their faces were blurred; featureless and blank. There was only one face he was trying to find, but they were not there.

"She never came," he said dully, staring at people who did not see him. He had never dared meet the eyes of another save for her, but that day he had looked and looked, within each gaze that passed him by, seeking the only eyes he had ever met, from outside of his prison and into hers, and he did not see them; she was not there. She never came.

The raven hopped on the gutter before him, the cock of its head speculative.

You learned what disappointment felt like, it said thoughtfully with that voice that only he could hear, but he shook his head.

"I learned what that felt like long before this. This was despair. She would not have done this. Not unless she had no choice." He closed his eyes, squeezed them tight, then opened them again, and looked down to the newspaper he now held. The articles were blurred, the text foggy, but the headline stood out as the falling snowflakes soaked the page to a soggy grey.

WHERE IS JACK THE RIPPER?

He let his eyes drift shut again; he remembered how, in his lost moments, he had seized this. Even in the orphanage they had known about Jack; had heard the whispers of the madman who tore his victims apart and stole pieces of them. The children had told stories of how the monster would come for them, to frighten each other, as if the act of spreading such fear could allay their own somehow. If only they had known how right they were.

"There were so many unanswered questions." Barty's voice was still dull, hollowed out, his breath steaming in the frosty air. "I had nothing else. I had to find out. But..." His silence choked him once more. He opened his eyes again and the world streamed past him in a blur even as he stood still. Closed doors, closed faces, heads shaken in denial and dismissals given. No one had answers for him; no one cared to give him any. He had struggled, and then he had turned to the last option he had.

He blinked as the world abruptly locked into place, and he found himself outside the office of The Times; the lifeblood of news and information, the voice of the people writ large in bold type and with the power of hysteria behind it. Originally, Barty had gone there to learn what he could, to find investigators who could provide him the means to find his own answers, but instead he had met a man elaborately called Charles Frederic Moberly Bell.

A frantically energetic man, once of Alexandria of Egypt, but now firmly in charge of The Times, he brought with him a ferocity built upon worldly experience that had been founded in war, discord, and seeing more of the follies of life than most. A large man, with a larger personality, he had come across a despondent Barty after his latest rejection in his offices and then, after a brief conversation, gave him a job.

"Find me a story, and I will print it. Give me things worth writing about, and I will tell it. You want answers? I'll show you how to get them."

It was the first time someone had given him a chance—and a pay cheque—and the true beginning of Barty's experience as a journalist. Barty learned how to dig for the truth and how to find ways of getting his questions responded to. He learned how he had learned near everything before, by his own intelligence and ingenuity, because there was no one there for

Barty, and no one he could rely on. His life sped by faster and faster, into dark places, into hidden corners, into meeting people who he could learn about and learn from, but the name of Charlotte was never far from his lips, the question of where she had gone ever in his thoughts and then—

The raven flew into his vision, except now it was larger, far larger, its eyes more human. It landed before him in what was now a grey, formless void. *Interesting.* Her voice came, thoughtful and even surprised. *There is nothing here.*

"What?" Barty felt disorientated. Dizzy. Years had rolled by and too fast for him to blink. He had been ripped from moment to moment, as though someone was rifling through the files of his thoughts and memories, dragging him heedlessly through motes of time that stuck in his thoughts. There were no nightmares of the orphanage on his heels any more, but still he did not feel safe. "What are you talking about?"

The raven hopped about on formless nothing, finding purchase where there was but grey, vague void, a fog of seeming that had no bottom nor end.

Your memories are clouded. There should be something here—something significant. A moment in your life that follows you, but there is nothing. The voice mused, curious. *But after this, you began to look for Jean Reynard.*

The name jolted him. In this place, that name had weight, cracking the moment into life and sound, colour and movement. The grey twisted, warping into otherworldly geometry. His head started to hurt—the first time he had felt pain since coming here. Sharp and bright behind his eyes, the nerves tearing as something ephemeral became tangible, turning jagged in his skull as he clutched at his head. His eyes screwed shut, even as he clawed at his face, holding in the growing need to scream with his fingers.

"Someone... someone told me his name. Said that... that he would have answers... that he would know." The pain intensified, turning molten, and he staggered.

Through his fingers, the grey began to take shapes. Chairs and benches. A corner, by the fire. All formed in lifeless shades. There were the sounds of clinking glasses, talking people, the smell of smoke and tobacco, of stale beer, the air thick and hot. A tavern dive, a place with no name and no meaning, but something here *mattered*.

He groaned, then cried out in pain. The broken glass running through his nerves grew harsher, crueller, burning him.

The raven cocked its head. *Bartholomew? What is wrong?*

He struggled to answer, the compulsion to speak fighting desperately to overcome the pain holding him back. "Something... happened here, I..." The flash of pain dropped into the fires of torment, and he screamed.

The raven gave a surprised cry, harsh and croaking. It flapped in the air, taking off and hovering before Barty, speaking intently. *What do you remember? What is hidden here, Mister Bartleby?*

It hurt, and then it moved far, far beyond simple pain. Whatever it was, as the memory rose up of its own, something sunk its claws into his skull and *dug* inwards. His cranium was cracking, his eyes were catching fire, his mouth and ears were filling with blood and he was dying—

No! Hands gripped his shoulders, hands with strong fingers, that held him upright as the woman spoke to him fiercely. *No! Do not run from it! The pain will only stop if you push through it!*

Every instinct in him told him to flee. To duck and hide like he always did. To shield himself from pain by finding a place where it could not find him. But there was no refuge here. His vision was red, the world filled with a dull roaring, the abyss was yawning before him. Somewhere, a woman was screaming his name...

"You look lost, young man."

It was a woman's voice. His eyes opened, and he was in the tavern. His forgotten dinner of beef pie before him, turning cold. He blinked, looking around. What was he doing here? How had he gotten here?

Oh. That was right. He had been following leads in his spare time on the Ripper case, and once again come up with nothing. No one ever knew anything, but then again, it had been years since the last killing. So now he sat, in this alcove corner of the tavern, far from everyone else, hidden away in the gloom, hoping no one would see him or find him. By the light of a single candle, he had been sadly poring over the clippings of the old newspapers he had gathered—all various articles of the Ripper case—looking without seeing anything new.

But someone had spoken to him. He looked up, and held his breath. A woman was standing over him in the darkened room. She was tall, taller than he was, and so, so still that she did not appear to breathe. Her face was hidden in the shadow created by an exquisite wide brimmed hat of deep crimson. She wore a dress of the same colour, but was cloaked in rich black sable.

She looked so utterly out of place in that dingy tavern that Barty felt his tongue tangle in his mouth.

There was a hint of a red lipped smile in the depths of that shadow. "Do invite me to sit, my dear. It is most impolite to stare." Her voice was as rich as her garb, soaked in honey and deep, deep mysteries.

Barty, unable yet to speak, gestured to the chair opposite him in his little corner. The woman sat with an elegance that would have shamed any queen into silence. She leaned back in the chair, her smile still coy amidst that darkness. There was a hint of a tooth, sharp and pointed, that poked into her lower lip, her incisor sharp and gleaming.

"I hear you are looking for someone."

Of course. He remembered now, as the world wavered once more. It was so easy to remember it when he thought about it. She had found him, and she had told him—

"You are looking in the wrong place," she chided in a friendly manner, giving a soft laugh.

She had proven to be a warm conversationalist, gently encouraging him and allaying his previously soured mood as they talked. He still had no idea who she was, but this woman was gregarious while measured, and surprisingly kind. She had skilfully cracked open Barty's awkward shell and he had opened up to her throughout the evening, growing ever more confident, talking about how he believed that Jack the Ripper was dead, that there was *someone* out there that knew about it, and that he was determined to find out who. And she had listened, even as he told her of Charlotte, of how he was hoping to find her again, and the pale woman with long black hair had laughed while covering her mouth and shaking her head.

She sat sipping on wine she had summoned with a casual and dainty raising of her wrist. She had even been so kind as to share it with Barty, and drinking it—a fine, rich red that was far, far beyond his ability to ever afford—he had grown ever more loquacious. Strange, he vaguely thought; she had told the barkeep precisely where the bottle was, on a certain shelf in the basement behind a certain barrel, and he had been shocked first to know he had such a fine vintage at all in his run down establishment, and that she had paid for it in full.

They had continued to talk—or more accurately he had talked, and she had listened—and her form remained shadowed, her face in particular. He never got around to asking how she had found him. Nor why a woman of such obvious prestige was in such a place, either. The questions simply never found their way out of his mouth, catching on his tongue, and each time they did she would ask another question about his investigations, and he would travel down that rabbit hole instead.

"The man you are looking for is called Jean Reynard."

She said it smoothly, softly, but in the aftermath the silence was deafening. Barty blinked at her, confused, but the beautiful woman sighed and eased herself forward, coming more into the light as she did so. Now she was looking at him directly, and for the first time, he could see her eyes. They were dark, the iris a brown so wickedly deep as to be nearly black, particularly in contrast with her startlingly pale skin. She looked into his eyes as her own turned a malignant, vibrant red; the room locked up, his heart stuttered in his chest, and the world turned hazy and uncanny—the frozen moment turning the homely scene into something suddenly disturbing. The pleasant smile vanished, swift as a door slamming shut, as all humour left her, and when she spoke, her voice was one of power, every syllable ringing in his memory like a bell.

"You will seek the man named Jean Reynard, though you will not know his name until it is told to you. The man who killed Jack the Ripper will give you the answers you seek, and your life will be changed by it forever. Because he will find you, Bartholomew Bartleby. I will make sure of it."

Every word hammered itself into his brain, drilling into his thoughts and burrowing into his subconscious. She leaned back into the darkened recess. His vision blurred—then abruptly, all was well again. Things once more turned jovial and friendly, and moments later she politely excused herself, thanking him for his hospitality. She slid out of her seat like rising smoke and vanished into the shadows before Barty could think of a way to convince her to stay. And after she was gone, he remembered the surety, the name on the tip of his tongue, that the man who killed Jack the Ripper was out there. But he did not know how, just as he never knew the name of the woman in red.

The pain came roaring back, but it was lighter. He could withstand it now, but it staggered him even as the world went back to its formless grey. The moment had cast him out. The false reality became fractured, shattering without form or sound and he was flung into uttermost nothingness, the space where no imagining could survive. Freefalling into shadows, a bleak darkness where he abandoned all else, to obey a command he had not known he had even heard, much less that he was following; find Jean Reynard, find him at all costs. Each day another step down that road to damnation, and ever as he went, a red lipped smile and an eye that gleamed with the same bloody crimson. He was falling, and now everything was scattered and lost. He was lost.

A flutter of wings, a flare of feathers, a deep caw and a woman's voice, strained with concern, thick with relief. *I have you. You are safe. I have you now.*

He fell into darkness, but now there was no pain. Just the void.

WHEN HE AWOKE HOWEVER, the pain returned with great fanfare, grandly announcing its unwelcome presence with the burning in his muscles and the needles in every joint. There was a dim, natural light in the room, but even that faint glow set to stabbing at his eyes so fiercely that they watered immediately upon opening, foiling him from making out its source. He was laying down on something soft and yet his agony would not allow it to be comfortable, the pain so great that when he moved, he bit his tongue to keep from screaming.

For the moment, he gathered himself as best he could, his breath huffing through his nose, his mouth clamped shut. He was back in the caravan, but in a second space beyond the first he had seen, placed on a bunk bed bolted to the wall, with barely enough space to sit up. There were books, cases, and a mirror—jewellery and perfume bottles were scattered about, and other feminine touches besides that identified this compact space as belonging to a woman. And it was a woman's voice he could now hear beyond a doorway—a door close to him at the foot of the bed.

"... I had no idea that would happen to him." The Romani woman was speaking, her voice terse. "That was not at all what I expected."

To his shock, it was Elanor that replied, her voice tense, struggling to keep it lowered. "He almost *died*. He was convulsing for God's sake! You don't even know if he will wake up!" She swore then, and he could hear the thump of a stamped foot. "What am I going to tell Father?"

"You will tell him nothing," the witch answered sternly. "If he wants to know he can take it up with me." A pause. "Eventually, at least."

Elanor groaned in exasperation. "Well, what are we going to do with him?" she asked in a grouchy tone. Barty's torn muscles tensed on hearing the question, and his already racing heart pounded harsher when he heard the answer.

"First, before making any rash decisions, we should see if he is still alive."

Barty attempted to push himself up, his arms shaking under the strain, trying to figure out a means to escape in his blind panic. But for all the frightened racing of his heart, his treacherous body was far too slow.

The door opened and Elanor stepped through, drawing in a

gasp that halted her in her tracks. "Barty? You're awake?" She hurried over the step it took to reach him, sat on the edge of the bed, and reached out to help him.

But Barty was having none of it. He flinched and warded off her touch by striking at her hand with what little strength he had. Pushing himself away from her, with a spasm that made him want to weep it hurt so fiercely, he pressed his shoulder blades into the walls of the caravan. All to put as much distance as he could between them. Trusting her had gotten him into this mess, had gotten him feeling like this. He was in no hurry to repeat the mistake. He shook his head, croaking a guttural, dry-throated, rasped, "*No.*" It was all he had the strength for.

Through his blurred vision, he could see her face. Her shocked confusion was wrought bare, her mouth half open as though to form a question, before his glaring eyes seemed to explain to her all she could have thought to ask. He was grateful for that, because he could not find the words as he shivered and shook; there were none, just the pain, and his visceral, gut wrenching anger at the hurt. *Look at me.* His thoughts were despairing. *Look what you did to me.*

"I see our guest is awake," the older woman said dryly, leaning on the doorframe, her arms folded across her chest. She had discarded her shawl, revealing a simple blouse in a rustic style, a sash of red cloth around her waist and a dark brown skirt. There was more light now in the caravan; the windows in the other room had been opened during his nightmare foray, and now the meagre sun was shining through. It was still daylight, but it was fading. Barty did not know how long he had lain thus. Elanor shot her a warning look, but Barty did not see it.

He was trying to keep himself upright but he had never hurt this badly before, through any number of beatings and broken bones. This was worse. All his nerves were screaming, and tears manifested from his pain, blurring his vision into a smear. "*What...*" He coughed, harsh and scratchy, and tried again. "What... what are you going to do to me?"

"Beyond making sure you are still breathing—nothing." The older woman sniffed.

Elanor made an exasperated sound and then held both her hands up, palm out. "We're not going to hurt you, Barty. Everything is all right now." She kept her voice soothing.

Barty, however, did not believe her at that moment. The sensation of knives stabbing him all over prevented it. His naked suspicion clearly disappointed Elanor, her downcast gaze one of shame, but he did not care. "Who is she?" He gestured with his chin towards the watching woman. Elanor sighed, lowering her gaze, but it was the witch who answered.

"*I* am Esmerelda di Bella Connistra del Erzsebelita Magdelena Vonnicari Magritte d'Amille," she said dryly, "but *you* shall call me, Mrs Reynard."

Barty blinked several times, as the name washed over him in a somewhat dizzying wave. His wretched state faded back temporarily. He looked to Elanor, his suspicion dulled for a moment as he sought a response that made sense.

She sighed, her manner subdued, and gestured vaguely. "Barty, this is my mother"—an awkward, guilty shrug—"she wished to meet you," she explained, somewhat meekly.

Barty could scarcely believe his ears. He stared at Elanor

then turned his gaze to Jean's wife, who now wore a knowing, but bitter smirk on her lips. "Well, she certainly bloody well did that," Barty managed to rasp.

"Pleasure to meet you too, my dear," Esmerelda—in truth the only name that Barty had managed to catch aside from her addendum title—said with a sardonic tone that seemed painfully familiar, so much like her husband that it now seemed obvious. She moved brusquely over to the cot, taking a seat beside her daughter, who still looked crestfallen. "Now that is all out of the way, how do you feel?"

Barty coughed again, the sensation wracking his entire body in a fresh flare up of burning misery. "Hurts," he croaked out in the aftermath, still trying to keep his distance from the two women. It did not matter if it was futile or not—he was in pain, and his body was trying to evade further cause of that pain. The wife of Jean tutted, and reached out to grab his hand while he struggled to escape.

"Shush," she said absently, unimpressed by his weakened flailing.

He stammered as she set two fingers to his wrist, her lips moving as her eyes closed. "What are you doing?" he groaned, too tired to pull away.

One eye flicked open to stare at him. "I am *trying* to take your pulse. Now be quiet." She closed both eyes again, and resumed counting as Barty shut his mouth, his heartbeat pounding in his ears treacherously. After what felt like an age, she looked back up at him, frowning. "Your pulse is strong, perhaps a little too strong." She stared into his face with an intensity that made Barty flinch, her expression unreadable as she still held fast to his wrist. "And I am still not sure of what it is you are hiding."

Barty grimaced, pulling his knees up to his chest and yanking his hand away with a wince. "I don't know what you are talking about," he said sullenly.

Esmerelda scowled, glaring at him. "You *are* hiding something. I saw you there, struggling against whatever it was that clouded you, and then there was a place where *something* was stopping you from remembering. You vanished from my sight, until the dream cast you out again. But after that? After whatever it was that happened in that moment I was blocked from seeing, you were searching for my husband as though the devil was whipping you to hurry. Why?"

Normally, Barty would have answered. Perhaps evasively, perhaps honestly, but not today. Today he was angry, and he hurt, and he was in no mood to cooperate with anyone. So instead, he glared right back with all the defiance that agony lent him, even though his anger made him hurt all the more. Instead of backing away from it, he leaned into it. It made the spite flow more freely.

"What I *know* is that you poisoned me, and then did... did *something* to me, after your daughter *tricked me* into being here in the first place," Barty growled, his jaw working, blinking back tears in his outrage. "What I *know* is that everything hurts, because of what you did. So why should I tell you anything at all?"

Elanor flinched at his words, hearing the venom in them. He did not care. But Esmerelda drew herself up imperiously. "You are here because I ordered my daughter to make it happen," she said coldly. "And because she knows better than to argue with me, she did exactly that. I wanted to know who you were, without there being any distractions, Bartholomew Bartleby." She frowned. "So far, I am not entirely unimpressed. You have a stronger will than you give yourself credit for; and stronger than I expected." For the first time, her gaze lowered, her vision clouding. "The orphanage of St Mary's has claimed far more lives than it ever saved. The Romanichal know that very well indeed."

This made him laugh bitterly, strained and aching. "Ah, then I am *incredibly* pleased to satisfy whatever standards you set, and just as pleased to tell you that *I do not care* what your opinion of me is, in the face of what mine is for the pair of you." He winced, a spasm passing through his body leaving him wracked and buckled over.

Esmerelda muttered something in a language Barty did not understand and stood up abruptly, exiting the room. Elanor replied to whatever was said sharply in the same tongue as she retreated. Her expression was downcast to where her hands fidgeted in her lap, as Barty struggled to recover from the spasming. She continued to look away as he managed to control his breathing, gritting his teeth so tight he feared they would crack under the pressure.

Silence hung for a long moment, before Elanor finally met his gaze with reluctance and spoke. "I did not know." Her voice was hushed. "Mother did not know either, Barty. She has never had anyone react to her *vraja* like that before." She made a face as Barty's blank expression betrayed his ignorance. "Her magic," she explained, grudgingly. "If you want to call it that.

She was as shocked as I was. This was not supposed to happen. She just lost patience and wanted answers."

"She could have tried *asking*," he growled. "You *both* could have tried." He turned away from her in his sulking rage.

Elanor sat awkwardly, before she spoke again. "I did not know about St Mary's, Bartholomew. I had no idea. You never..." She trailed off into anxious silence.

"There's nothing to tell of it," he said sullenly, his tone turning wooden. "I went in. I came out again. Most of the others did not. That is the end of it." He was in no mood to pry open that door again. Absently, he looked down to the palm Esmerelda had sliced through. There was fresh stitching, much finer and much cleaner than what Adam had managed. He barely felt it, but there was a whole list of other pains warring for his attention. Truth told, a twinge in his gut berated him for being unfair. Talking about his past was not easy for Barty. He preferred to deflect from any discussion on the matter, much as he had just done. How could she have known any other way, other than what she had done? But such rationalisation was drowned out in his hurt and disappointment.

Esmerelda returned, pushing through the door with a steaming teacup held in both hands. She offered it out to Barty wordlessly, who stared at the cup, then at her.

"If you think I am going to drink something *else* you give to me after what took place the first time, let me inform you that your chances are small."

She rolled her eyes at him, exasperated at his defiance. "If it will make you feel better, I will have Elanor pin you to the bed while I pour it down your throat," she said sourly, holding it out to him. "It is purely for your benefit; I made it to dull the pain."

He remained unconvinced. "With what, exactly?" The concoction did not smell terribly good, which did not allay his suspicion, nor lend it any greater appeal.

Esmerelda sighed and then spoke swiftly in that strange language before switching back to her accented English. "There. That should explain it. Now take the bloody thing and drink it already before you collapse. Go *on*." She held it out to him again.

He remained reluctant, and cursed himself for a weak-willed fool—but if it promised to lessen the pain, he could only fight against it for so long. He took it, the heat of it flaring in his two handed grip, before he had himself a sip that numbed his lips. There was a sharp shock of a taste he did not like, but it faded swiftly. Taking a deep breath, he drank the rest of it. It was just on the side of being too hot, but what was one more pain on top of all the others? He exhaled, setting the glass aside with a shudder, as the brew did its promised work. The nerves of his body stopped screaming, and the fire ebbed. His breathing eased, soothed by the absence of the ache that had impeded it.

Esmerelda was watching him steadily, her brow furrowed. When she finally spoke, her voice was subdued. "For what it is worth, young Barty—this was never what I intended." She sounded genuinely apologetic—or at least as apologetic as he was going to get. "While I have heard of such things before, they are extremely rare." She cocked her head, as he tentatively opened and closed his hands—they felt numbed, a little distant, but it no longer felt like grinding glass between his joints. "What do you remember?" Her tone was curious, but intent.

"About what?" he grumbled back.

Esmerelda sighed and with great patience, tried again. "About the moment where things went blank, when the pain started. I said Jean's name, and you reacted like you had been stabbed. *Something* happened then. What can you tell me?"

He grimaced, shaking his head. Just mentioning it made his body twinge, either from the memory of the sensation or the reawakening of it all over again, he could not tell. But the tea, whatever it was, made things easier than the last time; it blanketed the pain, buried it, and made it just distant enough. But he did not want to push it too hard.

"There was... something. Someone. Someone told me about your husband, and I..." His words failed him, tongue twisting in his mouth as the effort to remember became too much. His mind was clouded once more, the moment of clarity that had come in those memories was faded, foggy. But there was something more, a jagged hole that ripped through where the answers should have been. "A woman, but I cannot... I mean..." He struggled with it. A smile without a face, a shadow without colour and no light to cast it. The more he reached for her, the more she and the conversation they had shared slipped away, the harder it became to recall.

He had laughed at something someone had said—this woman he could not picture. Strangest of all, he remembered how their conversation had been the *only* sound—how when they were talking, the entire taproom and bar had been near silent, as though everyone in the place had been stunned into wordlessness. It was something he had not noticed before, but it was all he had now. He could not recall the rest.

But he did not want to talk about it in that moment. He was tired, he was sore, and he had been lied to enough already. So he bit back his revelations and instead shook off the malaise, reaching down into the anger he carried instead as he affixed a glare back at Esmerelda. "Why do you want to know all of these things anyway? What does it even matter to you?"

She frowned in response. "I wish to know if you are a threat to my family. To my husband, and to my daughter. If you were able to find him, I want to know how, and I want to know why—and in so doing, know *who*. My husband has far too many enemies for me to be comfortable with, and a newcomer at this point in time? I wish to be sure of you." Her tone was cold, but it did nothing to halt his rising outrage and indignation.

"If you had wanted to find this sort of thing out, why did you not just come to the Lodge and *ask* me about it? Why the wretched game of charades that nearly killed me?" He waved a hand around furiously, his tone bitter.

Elanor shifted at that, flinching as though a sore point had been pressed. She pushed herself off her edge of the bed, taking a pace away, as Esmerelda's demeanour hardened somewhat, her back stiffening. "I cannot see my husband. Not yet." She shook her head.

Barty was confused, and his confusion made him snappier. "You went through all of this to protect your husband, but then refuse to go near him? Why? Do you despise him, or is it a habit to serve poisoned tea every time you wish to ask his associates a question?" He could not keep the acid from his tongue, lashing the air.

She gave him a flat look of indignation, her eyes tightening. "No. I love my husband very much," she responded simply, with a shrug.

Barty was baffled. "Then why?"

"Because he shot our son." She said it in that same simple, matter of fact voice, but her head tilted as her jaw tightened. "You know little of the ways of my people, Bartholomew Bartleby, so I will excuse you for this, but only the once."

This made him pause. He took his anger and shoved it aside for the time being, forcing it down. It was something he'd been required to learn from being in Jean's company. "Very well." He swallowed, quieter now, the venom fading. "Then... please. Help me to understand, if you could be so kind?" He kept his tone measured—the closest to respectful as he could get.

She enfolded her hands across her stomach, her expression turning within, doors closing in her eyes as she became her pain, wrought manifest. Barty had seen this before in Jean, when talking about James. But where he bore the wound in his heart, letting it bleed out into his actions, his words, even as his face went still and cold, Esmerelda shut down all parts of herself. She became shadow, the air around her darkening, as she intoned her words with the hollow, lifeless ache of a funeral rite.

"When there is a death, our people swear oaths upon those that took that life," she said slowly, her gaze as empty as her voice. "When my husband informed me that he had killed our son, I made my own oath—until he ended the life of the one who had cursed our son, I would not forgive him. And he would not see me again. That is the only way that I shall not take my vengeance upon him. Either he brings me the heart of the one who took my child from me, or I will take his."

Barty was shaken, unable to hide his shock from his face. "He murdered his way across France to find them," he said in a hushed tone.

Esmerelda did not meet his gaze, but shrugged. "But not the heart I demanded," she said in a neutral tone. "Until he pays that price, my oath remains."

Barty shuddered. He did not dare turn to look at Elanor, who hovered with her back to both of them to hide her expression. "He may never know if he has gotten his vengeance, or not," he said, his anger drained out of him.

"Then he shall never see me again, unless it is to take his life." She stated it simply, in a matter of fact voice, devoid of whatever true emotions she felt; the closed door of her features showing not a glimpse of her heart.

Barty swallowed. "You said that you loved him."

To this, Esmerelda gave a slight and bitter smile that held the sort of sorrow one such as he simply could not grasp, a depth too terrible and too dark for him to peer into. "You will learn someday, Bartholomew Bartleby, that the deeper the love, the deeper the hate can be. I do love Jean Reynard—I will always love him—but he shot our son, and I cannot forgive him for that. Not yet, at least."

As the afternoon light faded, the world grew darker and a heavy silence enshrouded the space. There was barely enough room for one person in this little cot—and three was far too many—with the weight of that revelation hanging in the air, bringing an unbearable pressure of its own. Elanor still stood with her arms folded across her chest, refusing to look at either of them. Her mother watched Barty with all the intentness of one of her ravens, and equally unknowable.

He swallowed then, his throat turned dry once more. "I do not know what happened," he stated slowly, his gaze lowering from that unyielding stare. "I cannot tell you why I do not remember." He shivered again, and shook his head. "But I do know I am not a threat to your husband."

"And why is that? Why then, do you follow him?" she replied, suspicion rising thick and fast in her words.

He gave a tired shrug. "You know why. You *saw* why."

"The girl who kept you alive in that place," Esmerelda said with a hint of begrudging understanding.

But Barty shook his head firmly. "No, though I do hope to find her yet—and Jean is the only one would could aid me in doing so—but no, that is not why." He set his jaw. "Your husband does not flee from darkness. He does not run away in blind terror to find safety that is not there. He faces it down." His voice shook in remembrance. "I want to know how. I need to know why. Perhaps like you, I will learn *who*. And maybe then I will know what happened to Charlotte, too."

Her expression turned inwards, but briefly this time as she turned her eyes towards him once more, pausing in deep thought. Finally she made a sound of exasperation, smacked her thigh with one hand in frustration, and stepped over to him so swiftly he flinched.

"Very well then. Then we can reach *that* common ground at least." She held out a hand to him, the one with the clawed thumb, which he hesitated to take for a long moment before reluctantly accepting. She helped haul him out of the cramped space that was surely her own bed, he vaguely realised. With the practised ease of one who had lived much of their life in the cramped, carefully managed space of her vardo, she assisted the stiff and shuffling Barty out of her quarters.

The ravens, still perched defiantly upon the antlers hanging from the ceiling beam, screamed balefully, hopping along their perch and pecking at it to show their anger at the presence of the interloper. Esmerelda paused, opening the window and making a croaking sound—much like their own—and the four of them alighted one after another to slip out the window and into the world with flaps of their great black wings. That short interruption passed and she once more steered Barty out and to the step that he had tumbled in through what felt like a lifetime ago. The sun was preparing to roll down the horizon to its rest, the last hours of the day soon to pass. Elanor, subdued and silent, remained a few feet behind, following apprehensively.

Esmerelda paused at the exit, putting a hand to Barty's shoulder that bit down and held him tight, much like the claws of her departed ravens. "There is more to your story yet. Something wants you to forget what you saw, Bartholomew Bartleby. Something that is not your friend." She gave a grim smile. "I say this, even as the one who caused you such pain today, but you must understand, it was not my intention." She sniffed then, her gaze lowering, turning critical. "Now go and get yourself fed. You are far too skinny." She patted his shoulder and pushed him towards the exit. Elanor passed her by, but before Esmerelda closed the door, she called out, "Oh, and tell Adam to practise their stitching! That work on your hand was terrible; I taught them better than that!"

And that, as they said, was that.

With the door to the vardo firmly shut, Barty and Elanor stood in awkward silence, surrounded now by the stillness of the caravans. Except the stillness had eyes; people watched them, peering out of windows and open doors, with neither welcome nor suspicion. Just the empty, quiet watching that let them know they were seen, while giving nothing away.

At least, Barty was being watched—they ignored Elanor, which was understandable, really. They knew her, after all. Being reminded of that fact, Barty once more felt a fool; an easily led fool who had nearly lost everything because of his idiocy. That anger at being trailed along once more stirred a fire in his belly and stoked his tongue to wrath, waking the spectres of his agony as though it was fuelled by his growing rage. But even as his thoughts ran hot and foolish, enough to stir his mouth into action, a croaking cry came from above him.

Just as before, a raven was watching him, looking down at him with beady eyes. It spread its huge pinions and shrieked a raucous scream once more, flapping its wings as though enraged. A single long black feather came loose and fell clear, turning in the air to tumble at Barty's feet before the bird turned, clicked its beak disdainfully, and took off.

"You best pick that up," Elanor said quietly from behind him. "It's a promise."

He frowned, looking back at her, then crouched and picked up the feather, protesting the straining it put on his joints with a groan. The tea was still in effect, but it didn't make things any less difficult. With great care he held the feather up, between thumb and forefinger, and glared at it. "A promise of what?"

She shrugged, coming up alongside him. "Who knows? No one could ever guess what a raven is thinking."

He turned the jet black length over in his fingers, his jaw tightening. "... I do believe I can relate to that sentiment all too well." He shoved the feather into his coat, and with all the authority he could muster with his staggering step, he strode away.

Elanor sighed, and followed him, but did not speak again until they exited the fairgrounds proper, heading to the road to catch a carriage. As Barty peered down the street, he could sense her trying to summon the means to say something. But for once in their sparring, he was faster, and like a snake he *struck*.

"You know Elanor, what with the apology and all, and the circus, I actually was enjoying today. I had seldom had a better one, after all." He shook his head. "I should have known better, I suppose." He raised his hand, waving to an empty buggy carriage down the road. The driver noted his frantic gesturing, and promptly ignored it, much to Barty's frustration, trundling on and away to some other endeavour.

Elanor grimaced, her expression bitter. "You have to under-stand why I did it, Barty. She is my mother—I *have* to obey her. She had her reasons, even if I did not agree with them."

Barty squinted at her, doubt pouring from his accusing gaze. He shook his head and scowled, raising his hand again as another carriage, a two seater buggy, turned onto the street. This one did heed his plea, and flicked the reins to bring their horse towards the pair. Vaguely, he was grateful, for this one had a roof up to protect the inhabitants. The air was heavy now with the promise of rain, and the clouds above thick. Adam's premonition of a storm had proven fruitful. But Barty was more focused on what Elanor had said, rounding on her with a finger raised, jabbing it towards her in a fury.

"You told me not to blindly accept what your father says; that I should not simply do what he tells me, and be defiant of his methods. And yet somehow, you are exempt from such logic, when it applies to your own mother?" He snarled as he spoke, his pent up rage feeling almost not like his own, his voice running away from him as poison and pain gave it terrible power. His tone turned to pure spite. "No apology, not even remorse, just excuses, even when you demanded I make none. You know, I wish James was here right now too, instead of you, because I am sure at least he would not be such a treacherous snake as you have been."

It was out before he had time to think how awful it was. As soon as he said it, he knew he should not have. Because James had died in Elanor's place. He had taken the guilt of that loss, turned that grief into a blade, and all but stabbed her with it.

She stiffened as though he had struck her. He had gone too far and he knew it, but had spat it out before he could stop himself. He had let the hurt take over his tongue and turn his words to venom, the built up rage not buried enough to stop it bursting free. She stared at him, her expression hardening into icy fury, even as she turned pale. The carriage drew alongside them. She pushed past him, and up the steps. He made no movement to follow as she closed the door on him.

"I would not expect you to understand, Barty." Her voice was cold, her eyes wet, but they were ablaze with anger. "After all, it is a *family* matter. And if I recall correctly, *you* have never had one."

He stared at her, blinking, as did she. She seemed to realise that she, too, had gone too far, as the weight of those words pulled his soul from his body and cast it into the gutter. But she hardened herself and turned to the driver. "Carry on, if you could," she said in a shaking voice.

The driver, oblivious, turned and squinted at the staring, pale faced Barty. "What about him, miss?" he asked, his tone unsure. But she shook her head even as Barty remained still.

"He shall be fine, I am sure. He can figure it out on his own."

The driver grunted, and the carriage rolled along the cobblestone street, back towards the Lodge. Barty stared after it as it went, before, in accordance to how everything up until then had gone, it started to rain, engulfing him in a cold haze of misery, alone and forsaken in a world that did not want him... and once more, he was all too familiar with that feeling.

CHAPTER 5

ALL THESE BITTER REMNANTS

The rain endured, drowning the streets of southern London in grey. Water swirled and gurgled in gutters as it gathered mass and then plunged into the deep darkness of the sewers, the unknown place where entirely different lives were lived. Barty walked along, wondering dully if he could be sucked down into that darkness and forgotten.

His anger was played out. In truth, it had withered as Elanor's carriage had rolled out of sight, the inferno of his anger given nothing more to burn. In the aftermath, alone in the privacy of his own thoughts, all he had left to him was bitter ashes and brutal self-recrimination.

He had called her a hypocrite, but in retrospect he was as guilty of it as she was. He had been angry at her mother—but it had been a frustration that he could not vent upon Esmerelda. And so, he had seen fit to release that purposeless fury on Elanor, and for doing something that, if he had been in her shoes, he would have done the same.

But hindsight was no friend to him now. Instead it beat down on him, heavier than any mere rain, as he wandered, soaked through and aimless. He lost sight of where he was, where he was going, and he did not care. The pale, hurt face of Elanor stared at him, her lip trembling, her fierce and powerful pride wounded to the quick by his words. Words delivered with a poisonous hate to them that was so foul it might well have come from Jean's mouth rather than his own. But they had been his and his alone, and it was he who was to bear the price. Gloom surrounded his thoughts, and perhaps because the memory of the orphanage had been dredged up so recently, he turned his inclinations towards despair—his oldest and most hated burden—knowing its embrace all too well and its efforts to drag him into oblivion better than he wished. The devil on his shoulders he had never learned to shake.

Barty wondered what the result of this would be. How quickly it would see him hurled out of the Lodge, how he would be told to forget all he had seen and heard—*if* he was lucky. And since luck was not something he ever felt he had too much of in any case, this was a small chance indeed.

But even if Jean did not bury him in a shallow grave, he would still be left alone and hopeless. And where then, would he find his answers? What mysteries would he solve, what untold stories would he unravel? Would he go crawling back to The Times, where they probably had forgotten he existed at all?

Would he ever discover what happened to Charlotte? That thought pulled him up short in midstep. All these questions mingled with his self pity and his shame to make Barty a very pathetic creature indeed, as he stumbled along in the growing darkness.

His wandering brought him along winding streets and murky avenues to an older part of London where the lanes ran as warrens, where you could step in and never step out again, or at the very least not do so unchanged. He barely noticed as he trudged on with his head down, a morose spectre of unanswered fears that followed his every dragging step. Dimly, he was aware of how much he still hurt, but it was a distant cognisance that was drowned out by the roaring of his thoughts.

He came out of a twisting lane to find himself near to the Tower bridge, still in the midst of his fuguelike state as he approached the path that overlooked the river. He set himself against the stone fence—an insignificant shield between one step and seething oblivion—resting his aching body, as he stared down into the befouled depths. The river was stinking less than usual, thanks to the influx of fresh rainwater to wash it downstream, but there was still no masking the perpetual haze of stench that added its stain to every corner of London, however faint it might be. This close, it was strong enough to reach out and grasp someone, and pull them down into the forever depths with all the other rotting corpses that littered its bottom, and worse besides. A necessary evil, with millennia of history and human muck layering its vast underbelly.

And yet, he felt a reluctant kinship to the river in that moment. Twisting and turning in its winding way out to sea, turned foul by that which it had come into contact with and then made its own. Just like he had done. He did not like this side of himself. He did not like talking like Jean, or thinking like him, or acting like him. And he did not like making Elanor cry like her father did either.

Pushing down the thoughts before he sank any deeper into them, and to distract himself from wondering what the hell he was going to do now, he reached into his coat to pull out the raven feather. A promise, Elanor had told him, as he turned it over in his fingers. The way she had said it had seemed significant. But a promise of what? He wished he could ask her about it, and properly. He doubted he would have the chance now. A wild urge came across him to throw it into the churning water below. Maybe, he thought morosely, he could throw himself in after it and save everyone the trouble.

"Here, mister. Do I know you?"

He looked around, and to his surprise a man was staring at him, head tilted, with a faint, indecipherable smile on his face. Barty did not know him. But he recognised immediately *what* he was.

The man who had intruded on his despairing thoughts was unshaven, wearing a coat that was too big for him, his boots shoddy and poorly repaired. Bloodshot eyes and missing teeth told of an unhappy past, one with an excess of pain in it. They were holding a smoking cigarette in one cupped hand with fingerless gloves, and Barty found himself looking for the knife, because there was always a knife.

Barty realised all too suddenly and entirely too late that he was alone, in a very isolated place at night, with no one nearby. He saw a second shadow move at the corner of his eye, detaching itself from a wall across the street to step closer. His previously foolish thoughts of casting himself into the river were banished as ice flowed up his spine. He wanted to live. He very, very much wanted to live.

But there was no running, even as he felt the rain-slicked stone against the back of his legs. He was tired, and sore, and the healing brew that Esmerelda had prepared for him was wearing off, but that meant nothing. These two were hunters. Worse, they *knew* he realised that he could not escape now. They had cut him off on both sides. The faint smile of the first was widening now, revealing more missing gaps where teeth should have been.

"Cat got your tongue, mister?" He took a sidling step closer, a subtle movement that might not have been noticeable. But Barty noticed it. However, he had been silent too long, so he shook his head and hastily put the feather back in his coat pocket, panicking as he realised that he had not brought his revolver, nor any of the weapons that Adam had helpfully suggested for this very eventuality. Truly, fortune had made an idiot of Barty good and proper this day.

"I—ah, I am sorry," Barty said hurriedly. "I think you have me confused with someone else." He tried to smile disarmingly, and failed in every aspect, even as the man with the cigarette laughed, rubbing his jaw with his free hand.

"Nay, nay matey. I *do* know you, see? Or more to the cut, my friend here does." He nodded, gesturing to the other, more shadowy figure. "You know 'im, don't you, Davey?"

Barty was shaking his head, trying to deny in an even shakier voice, before the other man stepped out of the gloom and his excuses died on his tongue. The other man had a ragged beard and a black eye—and Barty knew him. He had been the lookout in Bugsby's Marsh, the one that Jean had knocked out with a vicious right hook before leaving him tied up and gagged. He glared at Barty now, curling his lip and spitting at the ground.

"Yeah. Yeah, I know 'im," snarled the man named Davey.

Barty raised his open hands, to protest, to say something,

to make some manner of excuse, but the other man stepped in close, bringing with him a practised, stiff punch that caught Barty neatly on the jaw, and folded him up into darkness. If he had space for thinking, Barty would have told himself he should have expected this. Instead, he was only vaguely aware, amidst the spinning in his head, that he was grabbed and dragged off, out of the world and out of sight, presumably never to see the sun again.

FOR THE THIRD TIME that day, Barty woke up wondering where he was. With his aching jaw, loose teeth, and the hammering pain in his head, this was possibly the most dreadful of the three. And it only got worse from there.

His pockets had been picked clean—of that he was sure. He did not have much, but whatever possessions he had once claimed were now gone. His hands were tied behind his back with his own belt. His ribs were aching where he'd been thrown around. His leg was twisted out of place and the cramp it created was what had woken him, which registered with the welling of tears in his eyes. This was followed with the realisation his mouth had been stuffed with a cloth. He was bound, gagged, and laying face down on stone, shoved under an overhang in a dark, stinking, wet alleyway. The rain was pouring harder now, heavy and thick as the storm built in its surly intensity.

And nearby two men were talking in hissed, whispering voices. He froze, and listened, trying to gather some knowledge of his forthcoming fate.

"—you know Old Lord Sawbones was wanting lasses. Paying a good price for 'em, sure, but skinny as he is this one ain't a lass, Harry." It was the grating voice of the man whom Jean had tied up—Davey, as the other had called him. Davey and Harry. He was going to die at the hands of men called Davey and Harry; what a miserable ending.

And who was Old Sawbones? Either way, while he did not know everything, he knew this much—one or both of them were part of the crew that Jean had thwarted from murdering Miska. The fact that such bloodshed was part of their missive did not lend much to his chances of survival, but it did make him wonder how he was still alive at all.

"I know, I know—but shut it, will you?" Harry groaned in annoyance. "I've got an idea here. They wanted lasses but what's the difference if it's all just meat anyway? You heard the other lads; he just cuts 'em to bits." Barty, afraid to move, started looking around where he was, his head still spinning, his vision still blurry. He hurt all over again, but terror lent itself anaesthetic that he desperately needed, and no witch-brewed tea could recreate.

Davey scowled. "Y'got a point. All he's got to do is say 'no' anyways, right?" He growled then. "Hope I find the other bloke next. I'll rip his guts out. Cut us out of a score and walked away? Bollocks."

Harry gave a rasping chuckle. "You're just lucky, mate. Lucky that Cripple Pete didn't make you pay in skin, and that the other bloke didn't gut you. He must have been a mean bastard to get the run on you."

"Makes me wonder what this'un is doing with him," Davey grunted. "Didn't look like much, didn't have nothing on him. Just a bloody feather. Some sort of nonsense that." He sighed. "How long till that cart gets here? We can't carry this runt up northside without bumping into Peelers. Much longer and I say we saw his legs off and toss him in the drink."

Ugly laughter ensued, then the flare of a match. It was a distance away—ten, maybe twelve feet—but it was enough to confirm to Barty that he was in the depths of an alleyway, probably not far from where he had been struck. Not that it would do him much good. How would he be able to run, and where would he even go? Not to mention the most important question; *how* would he escape the murderous pair who had captured him?

Nevertheless, his mind was working very fast now. He was awake. His senses were alert and active, cataloguing information that he could utilise. He was dizzy enough that he felt on the verge of throwing up, but he could *think*. And he knew the first thing he had to do was get the gag out of his mouth. Not to scream for help, no—no one would hear him here—or more accurately, no one would care; not if he screamed at least. No, he had something entirely different in mind.

Without making a sound, knowing that if he tried to spit or otherwise struggle they would return—with the fists and boots to shut him up—he started to scrape his cheek and lips against the stone. It was like grinding his face against a cheese grater; he could feel his teeth scraping against stone. But he had learned in the orphanage to be silent on waking, just in case something was near and listening. It would save his life here too. All he had to do was forget the pain, bury it down, bring it back later and let it pay then, but right now, he had to be silent. Until the right moment. Until it was time to make a noise. The *right* noise.

Rain poured, great sheets of water cloaking the world and creating a waterfall at the entrance to the alleyway where they had holed up, obscuring them from outside view. The duo were arguing about something else now—some other mean spirited discussion about money and the nasty, cruel things with which they occupied their life. He ordered his broken thoughts to remember the names of these two men and all they had said, for the slim and desperate hope of salvation. And for once, hope was not proven false as he felt the cloth in his mouth fall away. God save him, at least they had done a poor job of that. He could freely make sound at last—and with one chance to save his life, this precious, single noise was all he had.

He took a deep breath, feeling a burning pang in his chest as he tried to settle himself. He had been practising this for a while now, much to the amusement of the one it was directed towards. But he had one chance—and one only—to get it right. So he closed his eyes as the hammering of the rain drummed harder above him, and began to whistle.

The first note was shaking, but it was high and long. The two thugs were confused, heads whipping around to identify who was making the sound, while Barty counted, his heart-beat pounding in his ears. He heard them swearing—they had figured it out by now—Davey telling the other to 'shut him up'. They both started towards him as he ended the high note, wriggling away from them to whistle, sharp and fast once, twice, and in the midst of the third, a boot caught him in the ribs and all the air was wrenched out of his lungs. His empty stomach tried to retch up what was not there. Another kick. And then another, before he went quiet, save for the agonised whimpering.

"Bloody hell," snarled Davey, giving him another kick for good measure. "What d'you think this is? Game o' bells an' whistles?" He spat on Barty and reached into his coat, looking to his companion as he pulled out a short, rusty blade. "Lets just knife 'im and dump 'im." He moved in, but the other stopped him. "You don't want to find out about his mate, first? He's the one Pete's really wanting, after all."

A begrudging grunt. Barty was rolled over and dragged upwards by the collar, his face brought within inches of the still snarling Davey, who set the knife he carried beneath Barty's eye. The rusted tip drifted near to the eyeball itself and so, so horribly close that Barty stopped breathing. "A'right, start talking. Tell us where to find the other bloke, or I'll cut y'blinkers out." To make his point, he pressed the blade beneath his eyelid.

Barty's tongue twisted in his mouth. His despair in this moment was complete alongside his absolute terror. The whistle had gone unanswered; the only one he could think that might have heard it had not come. There was no hope for him. Everything had gone wrong and come to naught.

And yet, his desperation would not allow him to die in silence. His strangled, frightened murmur was his testament to the uncaring rain. The merciless beasts before him offered no solace at all, and heeded it not.

"Help me..."

A snort, a sound of contempt and disdain, and Harry laughed. Davey's expression soured further into the blunt, small minded rage of a man to whom fury was a second nature but without refinement or control. His mouth curled, and Barty saw the hand on the blade tighten, before there was a sound that stopped the world—even the rain seeming to take pause.

A whistling tune was heard, echoing with a haunting drift through that miserable alleyway. Exquisite for all its discordance to the situation at hand, whereas his own had been scratchy and desperate. It danced amongst raindrops, spun on the breeze, skipped over stones and twirled amongst the three who had frozen upon its arrival. A shadow had appeared at the mouth of the alleyway, obscured by the sheet of falling water, a veil between one world and the next. Davey froze, the knife he held remaining rigid, his mouth forming a curse, as a familiar voice spoke.

"'Help me', he cried, the lost child of stone and dreaming heartbreak." A luxuriant tone, triumphant in its mocking resplendence. Even though it was exactly what Barty had been hoping to hear, it terrified him as the speaker went on, "And lo, the Prince of Midsummer answered, as is his want." The figure spread their hands like an angel of supplication, stepping through the veil of rain and into the alleyway, grinning that wide, sharp toothed smile, with eyes glittering like silver lamps, feral in their unabashed glee.

Puck looked far, far too pleased. He sauntered forward, his

soaked hair plastered to his skull, the grin all too wild, idly picking at his long but flawless fingernails as he approached. "Really, Barty. You worry me with the company you keep—or does this company keep you, instead? Questions, Barty, many questions."

The two brutes exchanged baffled looks. Then, reaching a wordless mutual agreement that this newcomer was to be dealt with first, Davey flung Barty down. He was hurled with enough force to make his head strike the wall and bring stars to his already blurry vision. He was dazed, but did not black out again, instead left merely stunned and dizzy on the ground.

"Who're you then?" Davey snarled, holding the knife pointedly at his side. "Push on, this isn't your business."

Puck came to a halt, setting both hands behind his back and leaning forward, tilting his head as he did so in an almost birdlike fashion. "A pretty toy you have there to play with, my plaything," he mused thoughtfully, eyeing the rusted knife. His gleaming eyes shifted to Barty. "I hope you did not damage my charge unduly. I think I would take offense." He still sounded cheerful, pleased even. As Barty stared at him blankly, Puck winked back at him.

Harry barked an ugly laugh, disbelieving and confused, but Davey, clearly still smarting over the beating that Jean had given him and wanting to vent his rage in *some* way, snarled and brought the knife around, waving it threateningly in the air. "Turn to th' road and go, or after I'm done carving this one's eyes out, I'll take yours."

Barty felt his heart quail and his stomach churn, much as most would when confronted with an enraged man making such threats. But Puck reacted as only Puck could; he laughed. High, clear, pure, and bright, the laughter bounced merrily off the walls of the alleyway as he straightened, and started to saunter closer, spreading his hands wide. "A most magnificent proposition, but I do believe I have an even more delicious alternative!"

He slid closer then, so fast that a blink would have missed the movement, his terrible toothsome grin wide and fixed. The thug flinched and gave a clumsy yet threatening thrust, but slid on a soaked cobblestone, losing his footing by just a fraction. It was enough. Puck *blurred* as he moved forward, and with a graceful, fluid motion more akin to one a dancer might make, deflected the knife with one hand, while the other lanced towards Davey's face. The fingers closed together, the nails glittering with silver to Barty's dazed eye.

There was a faint, damp tearing sound. Faster than could be followed, Puck yanked his hand back. His fingers were dark with blood, and something dangled between them—at least, until, with that same demented grin, he brought it to his mouth and chomped down on it, chewing with wet, horrible sounds as his shining teeth turned red.

For a heartbeat all was still, as Puck slid back again with gracious politeness, to give the immobile and frozen Davey room, as though he were a considerate house guest, due to make his leave. Harry, standing a ways behind him and with his vision obstructed, was confused, tilting his head as his companion remained unmoving. Until he started to tremble with increasing violence.

"... Davey? Davey, what'd he do to you...?"

The man called Davey did not answer with words, but rather a keening, animal sound that grew in volume as he dropped his knife and reached, with shaking hands, up to his face. He collapsed in a ragged heap, folding up one joint at a time, holding his now empty eye socket as he screamed and howled so shrill and high that his voice broke and tore in his torment.

"All this talk of eyes made me *hungry*. But you were so kind to oblige me!" Puck said, sidling along in a gleefully energetic sidestep as the wretched, doomed Harry stumbled, falling onto his backside in horror.

Barty slowly levered himself up, wriggling about to sit upright, biting his tongue with the effort. Puck paid him no heed, the shark smile he wore paired with his unblinking eyes as he drew ever nearer to Harry, who was shuffling backwards, unable to tear his eyes from the nightmare following him. The shadows seemed to follow Puck, turning the alleyway darker with each step forward and as Barty watched, they engulfed the shrieking figure that was Davey, still clutching his face as blood spurted between his fingers in a desperate, futile effort to stem the crimson eruption. But it was all for naught, for the shadows then swallowed him whole, covering his writhing body in utter darkness. There was a final shriek—terrified and despairing—that fell into nothing, leaving not a trace of him.

"Come, come! Dance with me, my dearest gutter trash, my sublime sewer filth!" Puck said between his grinning teeth, stalking the hysterical Harry. Barty's vision was full of spiralling stars and blurred lights, yet he watched as Harry crawled away on all fours, pleading, begging, unable to form words, just frightened, terrified syllables. But Puck was having none of it;

he was enjoying himself far too much. "I shall make a song out of you that will leave sweet tasting babes yet unborn afraid of the dark, dearest lickspittle—you shall be the dream that stinks of the piss and sweat of the broken. What *fun* we shall have."

Barty could only blink slowly. His ringing skull impeded his thoughts, the blows he had taken making coherency difficult. He watched as Puck leapt through the air like a pouncing cat to land on the screaming Harry, screams that soon gave way to strangled gurgling, and then to wet, meaty tearing sounds, mixed with savage, hissing growls. The shadows only grew deeper, curling along the ground and covering the scene, muffling the horrors. Barty stared at the blurry scene for a while, then looked away, still befuddled by it all. Shock was settling in, wearing him down at last.

The shadows started to thin around him as he looked down, still feeling disconnected from the world around him, and focused on something familiar. At his feet, remarkably untouched by the rain, was the raven's feather. *Funny*, he thought in his dazed state; the moment he had considered throwing it away was when this had all started. That hazy thought took root in his mind as he reached out, holding the quill in one hand, and staring at it.

The shadows flowed like smoke, and two gleaming silver eyes with a smile that was far, far too wide, far too bright, and terrible appeared. Puck was there, crouched before him, his teeth dark with blood, his chin and cheeks smeared with the crimson horror. He seemed intoxicated with glee, mad with a fierce, malignant joy. Barty, too battered to register, stared at him blankly and without understanding.

"You called, and so I came," Puck purred in a low voice, reaching out to adjust Barty's collar fastidiously. "You pleaded for help and thus it was given, dear Barty. But now you *owe* me, Mister Bartholomew Bartleby. What shall you give me for my aid, for the lives that are now mine?" He sniffed, a bit disdainfully, the grin flickering then returning wide once more. "They were poor lives, crude and useless perhaps, cruel and unthinking things, but they *are* a price to be paid. What can you offer, in the here and now?"

Barty was confused. He had not had much on him before getting his pockets looted, and now he had even less. "I don't have anything, I don't think..." he said, his words faltering.

Puck's head tilted then, twisting birdlike on his neck as the gleam in his eyes grew brighter. The grin stretched wider, his voice turned more sibilant even though the cheer remained. "A price must be paid, dearest Barty. A bargain must be struck. That is how these things must go; by the first laws that were made, carved in the soul of the world. What price will you pay?"

But he remembered then, what he held in his hand. Elanor had told to him, after all. "... A promise," he rasped groggily, and held up the feather between them. "I can give you a promise."

Puck retreated, blinking as the grin faded, and the menace vanished with it. A curiosity covered their features instead, as the all-swallowing shadows retreated into the ether. "The promise of a raven, from a witch's wing," he said with a note of curious wonder. "Fascinating, that you would be granted such. They are not given to just anyone, Bartholomew Bartleby. You must have earned respect, however grudging."

Barty did not understand, staring first at Puck, then at the feather. Slowly, he offered it to the silver-haired coachman—whatever he actually was. "I... do not feel I deserve it," he said slowly, the words forming with difficulty. "I have been a fool, Puck."

Puck stared at him, then at the feather, an uncharacteristic frown on his face as he reached out with gentle care and relieved it from Barty's grasp with bloodstained fingers. "You are correct in every way, dear Barty. A very foolish creature, Namer and Named," Puck said wryly. "Innocent and yet knowing, perceptive and yet blind. You confuse even one like me." He sighed then, and inclined his head. "But you continue to both fascinate and endear me, child. I shall keep your promise, until it is earned. I shall be its guardian."

Barty simply nodded. This all had a dreamlike quality, a sense that everything was happening far away. It had to be a dream; there was no way this moment of madness could possibly be real. He understood nothing of what was going on—not even his own responses in this weird, blunted state. He wanted to rest. To just lay down in this dark, cold alleyway thick with the copper smell of blood, and the last echoes of despairing screams. It had to be a dream after all, and thus reasoning said that he should be asleep to suit the state.

But Puck would not allow it. His long, bloodied fingers lightly flicked Barty's ears as he mumbled and groaned in protest. Puck then took him by the collar and hauled him to his feet with both grace and ease that far belied his slender frame. "No sleeping, fearless Barty," he scolded, like a schoolteacher with an errant, misbehaving child. "You have taken a bump too many to that fragile, bouncing skull, and I fear you might dream a little too deep, a little too deep indeed. So, awake!" He looped an arm of Barty's around his slender shoulders and with a light step, carried him out of the alleyway, the movement rousing Barty even with Puck's graceful steps being more akin to that of a dancer.

The falling rain was washing the blood off his grinning face as they half danced out of the alleyway—Puck leading, Barty stumbling—and the four horse coach drew alongside with the smoothness of silk and barely a whisper. Barty was bundled into the back of the coach before he could protest, propped up with his face resting against the glass of the window. All the while Puck was humming, a low melody that—while oddly hypnotic—kept Barty's eyes from closing. And so he stared without seeing, as the coachman slithered into place, still lulling his charge with the disturbingly strange song.

The coach slipped away from the alley that still smelled like blood and death, though if any came by they would find nothing; no trace or sign save for a discarded, rusted knife, and the lingering echoes of a song drifting over the river, haunting all that heard it without explaining why.

BARTY BLINKED, his vision dark at the edges. He had not slept, but he had been drifting so far out of alertness that the world had passed by in a blur. He had yet more trouble concentrating, let alone remaining conscious at all. Even the strange song of Puck, that crawled through his ears and set jagged shards into his brain, was wearing off in its effectiveness. At one point he had started to drunkenly chuckle to himself. Almost killed twice in one day, and perhaps with no home to go back to at the end of things. A fine day indeed.

As if to emphasise the moment, it was at this instant that the sky split open. A great bolt of lightning carved a path overhead, incandescent and enraged. The rumble of thunder that followed set Barty's teeth to dancing. Even the air felt alive, humming and vibrating. A storm was coming, he had been told. The rain had merely been the harbinger.

He was hauled from the coach, barely alert, and made to stagger up the steps. Puck cheerfully propped him up against the door, then knocked with a dramatic and loud tempo, before—like a child causing trouble—he went skipping down the steps and to the coach, giggling happily at the mischief caused. Barty, leaning with his head against the doorway, groggily called out to him without turning his head.

"... Thank you, Puck." It was muffled, but the air hung still in the falling rain, then—with a scuff of light steps—Puck danced back up the stairs and ruffled Barty's hair, giving him a kiss on the forehead.

"No no, dear Barty! Thank *you*. This was an exquisite diversion. Until the next one!" And with that, he scurried off into the gloom, leaving Barty slumped face first against the closed door.

Dimly, Barty could *feel* a marching step approaching from

the other side of the door. Someone was coming, with anger in their steps, slamming down each foot in their annoyance. Barty recognised that stride. Belatedly, he wondered if he should move away from the door.

This presented a fresh problem; he had, for the time being, forgotten how to move. Nothing seemed to work—his arms and legs were not listening to him.

Fortunately, the problem was solved and the day was saved from the issue of Barty's overall lack of motion as Jean yanked the door open—ready to unleash seven kinds of verbal hell upon whoever was banging on it. Instead, he got an armful of Barty, who fell forward onto him, boneless and lingering on the edge of consciousness as Jean was—most unusually—caught off guard for one of the few times since Barty had known him.

He was barely aware as Jean dragged him inside, setting him against the wall and upright even as he slammed the door shut with a curse. He pinched Barty's cheek then, hard, the pain rousing him from his stupor briefly to realise Jean was speaking to him.

"—can you hear me? Barty?" There was concern in his voice—genuine, honest concern of a kind that Barty did not recognise. He shook his head and Jean called out to someone, the shout a blur of words and sounds that Barty struggled to comprehend over the ringing in his ears. A shape appeared on the stairs, someone familiar he could not name, but he heard a feminine gasp of shock.

Jean picked him up off the ground again, getting an arm under his shoulder. With the great and ponderous seriousness of a drunkard deep in his cups, Barty wanted to tell him that he was not as good at carrying him as Puck had been, but at the same time, he was growing tired of being hauled about like a sack of beef. If only he could remember how his arms and legs worked; it all seemed so difficult right now.

Jean was not deterred. He half dragged Barty along to the elevator, holding him upright and yanking on the release to send the box plummeting down into the depths of the world. Barty, still lost in his precarious state, was entirely captivated by the way the walls of the elevator shaft seemed to shoot up past them, lacking the equilibrium to feel the descent. As they plunged on, it seemed quite fascinating.

Jean hauled the door open with one hand, calling for Adam as he pulled Barty into the cavern of the armoury. He heaved his battered assistant to a table and, with a fine display of his strength, lifted the young man bodily and set him atop it, sweeping things out of the way and to the floor heedlessly as he did so.

Barty's tongue finally started to work again. As he stared blankly at the ceiling, he spoke forlornly, his words slurred as his unwieldy tongue labored to keep up. "I... really do not want to be... any more dramatic, Jean... I am sorry."

Jean did not pause. He was busying himself, opening Barty's shirt and coat, inspecting his torso, and then with forefinger and thumb forced Barty's left eye open to get a closer look at him. "You've got a head injury, but you're not bleeding out," he said brusquely, as Barty pulled his head away. "You are most certainly concussed." He started running his fingers through Barty's hair, touching the lumps and bumps that had been formed by the assault. "No fractures, near as I can tell," he said to himself, as Barty cringed away from his touch reflexively. Jean swore then, muttering as he went, before he finally shouted over his shoulder, "Adam! Where the devil are you?"

Barty winced, shying away from the noise that rang painfully in his ears. He turned his head as Jean continued his assessment, looking down the hall of the armoury, before he spotted a familiar shape.

"Oh. There they are," Barty said as helpfully as he could manage—which was not all that helpful, in that moment. He blinked, puzzled, as his confusion grew. "Are you supposed to be glowing like that?"

Jean paused at this. And then, very, very slowly, he turned around to see what Barty was looking at as thunder rolled above and the lights flickered.

Adam's massive frame stood in silence. Less standing and more frozen in motion, one hand extending somewhat towards the absent sky, seeking something unseen—or not there at all. It was unsettling, as though for them the world had simply stopped, but their long, lustrous dark hair was lifting and turning, shifting under an unfelt breeze to float upwards. And—as Barty correctly pointed out—they were glowing.

It was faint, but nevertheless present; arcs of energy, little bolts of lightning, running across their frame—the massive leather coat they wore, starting to smoke and char. Jean turned towards the sight with a careful, dread wariness, as the lights on the walls ceased their flickering and instead flared brighter and brighter, in ever increasing warning.

Barty, still unable to understand the strange situation, smacked his lips together. "... Why do I taste metal?" he asked with innocent confusion. And then Jean was grabbing him, yanking him off the table and throwing him underneath it, before diving over him protectively, just as the world turned incandescent.

Barty's vision turned white. The sound was so loud that it went beyond mere noise in that enclosed space, as lightning *crawled* along the walls, arcing off the many swords and weapons and other various devices—bits and pieces and more besides that made up the armoury. There were flashes of fire and explosions as various flammable things forcefully ignited.

All of it was pouring off of Adam, burning their grand coat to ashes as they stood, arm still outstretched. Arching bands of raw, unfettered energy blazed as they tore the armoury apart, ripping chunks out of the walls and ceiling, and shattering the light globes as they burst. And in the midst of it all, Adam screamed. But not with their own voice.

As the world turned black for Barty, and he faded into final unconsciousness, the last thing he heard was the agonised, despairing scream of a woman, driven to madness and far beyond it, coming from Adam's mouth.

Chapter 6

The Sorrowful and Blessed Mistake

Whatever dreams Barty languished in, they were obliterated from his memory the moment he awoke; there was no room for them amongst the pain that flooded his wretched body. It was so severe, so all encompassing, that he jolted violently, stars bursting in the darkness of his vision; the birth and death of worlds and galaxies held in those shattered blinks. He whimpered, pitifully, too pained to be ashamed, as a shape moved into his line of sight. Someone spoke, an entity he recognised, but could not put name to. He passed out again, the world turning to black, razor-bladed silence once more.

To him, only a heartbeat passed before he blinked his eyes open again. He felt different now—there was a dull ache, constant and miserable, but withdrawn, the pain lesser by far, as he floated above it in a body that did not feel like it belonged to him. But he could breathe again. He opened his mouth, and tried to summon his words, but instead what came out was a near silent rasp.

The shape that had haunted his delirium appeared above him once more. It was someone he knew, and he tried to say their name. They held something to his lips, and he swallowed. Blessed, blessed water, cool and life-giving, bringing him back as he drank greedily and tried not to choke. But the pourer was careful, supporting his head, until Barty finally drained that marvellous ambrosia, setting the cup away. Barty swallowed a few times, and was able to speak at last. "Thank you, Benji." His voice was rusty, weary, but clear.

The young wolfblood supporting him chuckled, and gave Barty a pat on the shoulder before replying softly, "S'all right, guv. But you didn't half give everyone a ripping great fright there." He sounded cheerful—relieved.

Barty lay back, closing his eyes a moment, assessing his state of being as best he could. "How long have I been... how long was I unconscious for?" he asked. Staring up at the ceiling he vaguely realised they were still in the armoury. He was comfortable, laying upon something soft and surrounded by blankets, well wrapped up. But the armoury was darker than he had ever remembered it being.

Benji rubbed his cheek, thinking it over. "About a day or so. Bit more. Bit hard to tell. You woke up a few times—mostly to cry out an' thrash about. We had to wait 'til your pulse got up before we put you on morphine though." He reached out, tapping a bottle to one side, which Barty glanced at blearily. "At least, that was what the others were saying." He peered down at Barty, his eyes reflecting orange candlelight. "How you feeling?" he asked curiously, his long, canine ears flicking briefly.

Barty gave a wry, pained smile. "Probably how I look." This begged a further question. "How *do* I look?"

Benji grinned, unable to help himself. "Like a lively bruise, if I do say so myself. You've looked prettier, guv, s'all I can say. Think you can sit up? Elanor said it was important you get moving when you wake up."

Elanor. Barty felt a flash of hot guilt, but let it pass as he nodded slowly. With no lack of agonising protest, he got his arms under him to push himself up—Benji assisted and, with care, helped Barty to a sitting position. "Why are we still down here, anyway?"

"Can't go up easy, is why," Benji said ruefully. "Adam knocked out just about everything down here." He gestured down the length of the armoury. "We're fixing things, but it was safer to look after you down here than take you up. And Jean wanted to keep an eye on you."

From his now seated position, Barty could see the results of the earlier night. The armoury was much changed; everything was a jumbled mess, there were piles of shattered materials, and debris shoved this way and that. The last time the armoury had blown up was during the Jekyll case, when Adam had accidentally discovered the explosive properties of Hyde's elixir and his blood. But that instance was nothing compared to this new destruction. Parts of the roof had collapsed, and tables, benches, desks, and racks had been blown apart. Every single light globe had exploded, the wires that had joined them melted into glittering copper that had oozed and run like melted wax. This was not a minor incident. The place was all but a ruin, a gutted shell of what it had once been. Like Barty himself, it was broken.

Scattered oil lamps and candles, placed here and there around the expanse, had been lit to create what light could be made. It wrought shadows where there had been none prior.

The destroyed remnants of what had been the armoury gave it an unreal air, making it feel haunted instead of homely, or as much as it could have been before with its many strange and wonderful creations, experiments and weapons. Now it was silent, dark, and ruined.

He had been laying on one of the few unshattered tables. Others were just scorched piles of splinters. The elevator was nearby, and the doors had been blown apart, the metal blackened and warped inwards. A ladder led up to the ceiling of the box and an open trapdoor—clearly how they had been getting back and forth, possibly with another ladder within the shaft itself.

Benji drew his attention back by holding up half of a sandwich. "Hungry? Guessing you would be, with all—" He did not get to finish. Barty grabbed the offered feast with the rapacious speed of the starving, as the sight of it ignited a fierce growling in his stomach. Ham and cheese, simple fare but hunger gave it a flavour beyond divine. He *was* hungry. And thirsty. And more besides. But he finally was able to see more clearly, and what he saw down the end of the armoury made him pause.

The forge that Adam liked to work at was now a war-torn battlefield. The carefully constructed kiln had been close to the giant when the energy cascade had begun, and the raw force of it had broken it like an egg, cracking the stones and brick that built it into fragments. And Adam still stood, wearing the tattered scraps of their incinerated clothing, one hand reaching upwards in a gesture that might have been a warning or a plea, turned away, and utterly immobile. They were exactly as they had been when Barty had last seen them. They had not moved, not one inch, frozen in that last moment.

And not far from them, sat with their back to Barty on a wooden chair, their legs thrust out before them, and arms folded, was Jean. He was watching Adam with the deathly air of one content to wait as long as might be, but nevertheless with the taut, sharpened patience of a hunter waiting for their prey. This was not helped by the fact that in his folded arms was a rifle, and on the bench beside him was a collection of retrieved weaponry of a terrifying variety of applicable violence. He was watching. He was waiting. For what, one could only guess, but whatever form that supposition took, it would have certainly involved carnage, and pain, in amounts beyond mere reckoning. Jean had not turned around as Barty and Benji were moving about, but Barty could nevertheless tell he was listening.

Benji nudged his shoulder. "Come on. Let's get you cleaned up, yeah? Set up a space back here for you." Once Barty was confident he could not only stand, but walk on his own volition, Benji nodded and guided his wounded charge down into the less damaged depths of the armoury. He showed Barty to a little corner that had been converted into a mixture of a bathing space and laundry. Some of Barty's clothes had been placed on a nearby bench. Elanor's coat hung on one corner of a screen. Someone had anticipated being here for a long time if necessary, and it was clear to Barty now that preparations had been made with that consideration in mind. For Adam, of course. But for him as well?

Benji seemed to read something in his expression, and spoke quietly, the distance and debris muffling his murmur. "The old man was worried. He likely won't tell you—vicious bastard that he is." Benji scowled, squinting down at Jean. "But he was. Still is. I don't think he's slept since this all happened, and he's had me and Elanor on shifts looking after you."

Again, Barty felt a hot rush of shame at her name. Benji, this time, seemed to notice the reddening of Barty's ears. He gave Barty a rueful look. "Yeah, she told me the two of you had a little talk." Benji scoffed and the sardonic understatement cut Barty to the bone. "If you weren't so poorly, I'd give you a clip across the ear." His wolvish ears flickered back and forth, a teasing mockery before they lowered in accordance with his tone turning somber. "You scared her half to death when you came in, though."

"I did not think she would care." Barty could not stop himself saying it, and Benji's expression hardened into a frown.

"Of course she cares, you bloody nonce," he said in a sharp whisper. "She acts tough and hard, because you have to when you're Jean Reynard's daughter. But that doesn't mean she hasn't got a heart. She hides it better than her brother did, but it's as big as his was. Just a little bit more battered." He shook his head, his expression turning regretful—it always did when he spoke of James. The two of them had been friends, after all. Something even Jean, with his burning hatred for all kinds of wolfblooded, could not deny nor disparage.

Regardless of that, Barty was silenced. He was still struggling with everything that had happened. But he nodded without looking at Benji. A nod said many things and nothing at all—for now, it meant that Barty had heard what was said and would take it to heart. A troubled heart, perhaps, but better than none at all.

BENJI HAD DEPARTED while Barty was taking care of things—vital necessities that needed taking care of after so much sleep, however imperative rest might have been. Once all such matters had been seen to, Barty made his way across the ruined armoury, picking his steps across the piles of debris and broken glass until he finally drew alongside Jean, seating himself with a muffled groan. He did not say anything for the time being, not quite trusting himself to bridge the gulf of wordlessness. So, for the time being they sat alone—save for the silent, massive figure of Adam.

Jean did not move. He sat still, legs stretched out before him as he slouched low in his chair. The rifle he held across his chest was a mean looking thing—a bolt action war rifle; not his preferred weapon for large targets, but the much heavier calibre, double barrelled rifle he normally used was—to Barty's knowledge—broken, perhaps beyond repair. To one side was a low bench that had a cluster of other armaments; shotguns, revolvers, and even a ludicrously oversized Tranter hand cannon, a revolver that fired massive rounds and did its best to break the wrist of the wielder. There were other more exotic weapons as well; vials full of substances that appeared to be various explosives, and one troublesome object that Barty eyed especially warily and with great distrust—a brass and glass syringe full of some dark, thick liquid, at once both innocent in appearance compared to all the weapons present, and also somehow far more menacing.

He stared at it overlong, the silence of the place growing more oppressive, until Jean spoke sourly, his voice rusty. "Before you wear your vision raw, or perhaps wander once more into some sort of disaster, I would be very grateful, Barty, if you could tell me what the bloody hell happened to you?" He finally wrenched his bloodshot gaze from Adam's frozen form, and turned his glare to Barty instead.

Barty, however, was not looking at him. At all times, Adam's presence arrested the eye, and this close, Barty's gaze had been dragged there inevitably, where even in the faint light the truth of the situation was far more visible. Terribly, horribly visible, and it was at last made entirely apparent as to why Adam had, until this moment, worked so hard to keep themselves covered.

Adam's body was a patchwork, much like their hands had revealed to be. Bones replaced with steel, nerves replicated with naked copper wiring, colourless flesh attached to both to give a semblance of falsified humanity. Ball joints with hydraulic hinges at the shoulders and elbows, the spine constructed from steel and bone and extending up the back, all with flesh and skin securely attached. They were a cross between a machine and a living being; a mixture of things that should not have worked together, and yet certainly did so. Or at least, they had. Now they were still, silent, and dark—mostly. As Barty squinted closer, he could see that along the exposed spine, little arcing sparks of energy could still be seen, dancing in steel cages along the vertebrae, leaping off copper wires. But still Adam did not move.

Jean was watching, as his assistant was struck into dumb silence, before he sighed, his flare of irritation subsiding. "Yes. That is Adam." He sounded sad as he said it, but Barty was barely paying attention. The sight of Adam—of how they actually looked—was both enthralling and abhorrent, a life that was not supposed to *be* and yet was. But there was something utterly sorrowful in them now, that uplifted hand with fingers reaching for something unseen. Jean went on, as Barty remained wordless, "Elanor is, as we speak, working on replacement clothing for them. Emptying my wardrobe to do it, but it must be done. When they wake, it will be important that they are clothed. For their dignity, if nothing else."

His tone was neutral, but Barty could tell he was uncomfortable from the way that Jean shifted, sitting further upright in his chair. Doing so brought attention to the fact that he still held the rifle, and Barty turned his gaze upon it. "Is that why you have brought such an arsenal then? For Adam's dignity?" He nodded to the syringe, placed prominently close at hand. "And *that* most of all? I know what that is."

Jean flicked a glare at him, his lip twisting, his moustache shifting in his irritation at the observation. Barty, was more than a little surprised at himself. He was used to doing what Jean said, what Jean asked, and little more. Over time, this had become a habit, one that he had not challenged. But Elanor had been right; sometimes Jean needed to be questioned.

"The Jekyll formula is only for a last resort, and nothing more," Jean said shortly. "To be quite honest, I am rather hesitant to use it for two reasons—one, it is the only sample of it that still exists. And two, I have no blasted idea what it will do to me." He glared at the syringe which, in the aftermath of the Jekyll case, had been filched from the rubble of Bethlehem mental asylum, where the twisted killer finally met their end. Until now, it had been kept hidden, locked in a case, with Adam rather reluctant to work on it while being the only one with the ability and the knowledge to do so.

"You would become whatever Jekyll turned into—his other persona, Hyde, correct?" Barty guessed, but Jean was shaking his head.

"Jekyll's blood was awash with the alchemical concoctions he had been imbibing for the duration of his miserable existence. They had warped together over time and remained in his body. This elixir was merely the trigger for whatever it was that it did to him—so there is no knowing what it would do to a normal man. I have no desire to find out, but even so..." He sighed, shaking his head.

Barty rubbed his brow. "That does not answer why you have all these preparations, Jean," he prompted pointedly, gesturing to the arsenal.

The hunter scowled again, exasperated, but with as much restraint as could be mustered, he explained, "Because this has never happened before. Not in my memory and certainly not in Adam's own." He scratched his slightly more ragged than usual beard as he went on, "They would have told me about it if that was the case. In the near seventy years since Adam first came into existence, they have not needed to sleep, nor even stop, not once. And now..." He trailed off, frowning, grimacing sharply as he shook his head. "You and I both heard it, Barty.

Before they... stopped, we heard them screaming. And that was not Adam's voice, so I would like to be sure of *who* it is that will wake up." His expression turned more intent. "I could not be sure in the aftermath, but I *believe* I heard whispers—a woman's voice once more—coming from within them, rather than being spoken. Like it was echoing out of a long tunnel. But I cannot be sure; I have heard nothing since."

Barty felt a shiver pass through his dulled frame, a spasmodic memory of the explosion, and of the horrific shrieking pouring out of Adam's mouth with pitch and power enough to rise above even the thunderous destruction. He leaned forward with a wince. "It still feels a bit excessive to have all this artillery for 'just in case', surely?" he said worriedly.

Jean did not look at him as he answered. "No... it is not nearly enough. Adam was—is—the most indestructible being I have ever encountered, and by far the most physically powerful. They are a marvel of creation—and a terrible one at that, for all the fact they are also the most decent being I have ever known." He stated it plainly, and simply, but it still took Barty aback in how emphatic Jean said it. It also reminded him that he owed Jean something. He rubbed his cold hands together, frowning.

"You saved my life. Again," Barty said quietly, to which Jean cocked a curious brow. Barty just nodded, embarrassed. "When it—whatever *it* was—happened, you put me under the table and covered me. It is the last thing I remember." He shrugged nervously, cheeks flushing hot. "Thank you, Reynard."

Jean grumbled, made awkward by the gratitude, his gaze lowering. But he spoke firmly thereafter. "Enough wandering around the subject, Barty, I asked you what happened, and I have answered a great many of your inquiries without receiving the same courtesy in kind. You returned here with bruises all over you, bloodied, and with a concussion of the brain. You were lucky not to have broken bones along with it. Serious injuries, that I would like to know the origin of. Now, illuminate me on your misadventures."

Barty knew he had evaded enough by this point. He rubbed the back of his head, feeling the ache there from when his skull had cracked against the wall. He decided to confess the truth—most of it, anyway. "Elanor and I had a disagreement," he began lamely, keeping his gaze averted.

Jean filled the moment of silence. "If she was the one who gave you the thrashing, I am sure she would have told me," he said in a sardonic tone, which made Barty blink before laughing weakly.

"No, no, it was not her. Not that she could not, I'm sure, I mean—" he stammered on while Jean watched him with, what Barty thought was, the faintest flicker of a smile at the corner of his mouth, but it faded before he could be sure. He took a deep breath before continuing. "We went our separate ways, and I... wandered for a time. Then someone recognised me." He rubbed his jaw, remembering with a scowl. "That fellow from the Beauchamp case—the one who was keeping watch on the Lady and Miska, whom you... dealt with."

Jean scowled, the smile well and truly vanished at the revelation. "Of course he got a good look at you—you distracted him so I could put him to sleep." Jean swore, as though in self-admonition. "They attacked you?"

Barty nodded, grimacing. "Him and one other. They struck me and dragged me off before I knew what was going on." He did not mention Esmerelda. He did not know if he should. The conversation between him and her regarding Jean, and what she had done upon the death of their son, was brought painfully back into focus.

Jean frowned. "Strange they did not simply kill you—the normal recourse of people of such an inclination."

Barty shivered, a convulsive reflex, as he reached to the spot below his eye where the knife had rested. "Yes, I suppose so." His memory curled in on itself then, as he looked past the trauma of his near maiming and worse. "I did listen to them talking however." He frowned, feeling his head throb warningly. "They were talking about... about something to do with young women." He struggled with it a moment more, before remembering. "They wanted to bring me to someone they called Old Lord Sawbones—but argued about the fact I was not female." He blinked then, once, twice, as the past flooded back and his blood ran cold, but not for his own wellbeing. "They were talking about finding women, and giving them to this Sawbones fellow to cut into pieces. That—that is..." Words failed him.

"Unusually hideous, even for the abominable underside of London," Jean finished for him, then growled, slowly straightening up in his chair. He was focused on Barty now, his eyes intent and glittering, the moment turning into something Barty recognised; that near feral, burning anger lurking beneath the surface. Jean pushed himself to his feet, and setting the rifle down, began to pace, grunting somewhat at stiffened body parts coming back to life.

"Recall everything you heard, Barty. Every piece of it. And every name," he said sharply. "Something tells me that this warrants investigating."

Barty could not help but agree, so did his best to recall the conversation and details of the now departed Harry and Davey, and the 'trade' of bodies and parts—a notion so hideous that Barty felt he would be sick. But it was the last name that he finally remembered, that made Jean stop and snarl.

"*Cripple Pete*," he growled, his eyes blazing, teeth bared. "If that miserable pile of excretion is sliding his filth covered fingers into places they should not be, I will bite them off his hand to find out what vile meddling he is engaged in this time."

Barty quailed a bit at the rage, but rallied himself. "You know of him, then?" Jean nodded, cursing under his breath. "He is looking for you, you know," Barty went on gamely. "After we helped the Lady Beauchamp. I guess he was the one who was waiting for them at the docks."

"He is only looking for me because he does not know it is *me* he is looking for," Jean snapped. "Unless he has quite gone and lost his mind, in which case I shall remind him of the folly of his ways, while taking my pound of flesh for his mistakes—close to the bone, if I am to make a choice," he finished, grinding his teeth. Barty did not argue; there was absolutely no way he wanted to know if Jean was being literal.

He took a deep breath then, realising that he had to say something else. If he did not, and Jean found out later, he had a feeling it would be met with an even fiercer outburst. He went on to speak hesitantly as he stared at his own feet. "I met

Esmerelda, Jean."

The man immediately stopped his furious pacing, the air going still.

"You did?" he finally responded, his voice oddly distant, but with the faintest note of yearning. Barty lifted his head slowly. Jean faced away from Barty, his posture rigid. It told him much of what he needed to know.

Over the time he had observed Jean, he had learned the man had an iron grip on his emotions. He locked them down, chained them in place, and held them tight to his heart with an almost inhuman ferocity. But the harder he did so, the more clear the emotion became that he was trying to keep hidden. The stillness told Barty that just hearing that name had hit Jean with the force of a lightning strike, leaving him potential-ly—dangerously—unstable. He would have to be careful.

Jean rounded on him, all emotion wiped from his expres-sion, leaving a blank visage of a hollowed mask, shattered and pieced back together but nevertheless still broken. How long had it been since he had slept, Barty thought? He probably had not at all. It was hard to tell with the man. His default state seemed to be perpetually haggard, after all.

"May I enquire as to what you spoke about?" His tone was as stiff as his posture, his eyes intent—holding himself back from what he really wanted to ask, to know, and Barty could see it.

He shrugged. "She wished to know about me. To meet me, as it were." He kept the full extent of what they had spoken about to himself, and pushed on. "She also told me the nature of your... estrangement," he said as delicately as possible.

Jean grimaced, his gaze turning aside. "Would you say, in

your own assessment, that she is well?" he asked slowly, his voice still measured, still reserved. Still holding on.

Barty hesitated, then nodded, taking pity on the man but knowing honesty was important right now. "Yes, Jean. She was safe, and healthy. Maybe not happy, no—but she was well." He sighed, rubbing at his face with one hand, wincing at the bruising that yet lingered. "She's a strong woman. Very strong."

Jean gave a snort that might have been a laugh, however defeated. "That she most assuredly is. Stronger by far than I." He looked back to Barty, a regretful look on his face and in his tone. "She is a woman so fierce as to split stone with her words. And then, with but a touch, bind them back together again."

"You must miss her a great deal," Barty said quietly. There was no question in it. It was a plain and simple fact. But he could tell Jean was wavering, that his resolve in revealing his feelings was breaking. And now Jean paused, as for the first time, the mask finally slipped altogether.

"If only it was as simple as absence, Bartholomew," he said slowly, heavily, each word bearing the weight, the burden of what was buried and dragging Jean down by the neck to the soil. "She is the mother of my children. We were married when we were younger than you are now—there was never any question of there being another for either of us at the time. And there never shall be, for me at least." He exhaled, listless, his hands opening and closing reflexively. "As pathetic as it is for me to ask such a banal question—did you gather if she misses me at all?"

Barty swallowed, off guard. This was not a side he had expected to see, not really. "She does," he said plainly. "She loves you still, that much is clear. It is just..." He bit his cheek. Jean sighed again.

"It is just that if she sees me again, and I do not have what she asks, she will kill me then and there, as she must." He sounded regretful, but his words were clear, even determined in their acceptance.

"I do not understand it," Barty confessed, shaking his head. "She would kill you, even though she claims to love you?"

"It is the way of her, and her people. I knew and accepted it of her then, as I do now," Jean said firmly. "My wife is of a people who, when they love, it is forever. It is the same as when they hate. In my case, one is both and the same." Bitterness clouded his words now, but he straightened. "It is as it must be. I love her for who she is, even if that costs me." He shook his head. "She will one day come for my heart. To either claim it, or set it free—one way or another."

Barty struggled with the notion. "That... after every-thing—with how you still feel about each other—that hardly seems fair, Jean."

The hunter barked a harsh, brief burst of bitterest laughter before he answered, rounding on Barty as he did so. "Fair? In what existence has fairness ever mattered, Barty? You should know that as well as anyone could, the same as I." He gestured vaguely to the massive, still silent figure who stood in vigil as they both argued. "Is it fair then, that Adam stands there, locked in their own body, unsure whether they will wake or know consciousness again? Fairness, justice—we open our eyes for the first time, and we close them again for the last, and in all of that account, be it brief or otherwise, we shall never witness a single manifestation of justice or fairness, Mister Bartleby. We shall never touch it, let alone hold it in our hand. They are fictions that we measure our lives by, that we live and die in expectation of, and yet they never exist at all. No." He shook his head, grimacing as he straightened his shoulders. "No, for all that we wish them to be true, there is no justice, and there is no fairness. There is simply what *is*, and how we act in accordance to that reality."

Barty held to the silence for a long moment, before speaking in a smaller voice. "There should be."

Jean squinted at him. "Should be what?"

Barty, his gaze downcast, raised his voice. "I am saying even if you claim those things do not exist, they *should* exist. They are something worth believing in."

"Even if they are a lie?" Jean said dryly, but his tone was more curious than it was scathing.

Barty nodded, but now he met Jean's eyes as he spoke. "Yes. Even if they are false, I would rather believe in them."

"Dare I ask why?" Jean asked, his tone sardonic, but for once Barty snapped at him.

"Because they mean *hope*, Reynard. Hope that things will get better. And you believe in them too—because if you did not, you would not have sat here for all this time, waiting for your friend to wake back up!" He pointed at Adam. Blinking at himself for raising his voice as he did. Jean seemed surprised, too, as Barty pressed on. "If—no, *when*—Adam wakes up, it will be a justification of that hope, Jean. And that hope is born out of wanting things to be fair, of wanting there to be some... cosmic justice in all of this. If you did not believe in that, in some way, you would never have been down here at all."

He fell silent, embarrassed at himself then, wincing at the fresh flare of pain as the morphine in his system burned away, drained by his outburst bit by bit. Jean said nothing for a long moment, eyeing Barty throughout, before he walked towards Adam. Standing closer to him with his hands behind his back.

"Well. At least you were wise enough to say I was worried about Adam, and not yourself," Jean finally said. It was not a very funny thing to say, but it caught Barty so off guard in that moment that he could not help but snort and choke on his laughter. Jean turned back, a faint smile on his face to see Barty struggling with the unexpected change in tone, before he returned to Barty's side. "You are right. I do worry for Adam," he said ruefully. "I am not sure what to expect, but at the same time..." He snorted, caught in his moment of doubt as he continued, "I am not sure what I would do without them, either."

Barty nodded, in full agreement, watching the giant figure in the hope he might be the first to see them start moving again. "You know, the first time I saw Adam, I—"

"Fainted on the spot," Jean interrupted in a blithe tone.

Barty rolled his eyes. "I was *afraid* of them," he finished tartly. "Their size, the stitches and scars, and those eyes, but..." He trailed off, and shook his head. "You tell me that they are self conscious about how they look, and yet..." He shrugged slowly, as a soft smile formed. "Adam is beautiful, in the end."

"In all the ways that matter," Jean said with simple agreement. "But come. Let us not speak in this manner, as though they are not here. It is rude, at the very least."

Barty blinked. "Can they hear us?" he asked, surprised, and the huntsman squinted in thought.

"I do not know—but whether they can or not, it does not feel entirely right to me, to act as though it might be otherwise."

"I would wager Adam would understand. They're far more intelligent than both of us," Barty argued, but Jean shook his head.

"Understanding or not, I still feel it is a discourtesy." He fell silent.

Barty decided to agree with him, but another thought occurred. "Be that as it may—I did not think there was anyone whom you would consider worth being polite around, Jean."

The older man grunted. "You would be incorrect. But be aware with every clever remark from your lips that the list grows ever shorter," he growled in a warning tone.

Barty could not help but smile however, and he relented, conceding the point. "You should get some rest, Jean. I can stay down here, keep an eye on things—I need a little longer to recover anyway."

Jean frowned at that, letting out a deep, grudging sigh from his nose, before he nodded slowly. "Fine then. But if anything happens, fire a gunshot into the ceiling. I can promise you that I shall hear it." He said it firmly, but Barty was doubtful.

"Even down here?"

The hunter grimaced. "Even down here." There was no arguing with the determination in that reply, so Barty simply let the moment pass. "Remember, rest. Tomorrow we shall be back to work," Jean said brusquely, and marched off towards the elevator.

Barty gaped a moment, startled, then called after him. "Work? What are we doing?"

Jean kept going, talking over his shoulder. "We shall be having *words* with Cripple Pete," he said darkly. "And I will be getting answers when we do. But it will take some doing." He reached the elevator door, and then paused in place, before turning back to Barty.

"A touch of advice, as a thanks for today, Barty... apologise to my daughter. Whatever your disagreement, swallow your pride, and speak to her. She takes too much after me, I fear. So be the one to cross the gap first." Barty blinked, then simply nodded. Jean grunted, then peered about the lamp lit gloom. "Keep the lanterns oiled too. I do not want Adam to awake in darkness, either," he finished, then climbed the ladder to the hole in the ceiling, and was gone.

Barty sat, listening to the hunter clambering up the shaft back to the Lodge, as the armoury turned to a deathly quiet, where only his breathing and heartbeat could be heard. He shivered, unable to help himself, as he set himself into place, and kept his eyes on Adam, preparing to wait. He could do this. He was good at doing nothing, when the occasion called for it.

Unlike Jean, he did not bother to look to the weapons beside him. Even if he felt confident in using them, he would not, simply because he could not conceive of *needing* them against Adam—and he was surprised at himself for that realisation. But over time, it had become clearer and clearer; Adam would not harm him, nor anyone. Barty just could not imagine such a thing being true. So he sat, and he waited, and he watched. And made himself ready for when his friend awoke once more.

Chapter 7

Amidst Rotted Dreams

Time passed, as it was wont to do. When Barty was about to nod off again—he had been slipping in and out of the grasp of slumber during his watch—he was relieved by Benji. It had been a difficult climb up the elevator shaft, and Barty had fallen straight to sleep afterwards, falling headlong into the soft warmth of his bed, glad to be out of the musty darkness of the armoury.

In that sleep he dreamt; dreamt that Adam was speaking to him, or trying to, but they always had their back to Barty and though he could hear their voice, he could make out none of their words. It had been a dream that had blurred with the reality, as the awkward stillness of the massive Adam had become only more haunting with the passing of the hours of Barty's watch. It was the main reason why Barty had refused to rest another evening down there, despite it being easier.

He did not like being afraid of Adam—he did not like feeling uncomfortable around them—but as the vigil had gone on, the sensation of both had grown imperceptibly but inevitably. Jean had been right—even though Adam seemed unalive, there was nevertheless a presence that yet lingered around them. It did not feel like they could not hear him, nor sense his eyes upon them. He had even tried to talk to Adam, so that they would not feel alone, like one might do to someone asleep amidst sickness. But the dull echoes of that lifeless chamber had robbed the strength from his voice, and he had fallen silent.

When he awoke once more, the sun was setting and he was feeling greatly refreshed. The scores of bruises littering his body still had their ache to them, but it was a more distant feeling now, easing back from his awareness. His youth and bed rest had worked wonders, and though his head still hurt, it was not the eye blurring, body weakening pain it had been. He was not at his best, but he was good enough to be useful. First however, he needed food—and he needed it badly, if his persistent stomach growls were any indication. He made haste for the kitchen, and the well stocked larder within, that it would give him all the weapons necessary in his battle against starvation. Thankfully, there were plenty on hand.

Taking the advice given to him repeatedly in the last few days, and aware that he had not eaten nearly enough in his resting, he piled his plate a little higher than usual. There were cold sausages on a pan sitting atop the stove, and short of no one claiming them, he decided to relieve them of their forlorn abandonment. In the midst of his ravenous devouring of bread, cheese, and whatever else he could get his hands on, he became rapidly aware of an approaching argument. A loud one, forceful, and a familiar sound in the Lodge—a father and daughter, once more at war.

Barty plaintively considered his previous conversation with Jean, whereupon he had drawn from the wisdom of knowing his daughter all too well, and had told him he should apologise to Elanor, when the door opened and Jean strode in. His daughter was doggedly at his heels as they shouted over each other with such a vociferous magnitude that anyone listening would be lost as to what they were squabbling about. They had that strange talent that comes from a family used to feuding with each other at such a volume and frequency that they could follow the other's sentences and thoughts; one would be in the midst of a vicious rebuke before they were interrupted with a merciless counter. It was fascinating. But mostly, it was noisy.

They came to a ceasefire in their tirade and stood facing each other, glaring as they got their breath back. As if planned, both spun on the spot to see Barty, a half-eaten sausage in one hand. Guiltily, he swallowed as Jean looked down on him. Elanor folded her arms and turned away, sticking her nose up in the air.

"Just the man I was hoping to find," Jean declared. "Eaten enough?"

Barty nodded, swallowing with difficulty. "I think so, but—"

Jean, however, was having none of his excuses. "Excellent. Get ready, we are heading out."

Barty did not even have the chance to protest before Elanor furiously rounded on her father. "He is in no condition to help you!" she snapped. "He was a ruined mess but a few days ago!"

"I think I will be all right—" Barty tried to manage, but Elanor was not done.

"And even if he was"—she shot a glare at him—"I am better at this than he could ever hope to be!"

Barty blinked at her flat dismissal of his abilities, before his gaze dropped. He probably should have expected that though.

He had not seen Elanor to speak a word to her, nor apologise—not that he felt inclined to at the moment. He swallowed the sting of her comment for now—but it still hurt, all the way down.

Jean growled. "I told you, I need you to remain here if Adam wakes up. So that is what you are going to do." He turned to Barty, reaching into his coat and pulling out Barty's revolver, the brass knuckles, and switchblade Adam had made for him, setting them down before Barty precisely as he continued, "You will be needing these, and I will not hear otherwise."

"Barty could do that. Benji could do that," Elanor said scornfully. "They would both be better suited to it in any case." She refused to look at Barty, who was keeping his eyes down on his plate and the weapons that he dearly wished he did not have to look at, let alone take up.

"It is not about who is better suited to what," Jean said evenly, his voice level but with an undercurrent of anger. "It is about what I have decided. It is not up for debate, Elanor. Do as you are told."

A vein throbbed at her temple and before she fully exploded, Barty decided he'd had enough. He set down the fork and sausage with a clatter upon the plate. "Before this pleasant display of contempt continues, I would like to make a decision for myself, if you do not mind." He was surprised at how angry he was, and how much force it leant his voice. Elanor's jaw worked, but she held onto her anger as Barty pushed himself to his feet.

"While you are no doubt more skilled than I am, Elanor—I have been here less than a minute and can clearly see that if you go out looking for answers together, the only thing you two will manage is alerting others to your presence by your incessant arguing as you approach." He picked up the revolver and stowed it, as Elanor snorted in anger but kept her tongue in check.

"A point I had not considered, but one I shall gladly accept," Jean agreed with a grimace. "There. An actual valid reason, Elanor." He gestured for Barty to follow him.

But Barty was not done. He collected the knuckle dusters and switchblade, putting them in his pockets. "While I *was* injured, I am feeling much recovered after my misadventure. Thank you for asking," he said sourly, fully aware that no one had. "If I was *not*, I would be refusing you, Jean. Just so we are clear on the matter."

"Entirely," Jean replied, with a brow raised. He appeared annoyed at the clarification, but finally shook his head. "Now, come on. We have a great deal to do, and the light is already getting away from us."

Barty nodded, as Elanor swore under her breath and stormed to the door ahead, pausing as she went. "I know exactly why you are not letting me go out there, Father," she snapped. "The same reason as last time, as every other time before that, over and over again." She scowled, pushing on. "When will you realise I am not a child any more?" She slammed the door behind her and went on her raging way.

"When you bloody well stop acting like one!" Jean shouted after her. He stood fuming for a long moment, as Barty waited patiently but nonplussed, looking away as Jean glared at him and snapped, "Not a word, Barty. Not one."

"Would not dream of it," Barty replied innocently as Jean set off, long strides with his coat billowing behind, forcing Barty to skip to keep up. The self control required to hold his tongue only held until they were outside and waiting for Puck's coach to arrive. "But if I *was* to say a word, what exactly would that word *be,* on the matter of her stating why you do not want her to go with you?"

Jean grunted, whistling high once, three times fast after. "You said it yourself, Barty. We argue a great deal. We have our methods of handling matters, and those approaches can conflict." The coach clipped around the corner as Jean stared it down. He refused to look at Barty, who did not need anyone to tell him that Jean was being evasive about the matter.

"That was not the reason why you chose to go against her," Barty pointed out. "You decided that it would be me the moment I woke in the armoury, in fact."

Jean grunted at the seemingly astute observation, but refused to answer or turn to face Barty.

Puck was smiling as the coach drew closer, that wide, ever wicked grin that said things unspeakable. Barty felt less comfortable in its presence than ever before, but could not remember precisely why; his memory was fuzzy, flickering with silver and flashes of red, of laughter and screams blending tightly in a crawling sensation up his spine.

Surely it had been but a dream, though?

But Puck broke the spell, giving a clear, bright and shining laugh that called not to cheer but to nightmares at seeing Barty's face. "So good to see you too, darling child, with worries eating your heart like worms in an apple core. Come to give me promise and feasts of fear once more?" He winked at Barty, and Jean paused, staring up at Puck and then turning to his stricken assistant, his expression unreadable. Unable to conceal his responses with his nerves so shaken, Barty flinched under that stare without quite understanding why.

To Puck, this was all simply far too funny for words as he cackled with glee. "Ah! But the story is untold, thus your song unsung!" He leaned over to Jean. "The little scamp was caught astray, huntsman. He called me to him, and I took payment in flesh." He shivered joyfully, a spasmodic movement of nauseating glee. "It had been so very long, I had forgotten how good fear tastes."

Jean stared long and hard at Barty, then, to his surprise, he simply nodded at the younger man. "I see," he said icily, a tone that revealed nothing. But Barty could tell he was wary now. The wooden expression on his face said more—this was something he did not want to talk about. And all the while Puck laughed and laughed, then abruptly rolled backwards to lounge on the roof of the carriage like a tumbling jester, opening the door from above with one languid hand.

"Whisper me your destination, darlings, and I shall take you hence. For a promise given and a decision made, by bones of iron around my heart, I shall do as you command." There was something entirely mocking in how he said it, the grin a little too wide. Jean said nothing, but climbed up into the coach. Barty, after receiving another jaunty wink from Puck, followed after him.

He opened his mouth to speak as he sat down, but Jean shook his head in warning, pointing to the ceiling and then placing his thumb to his mouth and drawing it across.

Not now, not here.

Barty took the hint, but was forced to wonder now just what he had done. Not for the first time, he had an uncomfortable realisation that there was much he was ignorant of in this new and strange world, just as he had begun to feel complacent about his newfound existence—and some of that strangeness and peril was closer than he cared to admit. If what had happened had not been a dream, then what was it?

"I never did ask you how you managed to escape," Jean said quietly, looking out the window. "Damn me for a fool, but I am missing even the most obvious of things these days." He shook his head with a scowl, sinking into his seat. "Tell me about it later though."

Barty could do nothing but nod, even as Puck's silver hair, and then the grinning face of the creature himself, came into view through the window beside Jean, upside down. He cackled and trilled. "You never said where we are going, dearest hunter!"

Jean stared back at Puck, unblinking and seemingly unbothered. He turned away, now comfortable in his chair, and closed his eyes dismissively. "Take us to the Wards, Trickster."

Puck cackled and withdrew, and the coach leapt forward. Barty grimaced, and patted his coat to make sure the revolver was still there. "The Wards?" he asked plaintively, hoping against hope he had misheard.

Jean did not open his eyes, but he smiled ever so faintly. "Yes. The Wards."

EVERY CITY STARTS somewhere. London started in the Wards.

Twenty five aldermanries from which London itself grew. The oldest part of the city, more than a mile or so across, was a twisting maze, the most congested and warped part of the metropolis as a whole. A thousand years of streets and alleyways, of buildings and dives, of generations of rivalries and wars. Gangs, families, industries, and more besides. The congealed maze of districts were a microcosm of London itself, concentrated down into the finest point—a hotbed of hatreds and bitterness. It was a place where inhabitants jealously and mercilessly defended each and every stone that they had, and would spill the blood of any and all who drew too close. It was a place where no sane person should have dared to go, and yet perfectly sane yet desperate people nevertheless did just that every single day. They visited the rookeries that started there and spread elsewhere, the slums that were either part of it or sprang up in other places.

Much of those slums were in St Giles, leading out from there to Whitechapel, and the hunting ground of the Ripper, or just nearby in Old Nichol. These were not part of the Wards, but it was where the districts began, with the gangs that would not die, shifting to other hunting grounds, and people forced to live crammed into tight spaces, building anywhere that they could. They were the slums of London, the centuries of life where one was forced to simply survive until the world itself devoured you.

Barty had avoided St Giles, or as it was otherwise known, Cripplegate. Built around a hospital of the same name, it was originally the home of lepers all the way back in the twelfth century. In many ways, even though the disease was not present, it remained exactly that; the place where the unwanted were made to go. And in the case of some, where others came to find them.

Jean moved with purpose through the streets, the inexorable stride of a man without fear. Barty was, however, fully within his fears—after all, St Giles was a place where one would be murdered for the mere possibility of what was in their pockets, let alone what might actually be, stabbed to death and left to rot before the sewers swallowed you.

Jean seemed to notice his hesitation; with the way the sweating Barty was looking around with furtive dread, Jean did not need to exercise his detective nature too stressfully. He stopped so abruptly that Barty ran into him in the middle of a dilapidated street. Having gotten his attention, he spoke, his tone interrogative. "You seem on edge, Barty. Whatever is the matter? When you came to find me, you were found here, if you recall." And it was true. Barty had almost forgotten.

"It was the first time that someone grabbed me off the street as well. And to have it happen yet again so recently..." He rubbed his head, exhaling. "I am sorry. I will get a grip on myself."

Jean gave a grim smile, with no humour in it. "Take heart, Barty. No one will touch you here."

"You sound quite sure of that?" Barty asked doubtfully, to which Jean barked a harsh, single laugh.

"Indeed. Because *I* am here."

There was a scuttling in an alleyway as they passed, and Barty glanced down it to see retreating shadows seeking deeper darkness. And he realised Jean was not lying.

It had been easy to overlook in recent weeks, as things had settled. Elanor's presence, despite the ferocity of their arguments, *had* been good for Jean; unable to wallow in rage and bitterness, he had been forced to confront it by virtue of the one person who could evoke it, without fearing consequences for it. Elanor had known that, and she had pushed that advantage relentlessly throughout. But it had made Barty forget just what his mentor, or employer, or whatever he wanted to call him, *was*. Seeing Jean move easily and without concern through streets where the brave dared not to tread, and the police did not come unless it was in force, he was reminded; Jean was the wolf. Everything else was either prey, or another predator to overcome.

"You did not say where we are going," Barty said, continuing to hurry after the striding man, knowing that he was not afforded the same level of almost mystical protection and terror.

Jean grunted. "To find a man I know, in a place I know where he shall be."

"That does not tell me terribly much." Barty's skipping step was hobbled by uneven, rain slicked cobblestones as he stumbled in the hunter's wake.

"It does not, obvious though that might be, I appreciate you endeavouring to point it out." Jean's tone was as dry as sun-baked sand. "But you were to tell me how you managed to escape your capture. Something I still find myself baffled I did not enquire about earlier."

"Well, you were a little distracted," Barty started, but Jean shook his head.

"Do not grant me excuses, Barty, please. Excuses allow us all manner of unforgivable evils in behaviour. Excuses are how we exonerate failure, and I cannot be afforded such a destructive luxury." He paused, sniffing the air and looking around. The street was a grimy, gloomy affair with all manner of offenses to sensibilities. It was only just turning dark but the skulking warren yet rejected light, transforming the street and its many lanes and alleyways into things of shadow and malice. And it stank, the low, foul stink of industry and desperate living. Barty was trying to hold his breath, and wondered what the hell Jean could be trying to sniff out.

Whatever it was, he seemed to acquire its scent by the way he turned on one foot and crossed the narrow, twisting street. "Regardless, I am asking now. What happened between you and Puck?"

Barty muttered to himself and set off after him once more. "I do not quite remember. Not fully." His tone was apologetic. "I hit my head quite badly, and it made everything sort of... muddled, from that point onwards." He frowned though, trying to recollect the details. "I... whistled for Puck, after getting my mouth free and then... then he came. They tried to threaten him, and he... he..." Barty blinked, stopping. Memories started to rise, breaking through the dark and blood-soaked surface into which horror had buried them. He remembered the screams. The sound of flesh being ripped apart and Puck's high, gleeful laughter as he did... *something* unspeakable. He could not properly recall the images, but the sounds, the smells, all of it came back with a crushing weight.

"Oh, God." Barty's voice was numbed as he stared off at nothing, the echoes of atrocity still ringing in his thoughts as he faltered.

Jean stopped at hearing that dread, turning to Barty wordlessly and, with a deadpan expression, filled in the void of the unfinished story with the cold truth. "He killed them."

Barty went on in that leaden, horrified tone, his face turned pale as he stared blankly into the middle distance. "He did not just *kill* them, he... he..." He felt his gorge rising, and he wavered, his knees turning weak.

Jean closed on him and steadied him with a hand on one shoulder, an iron grip that tightened and anchored Barty back to the present as Jean's gaze bored into his. "Steady. Breathe, Barty, even if it stinks to do so here. Breathe, and get a hold of yourself." Barty shivered, then dipped his head, taking a few deep breaths. Jean watched him critically, eventually he nodded, and released his grip. "So now you have seen the truth of the Prince of Midsummer," he said darkly, turning about again, and continuing on his path. "Better late, perhaps, than never."

"What *is* he?" Barty asked in horror. "I mean, I knew he was something more, something *else*, but what is he, actually? And how do you have him in your service?"

Jean passed an alleyway, peering, as though looking for something and then pressing on. "That, I am afraid, I cannot speak of," he said firmly. "For a number of reasons you shall have to trust me on. Just know that you *do* owe him now. I am surprised he has not already collected something from you for that intervention."

Barty hesitated, before speaking. "He did. He took a feather that was given to me by one of Esmerelda's ravens."

Jean halted midstep, rocking in place as he spun to Barty. "You gave him a *promised feather?*" He sounded as though this was something incomprehensible.

"Someone is going to have to explain to me what that means," Barty said plaintively. "Elanor and Puck both said it with some significance, but I do not understand it myself."

Jean covered his face with one hand and gave an exasperated sound, before speaking with as much patience as he could muster. "It is an old, old tradition amongst my wife's clan," he said testily. "A promised feather of a raven is an admission of a debt owed. Very rarely given, very rarely considered. It means that the clan will, at request of the holder of the feather, oblige them of one wish or assistance that they can give, in whatever capacity, or be called promise breakers—or in other words, outcast." He took a deep breath. "Esmerelda must have felt she *owed* you something, for some reason, something she felt obligated to repay. But you gave it to the most unpredictable being in all of England. Heaven nor Hell could guess what he will do with the bloody thing, but it *was* given to him, and thus it is now his."

Barty blinked a few times, suddenly feeling very, very awkward. "Oh." The significance of what he had done was not fully understood, but the realisation that there was a weight to it, one that was far, far heavier than he otherwise cared to admit, was sinking in. What exactly had he gone and done, or set in motion?

"Yes, indeed. *Oh*," Jean growled. "Some things do not change it seems, Bartholomew Bartleby. You remain a damnable inconvenience by measure of your ignorance." He ground his teeth a moment, then appeared to bury that rage back inside and continued on. Barty hurried after him once more, at a loss for words as they descended deeper into the rookery of St Giles.

There were people around now. The streets became narrower, the rubbish and detritus of cast off civilisation growing more noticeable. And in corners and shadows, doorways and arches, were the shadowy inhabitants of the Wards. They wore tattered clothes, with grime worked into their skin so deep as to be a tattoo, and they said nothing, staring with eyes that reflected no light and had no hope. Some would watch the pair pass with the gaze of a predator, only to slide away as they recognised a threat too great to handle, and stare after Barty instead, like crocodiles in a river, hoping the calf might separate from the herd so they could single it out, drag it into deep waters, and rip it into pieces. He kept close to Jean and kept his head down.

As they delved further, they started to see other lurking ne'er-do-wells. These however, while less threatening, nevertheless made Barty feel uncomfortable for entirely different reasons. They would stand or sit in lifeless, empty ways, staring or giggling at nothing. Sometimes Barty would see cracked lips split into a rotten toothed smile, eyes as vacant as the heart of a workhouse overseer. They increased in number as time went on, stumbling away from or towards something. Whether one or the other, it was the same direction as where Jean was going. Whatever it was that was dissolving the minds and more besides of the lost and the damned wandering St Giles, it was undoubtedly what Jean was looking for.

"I cannot entirely begrudge you your ignorance, Barty," Jean said as he pushed past a tottering, giggling figure who fell on their side to the ground and lay there, still chuckling as Jean pressed on. "It will take years of time and study to know all there is that I can teach you, and *that* will not nearly be enough." He paused, sniffing the air again. "You will need more than that. You will need to use that thing in you that I value, and you need to take more care of. Your mind." He half-turned, tapping at his temple. "You have demonstrated already that you *have* one, and I need you to be more aware of it." He rounded a corner, sniffed once, and turned to his left.

"And how would you suggest I do that?" Barty did not wish to sound irritable, but it was at times difficult to stop himself. Jean, in the midst of his focussed tracking of whatever it was that had his attention, did not seem to notice.

"In this life, Barty, if something seems unusual, it is often by such strange nature also important in some fashion. This may not be immediately obvious—but if things feel like they are significant, then they likely are." He paused at the mouth of an alleyway with a single lantern above it which was rather notably, in lieu of such a statement, unusual in the otherwise dark and shadowy street—a lone light calling like a beacon, in a place no one seemed to need to go. Jean ducked into it, needing to turn and sidestep to fit down the narrow gap. Barty, feeling a gorge rising sense of claustrophobia, nevertheless followed without hesitation rather than remain amongst the waiting jaws surrounding them as Jean went on, "A witch and her ravens are significant. The feathers from such birds are cut from the same cloth of importance. Remember that moving forward."

"I will do my best," Barty said, cringing with the effort of trying not to touch the walls closing in on each side, covered in centuries of layered filth to create a hideous patina. He was not doing a very good job.

"Do better. Thus far your best has proven insufficient," Jean replied bluntly, as he exited the alleyway, and gave a grunt of satisfaction. "In any case," he rasped, reaching into his coat for a cigarette and match, "we have found what we seek."

Barty glared at his back, shuddering at the cold, slimy build up that he had come into contact with, but looking past him, he was confused. They were at a nondescript building, much like any other, with a single candle at one window, and an open door that led into a dark, empty void. There was not a sound to be heard, nor a soul to be seen. "And what is it that we are looking for?" He was puzzled.

Jean inhaled through his nose, then glanced to Barty, and gave a grim smile. "Savour the air, Barty. Taste that smell?" Barty blinked, sniffing like Jean did, and behind the usual scents detected a pungent, smoky smell with a strong flavour. His nose wrinkled. Jean grinned, or rather bared his teeth, for there was no humour to be found. "That is the scent of the dreaming, Barty. That is the aroma of reality rent asunder." He chuckled menacingly, and set off for the darkened door. Barty rubbed his nose in a futile effort to get the stink out of it. He now knew what this place was, as he followed Jean into the void.

The interior was drowning in smoke, lit by fitful candles. It descended down stairs from which there was more light, but only barely. A large figure dozed by the doorway, perking up as Jean descended, reaching for an iron-bound club. They looked worryingly simple, the sort that was difficult to trick once they had a task they could devote themselves to, such as beating interlopers into a fine paste. But Jean was unphased.

"Tell Tommy he has a guest," he said, coming to a halt before the figure, Barty close behind him.

The brute worked a jaw that a sledgehammer would bounce off of. "And who is doing the asking?" he rumbled—at least that was what Barty thought he said. For all he knew the thing had not spoken a language at all, merely collected syllables and passed them through the rock crusher they had for a throat, but Jean appeared to know full well.

"Tell him it's the Huntsman. He will know." The lumbering figure paused at that, the faintest light of understanding making its presence felt in his expression. Jean nodded, recognising it. "We'll wait inside." And with that he passed through a curtain and into the miasmatic space beyond. Barty once more assessed his choices, to remain with the thug or to follow after Jean.

Better to be at the side of the Devil, than in his way—or in his wake.

Barty had never set foot in an opium den. He had never offered up prayers of thanks for that before this event—this had been remiss of him.

The light was dim, but there was enough to make it so he could see things around him, which made Barty wish that he could not. The roof was low, and cots and bunk beds lined the walls in rows, shoved into every available space of the den. Huddled shapes lay upon them and paraphernalia of blissful, empty, and destructive dreaming could be found strewn about each. The air stank of sweat and raw, desperate addiction. It was thick with the stink of the drug being burned, and he covered his mouth and nose with the lapel of his cloak to stop it from choking his lungs.

He followed after Jean, who headed to a cluster of tables and chairs which were occupied by a few scattered, insensate beings of abject misery, who were not even afforded a foul smelling bed as they dissolved their mind and soul in plain sight of uncaring eyes that rotted with the same sickness.

Jean dumped a man out of his seat where he lay, slumped face down. The man barely made a murmur as he pitched headlong for the floor, and then sort of melted into a supine shape as Jean sat down. As ever he looked unphased, unbothered by the outright squalor of his environment. Barty, bereft of options, gingerly took an empty seat and sat, his hunched shoulders an unsuccessful shield against the disturbing reality surrounding them.

Jean was watching him, a flicker of amusement on his face. "Something bothering you, Barty?" he asked innocently. At his feet, the man he had dumped onto the ground murmured and whimpered as some dark dream took him. Barty tried not to look at the ruined creature as he kept his breathing shallow and stared down at the rotted table.

"So what sort of man is worth us being here?" he said haltingly, his voice soft and subdued. The sweat in the air felt like it was condensing and dripping down his back, making him shudder.

"Not a very worthy one at all in truth, but a necessary evil." Jean shrugged. "This is one of his establishments. I expect he will be along shortly." Indeed, the brute at the door had dragged out what looked like a ragged street urchin, who scampered up the steps and out of sight as though glad to be rid of the place. Barty could not tell if it was true or merely his own projected desires.

"Whoever they are, I am not confident of their character," Barty said darkly. "This is an evil place." He looked around. No one was paying any heed to them. They did not seem to notice they existed at all. But Jean affixed him with a hardened stare.

"Perhaps," he said quietly. "But you know as well as I do Barty, that the world has many ways of breaking people. Sometimes it is easier to let the pieces lie, than try to put them back together. Sometimes there is just no putting them together at all, and that is where you will find people like this." He gestured briefly. "People who have not yet worked up the courage to die—who would rather dream, than face the world for what it is." He snorted, slouching in his chair. "And yet, it is short-sighted to call it evil."

"Then what would you say it is?" Barty asked doubtfully, still peering about. Jean rubbed his jaw as he contemplated for a moment, then spoke in such a low voice that Barty had to lean in to hear.

"Well, in order for there to be evil, there has to be good to oppose it, does there not?" Jean raised a brow at Barty, who simply nodded. "Excellent. Now what is good?" He pointed at Barty with an accusing finger. "Are *you* good? Are you the measure of what is and what is not righteous, Bartholomew Bartleby?"

Barty opened his mouth, then closed it again. Jean gave a grim sort of smile, seeing his discomfort, as he went on, "It feels somewhat delusionary to make that claim out loud, does it not? Plenty do just that of course, but you, thankfully, are not so foolish." He sniffed. "Most of the time, at least."

Barty felt that was uncalled for, but Jean continued, unperturbed, "It is entirely simple for someone to convince themselves they are good, Barty. Humanity is exceptional at it, and does so all the time, and all it requires is a little bit of gentle self-deception. To be blind to self-critique, to introspection. So simple, and so easy." He gestured to the room. "But sometimes it becomes too difficult to do even that. There is too much reminding us to be ashamed, to hate ourselves for what we are and where we have failed. And thus, you get places like here."

Barty frowned, looking around the den. "Then what exactly would you call these people?" He grimaced. His vision strayed to a nearby cot, and the blank, empty gaze of the inhabitant, gleaming hollow and bright in the shadows. They were holding a pipe tightly as they looked through Barty into some unspeakable place of dark forgetting. Barty might not have even been there, for all the difference his presence made to that vacant stare.

Jean looked around with a speculative squint. "I could call

them any number of things. Failures, perhaps some of them. People ripped apart in the gears of the machine that is life, for no other reason than it wished to show its unfairness. People who have things that they must forget. Those that are just looking to die, and want it to be painless. Maybe some just need sleep without dreams—or nightmares. Who can say?" He shrugged once. "But I would not call them evil. That would be a cruelty too far."

Barty struggled with this, and Jean watched him wrestle with it. The place simply seemed so ghastly, so *horrible*, that he could not bring himself to think of it as anything else. Jean went on, setting both hands behind his head as he leaned back into his customary slouch, both legs stretched out before him.

"You know the simplest way to think of ourselves as good, Barty? By measuring ourselves against those that have wronged us, or oppose us, or even are just *different* enough from us. If someone leaves us, betrays us, or causes us harm, we can say, that person was wicked for what they did. They were evil, and if *they* are evil, and I am opposed to them, ergo I am good." He snorted. "It seldom occurs to such people that not only does that fail to take important facts into account, they also do not like to contemplate, much less admit, that they perhaps deserved it."

"I do not think innocents who suffer under the indignities of the cruel are mistaken in believing their oppressors are evil," Barty said stiffly, frowning. Jean chuckled. The soft sound of humour out of place here, in this room where joy had long since died, stifled under pestilential smells and brain decaying fogs.

"There are many degrees of such things, Barty. I do not disagree with that point; by the measure of those who cry out from the pulpit, and by whatever morality it might impose upon our wretched souls, such malice can only ever be attributed to vile cruelty. But that is not the sort of sin I speak of." He settled further into his wobbling chair, yawning. "I speak of the banal, the trifling malevolence, the everyday evil that every soul out there suffers from. The sort of wickedness that looks at places like this, and tells themselves that because they are not under its merciless yoke, that they are, by that merit, good and righteous, upstanding and God fearing." His expression soured into a grimace. "By our station, we are good. By our wealth, we are good. By our connections and approval of those with the same ideals, we are good. For if we are not, then we do not deserve such affluence, such privilege, and our shame at our own wretched self-deception will, eventually, see us down here—in this dark place, under this darker embrace, trying to abandon who and what we are, because to forget is easier than to confront the truth."

Barty was fascinated. Fascinated, and horrified at this insight into Jean's dreadful mind. "And what truth is that, Reynard?" he asked hesitantly, turning his gaze back to the figure that had been staring at him without seeing him.

"That we are in love with our own ego, with the idea of ourselves Barty. Not by our own deeds but by measuring them against the failure of others," Jean said slowly, his tone distant. "Failure that may not even be their true fault, just the world grinding them under its uncaring heel. And by that merit, not by what we achieve, we call ourselves righteous. Blind to any and all fault, lest our shame drown us—or we seek a means to drown it."

Barty looked at the broken figure who still stared, his disgust transforming into something else entirely as he listened to Jean's words. He blinked as he realised that his disgust had shifted, and changed, into pity. Jean was in so many ways correct. How many of those down here had lived as he had, and found themselves trapped here in the aftermath, unable to escape the prison of their own mind? *You could have been here yourself, were it not for chance*, he suddenly told himself. *Nothing more than chance.*

"What about you, Jean?" he asked in a hollow voice, as he envisioned that awful future.

Jean's own stare was anything but distant as he focused on Barty intently. "What about me?"

Barty turned to face him. "What side do you find yourself on? Do you think yourself a good man?" He was not sure what the answer would be. He was not sure what he *wanted* the answer to be.

Jean stared at him, incredulous, before he gave a sharp, barking laugh, teeth flashing amidst his beard and moustache almost merrily. "Oh, Lord save me from fools. Ha!" He wiped at one eye, shaking his head. "Oh, no, no, no Barty. I do not. I am as terrible a man as there ever was."

Barty struggled to understand, biting his cheek in momentary frustration at Jean's mocking response. "Why would you say that about yourself? By what measure do you judge yourself?"

Jean stared up sightlessly at the sagging ceiling as he considered his answer. "For events of my past you are privy to, would be the first reasoning.. The second?" He shrugged. "I enjoy killing people too much," he stated blandly.

Barty shuddered at that. He was not sure if Jean was joking—he hoped he was. Because if he was not, and he was entirely serious, then what did that mean for him? Was he, because he aided the man, an accessory to such things? Did that not make him as terrible as he was, in the end?

"I do not think that is true, Jean," he said with small defiance.

The huntsman shrugged again. "Does it even matter what you believe? There are plenty of people out there who will disagree with you. Are you going to say they are wrong? And if you are, does your opinion somehow weigh more than theirs?" He sighed, and shook his head. "Enough of this. All this smoke is making me too light headed to continue down this useless line of inquiry so avidly."

Barty swallowed his words and looked away as the moments ticked by. But doing so meant his eye wandered again to the huddled shapes of people doing their best to die slowly, and perhaps a little less painfully. He mentally fled from this understanding, but not out of inherent disgust—he was all too aware that had his path in life differed even slightly, he might have well found himself amongst their number. The realisation was haunting, and he strove to move past it.

"So who is this man, anyway?" he asked. Jean grunted, but did not answer, his eyes shut as he seemingly relaxed. Barty pressed on, irrationally afraid Jean was about to fall asleep on him. "You said his name was Tommy?"

Jean twitched his upper lip in a sneer of annoyance, his

closed eyes tightening amidst his twisting scowl before he finally relented. "Tommy, indeed. Tommy Two Bob, the ragged king of St Giles, the lord of the rookery," he said dryly. "He's a man you come to about things like this. Especially when it is about one of his own."

Barty shivered at this. Suddenly the knowledge that there was only one way out of the place seemed worrying. He heard movement then, the creaking of hinges, a door opening above.

"Why do they call him Tommy Two Bob?" he asked, amazed that his voice somehow did not squeak.

There was a thumping of steps on the stairs leading down to the place. How many pairs of feet were moving? He could not tell. Jean, eyes still closed, slowly let a smile form on his face as he spoke, raising his voice. "They call him Tommy Two Bob, because for two bob he'd have you with your throat cut at the bottom of the river, with a brick tied to your feet." His eyes opened as he continued on, staring at the curtained doorway. "Is that not right, Tommy?"

A slender man of average height came in through the curtain. He wore ragged clothes that must have been expensive once, though now his richly embroidered vest was marred by stitched up knife holes, while his fingers were adorned with rings dark with old blood. He stepped forward with a confident swagger, his ratlike features twisting into an arrogant smirk. A single eye looked down his nose at the pair as he approached, unphased by the human refuse scattered around him—the other eye was white glass, the eyelid peeled back where it had been cut away. He saw Jean, and the smirk widened into a grin.

"Come on now, hound. Y'know that my prices have gone up

since then *substantially*." He picked at his yellowing teeth with one filthy fingernail. "So, what's this all about then?"

Chapter 8

The Tale of Tommy Two Bob and Cripple Pete

Tommy Two Bob tapped one booted foot with an air of impatience. "Well?"

Jean was still slouched in his chair, hands behind his head. He was grinning, but it did not reach his eyes. "That is a spectacular vest, Tommy. Picked it up recently?"

The one-eyed man gave a nasal laugh, lifting his arms and turning to show it off. "You like it? I had to persuade the previous owner to let go of it using my superior skills of negotiation." The knife marks had not been properly repaired, a cluster of them arrayed where the kidneys would have been. "They were terribly attached to it, but nevertheless"—he spun back to face them—"I was able to pry it out of their hands." He smiled the oily smile of a liar as he took another couple of steps closer.

"Now then, unless mine ears do deceive me—and they are very good ears, ears that can hear a penny drop down a drain from a half mile off, I tell you." He tapped his left ear to demonstrate his point. "You have as of yet, *refrained* from explaining what the hells you are doing on my turf, Reynard." He dragged a chair over, spun it around and sat between Jean and Barty, crossing his arms and resting them on the back. "But since I am the most polite of men, I will give you a chance to correct your mistake."

"Still piss and vinegar, Tommy," Jean grunted, seemingly amused despite himself. But there was an edge to the air now. Barty was not sure what to make of it. "Still king of the muck heap I see too. Would have thought life would get more difficult for you, after the whole debacle with Jack."

Tommy snorted, leaning away. He then twisted in his seat as he called out to a gathering of shadowy shapes that Barty had not noticed before, hovering at the rear. "Bring us a bottle, one of you." He looked back to Jean, as whatever the shadows were slithered and slipped up the stairs they'd come from. "You'd share a drink with an *old friend*, wouldn't you, Reynard? For old times sake?"

Jean shrugged. "Why not?" To the unfamiliar eye he appeared relaxed, but Barty knew him too well for that. There was a coiled sense about him now—he was waiting for something, preparing for it. But for what, Barty did not know.

Barty was used to these knife edge situations; he often found himself speaking for Jean, having a more genteel touch that often proved useful in the face of Jean's abrasiveness. So, seeing as things did not seem to be progressing in a helpful direction, Barty thought it time to say something. "We came here because—"

Something bright and silver glittered an inch from his eyes, and his tongue tangled itself into a hiss of silence.

"Who's the mouse?" Tommy asked with a squint, not looking to Barty but waving the knife he held vaguely in his direction. "You mind stopping him squeaking?" That single eye slid to Barty now, bloodshot and yellowing. "You might get your tail cut off, mouse. I ain't speaking to you. I'm speaking to the hound here, and waiting for him to *bark*."

Barty bit down on his tongue. It was either that or swallow it. Jean, however, appeared entirely unmoved. "I am here to do you a favour, Tommy," he said with that faint hint of a smile. "One that you are going to owe me for, and I *will* be collecting on it."

Tommy snorted, and the knife he held flickered and spun before being stabbed into the table next to Barty's hand, making him flinch so forcefully that his body ached. "Now *that* sounds like a tall tale, a big order, Mister Reynard," he drawled, tapping a single finger on the pommel of the tabled knife. "You know full well I won't have nothing to do with toffs. Toffs is trouble."

Jean grunted, rolling his eyes. "Still think of me as that then, after everything, Tommy?" He raised a brow, still unmoved from his relaxed posture.

Tommy squinted with his single eye. "Well, you know what they say about ducks, yeah?" He yanked the knife back out of the table. "If it looks like a duck, quacks like a duck, hangs around other ducks, lives in a big pretty duck house and wears duck clothes, then yeah, I'd say it's a bloody duck, wouldn't I."

Jean snorted. "You sure know how to make friends, Tommy." His tone turned dry.

The ragged king of St Giles shrugged. "Lots of friends. Just not with toffs. Better to piss on 'em and be done with it." He grinned, his teeth foul as his breath. "Leaves us with a bit of a, what you say, *problem*, doesn't it?"

"Same applies to your crew then, all those under you?" Jean

asked conversationally.

Tommy snorted, easing back from his hunched over position. "They know the rules. Stick to the Wards, stick to who you know, what you know, and don't cross paths with the bastards that don't even see you. Which, I remind you once again, *don't* include you. Leastaways, not on the dealing with side of things." He pushed himself to his feet, as though to signal an end to the conversation.

"And what about Cripple Pete? That include him too?" Jean asked in that same deceptively benign tone.

Tommy froze, just for a moment, before he recovered and shrugged. "O'course it does. Pete's a good lad, little too fierce for the likes of you and your mouse here though. But he's loyal to his lord, as it were."

"Good to know, good to know." Jean nodded, his gaze lowering to the floor as he shifted, leaning forward in his chair. "But that doesn't explain why he's doing work for Lord Beauchamp, and crossing paths with *me* as a result, Tommy." His voice had turned into a growl, and now his eyes blazed, all friendliness gone. "Let me remind you Tommy, how it goes when that happens. You *remember*, don't you?"

The rat-faced man rubbed at his cheek, fingers tracing up to his glass eyeball with a grimace. He was quiet a moment, then hawked and spat. "Yeah, Reynard. I remember all right." He let the moment hang as his henchman returned, bringing a bottle that he held out to Tommy—the man held up a hand, refusing, as he shook his head.

"Nay, not here. Not amongst the lotus eaters, yes?" He chuckled, a nasty little sound from the back of his throat, and turned to the exit. "Come 'long then, hound. I'll hear your barking upstairs. Let the dreamers dream." He paused and murmured something into the ear of the hard-faced man holding the bottle, who nodded as he passed it to Tommy.

Barty was left to wonder what *that* was about, but as there was no time to question it now, he set off after Jean, and the pair of them walked out of the foul misery of failed dreams and broken hopes. He took a deep breath as they came out onto the street again—it was hardly clean air, the soup of fog starting to crawl out of the ground and turn thick as treacle, but he would have taken a deep breath in a sewer after that entire affair. This side of the life with Jean he had not yet experienced and he hoped he would never have to again, but the lingering voice in the back of his head made a mockery of such hope, and told him that this was just the start.

Tommy Two Bob was in energetic spirits as they walked along the alleyway, his step springy. "You interrupted me at the height of my evening entertainment, Reynard," he said grandly, but with petulance. "I had five pounds on Mangler Roberts to put Stacker Simpkins out in the sixth round! O'course, I had to be there to make sure my boy had the right *incentive*." He chuckled.

"Did not think you would be the one to fix a fight, Tommy," Reynard said dryly.

Tommy rounded on him, affecting a look of hurt pride as he put one hand to his chest. "Me? Skive a flint like that? I could never show my face again, no sir indeed, ain't that right, boyos?" he said, looking around with a grin. The various figures that followed, large men in large coats and with hats that hid their faces, gave various grunts. Sounds that might have been the last thing many a person had heard before, as Tommy laughed and nodded, turning on his heel and carrying on. "O'course not, Reynard. All I did was give him *motivation* to win, and the knowing of what would happen if he didn't!" He laughed again, but there was an edge to it. "You know as well as anyone, Reynard, what a man will do with proper motivation. He can find depths of himself that he did not know existed." There was nothing amused about his voice now. He switched moods like a rocking ship in a storm, dancing on the edge of a knifeblade between one emotion and the next.

"I am familiar," Jean said evenly. He did not elaborate. He did not have to.

They turned down another alleyway, and Barty saw a large warehouse door lit by flickering, uneven light spilling out from within, with people wandering out and into the deepening night. They made way for Tommy and Jean, but not Barty, and he had to duck and shift to slip in after the duo.

The warehouse was a nasty affair, with only a few people left now and the scent of sweat and blood still lingering. Boxes and crates had been set around a crude circle of sand and dust, which might have been clean and well laid at the start of the night, but was now a distasteful mess of soaked up gore.

Tommy was in his element, shouting everyone out and waving his hands to banish the few remaining hangers-on that lingered. His men pushed and shoved, then followed out after. Tommy took a seat on a crate and pulled the cork of the bottle as the door slid shut. "Take a seat, gentlemen. We have words to share, it seems." He downed a mouthful, then set the bottle at his feet.

"First things first." He squinted at Barty, wincing at the taste of whatever horrible liquid he had partaken of. "Give the mouse a name, would you? Don't give him one and I will."

Jean dragged a crate over and sat down on it. "That one's Barty," he said with a vague gesture. Barty hesitated, then went looking for his own box as Tommy snorted.

"What a waste. Should have called him Squeaks." Tommy laughed at this, a nasty, snarking sort of laugh that left Barty feeling a bit taken advantage of.

Barty felt his hackles rise. "Is that how Cripple Pete earned his name then? A clever play on physical condition?" he snapped, not enjoying the jokes at his expense.

Tommy's expression slowly slid out of humour. He picked up the bottle, holding it out to Jean. "Nay," he replied with a sardonic smirk. "He got it because he comes out of Cripple-gate." He shrugged then. "Though the fact he likes to take a hammer to the ankles of those that owe him money might have something to do with it too."

Barty felt his stomach try to crawl up and strangle his lungs at that notion and how that could have been his own fate. Jean merely grunted, taking the bottle and squinting at it before raising a brow at Tommy.

The self-proclaimed lord grinned in reply to that stare. "Only sort o' poison that you're used to, hound. Don't let it knock you about."

Jean grimaced, and took a mouthful, the scowl deepening as he passed it back. Barty was grateful that it was not offered to him as Tommy took another swig, then set it down, frowning.

"However, let's stop the messing about. What's ole Petey boy gone and done now?"

Barty huddled on his box as Jean leaned forward and explained, "Your associate interfered in my work, Tommy. Under normal circumstances, I might overlook that—but then he decided to take it one step further upon my *own* people." He gestured to Barty, but Tommy did not even look his way, his single eye fixed with a manic edge to it on Jean.

"Quite so, quite so, as you say so, hound—but that's your business, and the business between you and him is also your business. So this is me, asking about *mine*, and my business is, I don't deal with the nobs. So." He, too, leaned forward. "Best be getting on to that part, yes?"

Jean's eyes narrowed, his jaw twitching, but he pushed on. "We competed on work for the Lord Beauchamp. He was running work for him, looking for someone, but not swiftly enough." He shrugged. "Considering your... known attitude to working with the upper class, I considered that you might not know about the arrangement—and if so, perhaps we could find one ourselves."

"Oh, and you would like that turn of events, wouldn't you?" Tommy sneered. "Tommy Two Bob and Jean Reynard, the famous hunter, who happens to work with the Chief of the Yard on a regular basis and rubs elbows with the hobs and nobs of the world." He snorted. "Even if we take our history out of the equation—you must be bloody joking. If you *are* taking our past into account, well—you must be mad, and I haven't found much profit in working with madmen."

"It will be far worse for you, I would think, if one of yours is playing both sides and you know nothing about it, Tommy," Jean said evenly. "I remember Pete from my last visit here, while I was working in Whitechapel. You and I *both* know he was ambitious even then, Two Bob. Ambitious enough to make allies in places he shouldn't, to make a play at the last obstacle in his way?" He gestured to Tommy. "His men were in Southwark, well outside the Wards. Where else is he working these days? What else is he not telling you?"

Tommy scowled, picking up the bottle and swallowed irritably as he weighed Jean's words. He then gave a dramatic sigh, throwing his head back and rubbing at his glass eye with one hand. "I will have to have words with my wayward laddy buck in that case," he said with exaggerated humility. "Ole Petey has been a good man, a very good man for me, brought me plenty of shiny lucre, and I can forgive him for his mistake once he explains himself, I'm sure." He sighed again, shaking his head and taking another mouthful, hissing in the aftermath a moment before he went on, "Bloody fool of him, but—ah, but we all slip up from time to time, don't we?" He gave a friendly smile that did not reach his eye. "You know all about that, from what I hear. Not your boy any more, I notice. You and he were thick as thieves going after old Jack, hound. He still around?" Still ringing with that false innocence, but there was a smirk in his smile now, and the single eye gleamed to see Jean's expression turn to stone.

"Careful, Two Bob," Jean said slowly, his voice twisting, becoming harsh and grating, the words forced out through smoking rage. "I can take that other eye of yours before your boys can make it through the door. Remember?" His eyes blazed, and he tensed, the coiling of a spring before the pounce. Tommy's smirk vanished in a flash of rage, the silent moment of tension burning sharp and bright as both men sized each other up. Neither blinked.

Tommy's upper lip twitched, and he looked away to reach for the bottle once more. "You know, my patience s'wearing thin here," Tommy said airily. "Here I was, hoping to have a quiet drink with an old friend and sort out a little issue, but now here *we* are, and I am reminded thoroughly that, well—I don't like you very much, hound. I don't like you very much at all." He pointed a finger at Barty while his eye stayed fixed on Jean. "And your little mouse looks like he's about to soil himself he's so worried, so before we have ourselves an accident we'll all regret, I think that I will make my way." He pushed himself to his feet.

The air, however, remained tense and Barty was reminded of the fact that there were plenty of Two Bob's men outside. Maybe more had arrived by now. Was this nothing more than a trap? Terror gave life to his tongue.

"Who is Old Lord Sawbones?" Barty asked suddenly.

Two Bob stopped then, going rigid as he was straightening up. "Who did you hear that from?" he hissed, his expression turning harder, colder, and far more intent.

Jean gave a faint smile. "I see that one pulled your chain a little bit. You know something of them?" He nodded to Barty in indication. "This one was near dragged up to this Sawbones on a silver platter. They were going to cut him into pieces, but he seems to prefer young women instead. Lucky for the lad, I guess." Jean leaned forward, his tone turning mocking. "Cards are on the table, Tommy. What have you got for me?"

Tommy paced, his expression ugly with his anger. "And why should I be *giving* you anything?" he snapped, as he boiled in his fury.

But he was rattled, and Jean pressed his advantage. "Because the last time someone was killing young women in this neck of things, it went badly for you, Tommy. The police tore through your operations like they were knives and you were butter. We both know how much it cost you." He let it sink in a moment, before continuing on inexorably. "If it is happening again, even if it is not happening here, you and I *both* know where they are going to look first. And I do not think you will recover from it." He paused, as a new idea came to him, and he chuckled in realisation. "Which, in all likelihood, is what your ambitious little lieutenant is betting on."

Tommy lashed out and viciously kicked his foot through a crate, cursing as he did so. After that destructive urge had been satisfied, he turned back to Jean, glaring at him. Abruptly, he sat back down again, his expression taut as he spoke in a controlled, harsh voice. "Before I go on with this, I want you to tell me you're going to keep your friends and the rest of the Peelers out of here."

"I am going to promise nothing when it comes to the police and the Yard," Jean said flatly. "But I will do what I can. You have my word on that."

Tommy's eye narrowed. "Your word? The word of the great Jean Reynard?" He spat it out, his tone disbelieving.

"Which you well know the worth of," Jean shot back. "And you also know it is the best you are going to get. So come on now, Tommy, stop playing about with these games. You know better than most that I have not the patience for them."

The ragged king looked less kingly and more akin to prey in that moment, and seemed to know it—and that enraged him. From just this short interaction, Barty knew that this was a very dangerous man; clever and ruthless. Giving away anything for free was not in his nature. But Jean had him—the better hunter had made the kill.

Two Bob scratched furiously at a scarred cheek before he spoke. "A month ago, a cagey fellow came to me and proposed a mutually beneficent arrangement—his words, the arrogant bugger. Payment for bodies. Women, of a certain age and look." He scowled. "Thought it was someone wanting working girls and tried to play it that way, but they wanted"—his expression turned to disgust—"not so fresh merchandise." He sniffed. "I didn't like how it felt nor sounded. T'was not for me."

"Did not think you the one to draw a moral line, Tommy," Jean drawled.

The one eye that could glared back, the lip beneath curling. "I've got a few. But the whole thing reeked of too much trouble. I didn't know 'em, and he wasn't working for any of mine, but offered more money than was sensible." He rubbed his glass eye irritably. "Pete was the leader of those saying I should take it, but I know a stink when I smell it. And I still remember Jack, as does everyone else with the sense to think."

"Sounds like Cripple Pete lacks somewhat in that department," Jean said with a sardonic tone.

An angry snort and a nod in reply from Tommy as he elaborated. "When the Lord was handing out wits, he sold Pete a short measure. But a stupid man has his uses, so long as you point him in the right direction." He shook his head. "Either way, I tried to get more about it, but they weren't giving me much. Now, normally you know me Reynard—I would have had that blighter toes first and with a hammer to get names out of him, but you also know if it's the business of nobs, then the nobs get upset when you break their toys. I sent him packing." He scowled. "Should have drowned him in a puddle o' piss and left him somewhere, it's seeming." A shrug, and then he chuckled with acid on his tongue as he tapped his glass eye. "Ah well. Hindsight is always sharper, isn't it?"

Jean grunted, nonplussed by the drifting of the conversation. "Be that as it may, you have not yet elaborated on who this Sawbones is."

Tommy's chuckle withered into a scowl once more. "After getting the offer and turning it down, I was curious. Had my folks do a little scouting, a little digging, and asked my birds on the street to get about whispering in my ear." He made a grandiose gesture to the wider world. "And lo and behold, I heard a name. Old Sawbones." His expression soured further. "I was not curious enough to find out more. But that is who was trying to acquire my services."

"The same services that Cripple Pete urged you to take. Same ones he's doing now, behind your back, just outside of the Wards so you do not take action on it," Barty said quietly, laying it out fully.

Tommy gave him a dark look. "Very well squeaked, my little mouse. Want some cheese?" Sarcasm dripped thick as lard from every syllable.

Barty flinched at that, but it was Jean who leaned in again. "Leave him be, Tommy. You would not know about any of this if it were not for him."

The one-eyed man grimaced. "I am not in the habit of *enjoying* owing people anything," he snapped. "Be it pennies or favours."

"You don't owe me anything," Barty said, surprising himself. "We want the same thing that you do—and that is all. We just want to find Cripple Pete, and who he is working with."

The statement hung in the air, Tommy's expression speaking volumes. After a moment he muttered, shaking his head. "Well, fact is, I don't know where he is." He rubbed his jaw. "But it so happens that I've a feeling I know who does." With that, he set his fingers to his lips and gave a sharp whistle.

The large warehouse door opened immediately, and the heavy set man who had been watching the door to the opium den lumbered in. "What d'you have for me, Gav?" Tommy called out to him. "Any takers?"

The giant, Gav—a name all too innocuous for a man that looked like he did—nodded. "We got two, in fact." Behind him came several more of the nondescript, thuggish looking brutes that had followed Two Bob, and with them they were pushing and shoving two ragged men.

Jean was looking questioningly at Tommy, who was wearing a grin that looked like a wound as he stared, unblinking at the two nobodies, and explained, "After you mentioned old Pete's name, I asked Gav here to look for anyone who suddenly roused from their dreaming and tried to scarper off. And look at what we have! Two fellows who are about to become my best friends and sing to me for their supper." He nodded to one of his lackeys. "Get a fire going, would you? I'm feeling a bit *chilly*." He made a dramatic show of rubbing his arms as if to banish an unwarranted shiver. "How about you, lads?" He walked over to the two men, leaning in close as they shied away in fear. "You feeling a bit cold?"

Both of them refused to look at Tommy. Barty opened his mouth to say something, but Jean caught his eye and shook his head once, his expression stern, more serious than Barty was used to seeing. He closed his mouth, and focused on the two opium addicts instead.

Both of them wore soiled clothing, dark with sweat and other filth. They were of sallow complexions, pale, wan, and sickly. Barty could not tell if it was from their affliction, or from the fact that they understood they were now at the mercy of a man who, in the brief time he had come to know him, had showed Barty he knew of none.

No wonder he and Jean clashed so much, he thought. *They have too much in common.*

He tried to banish the treacherous notion as soon as it occurred, but it lingered regardless. Jean was now standing somewhat in front of him, as though to shield him. He was not sure what to make of that.

Meanwhile, Tommy was standing with his hands in his vest pockets, uncomfortably close to the two luckless victims of his curiosity. Behind him, two men dragged over a heavy iron brazier, the crude sort of invention that would keep a place like the warehouse warm while a fight was going on. The sound it made as it scraped across the ground was loud and threatening, as was the deliberate way the two men fuelled it with pieces of wood, before dousing it in lamp oil and setting it ablaze with a loud *whoomph*. The flames burst to life and then died down, the warehouse now lit by its orange glow.

Tommy stood between the inferno and the pair that had tried to leave the den. The fire at his back turned his features to shadow save for his glinting glass eye, as he spoke not to them, but to Jean and Barty. "See, it's a funny thing," he drawled. "No one at this hour, in the depths of the poppy's embrace, is going to be going anywhere until dawn, usually." He tilted his head before he continued, "They get their dreams and their silence, and then they crawl off to beg again. *Unless* they've got a pressing need to be somewhere, or to see someone. Someone interested in what they've got to tell them." He spread his arms. "Lucky lads you are, for you have found someone *very* interested in what you've got to say. Where were you going, boyos? Care to tell old Two Bob?"

Neither one would meet his venomous gaze. Both of them mumbled things that Barty could not hear, but he did not need to. They shook their heads as they pleaded their innocence. He felt his blood turn colder.

"What is he going to do to them?" he whispered to Jean as the fire crackled, spat, and started to roar, smoke billowing forth. But Jean only shook his head. His jaw was set, and Barty could see that one hand was straying to his coat, not so close as to be a threat—but just enough to be ready.

For what it was worth, Tommy gave them time. He waited patiently, and then sighed, shaking his head. "Well, since I am in a generous mood, I'll give you both one more try at this." He stepped between them, putting an arm around the shoulder of each, and walked them both towards the fire, coming to a halt just in front of it, before speaking again. "You tell me where Cripple Pete is holding up, where you were going to go and tell him someone was looking for him, and we'll call it even right here. What do you say?"

Again, the denials came, but Barty could now hear them clearly. Not because they were closer, but because their voices were raised in panic. Each man talked over the other, denying, promising, begging. "Don't know who that is, Tommy, promise I don't! Wasn't going nowhere! Was just going home!" Pleas of family, of mothers waiting, of wanting nothing to do with whatever was going on. The litany of liars from time immemorial, who know they were caught, but had nothing left bar falsehoods.

And through it all, Tommy Two Bob listened patiently, looking at one and then the other with an unreadable expression, his glass white eye glowing red in the firelight. The warehouse was filling with smoke at this point, the inferno fierce in its raging hunger. The denials and pleas of the accused grew more desperate, before Tommy sighed, and let them both go, taking a step back.

"All right, lads, all right. You say you know nothing. Maybe you don't, maybe you don't..." He rubbed his jaw. "But maybe you do." He gestured then, and both of the addicts were seized and dragged. "Start with that one first," Tommy said with irritation, pointing to the leftmost man, whose tears of terror had cut tracks through the grime on his face.

"Please! Please Two Bob! I don't know nothing!" the man

screamed as one of the thugs grabbed his ankles and tipped him over. He landed face first with a crack of smashed teeth, as another brute came and seized his wrists. The grim-faced thugs lifted him up and carried him, stretched out between them—and over to the fire.

Barty watched. He tasted bile in the back of his throat, and his spirit turned to ashes, but he could not tear his eyes away. After seeing so many awful things in his short number of years, after surviving things that made him shudder to remember, there was something utterly inhuman and *worse* about the clinical, calculated way that these men went about their business. Something about it reminded Barty that the inhumanity of man to itself was yet greater than he could have ever imagined. In a world with monsters that were horrible beyond belief to most, there were still ways that mankind could remind even them that they had a long and awful way to go.

Tommy cast his single terrible eye towards Barty and Jean. He grinned the horrible smile of a man who was enjoying his cruel work all too much, as he winked at Jean. "Want to stay and watch?"

Jean shook his head. His tone was cold. "No, I think Barty and I can be spared the entertainment. We shall wait outside." With that he turned on the spot, even as the struggling victim squealed and screamed, and the other man, now forced to his knees, looked on while his arms were held, staring in open-mouthed horror. Barty was affixed in place by his gut churning nausea, but Jean seized him by the shoulder and dragged him away, out of the warehouse, and down the alleyway. The great sliding door boomed shut. The screams became muffled and distant. But still all too close.

Barty struggled not to throw up. He staggered over to a wall, holding himself up with both hands as he sucked in ragged breaths to force the bile building in his throat back down. Jean stood nearby, arms crossed in stiff, rigid silence. His expression was grim as he stared at the ground. Neither of them said a word. There was nothing to be said, as howls echoed from within, filling the alley with pain, and haunting them both to muteness.

As Barty fought to regain his composure, a fresh thought occurred to him, as Jean continued to stand utterly still. "You lied to me, before," he croaked. Jean turned his head, blinking at Barty slowly, as though he had forgotten he was there. "Back at the... place. You said you liked killing too much," Barty explained, wiping his mouth with the back of his hand, the remnants of his regurgitation yet lingering.

Jean grunted, looking away again. "This is not the same, Bartholomew," he said at last. "But perhaps to those to whom it matters, there is little difference."

A high pitched shriek came from inside. Barty shivered, and huddled down into a squat against the wall, his stomach still heaving as he considered Jean's words a moment, then shook his head. "No. No, Jean, I think you are right. This is not the same. Not at all."

They were both quiet after that. There was no desire to debate the matter further as Tommy Two Bob got what he needed in the only way he knew how, staining every soul that could hear as he did so.

Not ten minutes later, the wide door was thrown open, and

Tommy Two Bob strode out, wiping his hands with a cloth. He looked pensive, as though whatever dark and terrible thing he had done inside had somehow left him feeling dissatisfied.

"Second one was singing before we even got started on the first one proper. But I had to be sure of it." He scowled, stuffing the cloth in his pocket.

Barty swallowed. "What are you going to do to them now?"

Tommy turned to him, his expression perplexed before he shrugged. "Sack of bricks apiece and a rope around the ankles; we'll toss the pair of them in the river."

"You don't have to do that," Barty protested, getting to his feet. "They can be just kept aside until—"

Tommy rounded on him with a lip curling snarl. "You want to tell me how I do things, do you? They made their choices when they decided to be more afraid of Pete than me. And I can't have that. I can *never* have that," he sneered, gesturing to Jean. "Ask your boss, boy. He'll know what I mean."

"Be that as it may," Jean grated, "where am I looking?" He stood with his broad shoulders back, chin raised. The look he gave Tommy was nothing short of disgust, which seemed to amuse the man from the way his vicious grin returned.

"All Saints, up around Kings Cross," he said with a chuckle, his mood shifting back to spiteful vileness from his brief flare of anger. "There's a warehouse against the tracks, a little way down from the ironworks there. A cosy little place for my old friend Pete. He's moving up in the world." He laughed, rubbing his chin. "Now, with that little scrap dropped at your feet, be a good dog and go see to my—I mean *our*—shared problem, won't you? And we can call it even." He winked, grinning wider, then jabbed a thumb over his shoulder, his leer awful. "Unless you want a turn or two at these ones before we send them off to the Lord Almighty?"

Jean fixed Two Bob with a long, blank stare. And when Jean spoke at last, it was in a plain, matter of fact tone without emotion. "One day, Tommy, you and I shall cross paths again at opposite ends. When that happens, I will kill you."

Tommy's eye widened as he took a single step back. But he rallied from the retreat and bared his rotting teeth once more. "But not today, Reynard. Unless you want to have a try at it right now?"

Jean appeared to consider it, then shook his head. "No. Not right now." He set his hands to his pockets, and started to move, pausing only briefly as he passed Two Bob. "But soon."

"I'll be waiting," Two Bob growled as Jean, with Barty scurrying in his wake, walked away. "I'll be waiting, Reynard!" His voice rose to an angry shout at Jean's departing figure. But Jean did not turn around.

Barty could not help but risk one last glance behind him at the ragged king, catching but a glimpse of a single gleaming glass eye amidst the shadows as Two Bob watched them leave. Then he and Jean turned the corner, back out into the Wards, and left the darkness behind them. But Barty could taste it still, reminding him of the two dead men, and the price paid to find a place for a name.

Chapter 9

Temple of the Resurrectionist

As they pulled away from that pit of destitute desperation, Barty got the distinct impression that Jean was glad to be leaving the Wards behind. He had no guesses on his own part. He very much wished to put his back to the place, and hoped never to return to the spiteful miseries he had been burdened to witness.

But rather than going directly to Kings Cross, Jean abruptly left the comfort of the carriage to flag down a pair of police officers doing their evening rounds. Barty was too far away to hear, hovering at the door of the coach which had itself come to a sudden halt, but he watched the expression of the officers turn from suspicion to intrigue as Jean spoke, before they both nodded and smartly turned in the opposite direction.

Jean barrelled into the carriage, thumping the roof to get them moving again. He caught Barty's puzzled, inquisitive look and shrugged, his expression sour. "I wanted them to bring me Creek for this one."

"You are expecting trouble? More than usual?" Barty asked in surprise. Jean had once walked into a bar full of werewolves with an armed bomb. Cautious was not his standard approach to problems.

Jean's upper lip curled in irritation as he settled into his seat and nodded. "I am not sure what to fully expect. My intuition demands that I am missing something, a piece that connects events together. But I will uncover it."

He brooded, glaring out at nothing. He was even more moody than he normally was, and much more tense. It filled the air around him, stifling Barty within the carriage. Barty's mind churned, wandering through the meandering lanes of recent, bloodstained memory following the crimson trail that linked it all together in his thoughts.

"If this was just a nobleman kidnapping women, you would have gone to the police and let them deal with it, Reynard," he said haltingly. "But you are not. You're putting this on yourself—why? To distract you from the situation with Adam?"

Jean shook his head with a grunt. "No—at least, not precisely." He rubbed his bearded jaw with a pensive thumb. "My instincts are telling me there is a thread binding this all together, and thus then to me also. What that element is in this instance, I do not yet know, nor presume to guess with so little knowledge. But *something* is telling me that I need to be involved in this."

Barty fell quiet at that, not sure what to add to that admission. A memory of the silent statue that was Adam flickered unbidden in his mind's eye, and it stirred a thought, something that he had been told months ago during the Jekyll case. "I was told that you had an arrangement with Adam," he said carefully. "That one day, you were going to help them end their existence." He let that sink in as Jean turned his gaze back to him, his eyes narrowed and his face a mask. "And yet you seem to be concerned for them. Very much so, I might add."

"Do I appear to be in the throes of hysteria?" Jean replied dryly.

"No. But I know you better than that. You would not have gone to Two Bob if there was another avenue to pursue. You are also in a hurry on the matter—you think this has something to do with Adam."

Jean's expression soured but he finally nodded, looking away once again. "I forget that it was your own ability to discern that led to me taking you on," he admitted grudgingly. "I do not know *how* yet—the only evidence I have is that voice we both heard during Adam's... incident." He frowned ever deeper, etching lines in his face. "I might be wrong. But I rarely am." He cast Barty a warning look. "However, despite what Adam might have told you of the... arrangement, as you so put it, that they and I share, I would very much appreciate you do not engage me further on the matter. Adam may tell you more if they so wish. But I, emphatically, shall not."

Barty bit his tongue in more than a little frustration, but he did not press the matter, save to give voice to one truth he knew to be absolute. "You care about Adam very much, don't you?"

Jean turned that squint back onto him, balefully. "What have I told you about the luxury of friends, Bartleby?" His tone was cold. "They are one that I cannot afford. Adam is my responsibility, and the responsibility of the Lodge. But in the immediate, there are people in danger here and now. If they are connected, very well. If they are not, then I will continue on regardless."

Barty leaned back, looking out the window as the dark expanse of London rolled past, drawing closer to where they intended, and rapidly so. A thought occurred to him. "Back in the Lodge, you said you heard whispers coming from Adam. What were they saying?"

Jean grunted, settling into his seat. "The most prosaic of phrases, but one even I, at times, am driven to respond to, especially when delivered in such desperation." Barty gave him a quizzical look, and Jean stared back. "*'Help me'*, Barty. That is what they said."

"The two men back with Tommy said that, too," Barty replied. He could not stop himself.

Jean's expression went wooden. He did not seem to breathe, he went so still. "I am sure those men whom Puck *dealt with* for you wanted someone to help them too, Barty," Jean finally said icily. His gaze went back out the window. "Bad luck for them, I suppose."

Barty did not say anything more. There was no shifting his tongue from that moment. He sat in leaden silence, smothered by the weight of his own guilt.

ON THE EDGE OF THE TRAIN YARDS, the air of Kings Cross was thick enough that you could chew it, laden with coal dust from the engines that came and went at all hours. The high pitched shriek of a steam whistle echoed out, slicing through the air as if it were a knife.

They went by way of the train tracks themselves; great twist-ing lines that trailed off into the gloomy darkness. Jean did not say what he was looking for, but he moved smooth and quiet, a drifting shade, with the far less fluid Barty in his wake.

What Barty found interesting about Jean's method of stealth was how *lazy* he made it appear. Sneaking about to Barty brought up furtive images of slipping from shadow to shadow, mad dashes into darkness to avoid any observation, hugging corners, and moving on tiptoes. Jean would have none of it.

The trick, Barty had learned, was that the watching eye was drawn to such movements. If you rushed, if you *appeared* like you were trying to hide, people who were looking for those inclined to *do* such things would notice it. Like a fox seeking the twitch of a mouse amongst wheat rows, its eye would be drawn to the hurried, the panicked, the frantic motion of one trying to escape without realising how obvious it would be to the observer.

So Jean did not rush; he did not run, he did not quicken his pace. He eased from dark space to dark space, but when he could be seen, he strode with nonchalance—the confidence of a man who belonged where he was so completely that no part of how he moved indicated he was somewhere he should not be. It was the sort of locomotion that one might regularly see on the busy streets of London, and easily ignore; you did not pay attention to it, because it was so *ordinary*. And so, to the casual observer, Jean was invisible. The same could not be said though, for Barty, who stuck out like the sorest of thumbs, a digit belonging to a blind carpenter who wielded a hammer with impunity and much regret.

"You will either learn the habit of *thinking* yourself invisible, Bartholomew Bartleby," Jean murmured as they carried on in the shadow of a wall, "or a passing huntsman will become so convinced of your erratic movement—that you are in fact a wild deer in disguise—and, overcome with instinct, will shoot you dead on the spot from a hundred yards away. Which will be very tragic in the immediate once the mistake is learned, and very amusing in the aftermath."

Barty blinked several times at that. "I beg your finest pardon, but what?" he hissed.

Jean paused, turning his head in the darkness until the gleam of his eyes was visible. "I am saying," he murmured, "that you are a hair's breadth from becoming a cautionary tale in the art of stealth to tell future generations. Calm down, and breathe, slowly. Remember you are exactly where you belong." He turned away again and continued, leaving Barty to resume his clumsy pursuit.

"But we *are not* where we belong, that is the problem," Barty responded worriedly, looking around in dread of seeing spectres appearing out of the gloom.

"What did I tell you earlier about self-deception, Barty?" Jean replied with amusement. "We do it to ourselves all the time. A little bit of applied thinking to the matter should not be so impossible." He glanced back, looked Barty up and down, then shrugged. "Confidence, Barty. It is a falsehood in all of us, but it is empowering to be so while aware of the dangers of hubris."

Barty was about to protest this, to debate how impossible it was for him to feel such things, when he walked into Jean, all but bouncing off the hunter's back. The man had gone rigid, staring straight ahead.

"Speaking of things that do not belong," Jean said slowly while Barty rubbed his sore nose with a wince. "There is something that stands out to the eye." He indicated to the rooftop of a nearby, large and blocky building.

Barty poked his head around the other man and followed the pointing hand, tracing it to a series of large poles ascending skyward. They were each taller than a flagpole, towering over every other structure and topped by a globe, set at the edge of each building. But Barty did not see the reasoning.

"What am I looking at?" he asked, baffled.

Jean now gestured to the left. "Wait for it…"

As the stopping place for nearly every industrial train in all of England, the train yard was a maze of tracks, stable cars, and all manner of other paraphernalia that London's mighty industriousness contained. It was also heavily guarded and the prime component of that guarding was a great blazing spotlight that inexorably illuminated many sins of the train yard in its laborious path. And when it came rolling past, it lit the tall poles and made them gleam a particular colour.

"Copper," Jean explained from the safety of their obfuscating shelter. "Solid copper, and quite a lot of it at that. That had to be expensive." He frowned. "It must have been recently installed; there has not been time to develop a patina." He rubbed his jaw.

"Might I ask the significance of all that information?" Barty was genuinely curious.

Jean shrugged and went on, "Copper is an excellent conductor of electricity—and it attracts lightning *significantly*, especially with that amount."

Realisation crept across Barty's thoughts. "Adam's incident took place during a storm."

Jean nodded, and said nothing more as they moved forward. There was a high wall around the building, too tall to jump over. The building itself was dark—ominously so. It lurked heavily, brutishly crude and without windows. Just a massive structure of bricks, and yet the silence of it was forbidding.

"There does not appear to be anyone here, Jean," Barty murmured but Jean held up a hand to silence him. He looked tense, intent. Something had seized his attention, and as he sniffed the air again, Barty caught it himself; a scent of ozone.

Jean peered around the corner, then beckoned Barty to follow him as they approached the gate. It was locked, wrapped with chains, and with a fearsome padlock. Jean reached into his coat, plucking out a small cloth package which he unwrapped, and selected some thin metal devices—well-oiled lockpicks.

Barty was acutely aware that they were within plain view of anyone who might be looking. He shifted on his feet as Jean performed his larcenous task, and hoped no one would see them.

"Remember what I told you about being invisible, Barty," Jean hissed as he worked the lock, operating not by sight, but by the sound of faint clicks, metal scrapings, and the feel of the pins within. "While you are failing entirely at the art of subterfuge, you are, however, performing exemplary as an alarm bell."

"We *are* right in the open," he replied anxiously. The darkened street felt like there were eyes in every shadow, stares from every closed window. Sweat poured down his neck and he jumped when Jean made a sound of triumph as the lock clicked open. Not nearly quiet enough for Barty's liking, Jean extracted the chain so that there was only a minimum of further racket. He pushed the gate open enough to allow Barty within before closing it behind him, then returned the padlock, but did not set it into place—leaving the way open for a swift departure.

Jean moved with long, light footsteps, covering ground quickly. The laziness from outside was gone, replaced with a predatory urgency, his strides sure and silent. He reached a great sliding doorway set on rails, locked and barred—but after a cursory inspection, Jean left it and went to circle around the back of the building, with Barty in tow. His discomfort at their burglary remained at the forefront of his mind, conflicting entirely with his instructions on obscurity. He hoped they would find a means of entry to get out of sight shortly.

They found a way in. An entirely unexpected one.

The rear of the building had a yard, with barrels and crates of various unidentified goods, and a hole—right through the wall.

Jean walked in a prowling semi-circle, his expression in the gloom difficult to read. He stepped amongst scattered fragments of bricks, spread out from the hole in an explosive array in all directions. Barty stared at it—the unconventional entrance measured about eight feet in circumference, and looking through the void of its opening Barty saw only an unknowable darkness. Silence emanated from that gaping maw, the echoes of disaster written into every broken brick of its making.

"Interesting." Jean's tone was one of subdued fascination.

"Whatever made it might still be inside," Barty said, expecting something to leap out at him from the darkness. But Jean was shaking his head.

"No. Whatever created this opening came from inside." He pointed at the pattern of broken masonry. "No chemical residue, nor trace of scorching to indicate an explosive. Pure concussive force did this." He frowned, crouching and squinting as he peered closer. Jean pointed towards the wall, on the other side of which was the train yards. "There's a footprint there. A heavy one, though… not large. Whatever this is, they have mobility, they were in a hurry, and they did not linger." His tone was contemplative. "I would wager they jumped over the wall."

Barty peered at the wall, around ten feet high. "That is quite a climb," he said. "With no hand holds."

Jean was shaking his head. "No, Barty. I said *jumped*."

Barty looked at the wall, at the hole, then back at Jean. "Oh."

"Indeed so," Jean said dryly. He stood back up again, then opened his coat, pulling out a small metal disc that he twisted in his hands and shook. There was a faint metal scraping and the small object turned into a slender cone with a single opening; a very basic—and very small—lamp. Jean filled it with oil from a small flask, and lit it with a match that flared bright in the depths of his coat where he kept it concealed. The cunningly wrought device was barely a hand's breadth long, but it created just enough light. Jean put it to use, stepping through the hole and into the darkness beyond, a blackness so thick it seemed to swallow him up. Barty's steps faltered in his anxiety, but he followed after him.

It was difficult to make anything out at first for there was no light, save for what Jean brought. No windows opened to the outer world, no skylight allowed even the obscured glow of the fitful moon within. The building was as dark as a tomb. The smell of ozone within was much, much stronger and Barty focused on it as his eyes adjusted.

Jean swept the pocket lantern around, then swore and held it out to Barty. "Hold this." He searched the depths of his coat with nimble hands. "Hold the lantern out, and close your eyes. Don't open them until I say," he instructed.

Barty, confused, did as he was told.

Jean grunted in satisfaction and plucked the lantern from Barty's fingers. "Remember. Eyes closed," he growled. There was a faint hiss.

And then there was light.

A searing incandescence so powerful Barty could see *through* his eyelids, the world turning red as the blood flowing beneath the skin illuminated with that terrible brilliance. He covered his face with both hands, shying away, as Jean cursed under his breath. "Should be all right to open them now. But do not look at it directly."

Barty opened his eyes hesitantly, peering over through his fingers. Jean held the little lamp up and away, but from the opening came a scintillating brightness. "A compound of magnesium and some other materials to slow the burning," Jean explained. "Adam designed it, of course. Now look around."

Barty did. And gaped in astonishment.

The interior was a singular open space, but for all of its size nevertheless felt crowded. From each corner of the roof slithered a plethora of twisting cables, passing through the ceiling and converging downwards, before vanishing via a crudely cut hole in the floorboards. They hung lifcless, the roots of some great and terrible tree, dark, silent, and dead.

Jean was moving around them now, taking care not to touch the cables as he weaved, holding up the bright flaring lantern before directing the beam to the ground. There was a large trapdoor set into the floor—at least, what remained of one. Now it was simply destroyed, broken outwards by a tremendous force. The iron hinges had snapped and twisted, the bolt resting amidst splinters at the opposite end of the room.

Jean turned, looking at the dimly lit hole in the rear wall, and then back to the shattered trapdoor. "A more or less straight line," he mused to himself. "They came up through here and did not stop."

"What do you mean by 'they'?" Barty hissed in shock.

"Is it not obvious, Barty?" Jean said quietly, approaching the broken trapdoor. "Something came out of this door, and through that wall using neither explosive, nor device. Some*one* did this damage." He paused at the opening, lifting the lantern to show descending steps. "Someone very strong—and very frightened. This was an act of desperation." He started down the steps. "And of panic."

"I can relate to that notion, well enough," Barty muttered, swallowing his dread. This place crawled uncomfortably in his marrow.

"Courage, Barty," Jean said sternly. "They are far departed. There is nothing here now but ghosts—and though they may be loud indeed, they shall not harm you either." His nostrils flared then, and he paused before reaching into his coat to withdraw his heavy revolver. "But you may want to cover your nose."

Barty leaned over the opening, and immediately gagged. The sickly odour of rot cut across his nose like a rust-bitten razor, fouled and cloying. There was a chemical scent as well, but this was the stronger. It wafted on a plagued breeze from the broken doorway, thick and disgusting. Jean appeared unaffected, but his grimace remained. Bearing torch and pistol, he paced down the steps. Barty covered his mouth with a handkerchief yanked from a pocket and followed, his nerves twisting tight under his skin.

"Formaldehyde, amongst other things," Jean said as he descended, his tone clinically detached. "Not enough to hide the smell—but there never is. I would wager the bodies have been here for a few days." He reached a door—open, for it, too, had been wrenched off its hinges. "Now let us—" He stopped, going rigid as he held the glowing lantern aloft.

Barty drew alongside, and sucked in a sharp breath; he could not help it, regardless of the stench of death.

The room beyond was long with a high, reinforced roof, the walls lined with shelves and shelves of large jars filled with green, noxious looking liquid, in which vague shapes were suspended. The cables that had been put through the floor above them clustered in a twisting nest, attached to devices that were connected to a human-shaped cage of glinting steel. There were panels and gauges, and scorch marks where unbridled power had arced and blazed along metal that was barely able to contain its wrath. Strange and unsettling machines, crafted of copper and steel, connected in some fashion to the cage apparatus at the centre, stood as if drained of power.

"God's blood." Jean's voice was a hushed whisper, and for the first time since Barty had known him, he seemed to be genuinely shocked. Steps loud in the breathless silence, he walked past the shelves and racks, the devices and the terrible cage—a sort of iron maiden—to three stone slabs, akin to mortuary tables. Three figures lay upon them, covered from head to toe in cloth. Where the stomach of each should have been was a dark, befouled stain of rotting, blackened blood.

As Barty walked past the forboding device and its dreadful cage to stand with Jean, the smell of death grew stronger, as well as his realisation. The stone slabs were also marked with copper and silver wires, all leading to the greater device that dominated the centre of the great chamber. The air smelled most thickly of burning metal here, and the repulsive rank of burnt flesh. It was an awful, choking reek, but Jean paid it no heed. His features were wracked with a blasted, hollow expression of grief and shame. He reached out to the cloth of the nearest figure and lifted it, to expose the face below.

It was hard to tell, time and decay warring against preservation as the body had laid untended and uncared for, but she had been young, and she had been beautiful, and she did not deserve to be down here.

"Who are they?" Barty asked, his voice a shatteringly loud thing amongst that dreadful quiet, feeling somehow blasphemous. Jean stared down at the dead girl, seeing through her, past her, and into something far away that carved out pieces of Barty's heart as he watched.

"They actually figured it out... they knew what it costs, and went ahead with it anyway." He sounded numbed, a thickening wrath crawling into his words, but for whatever reason he buried it down. He did not answer Barty's following question, but it was, in that moment, hard to believe he knew Barty was even there. He shook his head, and put away his revolver into his coat, as though to keep it from distressing the dead, who had already suffered enough. His fist clenched in a moment of repressed rage, but when he covered that silent, still face, he did so gently, like a father trying not to wake a sleeping child whose blankets had slipped. He made sure she was concealed once more before he spoke in a detached, dulled tone.

"Did you know, Barty, what a woman fears most? What tends to end their lives so unfairly, and swiftly?" Barty shook his head, but Jean did not even look at him. "Men. In one fashion or another, they bring death to their door. And one way that begets from men most of all... is childbirth." He took a deep breath, steeling himself and lifting the cloth at the midsection. Barty turned his head, but not in time to look away from the great cavity that had been carved into the body where, in circumstances without trauma and without fear, might have held a life of innocence. Now there was just horror.

"But it does not end there," Jean went on in a tone as black as the pit. "It is not simply the terror of giving birth that ends their lives. For some, it happens in the circumstances around it. A child born out of wedlock, because some all too tricky lad who lacks a soul was clever with his words and not with his actions, who convinced some poor, innocent thing that he loved them before it was too late for her to realise what he was." He gritted his teeth. "Sometimes it is not even that, but someone who cannot be told no. And each time, they are not the ones who pay for it. At least, never enough to satisfy." He paused, his hand gentle as he rested it on the covered forehead of the dead girl, looking to the others.

"Who are they?" Barty's voice was hushed as he asked it again. But he was starting to understand... as much as he wished it otherwise.

"Suicides," Jean said heavily, bitterly. "Lives that were ended because of a mistake, or a misdeed, or whatever someone might want to call it—it does not matter. Lives that were ended by those that felt they had no other choice." He shook his head, his tone turning flat with his anger. "Because, of course, they are the ones who take the blame. All for a small mistake, that was not even one they themselves made most of the time, but instead bore the brunt of. But it is easier to condemn than it is to care."

"But why?" Barty asked, shivering. The three silent corpses judged him with their stillness. Why were they here, when men like Two Bob and Cripple Pete and even Jean himself were still alive? When Barty was still alive, and they were not?

Jean shot him a caustic, sideways glance. "Because they were pregnant, Barty. And because the weight of that, in the circumstances they were in, for whatever reason was so vast and terrible that they felt this was the only option left to them." He exhaled, shaking his head. "I wondered why I had heard nothing of any missing women. Now I know. After all, this happens too often for authorities to bother reporting on." His tone was thick with bitterness, staining every syllable. "The uncared for, the forgotten. Nobody gives a damn about such 'regrettable and embarrassing incidents.'" He said the last through clenched teeth. He closed his eyes and took a steadying breath before he continued, "The men who found you—you said it was at the shores of the river, did you not?"

Barty was starting to understand too. "They were lookouts." He said it with a numb sensation trickling down his spine. "For young women in such—"

He wanted to say something like 'an unfortunate position' but such a delicate phrase in the face of such needless death was an insult too foul for him to voice. This was a tragedy thrice. Nothing less than that.

Jean simply nodded, his expression twisted with distaste. "Not to save them. Just to take what was left afterwards." His tone could have etched lines in granite.

"But *why?*"

Jean cast him a glance as though finally remembering Barty was there, and blinked once as he regathered his thoughts, then looked back to the bodies. "Because of the neverborn," he said finally. He continued as Barty's blank expression betrayed his bafflement. "Stillborn, miscarried, whatever the circumstances may be, the spirit of a neverborn child has... potency. They are used in magic—very, very forbidden magic—but to harness it, you need the form itself."

Barty felt nauseous, too sick in his stomach to dare to ask more. He shook his head. "This is vile, Jean." He had to force the words out as disgust choked him, his proclamation thick with his conviction. He did not want to know about whatever dark horror it was that lay before him.

"Why *three* though? That I do not understand," Jean muttered, inspecting each body and where they were set. "What is the significance? What were they hoping to create?" He was not asking Barty, speaking instead to himself.

"Does it matter?" Barty asked numbly, unable to look away from the three women. "They should not be here."

Jean scowled, ignoring Barty as he began to examine the twisted equipment of the laboratory. "A lot of residual charge in the devices," he growled, tapping one large tangle of apparatus covered in dials, levers, and gears that Barty could not make sense of. "I cannot tell if they went too far, or not far enough. But they did *something* here." He continued to stride around, frowning as he went from one machine to the next, before returning to the central device and the empty cage that all the other machines lead to. He stood at the closed cage, reaching out with both hands as though measuring it. The sarcophagus structure suddenly gleamed as an arc of energy tore across its frame, and Jean sprang away with a curse.

Barty barely reacted. He was still staring at the three women. Something about this unforgivable violation of the women and their unborn spoke to him; as an orphan, his story began in a manner he had no way of remembering the particulars of. How close had he come to being of the same fate as this? Neverborn, Jean had called it. Never known. Never given the chance to *be*. And yet, seeing the three still shapes, he was struck by the weight of the decision he had been unable to understand then, and still did not. While he had dared to hope that the choice to give him up to the orphanage had not been frivolous, he had not understood the difficulty of that choice either. Now, with the burden of three deaths so common that no one felt it worth reporting, he was forced to contemplate questions he had not faced before.

A hand came to his shoulder and he flinched. But Jean was there, saying his name, rousing him from that dark stupor, fixing him with a piercing, unyielding stare, speaking firmly as he did so.

"Neither you nor I can change the circumstances of their deaths, Barty. You and I know the wrongness of it. You and I know this is cruel, and unfair. *Nobody* should ever be forced into the choice that they made." His jaw tightened. "All we can do now is try to make this awful violation mean something—and in so doing, see vengeance done."

Barty simply nodded, not willing to speak about his own revelation, before something clicked into his own understanding. "You know about this, do you not? You have seen this before."

Jean stiffened, but he nodded as he turned away. "Unfortunately, I do. And now I understand the missing piece... the connection to Adam."

Barty's head jerked around at that, his attention sharpening to a point. This, more than anything, cut through to him. "I beg your pardon, what?"

Jean stood at the cage once more, glaring at it, as he answered, "This is a laboratory of a resurrectionist. In a place such as this Adam was made—the first, and until now, the only one of their kind."

Until now. The words were enough to send Barty's already

quickened heartbeat to racing. He was about to voice his concerns, when a loud, grinding scrape came from above. While he stood stunned into silence, staring upwards, Jean moved quick as a serpent and snapped shut the lamp, plunging the laboratory into darkness. He made not a sound despite his swiftness, as the rumble of heavy feet and rough voices came from above.

Someone had entered the building—men who were loud, who filled the air with impatient curses as chains rattled and doors opened. Barty felt himself seized by one shoulder and dragged towards the darkened slabs with the shrouded corpses, and into shadow. Blinded in the darkness, Barty felt Jean touch his lips with one finger, and though Barty could not see, he knew silence and how to hold on to it. He crouched down, and waited.

Between the devices, racks, and mechanisms, it was hard to make out the shambling figures who entered the chamber, but it was possible to hear them—one in particular, louder and deeper than the rest, a voice with a snarl in it, thick with animal fury that swept through the room. They barked commands, interlaced with curses, and then that deep voice bellowed a final order. "Open it up!"

The basement was beset with a rattling of cranks and chains, shifted by a grunting, desperate effort. Barty watched from his crouched position, mouth agape, as the ceiling split down the middle and began to lift. Hoisted by chains set into bolts, the roof opened up before settling to each side with a loud, reverberating boom. A yellow glow of crude fuel from dirty lanterns above, but Jean and Barty were secluded from it, tucked away in an alcove made by overhanging beams, out of sight. Barty huddled closer to the wall in fear, as though to push through it. Jean, however, his eyes gleaming in the dark and fixed upwards, lowered further on his haunches. Barty knew that look.

Jean was hunting.

"Lord save me, them lassies are stinking now," spat the foul voice from above. "Lucky for me, eh, that you're the ones handling this lot. Get you down there and get to it."

There was a whine of protests, cut off by a sharp sound of fist striking flesh and a cry of pain to follow. "No arguments," snarled the deeper voice. "You heard his lordship. Want to be paid? Then get to work." A moment of discomforted silence followed, before the sounds of movement could be heard. Multiple footsteps. People were coming down into the laboratory.

Heart beating against his chest, Barty turned his head to Jean to ask what they should do, but the words died in his throat. The man was gone. He had not seen it or even sensed it; he had vanished into the gloom. For a brief moment, Barty felt he had been abandoned in that terrible place, but a far more pressing realisation came into play as he ducked, hoping no one above was looking for him, and slipped amongst the machinery to place himself behind a panelled, boxlike array of steel, wire, and glass which offered better cover from anyone entering the opened chamber.

Four men stamped down the staircase with the reluctance of those who are tasked with an awful job, and no enthusiasm to do it. They were indistinct to Barty as he peered around the device that kept him concealed, seeking shadows and darkness, holding his breath lest it betray him. There was no sign of Jean.

The figures were more visible now in the half-hearted light of fell deeds and dreadful secrets. They were men that bore the ugliness of their souls on their faces—scars, foulness, and breath rancid enough to stain the air they breathed. Barty had seen men like them before and knew them all too well. They would be considered cruel, if only they had the wit for cruelty. And now they gazed with the dull-eyed stares of the unknowing, at the various machinations of the laboratory, drawing nearer to Barty, who crouched in terrified silence behind a large, boxed contraption. He identified the dragging steps of one, now standing close enough that he was sure they could hear his terrified heartbeat.

Barty perceived a grunt of bafflement and disgust, and closed his eyes. He nearly yelped as he heard a loud thump above his head—a hand slapped down on the device he'd taken shelter behind. A whining buzz emanated from it at the blow, making the hairs on Barty's neck and arms stand upright. The air tasted suddenly of metal and ozone.

It enraged the voice above, who roared in fury. "Don't bloody touch that! It's been building up a charge all day—you drop that lever, and there's a chance you cook us all." Barty could *feel* the figure near him flinch and back away, and he breathed in relief, even as the snarling, spitting, hate-filled voice above continued, "You lot know what you're here to do. Get those corpses out of here, or you're going to join 'em in the dirt."

Sour but fearful grunts were their muted replies, but then

came movement. Heeding advice given earlier, Barty willed himself invisible. There was noise from up above—loud, heavy sounds of something metallic screeching as it was dragged. Barty risked peering around a corner of the device to see the crude labourers making their way to the covered bodies. Their backs were facing him, but even in that dim darkness he was too afraid to chance his way out. He felt his heartbeat race and his blood surge as he asked himself,

Where was Jean?

For he was down here, trapped in this not nearly large enough space with three thugs, and another above, and—

His panicked thoughts stopped short. His breath hitched.

Three. He could see three brutes. But *four* had come down into the laboratory.

The three men seemed to realise this the same time Barty did, and called a name that he did not catch. Two shrugged, and set to manhandling one of the bodies, while the other cursed, abandoning his duty to search for his missing companion, stepping out of Barty's sight.

The darkness flickered. There was a soft sound in the shadows. And then there were two.

The remaining thugs started to realise something was wrong, letting the corpse fall from their hands as they replaced it with lanterns to peer about. Barty wondered what sort of creature Jean Reynard was. From the first he had known him, he seemed more comfortable in the shadows, more part of them than the waking world. Jean looked into darkness, stared it down, and then made a home for it within himself. And with that darkness he opened wide, and pulled others down into it where they would never be seen again. He was the man who hunted monsters. But tonight, he was a nightmare all of his own, and all the more dreadful for it.

Barty did not see him move. He saw a lantern tumble, shatter, and obliterate the light it made. The last of the body snatchers called out in terror, a high-pitched, unmanly shriek with his tongue cleaving to his mouth and robbing him of words. But no amount of words would have saved him as his cries turned into a cut off sigh and gurgle. The pit was rendered dark, pulsating with the last fears of those who had been devoured by Reynard's wrath.

There was a thudding of steps and loud cursing at the dying screech; the leader of the four silent souls rendered unto darkness entered the laboratory to see what had become of his miscreant crew. There were no answers forthcoming. The darkness breathed, but it told only terrible, bloody secrets.

Barty was huddled in hiding as he heard the vicious swearing, incoherent in its bestial rage. There was sharp light, bright and fierce, a carried lamp of a far more potent variety than what had been lost and broken. Barty thought he was well hidden; an illusion swiftly shattered when a vicious hand seized him by the shoulder and yanked him off the ground as if he were a child. Barty squeaked as he found himself face to face with a visage he could have lived his whole life without ever seeing—and certainly not from this close.

Brutal, slab-like jaws propped up lips mashed from bare-knuckle fighting. Half of one ear and less than that of the other, both ragged and torn. The teeth were bared fully and they were as foul as the breath which passed through them, which was awful enough to tarnish silver on contact. The man looked more scar tissue than skin. He appeared shocked to see the captured intruder, but the way his brow furrowed made Barty realise he was swiftly moving to spite-fuelled fury, and with it would come the burning, jagged pain that simple cruelty could evoke with ease.

"Who the hells are you?" He spat more than spoke, sickening phlegm spraying forth in a disgusting miasma.

Barty tried to speak, his tongue sticking to his teeth. "I... I..." But fear drowned his words until, over his captor's shoulder, he saw the shadows behind the brute move. He swallowed, and stuttered, "I am... not the one you need to worry about."

This was clearly not a good enough answer. But the monster never got a chance to comprehend Barty's words, as two gloved hands splattered with blood appeared out of the darkness to clamp down on both sides of the man's face, yanking him backwards and off his feet. Barty was dropped and he stumbled, falling behind the machinery he had used to hide himself. Sounds of struggle and violence came from around the corner, and then an agonised scream cut off into a teeth gritted groan as Barty crawled out into the space and laid eyes on the scene before him.

At first, he had wanted to breathe a sigh of relief, wanted to say something with effusive gratitude, a remark of annoyance to feign irritation, he couldn't decide. But he could see Jean now, having turned the brutal man into some complicated knot of joints and twisted limbs, and pinned him with a knee to the back of his head, one huge arm held in such a way that it looked ready to tear clean off the shoulder. He had seen the hunter angry before. He had seen him wear so many expressions of wrath in those dark and hateful eyes that it had made Barty shudder. But now, seeing him, Barty knew only fear.

The fallen lamp nearby provided enough light to paint the face of the nightmare. But those eyes were lit from within by whatever hell resided in Jean's soul. At long last, Barty fully saw it; the man that everyone feared, a man that would kill God if he could, and even if it was not possible, would try without hesitation; his hatred was a blasphemy upon the Earth. But if it was to be called thus then, in its defence, what this dread cellar had been used for was anathema.

"You knew what this place was." Jean's voice was as thick as the congealed, cold blood of malice. "You knew what it was for. You knew all of it and yet you still brought them here. You *bastard*." His teeth were bared, venom adorning every word. The trapped figure writhed and cursed breathlessly, trying to rise and failing. "Ah, *Peter*," Jean growled, revealing at last the identity of the trapped figure. "Even you could not be so stupid as to think I would not come for you, for this."

The wretched Cripple Pete writhed and tried to speak, spitting the words between his bloodied lips from where his face had been ground into the stone floor. He snarled in a mixture of pain and rage. "Reynard? I'm not telling you nothing you—"

Jean twisted that already straining arm with a wrench. From where he huddled, Barty could hear the *pop* and then the cracking, muffled *snap* of bones breaking and joints leaving their sockets. Cripple Pete made a nightmarish sound, a deep-throated squeal like a boar in a slaughterhouse being butchered alive.

"You misunderstand me, Peter," Jean growled as his prey went white and choked on his agonised scream. "I am not here to question you. I am here to *judge* you." He tightened his grip, and twisted further. The hideous cracking symphony continued as Cripple Pete howled in animal agony.

"Well, if that is the case Reynard—turn about should be fair play, do you not think?"

It was another voice, educated and clear, despite the inherent sneer within it. Jean and Barty both looked up to the opened ceiling into the larger warehouse as lights blazed bright in the upper structure, illuminating all of those below.

Dark figures, enshrouded by the lights behind them, looked down at the scene. A half dozen at least, and armed. They were not police. But they all wore the same outfit—black, long coats, trimmed in silver. They looked wealthy... They looked dangerous. Each wore a classic bowler hat with a black handkerchief tied around their face to obscure their features. All but one; the one who had spoken.

"How wonderful to see you again, Reynard." His oily voice echoed with a tone both mocking and reeking of false manners. "It has been far too long, has it not?"

Jean remained where he was, his hand frozen in the act of reaching for his sidearm. His expression flattened into a cold, murderous focus as he looked up at the man who had spoken.

"Sir Blake Wyrmwood," he said in a controlled voice that sounded like it took an impossible amount of effort. "It has indeed. And not nearly long enough."

Chapter 10

The Turning of the Worm

Blake Wyrmwood knelt at the edge of the pit that was the laboratory. He was in his thirties, with oiled, slicked back hair that glistened in the light shining on the scene. Thin lips were warped into an arrogant, knowing smirk that twisted a delicate moustache, and his cruel eyes were dark and sly, his nose twitching with suppressed, malicious humour.

He was, in short, someone whose entire appearance evoked distrust—a weasel more than a man. Barty did not like him on sight and could gather, even out of his line of gaze, the feeling would be entirely mutual. Barty was reminded by his bearing of Lord Beauchamp—cruel, spiteful, and sadistic. But unlike the wretched Beauchamp, this man seemed far more alert, and far more dangerous.

Jean pushed himself to his feet, untangling himself from Cripple Pete, releasing the stricken brute's arm which flopped boneless to the ground. Before the wretch could crawl away, Jean brought his right leg back and kicked hard into the side of Cripple Pete's head. The thug went limp, twitching in his unconsciousness.

"A touch rude, would you not say, Reynard?" Wyrmwood chided from above, a brow raised. "He was not going to be much trouble."

"I cannot stand whimpering in the midst of a conversation," Jean replied sourly. He straightened, turning his eyes from one man to the next without shifting his head. His hands were at his sides, loose but ready to act—Barty knew how fast they could be. Yet Jean hesitated. "I take it then, that this is all your doing?"

Wyrmwood chuckled, shaking his head. "My, you do like to fish for answers, even when you have no bait, Reynard." The condescension in his tone was laden with spite, his lip curling. "Though, for once... I do like to see the great hunter wriggling on a hook."

Jean hawked and spat to one side with the lazy contempt one has for someone they truly despise. "You still like to hear yourself talk, I see." For all his seeming boredom, he was nevertheless scathing. "You would think with all these lackies around you, you would get tired of it." He peered up at the wordless observers. "I would wager they certainly do." There was a shifting then, as though some of the observers fought the urge to nod in agreement. It was barely noticeable, but Barty felt it, as blatant as the raw, virulent hatred these two had for each other. They clearly knew one another—knew each other well—and it had lent them no affection. This did not bode well for Barty, who hardly dared breathe as his eyes darted around the room, trying to find a way out, but one did not avail itself.

Wyrmwood gave a strained sort of laugh at that, but it was forced. Jean, however, pressed on. "So all of this here is yours, I take it, you and your Blackcoat friends in parliament?" His tone was accusing, but Wyrmwood put a hand to his chest and affected an innocent air.

"Mine? Heavens no, but this is something *clearly* in the jurisdiction of the Department of Eidolon. And so we are here to investigate it."

Barty flashed a glance to Jean. He had spoken little of the group, but Adam and Elanor had told him enough. The Blackcoats—or Eidolon, as they now seemingly called themselves—were a group that operated with the backing of the law and the Crown. They pursued their goals with methods both mysterious and vicious, and quite in conflict with the Society as a result.

Barty was as of yet unnoticed, having huddled back in his corner of hiding—a most convenient corner it had been thus far—with the device that Pete had warned his men about doing a marvellous job of obscuring him. As he looked at it, he noticed, not far from his foot, a series of large latch lever controls. What had Cripple Pete said? The charge had been building all day?

Jean grunted, as Barty grappled with the mechanics of a machine he did not understand. "Eidolon. And that stands for?"

Wyrmood smirked. "The Department of Esoterica In Defiance Of Law Or Nature, if you wish to call it by its full name." He sounded very proud of it, but Jean barked one of his blunt, caustic laughs in response, rippled with amusement.

"Oh, someone must have *really* thought they were clever when they came up with that one," Jean snorted with blackest contempt. "But I thank you for the clarification. Now I *know* you were not behind what happened here. I fear that this is well beyond your capabilities." His teeth flashed sharp in a smile that was near a snarl.

Wyrmwood stiffened abruptly and went quiet for a moment, as though calculating. Then, slowly, his smile returned, building with malice as he spoke in an amused, vindictive purr. "Oh, Reynard. I've missed your little jokes." His lips split into a sinister grin, his eyes gleaming. "Though your son was better at telling them, last I recall. It's too bad he is dead, is it not?"

Jean locked up, then his hands moved in a flash to his coat, whipping out his handguns. But as fast as he was, that mere moment of raw hatred had been too long; revolvers and rifles were raised and took aim. Jean froze as hammers were pulled back. But no one fired as Wyrmwood raised an imperious hand.

"With that said, this *does* appear to be a fortunate circumstance. Here we are, investigating a *most* unnatural disturbance, and what do we find? A man trying to hide the evidence." He shook his head, clicking his tongue. "This does not look good, Mister Reynard, from where I'm standing. Not good at all. Now why don't you put those guns on the ground, and come quietly—or, we can see if your legend can stop bullets."

Wyrmwood smirked, an expression that came as natural to his visage as breathing. It was the smirk of a confident, hateful man, who took pleasure in watching others who were within his power squirm. An ugly expression for an ugly person, he watched Jean seething as he tried to formulate a plan, trapped in place, with the joy of a true sadist. But his attention was so fixated on Jean that he failed to realise he had miscalculated.

Barty had not been listening to the argument; instead he had turned his attention elsewhere, to the still humming machinery beside him.

The entire apparatus was encased in metal, with many different dials that he had glanced at and seen were pointing steadily towards the upper aspect; a pressure was built within that device. In this moment, with the crystal sharp focus of a mind expecting to die, he could *feel* the energy pouring off it—the intensity of the charge. Electricity had been used in this laboratory and, though Barty was no true expert in its use, he had intuition enough to know that this had something to do with the great device which was the focus of whatever dreadful things had happened here. He could see thick copper cables leading to the central cage, from which the wires reached up to the roof beyond. And he had an idea.

It was not, in truth, a very good idea. It was the sort of idea that Barty had the habit of coming up with, the sort of desperate gamble he knew would get him into serious trouble later—the sort that would get him out of one problem and into an entirely new one. But seeing what his other options were, he made his choice.

There were two levers—he would need to move into sight to snap them both into position, but he could read the labels over each, 'Safety' and 'Charge'. And in red, bold letters above them both was 'DANGER'.

Well, there was plenty of that in the moment. No point in holding back now.

As Wyrmwood raised his hand and opened his mouth—to order Jean be arrested and dragged off to whatever vile dungeon they had prepared, or to fire, he would never know for sure—Barty leapt, both hands outstretched. He heard a man shout. No doubt guns were being raised as the world slowed, surging adrenaline bringing time to heel. If this did not work, it would not matter what Wyrmwood said, the likelihood that he would feel hot lead tearing a hole through his body was a certainty, but faced with the alternative, Barty had lived in fear enough to know that the only option sometimes was to rage against it.

There was the *boom* of a shot, a shower of sparks close to his face as a bullet bounced off steel, but he would not be stopped now as he grasped each lever and pulled both of them down with all the force he could muster.

Many things happened very quickly.

Barty would realise later that the purpose of the machine was to build a charge, and contain it. How it did so, he did not understand, but it was designed to send that energy up through the apparatus and along the cables to the ceiling. This charge would then travel to the copper poles that had been arrayed outside of the structure to attract lightning from the sky above, to channel an incredible amount of force back down through the lines. Some manner of alchemy was certainly involved, that unnatural art of the unspeakable and the divine, but now its results were immediate, potent, and exactly what was need-ed—chaotic.

Arcs of energy exploded from every available metal surface connected to the apparatus. An overwhelming surge of bright light erupted into sparks as the charge travelled up the ca-bles, sending incandescent sizzling energy this way and that throughout the laboratory, with ear-splitting cracks of thun-derous retort. Whatever Barty had unleashed had gone mad.

Barty was seized yet again by a strong hand—though this

one was here to save him—and pulled to his feet. He had not remembered falling. The laboratory was disintegrating around them, surging energy lashing at bottles and other vile ingredients of whatever had been crafted in that nightmarish pit. The resulting contact caused a blazing explosion of foulest flame and smoke. Barty's hands were numbed after cranking the levers, buzzing with the energy that had passed through them, but it had done its terrible work. Gunshots boomed, but they were fired blind and wild as screams and shouts of panic filled that awful place.

Jean dragged Barty up the stairs with the inexorability of a bull. A figure stood at the top of the stairs, struggling to bring a weapon to bear, but Jean rose from the darkness like a demon out of hell and struck a right uppercut that turned a jawbone to dust and teeth to shards, lifting the black-clad figure near out of their boots from the impact. He did not stop storming onwards, Barty bewildered but trying to keep up as Jean pulled him along.

A shot rang out behind and something hot and fierce grazed Barty's collar. Too caught up in the moment to even cry out, he could see Wyrmwood, a revolver in his hand, pulling the hammer back to take another shot. Jean barrelled through a door to the outside courtyard but there was no freedom; men were waiting here too, and they were ready for them—or so they thought. Few indeed could truly be prepared for a snarling madman dragging a terrified assistant along with him like a boy flying a kite, driven by a wild fury and an overwhelming need to not only escape, but to cause harm in the process of doing so.

Barty tumbled aside as Jean grasped the nearest rifle and turned it, pulling the wielder into a lowered forehead with a wet *crack* as a nose was transformed into jelly and front teeth were made lacking. A pistol was aimed but it was with a shaking hand, and Jean weaved aside, pushing the shooter into the line of fire of another. He was too fast, too sure, and that moment of surprise had been all he needed to wreak havoc. But even as he continued his terrible dance of carnage, the weight of numbers against him demanded aid, and Barty, with all his helplessness knew it. He pushed himself to his feet, reached into his coat, and then—

Click.

"Unless you want to lose another charge, Reynard. You should stop there." Wyrmwood's voice had an undercurrent of deeper malice in it now, but that smirk did not falter as he pointed a revolver at Barty's temple, so close that Barty could feel the chill of the metal barrel against his skin. The hairs on the back of his neck stood up as his flesh crawled. He knew what sort of man Wyrmwood was; to be at his mercy in that moment made him feel sick.

Jean had one man in a headlock, driven to his knees, and had his own gun pointed at a second. He did not lower the one nor release the other, locking eyes with Wyrmwood as Barty held his breath.

"You appear unable to count, Wyrmwood." Jean forced the words through clenched teeth. "I have two of yours, you have one of mine." He tightened his grip, face white with fury, but Wyrmwood was already chuckling.

"The issue, Reynard, is that I know you all too well, and the difference between us." He slid behind Barty like a silken viper and kicked his legs out from behind him, forcing him to his knees with an agonised cry. Barty felt his hair gripped by a merciless hand and his head was yanked back, the barrel of the revolver now pressed with relentless, cruel harshness behind his ear. "I can lose a few of my men, in the course of duty. You, on the other hand, always seem to have trouble with it." His voice turned colder. "Now give it up. Because unlike you, I *don't* need this one here."

Barty thoughts raced, and he felt like his heart would stop in his panic. He closed his eyes. His captor was right; Barty was not important, was not necessary. He did not matter, and never had. Orphaned from the start, unwanted since this all began. Not even Jean had wanted him around. On the weight of that, what hope did he have? Jean would not back down. And this man would kill him, but perhaps Jean would take his vengeance—the only thing that mattered to him, the only thing that was important, but Barty would be dead—

The clatter of a thrown revolver shocked Barty out of his stream of frightened thoughts. He opened his eyes to see Jean raising his empty hands with an expression set with cold, sullen anger. The two men he had been grappling with got their revenge with a clean punch to the face and a kick to the stomach to drop Jean to his knees, but he did not make a sound.

Wyrmwood gave a chuckle that hovered on the edge of a giggle, as he shoved Barty away from him as though finding him distasteful. "Now then, with all that sorted... What are we going to do with you?" He grinned, sauntering over to Jean as Barty felt himself yanked to his feet—something he was getting most tired of—still chuckling and tapping the barrel of his gun against his cheek. "I admit, just arresting you for these *dreadful* events and goings on here would be a start, but there's so much more, don't you think?" He bent at the waist as he stood above Jean, bringing himself level with him and using the barrel of his revolver to raise Jean's chin to force him to look at him. "What do you think, houndsman? What do you want to happen next?"

Jean stared back, his cheek reddening from the blow struck, then cocked his ear. "Well, for a start," he growled in a bored tone, "you could let us both go."

Barty's hearing was troubled by the ringing in his ears and pounding of his heartbeat. He was not sure if the furious ringing of bells approaching was just another element of his distress. A ferocious upheaval of noise, of shouts and the clop of charging hooves, it grew louder until it could not be denied. Wyrmwood was straightening, his expression twisting, as it swiftly grew into a thunderous sound.

"What in the Devil's name is that?" he snapped, bringing his gun to the back of Barty's head once more.

Jean rolled his shoulders, then spat blood at Wyrmwood's feet. "My colleagues."

London's finest did not so much arrive as they did stampede. Foaming horses dragged thundering carriages and wagons loaded with uniformed officers, who poured out before they had even stopped rolling and charged into the yard. Everyone was shouting all of a sudden, the air full of fury and fire as the courtyard filled up. Jean and Wyrmwood kept staring at each other with a hatred so fierce it could have melted iron under its heat.

Barty was painfully aware of the gun at the back of his head, which had not moved. Wyrmwood remained immobile, stiff in his outrage, as a familiar voice was heard cursing and barking orders as it pushed through the throng.

Inspector Creek was a man who was defined by his moustache; it was large, it bristled, and when he was angry, it wobbled. When he spoke it added emphasis and emotion. He gave the very real impression of, rather than being a man wearing a moustache, he was a moustache wearing a man, and right now it was in fine form; it vibrated so fiercely it threatened to fly off his face and beat the nearest man to death for existing in the wrong place and time. "What the bloody hell have you gone and done this time, Reynard?" He scowled, setting his hands into his great coat as he stomped to a halt. "Do you know what time it is?"

Reynard flickered a slight smile, but it was Wyrmwood's voice that spoke. "Your intervention is welcome, *officer*," he said with the venom of one finding something distasteful upon their boot. "But I have the matter well in hand." He had still not lowered his revolver from the back of Barty's head.

Creek was nonplussed. He narrowed his eyes and drew himself up before responding, "I do not have the slightest notion as to who you are. This your property, then?"

Wyrmwood straightened, his nose lifting. He was not a very tall man, and Creek was a bulky fellow with the height to match it. "*Captain* Blake Wyrmwood, at the behest of her Majesty and under her orders, and no, I do not own this property, my men and I—"

"—was trespassing, is that right? Having a bit of a ruckus,

were you?" Creek said, with a horrible grin with no humour in it. "In my jurisdiction?"

Barty could already see what was happening; Wyrmwood had started things off on the wrong foot from the outset. Creek was an inspector, but before that he was a *policeman*, and few things are more difficult to deal with than a copper playing dumb to get the wool over your eyes. Creek, it seemed, had been an expert in the game for years. Barty's hopes, once dashed, were further rekindled.

"What? No!" Wyrmwood snapped back. "I am here under authority, and I am taking these men into custody. *My* custody. I order you and your men to depart to let me handle this."

Creek gave a grunt and a nod, and Barty felt that hope waver. "Fair enough, fair enough, *Captain*." He moved closer to Wyrmwood and Barty, but he did not even look at the latter, his eyes fixed on the greasy Eidolon officer, who seemed to relax at the note of assent, before Creek spoke again. "You have any sort of writ of authority, or identification towards that effect?"

Wyrmwood recoiled as though he'd been stung. Because of course he did not; he and his shadowy men were people who operated in darkness, outside of the truth, outside of knowledge, hoping no one would ever know they existed, and removing those who did. To ask them to reveal their hand, and who they were, was anathema. Barty knew it. So did Creek. He watched the snakelike Wyrmwood, and he did not blink.

The captain of the Blackcoats leaned forward, and lowered his voice, so that only Creek and Barty could hear. "Stop pissing about, inspector. You know who I am."

Creek smiled, but the words that came from behind his

moustache were through teeth clenched with fury. "You're a man in my streets with a gun pointed at someone, and nothing more, *my lord.* If you don't lower it right now, I'm sure afterwards there will be a lot of apologies and a lot of regrets, but you *won't* be here to hear them."

There was a long, aching moment of silence and stillness before, at last, Barty felt the gun at the back of his head lower. He dared to breathe again, sagging but not allowing himself to fall. Before he could even wonder what would happen next, Jean decided to do what he did best, and complicate matters.

"Inspector Creek—I wish to report a crime."

Wyrmwood went so stiff as to be carved from stone. More men were coming out of the warehouse and the laboratory within now, and though the police sincerely outnumbered the Blackcoats, there was nevertheless a threat of violence on the air that was only building. But Creek, either oblivious or refusing in his stubborn, bullheaded way to back down, nodded to Jean instead. "Go on then, Mister." Playing the part of not knowing him, even though the pair had worked together for years. "You've got something to tell me?"

Jean's eyes flicked to Wyrmwood, and Barty felt the gun at his back shake with its holder's frustrations. All Jean had to do was reveal the monstrous crime within, the dead women and more besides, and the hand of Wyrmwood would be forced to action. Barty shook his head, but Jean ignored him and smiled, while talking to Creek. "Indeed so. Trespass."

This was not what Barty expected to hear, and it got worse from there. "My associate and I trespassed upon these grounds. I wish to report this crime—and throw ourselves on the mercy of your custody."

"What?" It was the same word, delivered in different tones of astonishment, from three different mouths—Creek, Wyrmwood, and Barty—all taken off guard by the kneeling man who seemed to be sadistically enjoying the moment of confusion.

Jean shrugged with his hands still raised and a smile on his face, despite the bruises forming on his cheek. "Indeed. I trespassed onto this property, and these... *individuals* saw fit to bring us to heel for our misdeeds." He looked to Wyrmwood, that smile doing nothing to hide the desire for murder in his eyes. "I believe then, that this is under your jurisdiction, inspector. And we should be arrested immediately for lockup."

The moustache wobbled with enough vigor to fly free. Creek knew Jean all too well, but it was still remarkable in how the man seemed to equally admire and be enraged by him. He took a deep breath, and gestured irritability. "Well, you heard the man. Confession, plain as day itself. Lock 'em up, boyos. We'll take them back to the yard."

Wyrmwood was roused from his surprise. He started forward, white with fury. "No! Inspector, I command you to turn these men over to me, under the authority of—"

But Creek was not having it. He turned on Wyrmwood, shoving a finger into his chest with the intensity of a bludgeon, and brought his furious moustache pugnaciously close to Wyrmwood's sneering face.

"You don't get to command me, *captain*," he snarled, his face red with his own sudden and explosive anger. "Habeus Corpus. I have detained these men, and thus they are *my* responsibility, and *my* charge, and I *will* see them safely behind bars. We can have a little argument about that if you so please, but I was roused early for this bit of nonsense, and my temper is short enough that if you do decide to press it with *one more word*, I'll make sure it is one you and your guttersnipes here regret for some time yet." His tone levelled out, the moustache trembled with the effort of suppressing his rage. "Are we clear?"

Behind him, Jean was being pulled to his feet and manacles were clapped around his wrists. Barty blinked as his unresisting arms found themselves in a similar bind, from an officer who then, not unkindly, put a hand on his shoulder and pushed him along.

Wyrmwood watched them go, before looking back to Creek, who had not budged. He took a step back, whey-faced with his helpless fury. "I understand, inspector. But this shall not be the last of this."

"Capital," Creek barked. "I'll mark it in my calendar." He turned and waved an arm. "All right, you lot! Clear out of this place. Hop to!"

Efficient, swift, and knowing not to question an inspector, Barty and Jean were bundled by the officers into a wagon with bars on the windows. The manacles on Barty's wrists were uncomfortable—there is no way to comfortably wear several pounds of unyielding iron—and an unpleasant sensation he did not want to become used to. He shuffled into place, huddling on a seat, as Jean—who Barty could not help but notice was seemingly far more at ease with this situation than he—sat beside him.

Creek was not far behind. He added Barty's own unused re-volver to Jean's firearms, already secured within his own coat, after which he sat himself opposite them, untroubled by the bars and cramped wagon interior. Knowing this incarceration was not for him clearly afforded him some confidence.

"You'll get these back on the morrow," he said in a surly voice, as he fixed his eyes on Jean. The carriage started to roll away. "Now then. You mind explaining just how much of a wasp's nest you just dropped me in, Reynard?"

Jean chuckled, leaning back on the crude seat he was on. "A substantial one. Thank you, Creek. I am in your debt once again."

"Don't thank me yet, Reynard." Creek scowled, shaking his head. "This time I might make you collect on it." He looked to Barty, squinting at him, then back to Jean. "What were you doing there? And what were *they* doing there?" He jabbed a thumb out the window as the wagon rolled along. Jean shrugged, grunting, but it was Barty who answered.

"Investigating a crime, inspector. The sort we tend to investigate."

The moustache wobbled once more, the inspector grumbling. "I gathered as much. How much of it are you willing to tell me?"

Barty opened his mouth to speak, but Jean raised one hand with a clank of manacles, his expression turning grim.

"Honestly, Creek—I am not sure on this one," he said in a serious tone. "I will need a day or two before I can clue you in; there is something in this one that I did not expect."

"You mean the presence of Her Majesty's finest gathering of gutter rats?" Creek snorted, irritably. He did not look like he appreciated Jean's response, but was biting his tongue with the ferocity of one who had learned not to bother arguing. "The Chief Inspector will have my hide when that one's master comes knocking on our door."

But Jean was shaking his head as he responded. "Unlikely. They crawl in the dark... you know that. The less attention the better. They'll find other ways. They always do –for now, however, you are safe." He rattled his chains. "Regardless, I thank you for your hospitality, but I would appreciate these being released—you can let Bartholomew and I off at the next corner."

Barty breathed a sigh of relief, straightening in his seat, but Creek was chuckling harshly, shaking his head himself. "What, let you go? Not on my life, Reynard. You're going to the Yard, and you will stay there 'til morning."

Jean stiffened, frowning. "Come now, inspector. This is not the time for jokes."

Creek glared at him, folding his arms across his chest. "I am bereft of humour at this late hour, Reynard. Montague wishes to see you, and he is currently abed and will not be roused—unlike myself, who was forced into this mad evening venture. So you are going to the Yard, you will have yourselves a tidy cell, and you will explain yourself to my commander so I do not get thrown in yet more manure on your behalf."

Jean's chains clinked dangerously. "I do not have time for this, Creek." His tone was cold, his expression colder still.

Creek was settling back with his eyes closed. "Then find some. There are twenty officers with me at this moment, and even you are not that good, Reynard"—one eye opened to peer at him suspiciously—"but I would not like to wager, regardless."

The eye closed again. "You have both had a long evening, and I am at the limit of my patience for your damnable disrespect. Now sit there quiet and for once, cease your self-righteousness."

Jean's expression reddened, his words halting, and at long last Barty found his tongue, warded to silence for too long. "What Jean meant to say, Inspector Creek, was 'thank you.'" Both men looked to him, as though surprised he had spoken, remembering his presence, as Barty went on, "That man had a gun to my head—regardless of what happens now, I will not forget that. Thank you." He meant every word. The hard press of the steel barrel at the back of his head still ached. It felt like it was still there, waiting to turn his world to instant darkness with the squeeze of a trigger.

Creek grunted, shifting and looking uncomfortable at the gratitude. "Yes, well." He did not quite know how to take the moment, and it had thrown Jean off guard as well. There was something in that too, as his rage settled and his eyes looked away—it made Barty think. But this was not the time for questions. The wagon rattled on, drowning the silence in rattles and clanks, as they carried on through the darkened streets to their destination.

EACH AND EVERY GANG had their own territory in London—the

back alleys of Whitechapel, the twisting warrens of the Wards. But the Metropolitan police of London had the entirety to deal with, and they had the largest, meanest gang of all—and like all good and proper gangs, they had their headquarters.

They called it Scotland Yard, though it had no yard and it was most certainly not in Scotland. It instead sat upon the bank of the Thames amidst the Victoria embankment. This was the New Scotland Yard, built only a few scant years earlier, and it was from here that the police waged their daily war against the unending forces of societal entropy that was the result of a world that hated the poor, and yet had to deal with their shattered remnants. Barty had never set foot in it, and never dared to imagine that he might do so. Things would have had to have gone very wrong in his life for him to wind up in Scotland Yard.

This thought loomed large and fierce in his mind as the lock-up wagon rolled into the interior of the tall, severe buildings. Lights shone from windows, even at this ungodly hour that was the time of criminals, murderers, and the police. There were few people about, but enough to notice that he and Jean were being stared at as they were pulled out of the wagon and guided through a great, ironbound door into the depths of the Yard. Despite the place even smelling new, of fresh stone and fresh paint, not yet stained by the centuries of tobacco smoke and horrors done in dark corners, it carried a presence. There was no bleak scarring, the bloody marks of when justice turned merciless and cruel, seeking confessions instead of justice—but there was a heaviness to the air. It felt oppressive, and though there was movement and voices and more besides, a bustling hive of activity even now that would burst come the dawn, there was something that kept Barty reminded of his place. A separation, a line written into the sand upon which he stood, and the police upon the other. Us and Them, that line said. We are one side of the matter, and you are on the other.

He tried to shake the feeling as Creek and three officers led him and Jean to the cells. While he expected chains and miserable, cold stone floors—and the floors were indeed cold and hard—the cell they were brought to was surprisingly not as terrible as he feared. There were two crude beds set upon the floor, a bucket, and a drain. It did not smell very nice, but there was a notable absence of rats. This, in many ways, was a step up from his childhood.

Creek busied himself by taking the chains off the pair of them, much to Barty's relief. Jean and Creek exchanged a look that spoke volumes, but whatever fury Jean held had withered on the journey over—there was no denying that Creek's position was impossible. He had done all he could with what little he had, and now his hands were tied as surely as Jean and Barty's had just been. What mattered was that he'd had gotten them out of trouble—they owed him this much. And Jean knew it.

The door to the cell shut, and locks were turned with a hardy clank, leaving Barty and his mentor alone. Jean did not bother to glare at the door, nor look for an opportunity to perhaps escape—he still had his lockpicks on his person. While Creek had confiscated their firearms, he had not bothered to strip either of them of their belongings—and so, with a grunt, Jean laid himself out on one of the crude beds, setting his hands behind his head and staring blankly up at the ceiling. Barty fumbled about in their cell, the meagre light coming from a lofty window set with bars above doing little to illuminate his efforts. He sprawled on his own bunk across from Jean, until he could lay himself out flat as the hunter had done, his thoughts unravelling somewhat.

After a few long heartbeats, Jean shattered the silence. "I can veritably *hear* you thinking over there, Barty," he said in a weary tone of voice, as though despairing. "Come now. Let forth your musings before I am deafened by them."

This rankled Barty somewhat. "I was trying to think of a way to say thank you, without making it awkward."

Jean turned his head in the gloom—Barty could only tell by the way that he could make out the gleam of one un-blinking eye. "Thank me, pray tell, for what? I do believe this evening was not one of the better ones an individual could find themselves partaking in." His tone was sardonic, even darkly amused. But Barty would not be deterred.

"When Wyrmwood had me, I expected you to keep fighting. I—" He swallowed. "I know I am mostly a nuisance, and hardly much value in a fight. But you did stop. He might have killed me had you not." He shrugged, glad the darkness denied his blush of embarrassment. "So... thank you."

There was silence in that shadowy murk that near crys-tallised, turning to a shade of awkwardness that Barty felt sud-denly writhing in his gut. Had he ever thanked the man before? Surely he had. Why then did this feel so strange?

"He would have shot you," Jean said suddenly, his voice sub-dued, but cold. "A man who allows the butchery and violation of the unfairly taken would have no hesitation. He knew it, and so did I." Barty felt his blood congeal at that, turning solid in his veins, but Jean continued, "With that said, I did once vow to you that I would not recklessly endanger your life moving forward. I intend to keep that promise, as much as it might mean or otherwise."

Barty remembered. While venturing in the hidden depths of the Under, the secret city beneath London where the unknown dwelt, where he had first met Benji, Jean had put his life in danger—and the aftermath had been that very promise. He had almost forgotten it. It startled him that Jean had not, and so emphatically. He had taken blows for it, and Barty felt guilty in a way he could not fully grasp.

"With that said," Jean went on, his tone turning gruff. "It has been remiss of me that I have not yet shown you how to defend yourself. The fact you have not yet learned to do so, means my teachings have been lacking. I will have to rectify that, for the future."

Barty bit his tongue. Jean had not, in fact, taught him much at all; most of what he had learned had been soaked up like a thirsting sponge as he had been dragged along. But perhaps that was simply his way. Not for the first time, Barty wondered if Jean simply sat him down and started telling him everything he needed to know, or could know, about the hidden world of the Society of the Hound, he might never stop. Perhaps there was no choice but this.

"Then I will endeavour to do my best to look forward to it," Barty finally replied, in a tone of voice that clearly indicated that he did not. Learning to fight had gotten him stabbed in the hand last time, and many stinging bruises besides. Something told him Jean was not nearly as kind a teacher as his daughter, whether she was in the depths of her anger or otherwise.

Jean gave a dry chuckle, indicating he understood all too well. Silence fell once more. But in that wordless gulf something loomed heavy in the darkness; a spectre of what they had both seen.

"Why did they do such a thing?" Barty's tone was a sort of bewildered horror. "I cannot bring myself to understand it. Why did they do that to those women?" Jean did not answer, and that void grew until Barty felt his tongue loosen itself once more. "You explained it to me, but even knowing that, it is such a senseless, horrible thing."

When Jean spoke it was in a subdued voice, the harshness gone, turned instead towards sorrow. "They did it for the same reason all men do wicked things, Barty. Because they could. They can lie, or give some other reason, but in the end that is all it is. They do it because they can, and because no one has stopped them." A grim tone returned briefly. "Not yet, at least."

The silence fell down again, marred though it was within the walls of the Yard. Barty, not knowing what else to do, closed his eyes. It seemed that was the end of the conversation.

"You are never a nuisance, Bartholomew Bartleby." Jean's voice was still quiet, maybe even on the edge of sleep himself. "Despite statements to the contrary I might have made in the heat of the moment, I do not think it fair to say you ever have been."

Barty blinked, his eyes widening in the darkness again. "Jean?" he asked, surprised, even shocked. But the hunter said nothing more. His breathing was already settling gently into the rhythm of slumber, leaving Barty alone in the dark with his startled realisations, until he too merged and ran with the black shroud of sleep.

CHAPTER 11

A TIMELY COINCIDENCE

The clank of the door was the ringing of a most unwelcome bell of waking. Barty floundered and even thrashed for a moment, forgetting where he was and aching all over from the stiffness in his bones. The stark light of the rising sun illuminated the cell now, the whitewashed walls making it seem more sterile, more lifeless.

Jean was already awake, and standing. He looked much the same as ever, except the shadows under his eyes were deeper, giving him a more cadaverous cast than usual. He was watching the door with the stony expression of one prepared for a fight the moment it opened, regardless of whatever shape the opponent might take.

The shape it took in this case was Lord Montague. The Chief Inspector of the police of Scotland Yard bore a most bristling moustache these days, reminiscent of Creek's own, peculiarly enough, but lacking the older man's personality and sheer presence. He was better dressed than his peers, something that never failed to distinguish him from said peers, but there was nevertheless a sharper tightening to his shoulders and eye than the first time Barty had met him—wearing clothes he had unknowingly stolen from a manor belonging to Montague at the time, knowledge that, when revealed to Barty, had set him to sweating.

The Chief Inspector had been green, throwing his authority around in a desperate attempt to establish himself. But he had been forged somewhat in the fire of the case they had worked together—the hunt for the Pariah—and now he was more subdued, more collected, more sure. Barty had to give the man credit—he had matured swiftly, and poured himself into his role rather than viewing it as a stepping stone into a career in politics. He even held a grudging respect for Reynard, a man whom he had, at first, violently opposed, enough to seek him out on occasion. Barty knew he would never admit it, but Reynard had learned to have his own regard for the Chief Inspector.

However, the pride of both of them tended to get in the way of things—much as it was doing now. Montague stood in the doorway with his hands on his hips, glaring at one errant inmate and then the other.

"Excellent to see you, your lordship." Jean's tone was frosty. "I trust we did not disturb your much needed sleep, or whatever it bloody well was you were doing while we were in here."

The shorter man bristled as much as his moustache. "Sorting out problems you created, is what. I have half a mind to leave you in here for another decade, by which time I should have *begun* to sort through all the difficulty you have gone and caused me."

Jean snorted, shaking his head. "Well regardless, you have seen me as you demanded, and now I have things that need seeing to." He snapped his mouth shut and strode to the doorway with the air of one who would walk through any obstacle in his way. Montague, however, squared his shoulders pugnaciously and did not budge, though Jean was an inch away from him. Jean's eyes narrowed.

"There are other things that need seeing to, Reynard. And we can talk about them here, or at my office. For the sake of decency, and so I do not have to chain you both up for a conversation, *ensure to choose the latter*," Montague said through clenched teeth. Neither man moved, glaring daggers at each other.

Barty took the moment to come up alongside, even as the various officers who had accompanied Montague were hovering in the corridor looked ready to intervene. "Will there be tea, inspector?" he asked hopefully. "I know it is asking a great deal, but some breakfast would certainly settle many nerves."

Both men turned their gaze full of bloody murder to Barty, who quailed quite a bit. But it did the trick. They exchanged looks that, while not the least bit apologetic, were nevertheless a bit more amenable. Settling, Montague nodded and grumbled. "That can be arranged. Come along, you two."

He stepped out of the cell with Jean, and then Barty, following him. One officer, a bit slower than others, reached out to roughly take Barty by the shoulder. Jean turned and a gleam came to his eye, in distinct and none too pleasant warning, but Montague gave an irritable wave of one hand. "Let them go, you lot, and clear off. I will be speaking to these men alone."

The slower officer looked perturbed. "But sir, these two were—" he started but Montague was looking at him now with the sort of look no one wants from a superior officer; a look that had latrine duty in its future, or some other mucky job. The officer nodded and mumbled, touching his forelock in deference and making his way from their presence in a hurry. Montague continued on, and Barty and Jean fell into step behind him.

"They listen to you more than they used to," Jean noted blithely, as they went through a door and made their way up some stairs. Montague snorted, but did not bother to respond as the trio walked through the surging, controlled mayhem of the Scotland Yard.

The chief police station of the biggest city in England was, by necessity, an extraordinarily busy place. It had uniformed officers coming and going; those who were in plain clothes nevertheless all but shrieked 'police officer' to the most junior of those upon the street, and those that did not, well... they were much more of a problem. There were rooms and halls and corridors, and everywhere Barty looked he and Jean were being watched with the careful, suspicious eyes of men who assumed the worst in people by default and imagined what their crimes might well be. It made the hair on the back of his neck stand up. Jean seemed unperturbed; as with all things, Barty surmised, he took refuge in the sheer savagery of his own audacity, meeting each stare with the insolence of a born criminal, daring each and every eye to arrest him, just to see what would happen. He was a man who invited incarceration with his very presence at the best of times. Barty huddled in his shadow with his own sort of embarrassed meekness, and hoped no one would remember him.

Montague's office was surprisingly modest. Barty had expected something far more imposing and elaborate, but it was entirely functional; a map of the city on one wall with tagged pins marking points of interest, filing cabinets and bookshelves, and a very crowded desk. A secretary was waiting outside with a handful of documents—Montague took them with alacrity just beneath snatching, then sent her scurrying away to fetch tea and toast, the fuel with which the engine of justice rolled onwards upon, and ushered the pair within.

Once inside, the door shut, his shoulders visibly slumped. "God's blood, I did not need this today," he said wearily. "If we are going to have an argument, I would prefer we got it out of the way now."

Jean seemed, uncharacteristically, taken aback at this. "I would have expected more of a vociferous response to how I handled Lord Beauchamp than that, I admit," he confessed, but Montague was shaking his head with genuine annoyance.

"Beauchamp is a miserable toad of a man, and absolutely unbearable to be around. His wife is, however, a friend of my own, and it was for her that I sent you on that errand. As far as I am concerned, it was a job well done, not least because that snivelling wretch will not bother me ever again in the aftermath." He waved the stack of paper in his hands with fury. "Do you know how much of my work is taken up dealing with nonsense like that? The peers of the realm are my brethren, it is true... but they are also small-minded, selfish, stupid, and blithely ignorant." He slapped a piece of paper in his hand disdainfully. "This one is demanding, in genteel language but nevertheless with a dagger between each syllable, that I see that a young lord be granted clemency for his crimes because of some notion of kindred." His expression darkened. Crumpling the paper in one fist, he tossed it into the fire. "While it will no doubt be thrown out of court, I will not be the one to do so. Some nights in the cells are the least of what he deserves." He shook his head with disgust. Barty's own inestimable curiosity drove him to speak.

"What did they do?"

Montague fixed him with a stare, then looked elsewhere, his cheeks reddening. "The youngest member of house Satchwell has trouble understanding what 'no' means at times."

He left it at that. Sometimes words did not need to be said. Barty, however, felt sickened, turning to look at Jean, who stood facing away from both of them. Either he did not care—or, more likely he had heard it all before, too many times to count—but Barty had to privately admit that Jean's fiercely clenched fists spoke eloquently to his feelings.

Jean was looking at the map on the wall, both hands held behind his back as he did. "So I take it then, you are going to help me with my own issues, if that is the case?" he asked over one shoulder. "Considering your erstwhile respect for law and justice?"

Montague swore savagely, throwing the last of his paperwork to the desk. "*No*, I am not going to help you. Not after what your foolish actions resulted in." He did not elaborate further as the door was knocked upon, then opened shortly afterwards. The secretary returned, a demure young woman with a lowered gaze, pushing a trolley with tea, cups, and buttered toast. Barty was making a cup almost before it stopped moving, as the bearer of such a bounty departed with a curtsey and a slightly hurried step.

It was not hard to understand why; Reynard and Montague were again glaring at each other, and once the door clicked shut, Jean spoke with icy, carefully controlled language, as Barty sipped tea and looked nervously from one to the other. "You will have to explain *precisely* why that is, Montague. You surely know what it was that was found in that place."

"No, damn it all, I do not," the Chief Inspector spat back in volcanic fury. "You understand the nature of things, Reynard, so surely you are aware that I have people that stand above me, yes? Individuals who, on occasion, give me orders on what I can and cannot do?" He pointed an accusing finger at the hunter, who remained unmoved. "I received just such a missive this morning, sealed and signed, to that effect from parliament. All investigation is to cease immediately. An unnamed part of the government will be handling the matter."

Jean gave a low, contemptuous whistle. "Goodness. They *did* pull hard on your leash, didn't they?" His tone was scornful. "Did you bark when they gave it a tug?"

Montague purpled and strode over, jabbing Jean in the chest with the finger as though stabbing with a spear. "Don't give me that, Reynard. You know as well as I do that there are lines I cannot cross. And right now, I am on the line."

Jean did not dip his head to that finger, but his gaze travelled downwards, and then back to Montague, a warning without words in his eyes. "How fortunate you are, to know the depths of your own limitations." His tone was frosty with his disgust. Barty could take it no longer.

"Are the Eidolon a government organisation then?" he asked warily, even innocently.

Montague snapped his head around at hearing the name, as though stung, wincing and shaking his head fiercely. "I would prefer you do not even say the name of that den of vipers." He scowled, stalking away to make himself a cup of tea in the meanwhile. Barty waited patiently. Jean glared after Montague as though he could burn holes through him, then returned to the map, staring at it as though it, too, offended him.

Barty set down his half empty teacup. "That *is* who this is about, after all." He spoke carefully, watching Montague as he did so. While a street officer like Creek could keep their emotions and expressions in check until it was the right time, Montague had tells that were words all of their own. His hand twitched slightly as he poured his own tea, and Barty watched it as he went on, "They were the ones protecting that place, and they were the ones trying to conceal what had happened. Do they have that sort of power?"

Montague added a couple of sugar cubes to his cup, stirring it before he answered, but kept his gaze steadily averted. "The *organisation* in question has been throwing their weight around the past few weeks. They are being more open than usual, more willing to exercise their authority." He took a sip of his tea, then walked to his desk. "They cannot yet tell me what to do entirely, but I would be lying if I said they are not able to exert substantial pressure to me, and my department." He exhaled, putting the cup amidst the scattered papers, looking through them with a trace of listlessness. "I was able to refute their demand to place you in their custody, but I will pay for it later, I am sure." He scowled. "A vindictive bunch, if nothing else. In any case, this *is* the last bit of protection me or the police can offer either of you. I cannot do more." He looked to Barty then. "As much as I might wish that it was otherwise."

His tone was firm, resolute but anxiety and frustration was writ large in his furrowed brow and helpless grimace. He had done what he could, and as much as he might wish to do more, Barty could see the man was more than just worried. He was *afraid*.

"What did they threaten you with, Lord Montague?" He asked the question without thinking, and the man flinched. He stared at Barty, features turning pale, and then looked away. He reluctantly reached into his desk and pulled out an envelope with a broken black wax seal.

"This was in my youngest boy's bedroom this morning," he said flatly. "The... request that they made, to keep you from being involved further." There was ash in his words, tempered by dread.

Jean strode over to the desk and snatched the letter up, reading it swiftly. His shoulders, set and stiff, softened ever so slightly. "You should have told me this from the start, Lord Montague." Jean's voice was quieter now, without accusation. He shook his head, his expression turned now to a different kind of anger. "But I understand. I will remove myself from the situation."

Montague and Barty stared at Jean in outright surprise at that, exchanging confused glances before looking back to the hunter, who was turning away.

"Just like that?" Montague asked, but Barty could see he was caught between relief and bewilderment. Jean was nodding without looking at him.

"Just like that. Coming, Barty?" He absently picked up a piece of toast, taking a bite as Barty pushed himself to his feet. Jean halted at the door, however, turning back to Montague. "Creek took my weapons from me, as was his due diligence. Where might I find them now?"

Montague, still dumbfounded, waved aimlessly. "Ask at the front desk, they'll be under your name," he said in a tone that spoke eloquently to his surprise. He continued to look confused, torn between emotions, as Barty and Jean departed the office and made for the main hall.

Barty was conflicted. Montague and Jean never really got along. He also did not know Jean nearly as well as Barty did. Which meant he did not realise when Jean was lying, like he had just done so.

"You have no intention of letting go of this, do you?" Barty asked worriedly, as Jean strode down the long hall to, presumably, the front desk of the Yard.

The hunter shook his head. "Not even remotely. If I did, they would have the means to curtail me in the future. I cannot have that. What I need to do is show them that threats against those around me are useless when it comes to stopping me." He grunted, his expression darkening. "In point of fact—they tend to offend my sensibilities, and *substantially* so." He took another, angrier bite of his toast, despoiling it further in his barely controlled rage.

Barty was about to enquire further, his internal sense for danger in that moment somewhat lacking, when a familiar voice, tight and cold, rang out.

"I should have known they wouldn't keep you in a cell,

where you belong."

Jean halted midstep, his expression twisting into something altogether more dry, and he spun on his heel. "And good morning to you as well, Elanor."

Barty had to do a double take. In all the time he had known Elanor, she had been dressed in her work clothes—functional and masculine clothing that allowed her to move and act as circumstances dictated. Standing there, in the midst of that long hall, she could not have been further from such depictions.

Her hair was tied neatly in a sedate bun rather than its wild, dark wave; save for a straightened line of her fringe slightly obscuring one half of her face, and the scar that resided there. She wore a dress of the current fashion, dark blue plaid and bell shaped, puffed at the shoulders with a collar high and laced. She looked every inch a London lady of leisure, and from her cold expression, hated every second of it.

Barty could not help but think she looked terribly pretty, and felt his ears turn hot at the notion while hoping to high heaven no one noticed. He then proceeded to kick the thought away into whatever corner it had leapt from—he was still upset with her, regardless of anything else, and she was clearly still furious at him as well.

Behind her hovered a worried looking Creek. Elanor strode forward, her boots beneath her dress striking the ground with each heel like a hammer, the sound rising through even the carpet. She peered up at her father with an expression of tightly controlled anger. "Your face is bruised. You've been fighting." She snatched the hand that held the toast fragments and turned it over in her own, frowning. "Possibly a fracture in the small bones, from the looks of it."

"Two," Jean corrected. "Necessities of the moment, as it were." His tone was sardonic but Barty was horrified. The man had not complained about them in the slightest.

Elanor grunted, then spoke flatly, pointing a finger at Barty, who recoiled as though she held a knife. "And you. Are you hurt as well, or no?"

He patted himself down as though to be sure he had not missed any, but mutely shook his head. He had his slight aches, but they did not seem worth complaining about. Elanor sniffed disdainfully, and turned on her heel without another word to stalk away, her mouth a tight line. Jean watched her go with a look strangely both resigned and amused, the faintest smile creasing his countenance.

Creek walked up with an uncharacteristic apology written into his every feature. "Forgive me for that, Reynard. I crossed paths with her at the front desk—she was asking for you."

Jean nodded knowingly. "She has had to find me in a lockup enough times to know to start at the top. And to dress the part as well to be heeded." He spoke dryly, but still wore that smile. "Come with us, Creek. There are things I wish to ask you while I fetch my side arms."

The inspector looked like he would rather be anywhere else. "Don't try anything, huntsman," he said, shaking a finger warningly. "I am under orders to keep my mouth shut on this one. I can give you nothing about what happened."

Barty, having dragged his gaze from the departing Elanor, spoke up. "Is that from Montague?"

"It is, and may I remind you, he is my superior, and I am

already in more difficulties than I am in the mood to entertain so, I would ask you to leave it at that. Take a page from the book, you two—ask no more questions, for you will get no more answers." He kept his tone emphatic. Jean glanced askew at the inspector, but nodded, setting off after his daughter. Barty, once again feeling entirely out of place and useless on this sort of stage, hurried after him.

They reached the front desk, where Jean began the rather tricky act of negotiation for the trio of firearms, with only the presence of Creek allaying doubts. The sceptical sergeant on the front desk gave the inspector the dubious sort of look that spoke of being owed for this sort of thing, preferably in whiskey. Barty stepped to one side as Creek and Jean continued to converse, until a thunderous voice and a presence to match made itself felt with, of all things, his name.

"Bartholomew Bartleby! As I live and breathe! Good God, man, what have you gone and made of yourself?"

Charles Frederic Moberly Bell was a man who very nearly defied description. Born in Alexandria, Egypt, orphaned at a young age and shipped off to England, he had by flight and frenzy found himself the managing director of The Times—the pre-eminent newspaper of London, the beating heart of communication and truth from a hundred perspectives so differing that they became a fresh kind of falsehood. Bell was charismatic, he was strong, and he had a keen and fierce eye, a booming voice, and a presence so potent that doors opened ahead of him wherever he went. He had noticed Barty, and for good reason—the man had been his employer, once upon a time. Having spotted a kindred spirit, a fellow orphan with drive but not the means, he had sponsored Barty and his journalistic endeavours. Between all the blood and the terror since then, it felt like another life to Barty now.

Bell had no candour. He strode up to Barty and clapped him on the shoulder with a wide smile and that sharp gaze that had the clarity to see everything hidden or otherwise. Barty felt himself flinch under that powerful grip, but remembered his manners. "Mister Bell, sir. It is good to see you again."

That strong hand smacked down a second time with force enough to set him to rocking as Bell laughed. "Here I am to meet with the Chief Inspector about recent goings on, and I see you have beaten me to it!" He chuckled, shaking his head and releasing Barty. "I was wondering what had become of you, since you quit my employ. I see now that the Ripper case still has not let you go, am I correct?"

It had not, but not in the way he thought, Barty realised. He nodded hurriedly, his posture bowed somewhat still. It was easier to lie, when there was truth enough yet lingering in it.

Bell grunted with the satisfaction of a man pleased at his own cleverness, as he continued, "Been hearing all sorts of terrible things as of late; a bird on the wind told me of some terrible business up in St Michaels—Lord Braithwaite's warehouses have had *quite* the police presence, and word has reached me about some young women—heard anything about it yourself, eh?"

He fixed Barty with a keen eye, brow raised. This was the way of the man—he carried ever onwards, speaking fearlessly, as though the newspaper was merely the simplest method of what he wished to shout from the rooftops—to lay bare what he learned through his his vast web of informants and secret keepers. He was a beacon of things uncovered, and took it as a duty to share it everywhere. Some might have called it lacking in decorum; Barty thought it bravery. And now he found it extraordinary in its usefulness, however unlooked for.

"I am sorry, Lord Braithwaite, you said?"

Bell's brow raised further, chewing his cheek as he nodded. "Indeed so. Man has been through enough, he and that suffering wife of his. Something like this, akin to a scandal I would say. But I thought it best to enquire with the Chief Inspector before going ahead with it." He patted Barty on the shoulder again. "But still, do not let me keep you! Do pass on my regards to your new employer, however."

Barty, still a bit dazed, was about to point out Jean, wondering how Bell knew of him, but the man was in full flow and far from finished. "While I was surprised to find you in the employ of a woman, she had the personality and wit to leave *me* in the dust, to the point that I envied your placement." He chuckled, but there was a puzzled edge to it. "Though you'll forgive me if her name escapes me as of this moment." There was an unaccustomed look of confusion on his face, as though some sort of broken memory, a hole ripped through the edge of his reason, was causing it to elude him.

Barty had gone rigid, his blood running cold. A woman? When? He was meaning to apologise to Bell. It had been six months since he had quit The Times, without sending word—he had simply up and left to Jean's employ instead. But there had never been a woman in that time whom he had worked for. Had there? Surely the man was mistaken. He had to correct him—a man so concerned for the veracity of the truth should be told of it, after all.

"I fear I have only worked for one other since leaving your employ, and I did not mean to do so unannounced, but—"

Bell cut him off, looking positively perplexed. "Whatever do you mean, lad? Nearly a year ago, as my eyes do not deceive, a woman came during the evening rush and informed me that you would be working for her as a part of a private investigation. Are you telling me that she played me false?" His voice tightened with suspicion.

Barty's mouth opened and closed under that ferocious stare. He finally shook his head as though to dispel cobwebs, and found his thickened tongue telling a lie with uncharacteristic difficulty. "Oh. Of course. But in truth I now work for, for—" He stumbled at the close.

"For *me.*" Jean Reynard's voice was cold, and he loomed large suddenly out of the shadows. He adjusted his long coat, hiding the panoply of weaponry that was his once more, and he looked down his nose at Barty and his former employer, with Creek hovering with impatience behind him. "And we are leaving, Mister Bartleby. Come along now."

Barty swallowed, even as Bell sized Jean up, looking him head to toe swiftly with a harsh speculation. He spoke to Barty as he continued to lock eyes with the hunter. "I fear you have moved from blessed to something altogether different in your employment, Bartholomew," he stated, a bit sardonically.

Jean grunted, but a flicker of a smile formed on his face. Elanor was at the entrance, but as they turned towards her she was already pushing through the various police that were entering and leaving the building, and Jean set off after her, expecting Barty to follow. But he paused after taking a step, and turned back.

"Mister Bell, sir—before I go, just how long was it since that lady told you I was employed by her? I want to be sure of my dates regarding a trifling matter," he asked without a note of tremor in his voice, of which he was quite proud of. Bell, nevertheless perturbed, took a moment to consider before shrugging.

"I would wager about ten months, if I was any judge. Somewhere around that time." He frowned. "Foggier than I would like to remember." He sounded troubled by it; the man normally had a memory like a bear trap. It was disconcerting seeing him struggle.

Barty, however, had enough. He reached out and shook his old employer's hand eagerly. "It was good to see you again, sir. Thank you. I best be off."

Bell was startled at the enthusiasm of Barty's grip, but he was a man who understood a good handshake and the power that they had. He returned it firmly, his expression turned sharp once more. "Good luck to you, Bartholomew Bartleby. Something tells me you shall need it." Barty was already nodding and on his way however, agreeing with the man, who was more right than he knew.

Ten months. But that, surely, was impossible; the sum of time simply did not match up, not properly. What had Elanor and Benji told him, during the Jekyll case? That he had not been home in three months? But that could not have been the case. Could it? His thoughts were muddled, his step unsure, as he walked out into the uncharacteristically bright light of a London morning.

The coach was there, because of course it was, with its terrible apparition of a driver, who grinned that knowing, wicked grin of playful malice, attracting stares that hurriedly looked away when his lantern eyes slid to meet them. Puck was in his element, a creature of chaos amidst an ocean of law, defying structure and reason with his very existence. The police trudging in and out of the Yard avoided him as though he bore a plague of madness in the air he breathed.

Creek was talking to Jean as Barty hurried down the steps to catch up. "I know it's a bad business, but you're better off staying out of it, Jean. For once, there is nothing gained by getting involved."

"I already told you, I agree with you, inspector," Jean said with subdued irritation. "I have been agreeing with you every pace down these stairs and beyond." He climbed into the coach, where Elanor already sat, looking away.

"I know, and that makes me feel *extraordinarily worse* about the whole thing," Creek said with utmost exasperation, looking harried down to his moustache. "I know you far too well to believe you."

"You have the soul of a policeman, Creek," Jean replied in a dry tone as he made himself comfortable, and Barty clambered in beside him. "And I commend you for your unyielding suspicion." He nodded as he shut the door. "Farewell for now." The coach sprang forward without a flick of whip or tug of reins, and Creek was left staring after them in consternation.

The coach departed in silence, with Elanor radiating her

cold, righteous fury at being forced to wear clothes she hated and for a cause that was seemingly unnecessary. Jean was gazing out the window, with an uncaring air of nonchalance. Caught between one and the other, Barty could not find his tongue. But whatever clock was counting down before Elanor exploded finally ticked over as she gritted her teeth and snapped. "Well? Did you figure out *anything* at all?"

Barty and Jean spoke in unison. "Lord Braithwaite." They stared at the other in surprise.

Jean sounded, for once, entirely mystified. "How did *you* figure that out?"

Barty felt his cheeks grow hot as he explained under that mutual stare. "Mister Bell let it slip that the warehouse we were in belonged to a Lord Braithwaite. How did *you* figure it out?" He wanted to bring up what else he had let slip, but there was no time to do so—insofar as he could see, anyway.

Jean shrugged. "Montague had a pin on the place where we found the bodies. There was a name written on a tag upon it—Lord William Braithwaite. He had not thought to take it down before we got there." He shook his head then, chuckling. "All that effort, and we find the answer we required from the start by mere happenstance. We have a name."

"But not an answer to *my* many questions," Elanor interrupted. She refused to look at Barty, leaving him in an awkward state as she went on. "However, if you tell me what you learned, I will give you something in return." Her tone turned into something smug then, and she leaned back with a smirk.

"And what might that be, daughter?" Jean replied dryly, but with a suspicious glint to his eye as he watched her.

Elanor's smirk only grew as she said, "A meeting with Lord Braithwaite." She stared at her father, who glared right back, calculating and weighing the matter, before he finally gave an exasperated sigh.

"Fine then. I will tell you what we learned."

Above, Puck started to whistle. Trying to put that haunting discordance out of mind, Barty listened as Jean explained and a plan began to form. The coach continued its journey, turning towards the west as they did so—back into the lion's den of the wealthy, the powerful, and those who had the means to live life as they so chose, no matter who they had to crush underneath to do so.

But Barty remained silent, his mind elsewhere; three months, and a woman he could not remember. A time where he was outside of time itself, and a secret, kept beyond his power to know. He stared out the window, imagining an image in the glass—a red-lipped smile, and an even darker red eye gazed back out of that reflection. He blinked and it was gone, leaving him in terrified bewilderment. The coach rolled on, and Barty contemplated how to ask questions he dared not speak.

Chapter 12

A House In Mourning

The Braithwaite manor was, to Barty's eye, a rather severe looking place. Most manors of the wealthy had affectations to give them a sense of the bloodline that they housed; statues and carvings were common, a coat of arms over a doorway, something to denote its importance and an effort to beauty in hard, cold marble or granite.

The Braithwaite manor did not. It was a large building, with a front door to the street instead of a long driveway as was normally the custom for such places—to give space from those who wished to enter, as the upper class was inclined. This building, this dreadful block of stone and silence that was ostensibly a house, invited no one. There was a brutal iron gate situated a short distance before the double doors that were heavy set and reinforced. The windows were dark, and drawn.

They had found the house by using the abilities granted to them—the power that Jean, Barty, and Elanor all shared; a talent for investigation and for questions, and the answering thereof. The trio knew the general location where to find the home of Lord Braithwaite, even knew of his recent circumstances, thanks to Elanor. A cathedral had been their first point of call, and Jean and Elanor had spoken to a priest within, who had told them a sobering tale regarding a death, and a burial. Father and daughter had then woven a few tender lies, falsified interest, and been skilled enough in their deceptions as to convince the hearts of those who wanted to help in their poor, misguided way, to give an address—an address that they now stood outside of, though they were now several hours deeper into the day, with the darkening of twilight already approaching.

Elanor was staring up at the place, her expression perturbed; the story they told had not sat well with her. Barty stood at her shoulder, with Jean behind him. He felt like he had to say something. "You did well to find this place." He meant it sincerely, but it sounded entirely patronising. He winced, his expression twisting with his sudden embarrassment.

Elanor glanced back at him, and grimaced. "I am about to lie to a grieving family, Mister Barty," she said quietly, her tone flat. "I am not sure you can convince me to feel good about it." She squared her shoulders, and strode forward, affecting a look of concern and sorrow as she found a pull rope at the gate itself, tugging on it gently. A bell was heard, barely, within the building, and they waited.

"Must be a devil of a thing not to get children pulling on the rope at all hours," Barty mused to himself.

Jean snorted. "In this neighbourhood? They would likely disconnect it in the evenings. We are fortunate that they are still accepting visitors." Jean cast a look back at his discomforted assistant. "Besides. Look at this place. If you were a small child, no matter what kind of troublemaker, would you tempt fate by ringing the bell without good reason?"

Barty frowned, looking up at the looming bulk before them that stood stark, lifeless and cold. He had to admit, the man had a point. He did not want to be ringing this bell *now*, let alone in his youth, even if it had never been so luxurious as to allow childish rebellion, but had instead been an endless procession of terrors.

There were other reasons, of course. Elanor had heard the name of Braithwaite, and that had started them on their course of finding this place. But the circumstances in which she had heard it remained in his thoughts; nay, at the forefront... This was a house of mourning. Grief clung to its walls, as surely as the slick film of rain, a miasma that exuded coldness. Grief, and something else—something altogether more poisonous, even if Barty could not bring it to name. But he could taste it, at the edge of his senses, cutting through even his doubt and fears, raised by the questions asked in his meeting with Bell—he buried them for now, as best he could, but they persisted, lurking beneath his feet.

The door opened with a rusting creak that sounded like a distant, dying scream. Barty nearly jumped but Jean gave him a short thump on his back to bring him to attention—they had a part to play after all. A figure appeared in the doorway, an elderly, bent man with a wispy combover and a watery gaze. He was dressed as a butler, but to Barty he looked ten years past his retirement and half that from when he should have been buried. He *worked* with a walking corpse that was more animate than this fellow.

"Who comes knocking at this hour?" There was a hint of a tremble to his voice. "Do you have an appointment with the lord and lady?" He spoke with not so much as a rasp as a groan, echoing as though from a graveyard plot.

Elanor stepped forward to respond. Her voice was kind, even sorrowful, and it had a different kind of energy that was as potent as it leaned towards vapid. "Good afternoon, sir. I was hoping to call upon the lord and lady of the house. My name is Sasha Briarwood, and these are my attendants." She casually gestured over her shoulder to the pair behind her. Jean reached up to tug his forelock as Barty did in kind. Their roles had been decided on beforehand by Elanor. Though Jean had not liked it, he had respected the merit of it, and there was no time to argue otherwise.

Elanor continued as the ancient butler observed, her tone turning softer. "I went to school with young Miss Braithwaite. I was—I was not able to attend the funeral and offer my condolences. I was hoping to rectify that—if I may be permitted."

The request hung in the air. The butler looked doubtful, looking from each face to the next with the rheumy gaze of one who can no longer see properly, but makes the attempt nevertheless out of stubbornness. He then nodded, and turned his withered frame about. "I shall enquire with my Lady." He did not elaborate further. With another protest of clinging rust and dying sorrows, the door closed.

They waited, for a time that was just long enough to stretch into the unknown guessing of what the response would be, before the door once more howled in its opening. The elderly butler, words quite beyond him, gestured for them to come inside with as much grace as he could muster. It was not much, but Barty mentally gave him points for effort.

They walked through the great door, and Barty was surprised as they entered a bright but cold interior. The décor was nothing short of severe—white walls, with lamps producing iridescent light. There were no paintings and little furniture. The Lodge was an old building, and while clean it nevertheless had its fair share of accumulation and clutter, borne out of its centuries of use. This place seemed older, but it had been scoured of everything that might give it life. All personality had been stripped from it; even the stone tiles were without carpets, making each footstep ring out and crack as boot descended. It reminded him not of a home, but a hospital—or a mausoleum. But beneath it all, Barty could feel *something* coming up through the very floor itself. The air tasted alive, a faint thrumming as though he were awash in the breath of some unseen entity, constant and aggravating, and it grated upon his nerves. Something about it was familiar, nagging at the back of his thoughts.

The butler led them down the austere hallway to a door which he opened with effort. The room beyond was a sitting room, almost as empty as the entrance hall save for an unlit fireplace, so unaccustomed to flame it was spotless, and a few couches with all the cushion and spring of an ice block. A bare table and desk stood to one side, and grey, featureless light poured in from two high windows that showed nothing of the street.

A middle-aged woman in black waited for them by that bereft fireplace. Barty expected a haughty expression, perhaps a fiercely cold demeanour. He expected her to stare down at them, to sneer. What he did not expect was this reality—a trembling, honest smile that fought through an unbearable grief, and tear-filled eyes that were so much kinder than he had imagined of a lady of her stature. She spoke with a gentle voice, bravely through her tears.

"Do come in, my dear. It is wonderful to meet one of Lily's friends. She—" Her voice cracked, but she fought on, with a strength that Barty could not even fathom. "She had s-so few, you see."

Elanor hesitated, and spoke awkwardly then, taken off guard. "Lady Braithwaite, I—" But the black clad woman shook her head.

"Please, dear—call me Elizabeth. Jeffrey?" She turned to the butler, who demurely lowered his head. "Please fetch some tea for our guests." The ancient butler bowed, and shuffled out of the room. He looked at Jean and Barty suspiciously as he passed. Barty tried to give a smile and reassure him with a nod, but the old fellow was having none of it. Barty could not blame him. Suddenly he felt ill for partaking in this deception.

Elanor, too, seemed to have lost her ground for a moment, but she composed herself with an effort to return her smile—however wan it now appeared. With a certain fragility, she sat upon a couch as offered while Jean and Barty stood mutely to one side. There was no chance of chatter—the room was eerily silent, coldly so, with not even the crackle of a fire to cover the pair whispering. This would be up to Elanor, and her alone.

They knew the name of the girl who had been buried. The only daughter of Lord and Lady Braithwaite. A young woman, who so few had seen, who had always been ill and sickly, confined to her house for more than a decade, clinging to a life that never wanted to be with a tenacity that outstripped her ability, until it finally failed her. When they buried her, the coffin had been so light that it had been wondered if anyone was in it at all.

Elanor had informed them about the story, remembering it in the papers—a tragic but mysterious affair. A funeral where no one had seen the deceased in years. The girl locked in her home. A prisoner from even the light as she struggled, and fought, and tried to live. Looking around this cold, cold house, Barty wondered how she had managed at all.

Elanor put on the best smile she could manage. "Lily and I were friends when we were little, and attending school together," she explained delicately. "I was not in London when..." She balked at the last part, needing a moment to reframe her words that was entirely genuine. "When she passed. I only learned after I returned from Germany."

Lady Elizabeth Braithwaite looked a little confused. "She—I am sorry, she never mentioned you," she replied apologetically.

Elanor gave a sad little shrug. "We were very young, but I did not forget her. Lily was... she was..." She struggled with the words. Some lies would not allow the tongue to speak. An understandable awkwardness hung in the air, bringing a pause with it.

Jean shattered it. He coughed, a hacking, rasping cough into one closed fist to break the silence, ending it with a crude thumping of his own chest and a sniff. "Ahem. Sorry, ma'am." His voice was harsher than usual, a low, more guttural sound.

Elanor rallied around something she always had strength in—being disappointed in her father. "Forgive my family servants—my father insists on coddling me in everything that I do, and would not allow me to leave without them." She gestured to Barty and her father with the sort of indication that they were, in fact, responsible for all ills in the universe. But Lady Elizabeth was shaking her head.

"It is perfectly acceptable. My husband would agree entirely, as he is—" She paused, and tried again. "He *was*, fiercely protective of Lily."

Elanor nodded. "As I understand it, he is a doctor, yes?"

Lady Elizabeth acquiesced with a quiet smile. "He is, a professor of medical science at Oxford. For all these years he sought to find a cure for her illness." She curled her hands together around a ragged little handkerchief, worn down by tears and sorrows. "He did all he could, of course. No man could have done more. But God would not keep his angel from her home forever, it seems." She tried to smile, but it was brittle, prone to shattering at the slightest touch.

Elanor—or Sasha as she was calling herself—wrung her hands together with difficulty. "May I ask about what occurred?" Her voice was hesitant. Despite her best efforts, all of this made her uncomfortable. "What became of her, how... any of this happened?" Lady Elizabeth tilted her head in the faintest display of confusion, but Elanor continued, a little hurriedly, "Please understand, Lady Elizabeth—I grew distant over the years from your daughter. It was a mistake—one I regret deeply. I feel like I need to... to learn all that I missed."

The black clad woman lowered her gaze to contemplate,

as Barty turned his head towards Jean somewhat desperate-ly, trying to figure out a way to ask what they were to do now—but Jean was staring about the room in such a level of fierce scrutiny that it was near scorching. Barty glanced back to the conversing pair out of the corner of his eye, as Lady Elizabeth rallied and recovered herself.

"Lily was... always taking ill, you see. From a young age she would have fits and other distempers, fevers and the like... it was a mystery to my husband, to the point that he gave up all other ventures and, while having tenure at the university, he retired here to make our home as suitable as he could for our daughter, and to study her illness." She clenched her hands around the handkerchief before dabbing her eyes with it, turning to the fireplace. "Ever it foiled him, but he never gave up. Neither did Lily. She was very brave, my dear daughter."

The conversation drifted into silence, the sort of sour, thick-ening silence that only mourning can create, before Lady Eliz-abeth found traction yet again. "My husband is, sadly, not at home. He could give you details of her illness, I am sure but he has been very busy since the funeral... Much that he has to do, he tells me..." She trailed off, then abruptly pushed herself to her feet. "Would you like to see Lily's room? Perhaps there will be something that might remind you of her." Her tone was bright as could be managed, but strained. Desperate.

Her clear discomfort cut through Barty's thoughts then, a different realisation beyond the grief that made the hackles on the back of his neck stand up. Her behaviour seemed wrong, somehow—the sudden shift was disquieting for some reason, but he could not place a finger on why. There was no chance to ask. He put it down to grief once more—for what else could it be? Grief was a madness in of itself, and it was want to do terrible things to the mind.

Elanor, taken aback at Lady Elizabeth's abrupt change of tact, had nevertheless recovered swiftly. She smiled and rose to her feet, giving a little bob of her head in a small curtsy. "I would like that very much, Lady Braithwaite."

The older woman gave a pitiful smile. "I did ask for you to call me Elizabeth," she said gently. "Please, right this way."

She led them back out into the high hall, towards a curving staircase. The cadaverous butler reappeared out of a side door, pushing a small rattling trolley with a shining silver tea set as they approached. He was sent on his long suffering way to the sitting room, as the lady escorted her 'guests' upstairs and into the room.

As Barty and Jean discretely tailed in after Elanor and Lady Elizabeth, Barty wondered if there had been a mistake.

It was a large, wide room, well lit by high windows. But dividing the room in half was a wooden fence, eerily reminiscent of a cage. On this side, there was a desk and table, with signs of wear, ink stains and wax marks, and all the other indications that someone had, for years, worked themselves day and night upon it. The chair too, tucked into the desk, was so worn as to be scuffed to the point of collapse.

The other half of the room beyond that fence was just as sparse. An ironbound bed, with its sheets fresh pressed and crisp. A bookshelf, without books. Another desk, with nothing upon it. It was, to all accounts, to all purposes, a prison cell. Even the windows were barred. Barty recognised the sort all too well—he had lived in such at the orphanage. But this was too much to imagine.

He was about to say something, when Elanor beat him to it, unable to keep the horror out of her voice. "She—this is her room?"

Lady Elizabeth had a sad smile on her face. "My husband insisted upon it. It was the most sensible place, you see." She nodded, as though in self assurance. But Elanor was not swayed.

"You kept her *caged*?" Her performance was wavering, anger flowing into her words, but before Lady Elizabeth could respond, a new voice interrupted.

"We kept her alive. Which was the only thing that mattered." The voice was rasping, severe, and cold. It belonged to a straight backed and shouldered man, rigid and watchful, his hair pulled back tightly to reveal a widow's peak and a blackened stare. He was well dressed, standing with his hands behind his back. At his presence, Lady Elizabeth's head lowered to look at the ground.

Elanor rallied, straightening up. "Lord Braithwaite, I presume." She curtseyed. "A pleasure to meet you."

He eyed her, looking her up and down with a cold look that made Barty's jaw tighten. "Quite." He stepped into the room. He did not look at Jean or Barty, who lingered to one side—Barty hovering with the perpetual air of the knowing unwelcome, Jean malingering with malice aforethought, concealed from his features but ever present. Lord Braithwaite bypassed them both and approached the gate. "There were reasons for keeping her thus. Her illness forced me to keep her in isolation, to treat it. She rebelled at this notion on occasion."

He remained where he was. Tall and cold. He reminded Barty of Jean in that moment, but where Jean was a tightly buttoned down ball of rage at the best of times, Lord Braithwaite radiated ice. His every movement was firmly controlled, his words clipped and precisely enunciated. The world shrank around him, turning frosty. His expression was that of a statue—contemplative, staring, and a simulacrum of life.

Lady Elizabeth coughed. "I thought you were still busy with your... other work, husband." She did not look up as she spoke.

He ignored her, not sparing a glance, and spoke to Elanor. "How exactly were you familiar with my daughter, and what prompted you to visit her home now? She is no longer present, after all." His tone was callous, and Barty felt Jean tense.

Before Elanor could answer, there was a curious sound, low to the ground. A loud, interrupting *mreow* came from the doorway, causing all eyes to turn. A cat was standing with its head tilted at the doorway. Not much older than a kitten, the black and white feline stared up at Elanor with a curious look in its green-eyed stare.

Lord Braithwaite made a sound of annoyance. "See to that thing, Elizabeth." His voice was flat and brooked no argument. "I will see to our... guests."

The lady of the house hurried towards the door. The cat swished its tail and sprang away lazily, dashing down the hall as it was pursued, effortlessly keeping distance. Lord Braithwaite continued on, staring at the empty bed as he had been doing, "The cat was a stray that my daughter managed to let in through the window. It has avoided capture since and I have not yet found a way to poison it." He turned then to Elanor, affixing her with that cold, cold stare. "My daughter's illness was such that I limited her contact with the outside world as to better isolate and understand the reasoning behind it. Nevertheless, she was a defiant creature, who tried to escape her sickbed many times, forcing me to take firm measures." He turned back to the bed. "But I am not sure why I need to tell you any of that."

Elanor straightened. "I was her friend when we were children and I—"

Braithwaite cut her off, his words a knife. "I am not talking to you, girl. This charade ends now, before you make a further fool of yourself. I am asking what *you* are doing here, Jean Reynard."

The atmosphere of the room changed dramatically. Jean pried himself off the wall, exhaling slowly but with a growl of menace in his breath. "Interesting. You barely glanced at me, but you figured it out swiftly enough—and you knew of me at all. Few do."

Elanor grit her teeth together, and marched over to her father's side, her expression white with anger and disappointment, as Braithwaite snorted. "My erstwhile associates hold you in an uplifted position of awe, hatred and terror, and describe you aptly." He turned then to face the three of them, his hands behind his back. "I find no such need to grant you such undeserved eminence." His tone was flatly contemptuous. "You have skulked into my home to ask questions you have no business asking. You shall answer mine before I demand that you leave. What are you doing here? The Chief Inspector was, I am told, warned of further involvement."

Jean shrugged. "I was never one for following directions—he gave an order, I chose to ignore it. In his defence, I did lie to him about it."

Lord Braithwaite sniffed with disdain, turning away. "As is the lot of you lowborn gutter dwellers; to lie, and to be where you do not belong."

Jean chuckled at that, but there was anger in it. "That is quite the turn of phrase from a creature such as yourself." He looked about the room as he stepped forward. "I would wager the butchery I found in that cellar was your work, considering you were also the one who imprisoned your daughter in this place, to wither away until she died. They appear from the same hand, to my eye." His voice rang with disgust.

Braithwaite stiffened, and whirled on Jean, his face darkening. "Speak not of what you do not know. If you say one more word, I shall—"

Jean cut him off. One moment, they were two men standing a respectful distance apart, but in the next Jean stepped abruptly closer, standing nose to nose with Braithwaite as they glared at each other. "Or you will what?" The two faced off for a long moment, as Barty held his breath.

"You do not frighten me, Mister Reynard," Braithwaite finally said through clenched teeth.

Jean remained where he was, his eyes searching. "No. I do not, do I? You buried all those fears in that coffin and left them there. What else did you leave behind, Lord Braithwaite? What have you done?" His brow furrowed, and he repeated himself, colder than before. "What have you done?"

Braithewaite's face tightened further, the teeth grinding as he glared hatefully. "What a father must. What a father is *duty bound* to do." He lifted his chin, clenching his jaw, veins swelling at his temples. "But to the rest of your accusations, I admit to nothing, and you cannot compel otherwise, and nor would it matter. The extent of what you can do in this situation is to leave. Now get out of my home."

The moment hung in the air. Both men stared the other down, with Jean refusing to move despite the demand. Barty made his decision. He stepped between them, a hand coming to Jean's shoulder, which he shrugged off immediately—but it broke the eye contact.

"We have done all we can do here for now," Barty stated plainly, and it was true. The moment of rage passed; Barty could *see* the steel door shut behind the eyes of Braithwaite, as he closed off whatever secrets he might yet keep. Barty had seen it enough to recognise it, but in the very man he was now trying to turn away. Jean did not look pleased, but he did relent.

Elanor was watching them, her expression pale and pinched. The look she was giving them was conflicted but turned to ice cold spite when it fell on Braithwaite. "And I thought my father despicable," she finally managed. "You imprisoned her here, for no crime at all."

The Lord Braithwaite's expression flickered then, and he stared at Elanor for a long moment. "I wondered why my wife took to you and your falsehoods so easily. Now I see it." He stepped forward, inspecting her more closely. "You look a great deal like Lily."

"I regret I was not there to save her from your leechcraft earlier," Elanor grated. Jean reached her then, putting a hand to her shoulder warningly. For whatever reason, a smile—however cold—had formed on Braithwaite's face.

"Yes. Would that you had." He turned away. "Would that someone had."

Elanor turned away, striding from the room with her father in tow. Barty cast one last look about the room. The lord stared at the empty bed, through the bars of the spartan cage he had crafted. A room so empty of life and joy made all the more so by that silent presence standing within it. He shuddered, and followed after the others.

Elanor was in no mood to wait. She strode to the door and pushed it open, holding her dress hem aloft in her fury. A yowling was heard around her ankles and she jumped as a black and white blur shot past her feet and across the street, in time with the sound of distress behind them. Barty turned, to see Lady Elizabeth standing there, a hand to her mouth, staring past him with tear filled eyes after the fleeing cat. His heart twisted a moment, and he hurried out—not to the coach, but in the path of the racing feline.

"Barty! Leave the animal be," Jean called out in annoyance, but Barty waved him off. This was important, in a way he could not explain. He did not bother to find the words, as Jean stood on the step of the coach and looked after him from across the roof of it, boring a hole into his back as Barty jogged into the depths of the alleyway.

It was like alleys everywhere in London. Light was as foreign to its depths as mould and foulness was wedded to it, a skulking place where secrets died. The dim overcast was cut off by the stretching buildings on each side, and what faint glimmering made it through was reflected off standing puddles amidst the cobblestones. But thankfully he did not have to delve far to find what he sought. And something more, something that crossed from the gentle shores of the unexpected into the turbulence of the impossible.

The cat, whose name he had not learned, had found someone, lurking in the shadows where the sun reached not, cloaked in darkness and secrets. A tall, slender figure, obscured by a winding sheet wrapped around their frame. Their crude, strange garb aside, they seemed somehow alien to Barty, so much so that he had frozen in place, his tongue cleaving to the roof of his mouth.

For all his own hesitation, the cat was untroubled. Its back was arched as it rubbed against the figure, purring so loud that Barty could hear it in the sudden cessation of sound amidst the rabbit rapid thump of his inexplicably quickened heartbeat. There was a disquieting element to the scene though. Something about the strange, still figure was so very wrong as to *twist* the air by their presence, skittering down Barty's arms and spine in feather light touches of spider feet.

The figure slowly, but with a disturbingly unnatural sort of grace, bent down. The sheet, which Barty could now see was filthy with grime and mud, parted to reveal a hand, but a hand unlike any other he had ever seen—save one.

It gleamed a dull gold of brass, shiny and bright even in this dark corner of London. Each finger, each joint, each articulated component, shifted with a faint sound of metal against metal as it slid free of the tattered, makeshift shawl to caress that purring, fearless cat with aching tenderness. The feline nuzzled the hand, meowing once more when those golden fingers opened and gently lifted them up and up, as the figure straightened to their full height, and then, finally, realised Barty was there.

They went still, so still as to be locked in place. He could see nothing in the depths of the sheet but a glimmer of whiteness, lines of what might have been a face, but all of it... all of it wrought in sculpted serenity. But most arresting were the eyes; two dimmed green flames, lit like gemstones with candles behind them, gazed at him without blinking. The moment hung as they stared at each other, Barty unable to cry out or breathe amidst his thunderous, frightened heartbeat.

And then the figure turned and ran. Awkward, stumbling steps, haphazard and unsure, but running nevertheless. Panicked and frightened, easy to recognise because Barty had run so many times like that himself. But it awoke Barty at last as he turned and screamed Jean's name over his shoulder, before he set off after them.

He did not look back to see if Jean would follow, but he heard the sharp whistle come a moment later, the roar of wheels turning over cobblestones an instant after. It was one thing about the man that Barty would always respect—he never hesitated. He was regretting his own moment of pause as he set off after the fleeing figure—still carrying the cat that struggled but could not get free, as it ran and ran, clutching the sheet that flew after them. They ran with a clumsy gait, like someone who had never run before, wobbling as they went, but they had a stride that far outstripped Barty's own, and that made a difference. He scrambled after them, picking up speed. The coach behind him could not follow him down the alley, but it would, he hoped, make its presence felt.

The shrouded figure plunged on. Each step they made was loud, ringing like a bell over the cobbles. They turned to look back over one shoulder just as a door opened in front of them into the alleyway. Barty called out a warning, pointing without thinking. "Look out!"

It was no use. The cloaked being struck the door at full speed. Barty expected them to bounce back from the several inches of solid oak, to tumble unto the ground. He did not expect the door to shatter into matchwood, and hurl the person opening it to the cobblestones with terrific force, so much so that Barty only got a glimpse of a figure and nothing more. The sheet ripped and tore, and the figure beneath was revealed fully, as they tried to cover their face and protect the terrified cat they still carried.

It was a woman. A girl, if Barty was any judge, but it was difficult to fully gauge. There was hair, long and dark, and covering part of the face, but it appeared a carefully made wig. As the gleam of the setting sun fell upon her, it unveiled a face of purest white ceramic... a doll's face. It was the delicate culmination of a masterwork of precise construction that was her body; a woman's figure, much akin to a sculpture, but made of different, flawlessly wrought pieces that all interlocked and wove together. A work of art and beauty unlike anything he had ever seen before, and somehow alive, animated, and moving.

The porcelain face was featureless, at least in colour, but the marks of a face—nose, lips, eyebrows, had all been wrought upon it in sublime craftsmanship. He could see that the eyes, however, were constructed of glass and metal, and they gleamed at him with a light from within that defied rationalisation, but nevertheless conveyed complete panic, fear, and more; confusion, terror... an agony beyond reason.

They turned and kept running.

Barty leapt over the debris and continued after her, keeping his stride. The figure scrabbled over the stones and turned so abruptly that Barty bounced off the wall to keep his momentum. There were sounds now, for London was always noisy, but they were approaching a louder part of the city now. The alleyway broke open into light and roaring cacophony, a gaping hole into the bright world, a world now full of people coming and going with the setting of the sun, each of whom could see what raced towards them. There was no way to avoid it, or to hide from it, and soon every single eye would be upon them. The running woman of metal and ceramic saw it too and skidded to a desperate halt, stumbling, with Barty just behind. She turned, crumpling to the ground as she did so, curling in on herself and the tiny feline she held in terror, raising one hand in a futile effort to stave off the peril. A desperate, forlorn gesture of panic and fear, the body responding in the only way its owner knew, to beg, to plead, to hope that no one was going to hurt them.

Barty had seen it before, in the orphanage; it had never worked. He had done it himself, and it had not worked then either. The plea for mercy was never heard. Only the truly, completely desperate were foolish enough to ask for mercy in this world, Barty had learned. Only the helpless dared to hope that those who wished them harm were fools, or kind-hearted, or understanding, when they never were.

But Barty was never the one who had been begged for mercy before. And he would be damned before he became one of the beasts that preyed upon those that pleaded for kindness.

He stopped, holding his hands up with the palms out, breathing hard as he found his voice. "Please, I am—I am sorry," he stuttered. "I did not mean to frighten you."

The cowering metal and ceramic girl looked up at him from her vulnerable position. The cat was clinging to her now, claws finding no purchase on the smooth frame. Beneath the meagre remnants of the sheet she was a mannequin, with gleaming brass at every joint and point of articulation. With hesitance, she met his eyes, staring at Barty in terror, naked even in those false eyes of glass, of metal, the iris a ring of shuttering brass that was open wide—it was impossible. In every way but flesh and bone, this being before him moved like a frightened, timid girl. With a mixture of horror, awe, and pity that turned his stomach, Barty realised exactly who she was.

"Lily," he said, dumbstruck, the name falling from his lips slowly. "You... you are Lily, are you not? Lily Braithwaite?" He did not have to ask. He *knew*. And that knowledge was given surety as the huddling figure, her eyes shifting again, nodded hesitantly. Barty felt his world tilt.

He steadied himself by putting a hand on his chest. "My—" he stammered helplessly. "My name is Bartholomew. Bartholomew Bartleby. But you can call me—"

She sat up straighter, astonished then as she kept the cat close, and finally Lily spoke. The voice came from behind the mask and sounded like it was far away—a girl's voice, echoing and strange, but it was yet full of the fear that those desperate eyes portrayed. "Mister Barty?"

Of all the unexpected shocks in the past few minutes, that was certainly one of the more dramatic ones. He blinked and took a step back. "Y-yes. That is me. Mister Barty." He could not keep the shock from his voice. "But how did you know that?"

The frightened girl shook her head. "I... I don't k-know," she stammered, then touched her brow and flinched as she did so, staring at her fingers. "I... remembered it. I... remember you." The unfocused orbs sharpened once more and looked at Barty. "I'm s-scared. I want... I want to go home."

Barty felt his heart wrench. "I don't know if that is a good idea." He hated himself for saying it.

She lowered her gaze. The alleyway darkened then, the moment turning to shadow and gloom, but as hope withered Jean was there, his hand reaching inside his coat. Elanor stood behind him, her blade drawn but tilted down. The rest of the alleyway mouth was blocked by the coach that had drowned out the lingering light, and the smiling terror of Puck. But Lily, the frightened girl in a body of machinery and impossibility, paid them no heed.

"I have... I have nowhere else to go," she said in a voice a breath away from breaking. "I want to go home. I don't..." She looked up at Barty, her face was impassive but her glowing eyes were in a hell he could not grasp. "Help... me." She sounded close to tears, that once started, would never stop.

Barty could bear it no longer. As Jean shook his head in warning and Elanor stifled a gasp, he ignored both and knelt down before the doll-like girl, gently taking her free hand, as the other held the wriggling feline. The figure stiffened, the metal fingers twitching, then they slowly wrapped around his own. She was strong; there was no give in that grasp, none whatsoever, and he could feel his bones grinding together, but he did not show it. He did not dare. He was not the one in this moment who needed reassurance.

"Then let us take you somewhere safe. And see what we can do to help you." He was astonished how much he meant it. But he did. He meant it as sincerely, if not more, than anything he had ever said in his life.

"Barty," Jean began, his tone one of warning and one that spoke volumes, but Barty emphatically shook his head, his response immediate and sharp.

"We are taking her to Adam, Jean. That is who she needs to see." Something beyond himself gave him strength and conviction enough, and he met Jean's narrowed eyes for once without blinking. "We are taking her home. She has been through enough."

Jean's hand was still in his coat, still holding the gun that Barty knew was there as he seemed to consider his response—to take brutal action, for all Barty knew. But it was Elanor who spoke, her voice strangely distant. "He is right, Father." She was staring at Barty, but with a look he did not understand. "And we should hurry. We're losing light."

Jean looked from one to the other, then cursed softly, as Barty helped the ungainly yet shockingly strong Lily to her feet. "Eidolon is looking for her," he stated flatly, in warning. Barty ignored him and gently secured the remnants of the ragged sheet around the docile Lily; seeing this, Jean gave in. "Very well." He grunted. "Let us waste no more time."

There were no further arguments. A moment of quick movement, a shifting of a coach and a shielding with bodies, and they helped the huddling Lily and her feline companion into the coach. Eyes were on them, curious and confused, but they saw the coach and did not argue, quelled by the lamplight of Puck's mad grin and knowing terror of being, the crawling whisper of a voice from the stones coming to all those who looked too long. No one asked questions, not yet, but they would.

The coach plunged into deepening twilight. Night would not be far behind.

Chapter 13

Tears Unwept

The journey back to the Lodge was a rather awkward one, to say the least. Barty, Jean, and Elanor sat on one side of the coach, staring at their newfound company. It was indeed a fair thing to say they were being rude in their unyielding observation, but in their defence, the automaton that called herself Lily Braithwaite was nothing short of a wonder.

The sheer precision and skill involved in her creation was so incredibly advanced that Barty could only marvel at it. He had knowledge of machinery and engineering—his ability to work with such things was something Adam had not only appreciated, but also encouraged, an innate knack to figure things out from looking at them. But the ingenuity of the construction of Lily's body was beyond him.

He remembered the touch of her hand—though hard as the metal she was crafted from naturally was, there had been a warmth to it that alluded to something more. She sat with a mixture of despair and poise—holding her posture elegantly, befitting a lady of her stature, but the straightness of her spine could not hide the tremble of her shoulders. But her chest did not rise and fall with breath, giving her the strange look of a statue—save that it was one that yet moved.

Each limb, the torso, and the face was clad in a layer of porcelain—though there were places where it showed wear from exposure, it nevertheless was melded fully to her form and was interlaced with lines of gold, broken up into sections for more stability and movement. The body beneath and at the extremities was made entirely of brass—hands and feet segmented, the neck and more. She could bend and move like a normal person—mostly, at least—as her mechanical frame allowed. There was no flesh, none that could be seen. Even the eyes were mechanical, orbs of glass with gleaming shutters behind them, and lit from within by that dulled green fire. The long black hair she bore was part of the ensemble, akin to a carefully made doll, a luxurious wig attached directly to the scalp, the hairs carefully glued in place by an expert hand. She was a miracle of craftsmanship. She was incredible. She was beautiful.

She was a broken thing, with a confused—probably angry—black and white cat in both arms, holding onto it like it was the only thing to keep her from drowning. She shivered and spasmed, each shuddering movement audible, with faint grinding and scraping sounds. She did not speak, but this close to her Barty could hear a thrumming that might have been an impossible heartbeat echoing forth. She curled in on herself, covered by her dirtied sheet, hiding her face from those that stared at her. Hiding herself from a world that would not let her pass freely. Barty had seen fear, had seen frightened things in his life... He had lived it, been a slave to it, and seen others writhe in its grip. But never before had it been so complete in its misery, as it was now.

Jean, for once, was dumbfounded into silence. His expression was speculative and hard, and though he had no weapon in his hand, Barty was confident that he could get his hands on one if need be in an instant. But he said nothing, and observed in that menacing silence that Barty knew too well, the jagged glass of his stare grating and grinding away at the air itself to ratchet the tension ever higher. He had to find a way to break it.

"What is the cat's name?" It was the simplest thing to ask. Every set of eyes snapped to him. He ignored all of them, save for the only ones that mattered in that moment, as Lily stared at him from the corner of her eye. Barty tried again. "I am sorry, we did not catch it before—I was curious as to his name."

There was a pause before Lily spoke, in the strange, echoing, distant voice that came from behind her unmoving mask. "Daisy. *Her* name is Daisy," she said slowly. The feline was calmer now, but her tail was slashing the air with the ferocity of a cat that is biding its time to freedom or vengeance, if not both.

"Daisy," Barty repeated, as though to solidify it in memory. The wayward feline gave him a knowing look, its ears flicking as Lily continued to hold it in her metal grip.

"Where are you taking me?" Lily asked without looking up, but it gave Barty hope. Questions showed awareness and purpose, even if it was an entirely valid self-interest guiding it.

"To a safe place," Elanor stated. "To our home. We"—she looked to her father, then back—"we will figure things out there." Her tone was kinder than Barty expected, as one might talk to a child.

"Someone we know has... knowledge about what has happened to you, and I am sure that..." Barty cut himself off, remembering how they had left Adam; unmoving, frozen in place. He vainly sought to figure out a way to relay this, but Lily surprised him then as she nodded.

"I know. They are waiting for me," she said simply. She did not look entirely happy about this, hugging herself tighter and tucking her legs in closer, protectively. "I can... feel it. After I saw you, I... I remembered it." She looked up then, her gleaming gaze drifting from one to the other. "I remember you. You frighten me." She was staring, unblinking at Jean. He stared right back, but said nothing.

"No one is going to hurt you here," Barty said, wanting to reach out, wanting to reassure, but stopping himself. There was something so very different about her, compared to Adam. With Adam, the fear stopped quickly. For all they looked a corpse, there was a kindness to them, there was expression, and there was a gentleness to their movements that showed their spirit. But Lily, all he could see was her fear. And fear could lead to many things, few of them good.

The awkward quiet returned, but Puck was pushing the strange, silent horses that drew the coach hard, which was devilishly uncharacteristic of him. He set the coach rolling along the road and skidding around corners, slipping between the traffic with the skill of a madman and the impossibility of an improbability.

"So then..." Jean started the conversation with that iron relentlessness that so defined him. "You said you *remember* us." Lily nodded, her posture tensing with a flinch. "How, exactly?"

Jean asked, his tone sceptical.

She shrugged helplessly. "I... I do not know." Her metal body screeched as she tried to shrink in on herself, but Jean was not satisfied.

"You understand the unlikelihood of this, if nothing else." He frowned. "Do you *remember* Adam then? That they are trapped and cannot move—did you have something to do with it?" He was leaning forward, the tone turning towards accusation. "If something you did harmed Adam, I would know what, because I will not have further harm caused to them. Do you know anything?"

The brass and porcelain girl said nothing, but shrank yet more, clinging to her cat. Jean leaned further forward in her retreat, his patience breaking. "I asked you a question. Do you know—"

But Barty had heard enough. He grabbed Jean's wrist as the hunter reached towards Lily. He could not move it, as much as he could bend an iron bar, but it was enough.

"Cease this line of inquiry, Jean," Barty stated firmly. "We will have answers soon enough—just be patient. Now stop scaring her." He was surprised at how steady his voice was.

Jean glared at him, then growled low in his chest and sat back, folding his arms across his body. "Hells take that kind heart of yours, Barty," he spat. "It is more akin to weakness than sainthood, but it makes a martyr out of you just the same."

"Better than a brute, Father," Elanor stated dryly.

Jean shot her a look at that, before grunting harshly. "A *despicable* brute, if I recall your earlier wording properly," he growled, turning his head to the window, his tone flat. Elanor looked ready to respond, but Barty again put his foot down, leaning forward between them both.

"Stop it, the pair of you," he snapped. "You have all the time in the world to keep ripping pieces off of each other, but *not* right now." He nodded to Lily, who had shrunk so much that she looked ready to let the world swallow her whole. All three ceased their bickering, until Jean spoke.

"Forgive me, Miss... Miss Braithwaite," he said. "Adam is a friend and I... I have worried about them." He kept his voice controlled, but the effort to do so was palpable.

A glowing green eye looked up from the crook of her elbow, before Lily's gaze shifted to Barty. "Are... are they always like that?" She sounded a bit mystified.

Barty, unable to help himself, nodded. "They are father and daughter—I think it is rather natural after all."

Lily's eye blinked off and on for a moment before she peered back to Jean and Elanor. "They are very angry at each other." The green light flared a moment, then she huddled in on herself. "I am sorry. I should not have said that." She said it quickly, in an embarrassed rush.

"I would argue it was precisely the right thing to say, myself," Barty replied, and despite himself he chuckled, the mirth bubbling out of him before he could catch it. Both Jean and Elanor glared at him for it, but it did not matter. Barty saw the clenching of Lily's hands loosen, if only a little, the glow in her gleaming gaze turning softer. It was a moment, nothing more, but it was a better one than those that had come before it.

They arrived back at the Lodge not long after that. With uncharacteristic haste, Puck wheeled the coach towards the front door with such speed in the turn that the wheels kicked up sparks as it drew to a halt, rocking in place. They exited, as above them the coachman let out a great, grandiose breath of exaggerated relief. "Thank the twisting aether and setting sun you are taking that *thing* out of my presence. It was making my song *itch*." He practically hissed the words, venom dropping from every syllable. It was so unexpected and vicious that the entire group of them froze midstep to look back at Puck, who sat fidgeting in their discomforted fury.

"That is not a kind thing to say about Miss Lily, Puck," Elanor started stiffly, but he waved a hand back and forth rapidly in furious response to her statement.

"No, no, *no*. Not her, though her notes are discordant and her dreams are things of *shattering*. Not her. *Them*." He pointed an accusing finger at Lily—or rather, what she was still holding. "I see you, guardian of the crossing, feckless hunter," Puck grated, a jagged note over broken strings. "You shall have no claws for *me*."

A long pause. Barty, Jean, Elanor, and Lily all exchanged looks, before Barty spoke the burning question they all had. "Puck—are you talking to the *cat*?" He could not keep the astonishment from his voice. But Puck recoiled as though stung, and hissed.

"Fie, moonlight take me down, but I do! Keep it from my countenance. I shall have *no* entreaty with it over what is mine by right." He scowled, and pointed again with a long, fierce finger. "I *see* you, sneakthief. *Mine*."

The cat, cradled upside down in its metal mistress's arms, stared at the apparition of the coachman and with deliberate, insulting slowness, licked one paw. The message was clear, though no one else knew it; war had been declared.

Puck seethed, but there was no time. Jean pushed ahead and guided the errant cluster in front of him forward. They passed through the threshold, with Puck setting the horses on with an irritated flick of the reins.

As the door closed, the cat, Daisy, wriggled. Lily bent down—one piece of herself at a time, moving with a deliberate slowness as though she threatened to fall apart. She released the long suffering cat, who immediately bounded away and climbed the staircase out of reach, before pausing and turning to look back, her tail swishing.

"She will be all right, won't she?" The strange voice of Lily had a pinch to it, an anxiety that twisted with every syllable. The fear that radiated through her would not abate, and Barty did not need to guess for a moment as to why. It was not every day that a girl, trapped in the body of a machine mannequin, met a walking construct of flesh and metal. A deep flare of pity welled in him. The girl, for that was what she was, regardless of what gave her form, was terrified.

"She will," he answered her. "The house is large, and safe, and she will not cause too much damage, I am sure." He tried to sound reassuring, to smile, but it was difficult when those glowing green eyes swept over to him, amidst that impassive mask of white porcelain. His tongue twisted a moment.

It was Jean who stepped in to help things along, quite unexpectedly, his gruff voice subdued. "Miss Lily—you have, I am quite sure, been through something not one of us could begin to understand. We still do not understand it. But we are here to help you, as difficult and as strange as all this is, and the only way we can do that is by getting answers."

Lily straightened up as though reacting to a blow, then slowly nodded, sagging again. She stood in place, looking vaguely about the Lodge, but it was impossible to tell her thoughts, her expression as ever immobile. Barty, Elanor and Jean exchanged looks as the brass fingers of Lily fidgeted a moment—then she took a careful step forward. "This place feels... familiar. Not home, but..." She wavered in midstep, and reached up to put a hand to her head. "It's... it is so loud," she quavered.

A pause, before Jean spoke. "We need to get her below."

There was at least one bit of good news as they reached downstairs—the elevator was working again. It rattled most uncomfortably and there was a moment or two where it might well have been on the verge of collapse, but it was far better indeed than using the ladder. Benji was waiting anxiously at the bottom, wringing his hands together, and did not take a breath until the doors were dragged open to let them all out.

"Had no idea if it would work or not!" he reported happily, which did nothing to settle the nerves of those present whatsoever, and earned a few sharp looks as well. But Benji paid no heed to it, as he was staring at Lily, his nostrils flaring and ears perked upwards in alert.

Lily herself was paying him no mind, nor any attention at all. She was staring straight ahead towards the still figure of Adam. Her posture wavered, and shrank as she wrapped her arms around herself, her golden hand raising up to her throat protectively. She looked at them with the cowering doubt of fear. "What... who is that?" Her distant voice shook with more than fear. "Who have you brought me to?"

"That is Adam," Jean said quietly. He stood to the side, watching Lily, his expression intent. "How long have you been... like this, Lily?"

Her eyes did not stray from Adam as she spoke. "Four days." She took a step towards Adam. Though she could show no feeling on her face, there was expression in her movement that worried Barty.

Jean was watching Lily as she approached and Barty made note of the hand that once more strayed to a holstered gun in his coat, soft and subtle as a whisper, ready to rise to a roar. Jean was still unsure, and Barty could not help but share his apprehension in that charged moment. "On the night you were... changed," Jean continued, "something happened to Adam. There was—"

"—a storm," Lily finished.

She was closer to Adam now. Barty started forward, but Jean reached out a hand to stop him, shaking his head. The four of them were a particular distance now from the pair, and Barty was confused as to why, until he felt it—felt it, and *tasted* it. The air was alive. The hair on his arms was standing up. There was a raw energy in the chamber, much as there had been when the storm had struck. As Barty watched, the little sparks of energy that ran along Adam's structure and spine seemed to grow brighter.

"I was... I was so frightened," Lily continued. "It was all so dark, and then it was all so... strange. There were people there. Things that looked like people and I... I ran. I ran and... I heard them. I could hear them; they were calling to me." Her voice had a dazed, dreamlike tone to it. "Adam."

She clutched the sheet to herself as she approached, and her steps became more sure as she did so. It was unexpectedly swift, so much that it caught even Jean off guard, but she stopped as she came to stand in front of Adam, staring up at the still immobile figure, reaching out with one hand towards the sky, frozen in place—the statue of machine and flesh interwoven. There was something significant in the charged moment, Barty felt, so much so that he found himself standing and waiting for it to happen, rather than approach—even if he could have summoned the courage.

Jean, the ever more suspicious of the group, swore under his breath and acted while everyone else was immobile. He seized first Elanor, then Benji, and finally Barty, who were too confused to protest and forcibly sent each of them scurrying beneath the very table that he had dragged Barty beneath when Adam had first exploded. They crammed together as Lily reached up with one metal hand and stepped in close, placing her palm upon Adam's massive, broad chest. For a moment—nothing happened.

This did not remain the case for very long.

The world turned white as arcing energy burst in all directions, crawling over the walls and floor. Jean covered them as best he could, but the trio he was protecting needed no further encouragement, with Elanor and Benji taking the chance to bury their heads and hide. But not Barty. He watched through shielding fingers as the storm raged. It did nothing to Lily, save incinerate her sheet to ashes. But unlike the last time, which had all but destroyed the armoury, the searing display did not last long. It turned inwards, focusing on Adam and sinking into them as a buzzing roar was heard, a sound of energy and fury that went on and on before it cut off, a silence that rang in the ears. After the flare of brightness, the darkness seemed so complete that at first, Barty thought he had gone blind. But he blinked a few more times as his vision slowly returned, and the hesitant four pulled themselves back up.

Adam said nothing as they lifted the massive coat that Elanor and Benji had made for them from a nearby bench, where it had miraculously escaped harm. But they did not put it to their own shoulders, instead draping it wordlessly over Lily, who sat despondent on the ground, shuddering. She was weeping, but there were no tears, just wracking sobs of sound, of confusion. Adam was gentle, attentive, as they covered her now naked metal and porcelain form. The destruction had been far less this time, but still significant.

Adam, however, was not even looking at the flesh and blood inhabitants standing in stunned silence. When they finally spoke, their voice was tightly, carefully controlled. "I would request that you all go upstairs a moment. We shall join you shortly." They lowered their enormous frame cautiously, seating themselves down cross-legged, one mighty hand gently placed upon Lily's back as she sat there. Their long hair concealed their face, but not their tone; Adam sounded strange, in a way that Barty had never heard before.

"Adam—" Jean started, stepping forward, but Adam abruptly held up one gigantic finger to silence him.

"Forgive me, Jean, truly. I will explain what I can in due time." The huge hand lowered once more. "But I must see to this young woman. I beg you, grant me understanding."

Jean grit his teeth, clenching his fists—then relaxed them amidst an explosive exhalation. "Very well. We shall be waiting upstairs," he replied, his tone curt. But he managed only two steps before he stopped. "Adam?" he called over one shoulder, as the giant turned his head towards him. "It is good to see you with us again."

Adam blinked at that, then the twisted face broke into a rueful smile, as they nodded. "It is good to be back, Reynard. Now hurry on a while."

Jean nodded, then snapped his fingers at the rest of the still somewhat dazed group. This was neither the place nor the time for them any further. The upstairs awaited.

THEY GATHERED TOGETHER in the kitchen, sitting anxiously around the table. Benji usually hovered off to one side as he always did when Jean was present but now, with that not possible, the wolf in the boy demanded he keep danger in plain view at all times and an exit close at hand. Jean appeared to ignore this. Barty, however, was never really sure if that was true. He and Elanor were regulated to placing themselves just far enough apart that neither looked like they were trying to get closer to the other—a tricky thing to manage in a modestly sized kitchen.

Jean was cutting slices of ham from a thick leg, pulled from the larder, along with slices of cheese and bread. He was not very good at it, each ingredient being cut far too thick to be fully practical, but Barty was too hungry to care. Elanor seemed to share this regard, as they both started devouring their messy ensembles without bothering to add a lick of mustard—an unthinkable act, at least if Adam was present.

"What I wish to know first," Jean finally said as he finished cutting and prepared his own sandwich with brutalist efficiency, "is how you knew." He rounded on the seated Barty, whose cheeks were bulging like a squirrel with its collected bounty, and only able to make a '*hrrmph?*' sound in reply. "How did you know that was Lily, when you had never seen her nor spoke to her before? I am curious."

Barty pounded on his chest as he swallowed, wincing, before affording himself an answer. "Who else could it have been?" He gestured helplessly as he went on, "She was near the house, we knew Lord Braithwaite was connected, and he made no move to hide it." He shrugged. "It was an educated guess, but when I saw her I knew. There was no other possibility."

Jean grunted, shaking his head. "I appreciate your candour—and you were right. It was good intuition."

Barty blinked. Between showing gratitude to Adam, and complimenting Barty himself just now, Jean was displaying most uncommon behaviour. "You *are* relieved that Adam is all right, aren't you?" Barty asked curiously, leaning forward. From his observations he was already sure of it, but he wanted to hear Jean say it.

Jean twitched at that, his jaw tightening. "Of course I am.

They are a vital component to my work, and have a degree of knowledge that I simply lack." His reply was stiff, his eyes narrowing. Barty recognised it. He did not push further, but he was satisfied with the answer Jean would not say.

"She would not go back to the house," Elanor said quietly. She was staring at nothing, her brow furrowed as she chewed thoughtfully. She had a spot of crumbs on the corner of her mouth, and Barty half raised a hand to brush it away, before he caught himself. He coughed instead to catch her attention and when she lifted her gaze to him, he apologetically tapped his own mouth to indicate. The look she gave him in reply was nothing short of withering, as she scrubbed her cheek with one hand. "As I was saying," she went on testily, giving Barty a glare, "she did not want to go back to the house. Does that mean she was unable to? That she had not yet done so? Do you think her parents are unaware of her, uh..." She struggled to find a word, before finally settling. "... return?"

Jean shook his head firmly at that, his jaw tightening as his own gaze went distant in memory. "Braithwaite showed signs of sleep deprivation, though he hid it well. There were also burn marks on his hands and some of his hair was singed." He frowned, took an aggressive bite of his monstrous sandwich, continuing on after he swallowed. "There were marks on his shoes and trousers as well, and he had not shaved that day. If I had to make an assumption, he had been out looking for Lily, on foot. Possibly alone, but I doubt it."

Barty blinked, quite astonished. "You saw all that?" He was ashamed of himself that he had missed it.

"That and more," Jean said. "The house lights—did you notice them? They were electrified, but quite unlike what one might find elsewhere, even in a house of the nobility. That, and the taste of the air. Do you remember it from somewhere else?" He pointed at Barty, almost accusingly. But Barty jerked upwards as he realised.

"The laboratory where we found the bodies," he said. "That... machine that created all the energy and lightning, it smelled like that." He could not believe he had not made the connection before now.

Jean's eyes had a gleam to them that might well have been pride. "Correct. I never got a chance to explain it earlier, but *that* was not normal, nor was it natural. *That* had an air of the esoteric about it, and so it was in the Braithwaite house." He shook his head. "Lord Braithwaite has gotten his hands onto something he should not have. Either Eidolon and that cretin Wyrmwood gave it to him, or something else, but he has turned his mind towards the unnatural." He grimaced then. "Amongst other things."

There was a moment of pause. But then understanding settled on Barty, cracking along his nerves. "Elanor was right though. Lily was outside, but she did not go home—her father was looking for her, and yet the moment she had an offer to go somewhere else, she took it." He looked over to Elanor then, who was staring at him, her expression tense.

"What did he do to her, Father?" Elanor asked. Her tone was neutral, but it was a leaden dread, a numbed horror as imagination crawled into the unknowns of the question and filled in the blanks with what might have beens that, fed by the intimacy with the awful, clustered together and intensified, growing worse with each and every heartbeat.

"I do not know," Jean said finally, as he lay down the knife he had been holding on the cutting board. "But I intend to find out." His expression hardened. "Because until now, the only created being in the world was the one who you all know. And the information of how they were made is held by only one, as well."

"Who might that be, then?" Barty asked, leaning forward, but he jumped as a deep, melodic voice answered from behind him.

"That is easily answered, young Bartholomew. The only one to have such knowledge, is standing before you. Only Jean Reynard has such, in the locked vaults of the Rock of Gwyar Manor. The fortress of the Society."

Adam was at the threshold. Crouched down as always to enter, wearing the new coat that had been made for them. At their side, huddled and wrapped in a thick woollen blanket, with only her eyes to be seen, was Lily, who looked at them all furtively. She awkwardly raised a metal hand and gave the tiniest wave imaginable. Barty, not knowing what else to do, waved back. So did Benji, but with rather more enthusiasm; it was in his nature.

Adam stood attentively to one side of Lily, at their full height—standing taller than Barty had ever seen them do before. "Everyone." Adam's voice intoned. "I would like to formally introduce you to Lily Braithwaite." Their massive hand came down to rest just behind Lily, a shield to guard her. "She has had a terrible, terrible experience, and is very frightened. But I have promised her that no one here is going to hurt her."

"And so shall it be," Jean replied firmly, but his expression remained as watchful as ever as he eyed Lily. He hid it by inclining his head in a formal little nod. "Welcome to our home, Miss Braithwaite. Though I fear our stay here shall be brief."

Barty sat up straighter at that. "It shall? Are we going somewhere then?"

"Of course we are," Elanor replied, but her tone was wry more than exasperated. "Adam just explained it. There is knowledge at home that we need."

"It is more than that," Jean stated grimly as he wiped his hands with a cloth. "Wyrmwood will, with a little effort, be able to find this place. And after today, I would wager it will not take them too long to do so." He grimaced, tossing the cloth. "The Manor is better protected by far. While normally enough, there is only so much we can do here." He winced then, gingerly rubbing his knuckles, reminding Barty that Jean had, in fact, injured them the previous evening.

Adam saw it too, and with that careful step they had, walked forward. "You have done yourself yet another mischief in my absence, Jean," they chided gently, reaching out to take Jean's hand with one of their own, dwarfing it utterly as they turned it over in their grip, a careful touch with the thumb that made Jean wince. "Two fractures, if I am any judge. How did you manage it?"

Jean shrugged. "Broke them on the skull of a stubborn fool."

Adam raised one twisted brow. "My word. I thought you had a monopoly on such things."

"Breaking things, you mean?" Jean replied dryly, but Adam shook their head.

"Of course not. I meant being a stubborn fool." Their misshapen features twisted into a grin. To Barty's surprise, Jean actually chuckled, shaking his head.

"Ah, Adam." He exhaled. "I have missed your company."

Adam was carefully wrapping a cloth around Jean's hand and fingers, pulled from their coat. "Likewise, my friend."

Elanor pushed herself to her feet with the air of someone who had made a decision. She strode over to the anxious Lily, who had shrunk against a wall as though hoping to be forgotten, and offered her a hand, which was taken carefully by metal fingers.

"While that blanket looks very fetching—I think we need to find you some proper clothes," Elanor said with the sort of kindness she rarely showed the men in her life. "Mine may not quite fit, but we shall figure something out. Did you want to come with me?"

The blanket lowered to show more of the impassive face, a gesture so characteristically human despite the lack of features, as Lily nodded. Barty looked to Jean, who was staring after the pair as they left and the door closed.

"How is she doing?" Jean spoke quietly, his tone sombre.

Adam sighed as they finished a tight knot. "About as well as you might think. She is stumbling through the aftermath of a traumatic event the likes of which you cannot grasp. Even I, with all our similarities, do not understand her trauma—not fully." They grimaced, then straightened back up to their towering height. "I have known no life but this one. She has lived one life, and now exists in another fashion—but utterly removed from what she was used to, or what I myself have endured."

"You are speaking of the fact she died?" Barty asked cautiously.

Benji crept from the corner to finally make himself his own sandwich, even as he listened as unobtrusively as possible. Jean or no Jean, Benji was as hungry as any of them.

Adam sighed. "Correct, but that is only a part of it; she does not remember much of her experience, and much of her memory is badly fragmented and distorted. But what is making things even more difficult for her is her new form." They gave a wave of a hand to them all, before asking a question of each of them. "Can you imagine why?"

Barty frowned as he considered it. "The construction was peerless... Each handmade piece a level of engineering I have never even *imagined* before. The detail of the movement possible, frankly, still leaves me shocked." It was true. His mind for engineering had been left astonished—Barty had a talent for unravelling the mechanics of machinery, and that knack had made it all too clear that the work gone into making Lily's new body was beyond his limits of invention.

Adam, however, was shaking their head. "There is more to it than that. I have senses—though they are dulled in many aspects. I have rudimentary lungs, for example—I can taste, I feel sensations when I touch things; however I have no understanding of how much that is in comparison to yourself. I would wager it is substantially less."

Barty's confusion must have shown on his face, because Adam frowned and explained further. "Imagine, if you would, Bartholomew—you wake, in a strange place, but you have awakened different. You can see, you can hear, but you cannot taste. You cannot feel. The world is neither hot, nor cold. You cannot smell the air. And when you try, you realise you cannot breathe at all. You go to open your mouth but you cannot do even *that*. All the parts of yourself, all the muscles you remember as surely as you remember your own hand, are all gone. You are in a body that is not your own—and you can feel *nothing*."

Barty stared at Adam, horror dawning in his mind and blossoming outwards as he felt the blood drain from his face. It was answer enough.

Jean was still watching the closed door that she had gone through with Elanor. "She is holding together well, all things considered."

Adam shook their head once. "No, Jean. She is not. She just has no way of letting all that she feels out, save tearing herself to pieces."

This made Jean scowl. "Difficult to get a gauge of her, without features to read. And she does not have full enough control of her body to get an accurate assessment."

Adam's tone turned firm. "She is not a threat, Jean."

The hunter's gaze shot back to Adam, whatever kindness that might have been displayed now displaced by cold, relentless pragmatism. "When she first woke, she punched through ironbound oak, then a solid foot of brick without slowing down. From the depths of her pressure marks, I would wager she cleared fifty feet on her first leap in her blind escape." He carefully opened and closed his bandaged hand. "She is a threat whether she wishes it or not. In her first moments she reacted with enough force as to warrant extreme caution. She has no idea of her ability."

Adam hummed with disappointment, but sighed. "I will ensure she brings no woe in such regard. I can handle it, if things come to that..."

Jean nodded however, satisfied. "I trust you shall do so—but see that you do, Adam. If she causes harm, the situation shall grow more difficult." He scowled then, leaning back in his chair. "But before we go further on that, I would appreciate you explaining just what *happened* to you?"

Adam appeared uncharacteristically embarrassed, turning away and giving a shrug with those enormous shoulders. "Truthfully? I have not the slightest clue. It still feels very strange." They frowned, looking at the ground as though remembering. "I was, at least for the most part, aware of what was going on around me. It was as though I was under water, or far away, but there *was* some measure of comprehension going on. I simply could not make full sense of it."

"When you had your incident, we heard Lily—her scream was coming from *you*, Adam," Barty said quietly. "I wondered who it was, but it cannot have been anyone else... That does not mean it makes any sense, of course."

Adam's expression turned speculative. "This denotes a sort of connection between us—if not the act of her awakening me from my slumber, if that is what we are to call it." They rubbed their jaw. "I admit, the instant I saw her, I *knew* her, as though I had my whole existence. One look into her eyes was all it took. Her creation, her life felt like memories, dreamed while I slept in the torpor she both pulled me into, and dragged me free from. I have no understanding of it—not yet, at least. Even her act of transference, which granted me back myself, is something neither she nor I yet grasp. It was instinctive, and yet it worked." They sighed, lowering their hand, looking to Jean with a troubled expression.

"I have, for all this time, refrained from reading my creator's notes," Adam said finally. "But it is fortunate that we are returning to the Manor. I do believe we have no choice."

"We do not," Jean said firmly. "But there are questions beyond this. We need to know the involvement of Wyrmwood—and Eidolon. I want to know why an agency of the Crown is trying to recreate the work of resurrection." He pushed himself to his feet. "For I would wager it is nothing short of nefarious."

"For myself, I wish to know who murdered her," Barty muttered, half to himself. It took him a moment to realise that everyone in the room was staring at him, and he blinked, looking from one to the other, with Benji frozen mid-bite of his sandwich.

Jean's expression had turned intent. "You are correct, Barty," he said at last. "That is something we must not forget, even if it is all too easy to do so." He nodded sharply, conceding a point Barty had not realised he was making. "The core of this is one thing above all else—the death of a young woman. And we would be no better than they who did this, if we lose sight of that."

There was an awkward pause, before Benji swallowed and spoke up at last. "So what are we going to do?"

Jean turned, squinting, as the young wolfblood shrank under

his glare, before the hunter muttered under his breath and squared his shoulders. "*We* are going to pack and get ourselves off to the Manor. But *you*, Benji, are staying." Benji's ears flattened, his downcast expression filled with hurt at this, but Jean was not finished. "You are to remain here and keep an eye on this place, keep it tidy, and keep your head down. If anyone comes knocking, ignore them. If anyone tries to force their way in, escape through the sewers until things die down. Use your nose and use your head. You have one as good as the other."

Benji blinked at that. Barty could understand why. It was a massive responsibility—and privilege—to leave the wolfblood unsupervised. He brightened then, his pointed ears perking back up. "Well, blimey, guv. You got it." He touched his brow in a deferential salute.

Jean nodded before he went on, "Now go see to Elanor and our guest. Let them know what we are doing—but be sure to knock."

Benji clutched his sandwich and hurried out. Barty was about to say something, but he could see Adam scrutinising Jean. "You have a reason for doing that, don't you? Beyond just needing someone here."

Jean grunted. "You'll figure it out. Don't forget our neighbours on the loch, after all."

Barty was mystified. "You'll have to explain that one to me, Reynard."

"Not tonight." The hunter shrugged dismissively. "For now, go pack. We are running short of time as it is."

"We won't be waiting until morning? It is already dark outside." Barty gestured to a window, but Jean ignored it with a sigh.

"If it was not clear to you, Bartleby, that is in fact part of the plan." He pushed himself to his feet, his expression speculative. "I would assume we will not get far without the notice of Eidolon, and night will afford us the best chance." He reached up to clap Adam on the shoulder almost jauntily. "Ready to ride by starlight again, Adam?"

The giant looked flatly glum about the prospect. "Not particularly, no. Especially when I consider where I will be perched throughout."

Barty was perturbed by this. "That is an odd way to describe travelling." He looked from one to the other.

Adam remained unhappy, but Jean wore that lupine grin that was part a snarl, and just close enough to either to be unsettling. "Fret not, Bartleby. The Prince of Midsummer is many things, but a boring navigator is *not* one of them." He made a gesture of dismissal. "Go on with you, and see what the others are doing. We leave in an hour."

Barty did not argue, there was no point. He sprang a quick step outside the kitchen and down the hall to a nearby door—Elanor's room. He opened it without thinking, ready to speak, but words died in his mouth.

Benji was standing to one side, with his back turned respectfully. Elanor had her arms crossed, her chin propped up by one hand as she looked speculative. And before her, awkward and fidgeting, stood Lily.

She was dressed in a white and grey dress, a summer garment from its lightness. A shawl was draped over her shoulders and a bonnet around her head, with long black gloves covering her hands and forearms, the few exposed parts of her body glinting in the candlelight. She looked anywhere but the full body mirror she stood before, shifting her weight from one foot to the other, as though cast under a spotlight and weighed down by her anxiety.

She looked up at Barty as he opened the door, and gave a startled squeak before turning away, hugging herself. As Elanor rounded on him with a blazing fury he remembered himself, and turned his back promptly, stammering apologies.

"You are *very lucky* she is dressed, Barty, or I would stab you again," Elanor snapped. "Knock next time! And apologise to Lily immediately!"

He stumbled on, facing firmly to the wall. "My sincere apologies, Miss Braithwaite!" His cheeks reddened, but part of him felt foolish for it; after all, she had not shown bare skin nor flesh in any regard, lacking such entirely. But that thought brought him up short. He realised what Elanor already clearly had; it did not matter of the specifics. What mattered was comforting a frightened girl—how she appeared, and what she was made from, was irrelevant. How she felt in that moment, however, was all that actually did.

"Jean wished to tell you we will be leaving in an hour," Barty said, with his back still turned. He heard a dismissive sniff behind him, before there was a movement of cloth.

"There," Elanor said. "I will be able to do more back at the Manor, but for now, with what we have—I think this is enough." Her tone turned cold again. "You may turn around now, both of you."

Benji was giving Barty an amused look as he turned around

to face the trio, a knowing look that was a trifle smug. Lily now wore a thigh length, long sleeved frock coat to go with her dress, alongside her shawl and bonnet. Her shoulders and neck were no longer exposed, and only her bare feet could still be seen. She stood bowed still, taller than each of them but yet trying to shrink herself down to nothingness.

Seeing her in that moment, Barty felt a pang. He was reminded a little of himself, lost and confused and bundled along by Jean into a world he did not understand. In those days he had longed for a kind word, an understanding one, and though they had come, they were few enough to keep him afloat and stave off drowning, and little more. He did not want to be the one on the other side of that experience, who offered no comfort.

"You look lovely, Miss Braithwaite," he said sincerely, his voice quiet. Her green glowing eyes lifted however, the light changing hue and softening. She unbound her hands and wordlessly performed a little curtsy. Barty, touched by the moment, gave an awkward short bow in reply. "I hope you forgive me for my intrusion."

She seemed to straighten up a little. "It is quite all right—but do please knock next time." Her voice was a little clearer, and if anything, Barty thought he could hear a smile in it, however fragile. "Please let the coachman know we shall be ready within the hour."

He bowed again and made his way out, closing the door behind him. The last thing he saw was Elanor watching him, and for once, there was a warmth in her smile. It followed after him, his heart giving an odd sort of beat, as he raced up the stairs to his room.

Chapter 14

———◆○◆———

A Flight By Moonlight

Barty did not envy Adam in this moment.

The coach of Puck was a large one. It was sturdy, well built—though the method of its making was a strange and subtle mystery—and had plenty of room internally for six people, if they didn't mind a bit of squeezing. This was not the case when one of those individuals was Adam, who took up as much space as four people on their own. Therefore, there was no possible way for them to seat themselves in the coach itself.

This was compounded by the fact that Adam was, well... Adam; enormous to the point of it being impossible to overlook, it meant they could not sit beside Puck as Barty once had, for every eye would be upon them and with it, every pointed finger. They were *too* big to ignore. And thus, the matter was turned towards the next best alternative, which was subterfuge and skullduggery—in this case, a disguise. Just not a very good one.

The result of this was that Adam was instead somewhat crushed under their luggage, laying contorted in on themselves on the roof of the coach. They made an impressively massive lump in their shape, but it was just enough of a lump as to not

345

attract attention. Barty could not see them—hidden beneath the cover of a canvas that was tied to the handling around the roof—but he could hear their long suffering sigh, as they were completely wedged in place.

Puck was not sighing. And for once, he was not laughing either. He was, however, glaring, fierce and accusatory as he was met with his newfound nemesis—Daisy, clutched in the embrace of her mistress. With arms folded he drew himself up to his full height, silver eyes flashing. "No," he said simply, his tone peevish.

Daisy, the most placid cat Barty had ever known, was not phased; she knew she had already won this fight.

"We do not have time for this, Puck," Barty pleaded. "I am sure whatever problem you have with, uh, Daisy here, is something you can work out, however"—it was a ludicrous statement, but the best he had at the present—"we have to get moving."

Puck scowled, pointing an uncomfortably long finger at the black and white feline. "I will hold you responsible for this one's crimes, Stoneborn." He growled the words at Barty, squinting, the finger remaining pointed at the cat. "A truce then, an accord, for the delightful dreaming boy with the delicious name." He jabbed a little closer at the cat, who flinched far less than her carrier did. "But I will be *watching* you."

"Yes, yes," Jean intoned with annoyance, as he offered a hand to Lily to help her into the coach. "But it is going to have to wait. I would wager our pursuers will be waiting for us the moment we exit the street."

That brought Puck up and around. "Pursuers? Some... miserable, ground crawling, dreamless worm believes that *they* will be pursuing *me?*" He shuddered, as though having touched something cold and clammy, revolted by the thought. "I? They believe that *I* am the one to be prey?" He sidled up to the window and glared once more at Daisy. "This is *your* fault somehow. I am assured of it."

Lily shied away, shifting her form so that her back faced Puck and Daisy was thus protected. Elanor drew alongside then, carrying an open wicker basket. There was a plaintive yowling as Daisy was placed inside and the lid tied shut. It was easier than the alternative, but seeing it made Puck's expression brighten maliciously.

"Regardless of who is to blame, the matter remains," Jean said sourly. "I do not think we shall get far before we are intercepted, and looking heavenwards, well—it is a cloudy night, Puck." He gestured to the scudding clouds of London. The silver-haired coachman sighed, craning his neck with a resigned expression.

"Unfortunate, but true. T'would seem I am cursed to find us an alternate route." His pensive face shifted like melting ice, turning into a wide lipped, bare toothed grin. "Do I have your permission then, to do what I must to ensure our escape? Do I get to *enjoy* myself for once, huntsman?"

Jean paused, his gaze lingering on the coach. Lily and Elanor were within, and to Barty's eye, Jean seemed more conflicted than he could ever recall seeing him. There was a look on his face of true consternation, before he steeled himself and took a deep breath. "Do what you feel is necessary, trickster—but within the boundaries of mortal reason." There was another pause as the air turned heavy with the weight of what that might mean before Jean turned around. "And by that, I mean get us to the Manor, *without* killing anyone, by direct or indirect means."

Puck's bare toothed grin turned downwards, but the teeth remained visible as he hissed through them, a sound like a sawblade grinding through flesh. He crossed his arms with a huff of disapproval and turned up his nose. "You take all pleasure from the dance, huntsman. But I shall abide." Jean seemed as satisfied as he was going to get.

"That is somewhat unexpected of you, Reynard." It was Adam's voice, spoken with an inflection of curiosity from their obscured position. Jean grunted, and shrugged without answering. He clambered inside, with Barty behind him—who paused as he did so and pulled himself up to get a look at the roof, and speak to the grand, canvas lump that was Adam.

"All right in there, Adam?"

A hurricane sort of groan greeted him from beneath the sheet. "While it is not exactly comfortable, primarily it is embarrassing—and that is saying something. Let us please be underway at the earliest opportunity, Barty. I would like to be getting on."

Puck's mad grin slid abruptly into view. "You heard the resurrected, Barty. Do be a sweet and get yourself settled—this shall be a sharp and shivering sort of journey." Barty did not argue with him, and hurried within, the coach leaping forward as the door closed.

Jean was sat with his arms folded, sunk into his coat, Lily and Elanor positioned opposite him. Elanor had a tense look on her, but Lily sat demurely, like a noblewoman might. Her immobile porcelain features, of course, did not move, but Barty felt the glow of her eyes brightened a moment when she looked over at him and gave a gentle nod, the gears and pistons that made up her neck and the interlocking plates of her spine moving smoothly. He was still not used to seeing it, but once again he reminded himself—she was a person, not an object. And it did not do to stare at her—though he did note she seemed to stare at him, in turn.

The coach plunged into the main street, the same way as it always tended to do—with haste and yet perfectly timed as to slide through whatever traffic might otherwise have obstructed the path, as though Puck moved his silent steeds to a pace that only he understood, or by the devil's own luck. But immediately he started to laugh, and Jean began to scowl as he slid in his seat to look out the window—a scowl that turned to cursing.

"Father, *please*," Elanor groaned as Lily shrank from such ungentlemanly speech. "What is it?"

"Wyrmwood, is what," Jean growled. "I expected us to get further away from the warding before they were on us, but they were waiting for us to leave."

Barty shifted about to get a look himself.

The wide street was designed for a lot of traffic. Even at this evening hour, London remained a hubbub of activity and the roads were no different, with coaches, carts, horses, and foot traffic making their way to and fro. But there were two black, unmarked wagons now coming side by side down the street at speed. Each were led by fast horses, and crewed by men of a soldierly bearing, wearing black, nondescript clothing, their faces covered. They ignored the traffic, forcing it out of their path and even off the road, and made no attempt to hide their effort of pursuit.

"They stick out like a sore thumb, don't they?" Jean said disgustedly. "No attempt at subtlety whatsoever."

"Coming from you, that is saying something." The words came out of Barty's mouth before he had the thought to stop them.

But Jean actually chuckled in agreement. He reached into his coat but rather than pulling out his pair of pistols, he produced a cardboard tube with a long wick coming from it instead, tossing it up and down in his hand. "You are quite right indeed, Bartholomew. But in the matter of audacity, these individuals shall learn something this evening." He thumped the roof then with three powerful blows. Adam groaned in annoyance, muffled but clear through the ceiling between them, as Jean raised his voice with power enough to rise above the sound of wheels crashing over cobblestone, and the panicked shouts of passersby and travellers. Puck began to cackle madly in the pleasure of the pursuit.

"Look lively there, Adam. When I take care of one, you take care of the other, won't you?" Jean called out. He turned his eye then to Lily, who was cowering in dread, with no cat to shield her as Daisy remained locked in her basket. Barty opened his mouth to reassure her, but was surprised when Jean beat her to it.

"Forgive me for this, Miss Braithwaite," Jean said with a surprisingly even tone. "This is unfortunate, but it shall be handled swiftly. Perhaps close your eyes a moment, yes?" The glowing green eyes showed hesitation, but she nodded and the glow winked out. Jean, holding the tube in one hand, reached into his coat and pulled out a packet of matches, which he handed to Barty. "Get ready to light one of these."

Barty did as he was told, but he was suspicious. "What is that, Jean?" He gestured to the tube.

The hunter gave him a face, the portrait of innocence. "A simple spot of illumination, Barty. To show our friends here the error of their ways." He looked out the window again. The pursuing carts were getting closer, their bells being rung loudly now by each to ward away travellers from the path. Jean tossed the tube up and down, gauging carefully. "They'll come up on each flank. Standard, really. Just the lack of inventiveness I expect to see from Wyrmwood, unimaginative little rodent that he is." He grunted in satisfaction. "Good."

"You really do not like that fellow, do you?" Elanor asked, her tone sardonic. Despite the unfolding situation, she looked more annoyed than excited.

Jean grunted, still watching out the window as the pursuers drew closer. "Not quite the word I would choose, daughter," Jean replied thoughtfully. "Loathe, despise, those are more akin to my sensations." He thumped on the roof again. "Right side for you, Adam. And slow down, Silver! I wish to converse with these men a moment."

Puck made an indescribable sound of displeasure, but their pace slowed. The two carts closed in, coming in from both sides. Elanor put her arms around Lily, and Barty cursed himself for feeling useless, as he wondered if he should unholster the gun he carried.

But Jean noted it. He gripped Barty by the shoulder firmly. "Light that match, lad. And be ready to close your eyes after."

Barty swallowed, then struck the first of the matches. It hissed as it ignited, bringing a Luciferian stink of sulphur as Jean took it and lit the wick leading from the tube, which blazed into terrible life of its own immediately.

The two carts were close enough to touch, the drivers of each at arms length, with men on the back preparing to climb from one moving cart to the coach. Barty could see them poised to leap before they saw the sparking light of the fuse, and panic ensued.

"The lesson in audacity they are about to learn, Bartholmew Bartleby," Jean said as he squinted, gauging, "is that I am *better at it.*" He tossed the tube out the window. It spun in the air, hovering above the charging horses with their leads already being pulled. There was a frenzied, pointless scrambling on the pursuing coach.

And the world went white.

The flare, as the tube revealed itself to be, ignited in a burst of light that blazed through even closed eyelids. It was a rather powerful one, designed to send a signal over many miles when set off. In this case it exploded about six feet in front of the cart driver and above the horses, who were both completely blinded by the blast and sent careening off the road, smashing into the mouth of an alleyway and hurling the cart—along with the men inside it—in all directions, where they were to lay groaning amidst more broken bones than was convenient to count in a hurry.

While everyone was gawking at this, Adam had settled upon

their own task. It was, in fact, shockingly easy—they thrust out one mighty hand towards the cart on the right, and reached down. The driver heard a rich voice speak—"Terribly sorry about this"—before, with a simple tug, Adam closed their hand around the closest wheel, and yanked it clean off with a movement so sure and swift that it did not register to those who might observe it. Instantly, the cart spun out of control, skidding and weaving haphazardly across the street as horses, remaining wheels, and physics fought a battle none of them were going to win. The bout was decided when it all crashed into a store front, leaving the horses broken loose and running madly. Puck's own unusually quiet steeds smoothly accelerated at just the right moment, leaving the wreckage behind them, and a state of absolute confusion riddled with near hysteria. All told, it was a grand mess.

"And you told *me* not to make a scene, hunter," Puck called down to them in a huff. Jean chuckled, his humour restored by his ability to cause mayhem, but Puck continued on, "I do however, hope you have a plan for the *other* two."

Both Barty and Jean poked their heads out of the window to follow Puck's pointing hand. They paralleled the foul-blooded Thames river now but, rapidly approaching from the southern bank, crossing a bridge to intercept them, came two more carts. They were close enough that Barty could make out the man in the lead—the glint of his oily hair left no doubt; Wyrmwood himself had come to try and capture them.

Jean looked thoroughly put out. Though he bit his tongue, he did not curse, yet the desire to do so radiated from every pore. "I shall think of something."

"Perhaps you should do so in a hurry," Barty said, a completely unhelpful addition that earned him a glare, before Jean turned his eye skyward, muttering to himself as he did so. Barty could not make out what he sought, for the clouds, while thinning, were still obscuring the sky.

But then Jean called out to Puck. "Take us north! Get us to clear sky, and evade them for now!"

Puck trilled a laugh, and that was answer enough. The coach swerved violently, sending Barty lurching out the open window. Jean caught him by his coat and dragged him in as they plunged down a new street, sending passersby scattering and screaming.

The pursuing carts shifted to intercept. The bells rang louder now with the approach, near enough to police wagons that people did not look too closely, but got out of the way in a hurry. They had been hot on the heels before the swerve, but they did not have the frightening ability to turn like Puck—to make nonsense of reality, to twist several thousand pounds of horse and coach through the air with utter disregard to physics—and so were forced to take a far wider berth and catch up.

Lily moved to the window, keeping her head low so that only her eyes passed the door lining as she peered outwards. "What do they want? Have we done something wrong?"

Barty, Elanor, and Jean exchanged looks behind her. Each of them wondering what to say, how to say it, but it was Barty who made the call. "They are after us—and after you." He was subdued as he spoke, not wishing to scare her, but feeling she deserved what truth he could offer. "I cannot say for certain what they want of you, but I—we—think they mean you harm. And we wish to protect you from it."

"But why?" Her voice trembled, doubting and unsure. She turned her head back to the trio and her bright green eyes fell on Barty as the coach raced and raged.

He felt his tongue twist a moment under the force of that inhuman stare, but he forced it to respond. "We do not know, Miss Braithwaite. But I promise you—we shall find out."

The glow dimmed, and she looked out the window again. Her gloved fingers alighted on the edge, and for a moment, Barty considered pulling her back from it before anyone could see her. But it felt immediately wrong, for reasons he could not explain.

The approaching carts were drawing closer now, finding it easier to pursue in the wake of the street clearing ahead of Puck amidst his mad race to freedom. Whipped on by a merciless hand, foaming horses brought a black carriage to cast its despairing shadow, causing Lily to give a high gasp, flinching back and covering her mouth.

Elanor took her other hand, interlacing their fingers. "What was it? What is wrong?"

The metal woman stammered, her echoing voice shaking as she pointed. "I r-recognise him. He saw me, and, and..." She shuddered, the emotion wracking a body that had no means of releasing it physically. "He was there. He was there when I woke up. He was standing over me." Her grip tightened, and Barty saw Elanor's face go white as she bit her tongue to stop the scream that must have been forming. It was not hard to see why; Elanor's fingers were discoloured, blood rushing to the tips and pale where she was held—Lily's grip was crushing her hand.

Barty acted fast. He scooped up the hamper with the angry cat off the floor between them and thrust it towards Lily, who blinked and took it, releasing Elanor's hand without realising the damage she had caused. Elanor reeled back and inhaled deeply with her tongue still held in her teeth, as Barty continued to distract. "Best you hold on to this, Miss Braithwaite. We do not want poor Daisy to be more disturbed than is necessary, yes?"

She nodded, looking down at her charge, but Barty was looking at Elanor, who met his gaze and nodded, rubbing life into her damaged hand as she exhaled. Barty was relieved. No harm done.

Jean had made no move. But he had observed, watching wordlessly throughout, with no sign of his thoughts save for the cold, hard nature of his stare. Interrogation had to wait however, as the coach swerved again, and then again shortly after. There were more bells now and more pursuers had settled in, though Barty could not tell if they were ordinary police or otherwise. At this point it did not matter.

Jean seemed to have had enough as he moved to the door and opened it, standing on the step to gaze at the pursuit, his coat whipped by the wind as he balanced in stoic observation. Puck had brought them to a more subdued part of town, with streets devoid of people, a park on one side and rows of dark buildings on the other. Jean looked upwards once more. Now, the clouds were breaking apart, thinning and wisping at the late hour. Through the haze, there was a glint of moonlight, and perhaps stars beyond that. He sighed, then barked, "Trickster! Do you as you will. Take us where the road goes not."

A low whistle, going high and then back to a low so deep that it danced among the stones and set them rolling was his answer. Jean went back into the depths of the coach, and sat with arms folded, staring off into nothing.

"What exactly are we going to do now?" Barty asked anxiously.

They were about to be cut off, forced to turn down streets to evade pursuit, but Puck was driven now, standing on his seat with the reins in one hand, the other sweeping out in a grand uplifting gesture as he began, most strangely, to sing. A song that was like music if it was made out of wind and water, turning the stagnant air fresh and bringing the scent of rain. There were words within it, old words that spoke of older mysteries, of the first spinning of the world where to sing and to speak were one and the same, and ancient things were not yet named. It made the world shudder and the air turn clear, sharp as a blade.

Jean was watching Barty, his expression unreadable as he sat. "Consider this next experience, part of your further education, Barty," he said, his voice somehow muted. The clouds broke above and moonlight streamed down upon them under the force of Puck's music. "You have seen the unspeakable, the unreal, and the strange. But now you are going to see for yourself something new."

There was a peculiar situation happening beyond the windows of the coach. The moonlight had turned hazy and bright, and the world outside had been muted by that light, rendered indistinct. The sound of the bells of the pursuing wagons had become weaker, dimmer, and was rapidly fading away. Barty wanted to look away but could not, as the world slowed to a state of thickened molasses. His mind rebelled against what his senses imparted on him so powerfully that it left him near on insensate.

"This is the impossible, Barty," Jean went on, answering a question Barty was not sure he asked. The bells were gone. The world was gone. There was nothing but the song, the glow of stars and the light of the moon, as London turned to fog. "This is the line between dreams and reality. The unexplained and the inexplicable." He smiled then, a grim, knowing smile.

The change was abrupt. The world seemed to *speed up*, all too quick and all too sudden, reality itself blurring into indistinction. There was a formless light, and sounds somehow stretched, distorting into indecipherability, a high pitched ringing at the back of the skull—before the whole thing snapped back like a rubber band pulled too far. And Puck was laughing, laughing even through the song, wild and free and dreadful.

For Barty, it felt like his entire body had been thrust through ice and into freezing water below. It *struck* the air out of him, and left him gasping and nauseous, unsure of his state. In his moment of utter discomfort, he could see that it left Elanor shaken as well, as her eyes went wide and she covered her mouth. Lily seemed unaffected, sitting still and holding the basket with her cat. If anything she seemed faintly puzzled at their distress.

Jean never stopped watching Barty. He did not even seem to blink. He finally nodded, and spoke in a distant voice. "You will get used to it."

There was a new sound now; the sound of coach wheels over gravel. The air was different, the outside clearer, the moonlight shining down on them all from above. It was when he caught the rich, pine and loam scent of a forest that Barty had the dizzying realisation that they were somewhere other than the stone-clad streets of London. Somewhere alive. Somewhere *far.*

"How?" Barty managed to croak at last.

Jean shrugged as he looked out the window. "The wrong question, lad. But only because I cannot answer it, and the one who can will not be telling you." He glanced meaningfully to the roof. Puck was still singing, in that beautiful and terrible voice, but softer now, without the world-rending weight it had borne. "The correct question," Jean continued, "is *where.*" He pointed then, and Barty saw it.

It was lit by star and moonlight, and by a single window that pulsed with the flickering flame that no doubt rested within a well fed fireplace. Atop a large hill with sheer sides, was a manor. It was closer to a castle on inspection, sturdy and strong, and it extended out over a great, still lake, upon which the pale skybound orb was reflected—a gently illuminating portal of white, the glimmering mirrored in the haunting architecture of the ancient, waiting structure. The lake was vast, and forest lined its edges, nearly encroaching on the manor itself—but with just enough distance to give the impression that they were afraid of it. It was a sleeping giant, a great behemoth at rest, and that single orange glow of one lower window took on the look of an eye, staring at the coach as it came closer.

Standing stones lined each side of the road—markers so old that wind and water had worn them down to featureless blocks. Rolling green fields that seemed well tended surrounded the place, hedged in by the forest. Barty could see that towering oaks flanked the front gate—tall, silent and mighty, older and stronger than any he had ever seen before.

"What is this place?" Barty's tone was hushed as they approached; the rattling of their impossible journey and the sight of the imposing, haunting structure had left him disorientated.

Jean chuckled, a little harshly. "*That* is the Manor—but if it had a full name, it would be the Rock of Gwyar, the ancestral home of the Society of the Hound," he intoned formally.

"This is your home?" He sounded disbelieving. The Lodge had been, to Barty's eyes, a grand and magnificent place. But this was something else; something older, and altogether more terrible. The structure did not sit in place. It *waited.*

"With all of its bloodstained stones, yes. That is my home—however unfairly earned," Jean stated sourly.

Elanor interjected at that however. "It *is* your home, and it *was* fairly earned, Father," she stated with exasperation. "There are no other hunters in England any more; no true ones at least."

Jean grunted and opened the door, standing on the step. "And yet," he grumbled, as the coach began to slow, then stopped, just as Jean leapt clear and approached the gate. "Barty, come help me with this."

Barty followed Jean's lead and hopped off, to open the great iron gate that barred the way—black iron screeched a miserable chorus as it was pushed aside. Barty happened to glance over his shoulder to Puck, who was watching him. The coachman grinned.

"My gratitude, for shifting those hateful bones from my path, dearest Barty." He winked. "I *do* hope you were not troubled unduly by your passage amongst the First roads—it was a much longer journey than the first time I made you wander the dream, was it not? Those tend to be a little, mhm... *sharper*." Barty blinked as the coachman laughed, but there were no further answers forthcoming. The coach was rolling again. Jean caught the back of it and rode at the footman's rest for the rest of the journey—Barty did the same, hauling himself up to join Jean. It gave the pair a moment to speak.

Jean glanced at him with a knowing smirk. "Someone is waiting for you here, you know," he said, a tone of mirth entering his voice. This was not reassuring. Jean normally smiled only when someone was about to be hurt.

"I have no idea who it could be," Barty replied, radiating genuine innocence, as the coach slid soft as a serpent to a stop. They were at the front door of the Manor—a series of broad granite steps leading up to a large, ironbound double door that looked more akin to a castle entrance than anything else. He hopped off, took a step, turned, and came face to face with one he had tried to forget, even though it still haunted his dreams.

It had been months since he had last laid eyes upon Cosgrove. Cosgrove the butler, who worked such a role for Jean Reynard and, presumably, for his household. Though to call the man a mere butler did him a disservice; there were plenty of other names he could be associated with, and as he looked down his hatchet-like nose, his face carved in a stony expression of frozen distaste, Barty could think of any number of them that involved murder in some fashion.

"Ah." His wintry tones withered the air with his scathing contempt. "You've somehow survived." He did not bother to try and conceal his complete disappointment, before turning back to Jean. "Very good to have you home, sir. I shall have a bath drawn and though it is somewhat past the hour, dinner shall be prepared directly." He bowed, sharp as a falling blade.

The coach came alive as people departed from it. Adam, with careful movements, was working their vast frame off the roof. Puck was slithering about, going to each of his ever silent horses as though to make sure they were remaining so. And Elanor was stepping down and holding a hand out to Lily.

Barty saw Cosgrove's eye move with cutting swiftness to this unknown factor. Jean noted it too and gestured to his daughter, who brought the mechanical girl towards the steps. "Cosgrove. This is the Lady Lily Braithwaite—she is to have a room to herself, and to be afforded any and all courtesy." His tone was neutral, but his expression was intent. The butler saw it, read it, and understood completely. He bowed to Lily.

"But of course, Lady Braithwaite," he replied in a polite, entirely well mannered tone. "Miss Elanor, would you both care to accompany me?" He gestured to the door—Adam was already there, carrying collected luggage easily with one huge arm as they pushed it open. Cosgrove was watching Lily—but there was nothing, absolutely nothing, other than professional, competent concern in his expression.

Lily's body language spoke volumes. She was shy and awkward, moving hesitantly—but Elanor remained at her side, supporting her with a nod here, and a smile there, to let the lady of brass know that she was all right. Taking Elanor's lead, Lily did her best to straighten, and nodded to Cosgrove. "But of course, Master Cosgrove. By your leave." Her strange voice only had a trace of a tremor to it.

The butler bowed again, and walked briskly through the door still held ajar by the giant. Elanor and Lily followed, with Adam taking up the rear. Jean lingered on the step, looking to Puck, who was watching the exchange with amusement gleaming in his eyes.

"You lead us on the roads of the moon and stars once again, Silverhair—I know it is not easy in the city." His tone was careful. Neither grateful nor sardonic.

The inhuman coachman laughed at that, high and clear, full of life, freedom, and edged all round in malice. "There is little I cannot *twist* and remake, given half the chance and less the time, hunter." He grinned as he went on, "Though one day you will give your little orders and I will have to decline, I am sure." The grin turned slightly feral. "An interesting evening, that will be. I would wager you dream of it—if I did not already know you did, of course." He winked then as Jean's expression turned hard, before glancing to Barty. He reached up, brushed back his hair, and flicked his wrist, bringing the long black raven feather out of the air itself. He ran it along the underside of his nose as he took a deep breath, exhaling a sigh in the aftermath, before his tone turned pensive. "But perhaps our accord may linger yet."

"Not just *our* accord, Prince of Midsummer," Jean growled, which made Puck grimace, before he masked it with a theatrical roll of the eyes and a graceful, pirouetting bow.

"Of course, of course. *Do* forgive me, master hunter—and excuse me." He bent his knees, and sprang up—executing a perfect, high backflip such as a circus performer might do, and quick as a blink, was standing once more on the coach, his arms spread amicably. "For now, I must depart to the wind, and make my rest where I am promised—there are charms to be whispered, songs to be sung, and poems to be *howled* to the sky." The coach began to roll then, with no command nor gesture, Puck remaining still where he stood, grinning all the while. "Until next you make your call." His eyes glowed like diamonds to match his too sharp teeth in the moonlight, as the coach set off into the darkness that waited for it, with Puck still standing atop it, smiling, hungry, and knowing. The gloom surrounding the Manor grounds soon shrouded all, and that gleaming wickedness with it.

"What did he do?" Barty finally asked. He had watched and said nothing, but the question remained. "How did we get here?" He looked around. "And *where* are we?"

Jean watched him, and carefully at that, considering his answer before he finally made an attempt at one. "We are a long way from where we were, and far further than the fastest coach might travel in a day. Our coachman has... abilities, Barty, afforded to him because he is of a unique nature," he said, choosing his words with care.

"I have seen *some* of what you are talking about," Barty responded with a shudder. Memories swarmed up from the darkest pit of his mind, visions of shadows edged in silver, beset with bright eyes and sharp teeth, the smell of blood amidst gurgling screams. He forced them all down. "But how?"

Jean shrugged. "I know *some* of what he can do. I don't know *how* he can manage it, not at all," he replied firmly. "But I know he can, if the moon is out and the sky is lit by stars, make a journey seem not a distance at all. That, is just one of the Tricksters *many* tricks." He grimaced. "And one of the few that seems without an unruly edge to it."

"That you know of, anyway." Barty said it without thinking about it. But it was a statement he could not help but make, for all he had seen so far of Puck, the more he came to fear him. This must have shown on his face, because Jean put a firm hard on his shoulder.

"Fear is something you bring with you, Bartholomew Bartleby. Do not do that with the Prince of Midsummer. Do not fear him, for it will give him power and opportunity over you—and he will not be able to help but take advantage of it—for that is his inevitable nature." His tone was hard, his brow furrowed. "Remember what you told me, when you fully committed to this road?"

Barty took a deep breath, and nodded. Jean was right. That fear was something he was supposed to be leaving behind. But how could he, when the more he learned of this new and terrible world, and all the awful things within it, the more that fear seemed to chase him. But he had to. He remembered the vision inside Esmerelda's wagon, and it came to him in startling clarity. He was tired of running from the dark. He straightened.

Jean nodded, a flicker of a smile that might have been approval flashing across his face. "Come then. I think it is time I took your mind off things." He turned to the door, expecting Barty to follow. "Welcome to the Manor of the Hounds, Bartholomew Bartleby," he said dryly as he stepped through the great doorway, holding it open for his assistant. "Do mind your step." Barty stepped through, as Jean continued with a dark chuckle, "There are all *manner* of things to trip you up in here."

Barty passed into the darkened maw, believing him entirely. The velvet blackness swallowed him without even bothering to chew.

CHAPTER 15

LILY

Barty did not remember falling asleep in the large, slightly dusty room which had been chosen for him. The room was quite spacious, with open windows that overlooked the grounds, and the road that they had taken to the front door of the Manor that slithered through fields until it was taken by the forest. It left little idea as to where they were in the lay of the land. Barty assumed that was the whole point.

He pushed himself awake with a grunt, blinking with confusion as he looked about. Motes of dust glittered like falling stars in the beams of sunlight breaking through the windows, showing a mostly featureless room—mostly, but not entirely. Beyond the cupboard, dressing table, and a large chest for possessions—empty when he had checked it the previous evening—there was luggage, his own meagre allowance for such with his few belongings, and a small bedstand table—upon which sat a silver tray, graced by a small plate piled with slices of toast, and a teacup.

He reached out to take a piece of the well browned and buttered toast—it was cold to the touch. The teacup also seemed to have lost its steaming quality as he picked it up to take a sip. A creak at the corner and the doorway leading into the room stole his disorientated, barely woken attention away. The door was drifting ajar ever so slightly, as though someone had peaked into the room. The same person who had left him the toast and tea?

He was confused, even baffled. In another house, he might have thought it was a ghost; in this manor he was *much* more likely to believe it was the case.

He sat there, chewing his toast and sipping his tea, eyeing the door in case it would move again. It did not do so, but he remained suspicious. The Manor had him spooked thus far... It had from the moment he had stepped inside. The place was *old*. The sort of old that had age in the air, a scent of ancient stones and wood and, trapped between them, a choking dust that was never quite swept clear. Each hidden, darkened corner carried the echo of the generations who had lived and died inside these massive walls. The floors creaked underfoot with the weight of their history, painted figures layered in varnish made dark with age watched as he passed, and he had been, above all, grateful to be inside his room—even if the comfort had been a false one. It had taken him a long time to fall asleep.

It was strange. Even with Adam walking around the Lodge back in London, and Puck dancing just outside, he had slept easily from the first night. There was something about the Lodge that felt like it welcomed him—but not here. The Manor did not welcome him—it had *waited* for him—but now it felt like it had swallowed him up into the cage of its dreadful stomach. Its ageless stones longed for his blood, to join the viscera of untold others who had died in this terrible place.

He was being irrational, he knew. But he had been rattled

by that abrupt awakening and the oddity of the open door, and he still felt uncomfortable. The hairs on his arms were raised, and he shivered. There was nothing else for it. He had to get moving.

There was little noise as he did all the things he needed to do, before tracking out into the hall. The Manor was enormous, promising dozens of rooms to explore. Barty did not feel the urge to peek about, however, for he could but guess what was in each of them, and his imagination filled the gaps with dreadful notions. He was dimly aware that he was in the western wing—it was capped by a large tower at its end, and held all the guest rooms on its several floors. The opposite end was where the rest of the household were staying, as well as seemingly everyone else.

He knew it was Cosgrove who had put him in this room, away from everyone else, to isolate and leave him bereft. The man had not liked Barty from the moment he had laid eyes upon the beggar boy at his door. Barty, for his part, remained terrified of the butler since their first inauspicious meeting, regardless of the fact that Cosgrove had never harmed him.

As he started to explore the corridors of the Manor, he realised that was not exactly reassuring. If Cosgrove meant Barty ill, he would never have known it—or anything else ever again. Jean's butler had the look of knives and shallow graves about his person, a look Barty had known before, and it had been as true then as it was now.

But now he was wandering the Manor. There was no one around, no one to guide him, and when he tripped slightly on a rumpled corner of a rug, he took stock of his surroundings as he regained his balance. The hall was long and quiet, lined with suits of armour who stood guard with swords and spears. There were statues, and paintings with unfriendly faces that judged him at every step. He crossed a hallway that had the entrance he had passed to enter the Manor on one side, with another great doorway leading deeper within to his other. He pushed at it, but it did not move. Considering that route foiled, he instead followed the darker corridor deeper into the eastern wing. Still, he could hear nothing. But despite that he could *feel* something, a much more tangible presence now, a sensation of eyes boring a hole between his shoulders, letting him know that something, or someone, was near.

There was a pressure in the floor beneath his feet, a sensation that a weight was pressing down on the carpet nearby, like a current flowing up his feet. He had felt it too many times in his life to ignore it. And so, blindly, he opened the first door that he came to, and stepped across the threshold in an effort to escape, the door clicking shut behind him.

All thoughts he might have had about being followed flew right out of his head and through the glass skylight above as he took in a new and terrible wonder.

At the Lodge, he had come to enjoy his time in the basement. It was a workshop and a storage combined in one useful place—it had everything he could have imagined a monster hunter would need to pursue their terrible endeavors. Standing here with his back pressed against the door, he realised it was but a pale shadow of what he could *not* imagine, and that was now well and truly before him.

The room was huge and, while open, had several floors

dedicated to the craft—there was a prominent forge against one wall, but the interior held an astonishing array of racks and tools, of machinery and science. A laboratory took up the entire upper level, which was accessible via a spiral staircase to one side, beneath which were cabinets, lathes, anvils, and hammers. Barty felt dizzy trying to take it all in. Whatever an individual could need to create something, to forge or weld, to concoct or brew, it was all here. There were benches with half completed works upon them—mostly firearms, from what Barty could tell. Pieces of the heavy double barrelled rifle that had been shattered during the encounter with Jekyll were there, on a table all of its own. But that was not what drew Barty's eye.

Laid out on one of the larger tables was a suit of armour. It appeared to be the armour of a knight, but different—thicker, and clearly heavier, made with straps to hold it in place. It had a somewhat cruder look to it than the refined suits of metal that he had already seen, but this seemed somewhat deliber- ate. It covered less of the body than plate armour might—the torso and head were well guarded, but less so on the limbs. He reached out to touch the bulky, bucket-like helmet when someone spoke at his shoulder.

"Making yourself at home, I see?"

It was Cosgrove who spoke. Barty did not recognise the voice as much as he did the tone—cold as death, and wishing murder upon this particular listener. Cosgrove, having passed noiselessly into his workplace with the stealth of a trained murderer, paid little heed to the floundering of his struck audi- ence, as Barty tried to pick his shattered nerves off the floor. "I would assume that you are used to being in places you do not belong, being as you are a *journalist.*" He spoke the last word with the same inflection one might use for a drunkard, or sewer cleaner.

"You shall have to clarify that somewhat, Mister Cosgrove," the baffled Barty said, as he dusted himself off mentally.

The butler's lip quivered into near a sneer, but he went on, his tone disdainful, "I see you are taking note of the bullet proof armour I am working on." He tapped the heavy breastplate of steel, the blackened metal making a dull sound. "Inspired by an astounding tale from Australia, of all places—a man by the name of Edward Kelly. Affectionately known as Ned." He raised an eyebrow at Barty who shook his head—he had not heard the name.

Cosgrove looked somehow even more disappointed as he went on, "He was a criminal, who went to war with the local—and seemingly quite corrupt—constabulary. Surprisingly, he and his gang almost won, and did so using suits of armour similar to this." He tapped the armour again. "I was seeing if I could refine the process."

"I would bloody well hope so," Jean said, and Barty jumped again. The hunter walked through the door that Cosgrove had left open while hunting Barty down in the workshop. He strode in now with a businesslike expression, barely glancing around the room as he focused on Barty. "It is still too heavy by far."

Cosgrove scowled faintly. "If you want it to absorb heavier rounds, I have little other clue on how to achieve such a thing," he said testily. "Besides, you're a strong fellow, Master Reynard. I am sure you'll manage it, unless living in London has softened you up somewhat."

Jean chuckled. "You *are* in ill humour today, Cosgrove. I've never known you to be so snappy." He glanced to Barty. "Towards me, anyway," he corrected.

"You never brought my Delilah to me in pieces before, either—nor have you left my family and myself in the dark as to your goings on for quite so long without message nor news, and—" Cosgrove cut himself short and sighed, before he straightened and got his tone back under control. "Forgive me, sir," he managed, exhaling. "I understand it has been difficult to send word, and you could give no warning of your upcoming arrival, but—"

"But I should have kept you better appraised, regardless of goings on," Jean finished for him in a subdued tone. "I do apologise, old friend. Things have been difficult, but it is no excuse."

"I trust someone has not been making matters *more* difficult for you in my absence, sir?" Cosgrove was eyeing Barty as he spoke, who withered under the butler's razor sharp glare, but Jean was shaking his head. Barty quailed and wondered if he was going to be stabbed with the blunt end of a nearby chisel.

"Quite the opposite, in fact. The lad has been doing better than I expected."

Barty was surprised, and felt a faint swell of pride to hear such praise. Unfortunately it appeared that this showed on his face, and thus Cosgrove was obliged to burst the bubble of self-satisfaction before it swelled overlarge.

"Somewhat better than entirely useless then, I take it?" he said in a frosty, sour tone. His eyes narrowed as he sniffed contemptuously at Barty.

Jean chuckled again despite himself, holding out a hand with thumb and forefinger about an inch apart. "Fractionally so, Cosgrove. Fractionally so. However"—he reached out to clap a hand on Barty's shoulder then, firmly and possessively, as Barty wilted entirely—"he also does not have time to be interfering in your workshop. I have need of him." He went to pull Barty along, but the young man resisted then, on an impulse.

"Pardon me, but if you do not mind, Mister Cosgrove... forgive me, for intruding on your workplace. I truly did not mean to. I was quite lost."

Jean paused at that, exchanging a look between the two, his expression mysterious. The butler bristled a moment at Barty's words, his eyes wary, but he relented, giving a curt nod. "Be sure to ask permission first, next time." His tone was frosty, but Barty seized the moment.

"Then I would like to do so now, if I may—I am very curious in learning about your work, if only to observe. May I do so, in the future?"

The butlers stare remained cold, but caught Jean's eye before he replied stiffly, "I shall consider it, yes. I will think on it."

Barty nodded, and answered with a slight bow. Jean gave a grunt that might have been of approval, then steered Barty towards a door to the left of the one he had come through—one quite large and grand. As he did so, he spoke out of the corner of his mouth. "What was *that* about?"

"Well," Barty responded awkwardly. "I rather think if we are going to be working together, it is high time I made an effort to know him better, don't you think?"

Jean grinned, but there was something wicked in the gleam of his eye. "Oh, that *will* be something to see. However, we do not have time for it at present. Someone is waiting for us." And with that, he pushed the door open before him, and Barty was made to gasp once more.

Jean carried on into the great, vaulted hall before him, before he paused to look back at the dumbstruck Barty. A knowing sort of realisation came to his face, and he nodded. "I tend to forget this is how people react to his place." He raised one hand and swept it across. "Welcome to the Hall of the Oak, Bartholomew Bartleby."

The roof was more than a hundred feet above his head. Sunlight streamed through the great glass and iron windows that both lined the arched roof and the walls. Four floors ringed the centre hall, and upon each were rows and rows of over-flowing shelves to make up a tremendous library. Thousands upon thousands of leather-bound tomes and more, a collection of knowledge, of art, and mystery as well, each one promising wonders and new horizons. And at the heart of it all, was a tree.

The expanse of the hall was dominated by a vast, ancient tree; petrified, turned almost to stone, its straining frozen branches reached outwards, almost to the ceiling and near to each of the outer tiers. It thrust out of the stone floor of the hall itself, its surface glossy with wear. The tree was long dead but it seemed more akin to a statue than a mere corpse, a monument to something long past.

Before the mighty tree were comfortable couches and cof-fee tables aligned, to provide space for a whole crowd of peo-ple so inclined to take in the sights. At the moment however, there were but three, gathered in a small group where each had enough space between them to be each of them respectable. Adam was lounging upon the ground with one knee raised and the other leg stretched out before them. On one of the couches, dressed once more in her utilitarian clothes was Elanor. And between both of them, sat demurely and with her head bowed, was Lily, dressed elegantly in the clothes that had been provided for her.

Not for the first time did Barty struggle with her doll-like figure; an embodiment of the elegant, expensive plaything of a wealthy child wrought large on the world, and as still and seemingly as fragile, her face frozen in the perpetual pale, benign smile. She kept her face lowered, but Barty could see her hands working slightly, rubbing over her knuckles pensively, the only hint of her anxiety.

"There you are, Barty," Elanor said with a hint of reproach. "We were wondering where you had gotten to."

Barty was unable to hide his surprise as his brows lofted upwards. "I was expected?"

Elanor frowned. "Of course you were. Lily told you, did she not? She insisted on bringing you breakfast to inform you—do not tell me you were not paying attention?" She narrowed her eyes dangerously.

Barty saw Lily look away, her hands clutching her knees tightly as if embarrassed. Barty recalled his cold breakfast, and his imagined encounter with a ghost—having discerned who it must have been, he quickly leapt to a conclusion, and then in so doing knew what he had to say.

"Oh. Of course—I am sorry, do forgive me," he said apologetically to all gathered. "Miss Lily explained, but I was entirely turned around and completely lost."

Elanor rolled her eyes and Adam chuckled. But Lily stiffened, her head turning around to Barty, her glowing eyes flaring beneath unblinking lashes in her sudden curiosity. He met her stare, and without knowing why, he nodded with the smallest smile, remaining silent. She jerked a little, and pulled her eyes away, yet their glimmer seemed, to Barty, to be grateful. But he could not help but wonder why Lily had been watching him. Whatever the reason was, he would not embarrass her further.

Jean was now the one observing him however, and there was, in that dark stare, nowhere to truly hide. He gave a grunt, and then, with arms crossed behind his back, he strode to stand before Lily, towering over her as he spoke firmly. "With all that out of the way, I do believe it is time we conversed plainly about matters, Miss Braithwaite. We have a great many questions—and while I am sure you do as well, we shall only have answers for them once ours are fully realised." He turned, sitting opposite her on the edge of the couch and leaning forward, clasping his hands together with his elbows resting on his knees—poised, intent, and tense. "Where would you like to start?"

Adam stirred. "Are you sure that this is a good idea, Jean? Lily has been through a great deal, and has scant had time to rest." Their voice was deep, and worried. Elanor shifted a little closer to Lily at that, reaching out with one hand to rest it on her shoulder. Barty, for the moment unsure of himself, took seat on a couch of his own that was between the two groups—facing both parties in a sort of neutral territory of his own.

"I do," Jean said firmly. "I am unsure of the time we might have—if some variable or problem might yet intervene if we delay. In truth, I am unsure of *anything* at present, and require illumination. This means, however regrettably, that Miss Braithwaite must be interrogated, however unkind it might make me. But until I am sure I can take my time, I must act as though I cannot."

"Do you not think you are being overly abrupt, Father?" Elanor said acidly. "I assumed this meeting was to teach Lily about the Manor." She flicked a glance to Barty, and grimaced. "Your assistant as well, I suppose." Her tone was frosty. "This sort of thing can surely wait, regardless of your fears—you should not scare Miss Braithwaite so."

"I can speak for myself." Lily's voice was small, but for all of its softness there was nevertheless something firm in it. Elanor and Adam both blinked, taken by surprise. But Barty saw Jean's lips twist into a faint, triumphant smile.

"Are you sure...?" Elanor's voice softened as she spoke to Lily, dropping the hand on her shoulder as she drew closer.

Lily nodded firmly, twisting her fingers together with a faint click of brass and porcelain. "It would be a relief to finally talk about this. But..." Her voice wavered into doubt. "I am not sure where I should begin."

"I tend to find that the very beginning, no matter how long it might take, is the best place," Barty said, bringing all eyes to him—all questioning. But he was only looking at Lily as he went on, "I think it is fair to say that each of us will be as patient as need be, to hear any and all words you might say,

Miss Braithwaite."

Shyly, she looked up at him. Whatever it was she saw in Barty's face in that moment seemed to give her strength, and she straightened up, nodding her head faintly to him, before she began to speak.

"You told me that you spoke to my father," she said slowly, to which Elanor nodded wordlessly. Lily went on, gaining confidence, "When I kept taking ill, he gradually became aware that my illness was... chronic, in nature." She frowned. "Eventually, he took me out of the hospital I kept returning to, and kept me at home instead, to better take care of me."

"We saw," Jean affirmed with a grimace.

Elanor nodded at that, her own tone turning dark. "We saw that *beastly* cage he kept you in for all those years—it was ghastly, and he was uncaring and cruel for doing so—"

"He was *never* cruel," Lily interrupted sharply, a fierce note coming to her voice. "Never. Not to me." She glared at Elanor, who blinked in surprise at this sudden anger. before Lily seemed to ease down. "Though... it must seem like that to others. And I cannot pretend I did not resent what my life became—but it was not his fault." She fell silent, sinking into herself once again.

Barty exchanged looks with the others, each betraying bafflement—save for Adam, who, instead, simply looked sad. "Perhaps then, you should explain it from your point of view—tell us your experience with Lord Braithwaite, Lily." Barty used the same gentle tone that had worked the first time.

It worked again now, as the anxious Lily made a small sound like a sigh, and continued, "My father spent every day with me that was possible. He took every measure he could to make sure I would not get worse. He helped prepare my meals, he educated me, and did everything he could to keep my spirits up. He was fighting whatever was wrong with me. We both were." She turned her burning gaze to the ground, but there was a softness to that fire. "He used to read me books, giving voices to all the characters. He... he was not very good at it. But he did his best. And when he was not doing that, he was studying my symptoms, writing things down, comparing them to other research—it was all very confusing to me, but he did his best to explain his research as he went."

"He... never discovered what your illness was?" Jean sounded quietly surprised.

Lily shook her head. "No. He described it as something that would change, shift into something else whenever he thought he had revealed the answer. It baffled him. And I was not strong enough to undertake surgeries, so..." She did not finish, but returned to the defense of her parent. "He would regularly fall asleep at his desk in my room. He did not mean to, just like he would forget to eat sometimes, but..." She raised her head to give Elanor a firm look. "Please do not ever claim my father did not care again, Miss Reynard. He cared very much."

Elanor met her stare, but relented with a frown. "Forgive me, Miss Braithwaite. The impression I had of your father was a rather more... severe person. I apologise for having the wrong idea about him." Her words were measured, and Barty wondered how much of her apparent change of heart was true—something told him Elanor was simply being careful.

The machine woman, however, relented, and lowered her

glowing eyes once more. "But all that aside—I assume you want to know how I... how this happened." She awkwardly held both of her hands out, staring at them as she flexed her fingers. "And I am sorry to say, I do not have much in the way of answers."

It was Jean who spoke, and Barty could not help but notice that, for once, the huntsman's tone was subdued, the usual snarl easing out of his words. "All you need to tell us, Miss Braithwaite, is what you *can* tell us. What did you... see? What did you experience?"

Her unnatural gaze settled on him, then shifted away, the lenses and irises of her glass orbs shifting to refocus on some distant point in time and memory. "I remember having tea with my mother," she said quietly. "Father was away for the afternoon, and on those days my mother and I would often take tea together." The light of her eyes softened, as though remembering brought a warmth back to her. "Mother was never very good at making tea, but it was a private time for just us, and she would tell me of the local news. She made me feel like I was still part of the world." She shook her head to dismiss the thought. "I felt very tired then, and I must have fallen asleep not long after—I often do, you see." A pause. "Or at least, I did. When I woke up everything was... different..." The gleam in her eyes darkened. A sort of weight fell upon the room; a note of portent, of a rising memory so terrible it cloaked all it fell upon with its dread and awful mass.

"Miss Braithwaite." Jean's interdiction was firm, and cut through the sudden silence like a blade. "While none of us here want to make you relive the circumstances of what led you to this—we also have no choice. It is important that we know what happened next."

"Why?" Lily's reply was ragged and raw. "Why do you need to know?"

"Because what we do not know could be dangerous for many," Jean replied steadily. "Because what you know may shed light on what has happened to you—and may happen still."

She stared at him, the fire behind her glass eyes flaring. "What would you have me say? That I awoke in a... terrible, strange place that I had never seen before? That I could hear screaming—my voice, screaming, as I woke?" She tore her burning gaze away and looked down at her hands. "I could *feel* everything and *nothing* all at once, and... and I ran. I could hear people shouting, and running, and there were lights and sounds, all loud and confusing and everything felt wrong, so wrong, and I was screaming and I... and I..." She trailed to a halt, clutching one hand to her chest.

"Something broke." She closed her fists with a sound of grinding metal. "I ran until I could not bear it any longer, and realised I had no idea where I was. I wandered and I... I wanted to go home. It had been so long since I had been outside. I stumbled down alleyways and hid myself from people, and tried to find the streets I could remember from my window." She clutched at air for a moment. "I found it—home, the place I had been staring out of for years and years and wanted to be anywhere else, but when I got there, I could not bring myself to go inside. I could not bear to... to *see* them look at me when I look like... I look like..." Her words failed her, leaving her bereft as she looked down at her hands, the metal fingers spreading wide. Her voice came again, softer, but there was something terrible in it as she spoke.

"Are you going to help me?"

The raw note in her voice was stronger now. Elanor was easing away from her. Even Jean was tense, and Adam had moved to their knees. Barty could sense why. The air around Lily was *charged*, like lightning was about to strike, like it had been in the cellar when the storm had erupted from Adam. As her emotions grew wild, as her voice grew stronger, there was a swelling danger around her. Much as Adam had stopped Elanor and Barty cold with their anger during their ill-fated sparring, this was a stark and terrible reminder that the girl before him *was not* what she behaved like. She was something more, and her emotions were barely contained by a body that could smash through walls and rip ironbound doors off their hinges without even trying.

"How do you want us to help you, Lily?" Barty asked, trying to keep the trembling out of his voice.

She whirled on him, standing abruptly, her eyes burning like twin green suns. "I want you to *fix* this! I want you to fix *me*!" She gestured at herself in her helpless fury. "Do you know what this is like? Do you? I cannot feel *anything*!" She wrung her hands together, giving a wretched, helpless sob. "I used to beg to feel no pain, I used to pray to God for Him to hear me and take it away—I would bite my fingers until they bled to stop myself from screaming, and now, at last, I can feel *nothing*. No cold, no warmth, no hunger. No softness. No touch." She brought one foot down with a nearly spasmodic movement and there was a sharp retort, but she carried on without seeming to notice. "I try to take a breath to calm myself, and when I cannot draw one I feel like I am *drowning* over and over. God heard me, and for my hubris in my pleas He has *punished me*." She broke at the last, covering her face with her hands.

Barty took a step towards her, but Elanor was faster, reaching out as though to embrace Lily with a gesture of comfort. A vast hand stretched out to halt her progress. As Lily stood, her face covered and shaking by soundless sobs without tears, Adam pointed downwards, to the spiderweb of cracked tile and stone beneath Lily's foot. Her thoughtless stamp had shattered stone. Her embrace might well have done the same to fragile bones. Elanor stopped cold, her arms lowering.

But Barty did not.

He walked the short distance towards the stricken girl, and reached out with one hand, setting it to her shoulder. A shudder ran down his spine as he felt metal—but metal that was strangely warm, that had an energy to it that seemed to writhe just beneath his fingertips. It was marvelling, and frightening, but he ignored it for the moment. She seemed to sense the touch, and stiffened, peering between her fingers, the glow flaring, then fading, as she slowly lowered her hands.

"We *are* going to find a way to help you, Miss Braithwaite," he said. "Even if we do not understand, we will find a way to do so. We will find out what happened to you—and why."

Adam gave a rumbling sigh, and nodded. "Mister Bartleby is telling the truth, Miss Braithwaite," they said with a firm note. They looked unhappy as they said it, their gaze lowered, and that misery brought with it a question.

"Except to do that, we must go to the beginning of things.

The *true* beginning." It was Jean this time, his eyes on Adam and watchful. "We must examine the research of the first true resurrectionist, and the most brilliant mind of the Society—and the most dangerous." He grimaced. "I am sorry, Adam. If there was another way, you know that we would."

Barty looked between them, baffled, as the pair exchanged looks. "Who are you speaking of?" he finally asked. Adam looked away, their expression twisting yet further.

"We are speaking of a former member of the Society of the Hound, who used to work within this very manor. Who taught and guided an entire generation of hunters—my mentor included," Jean said grimly. "Mary Wollstonecraft Shelley."

"My maker," Adam finished, their expression filled with the quiet, deep regret of grief. "And in all respects save one, my mother as well."

Jean pushed himself to his feet, adjusting his coat. "Well. There's no time like the present. We had best be making our way." He turned on one booted foot and marched off towards the far end of the hall.

Barty looked to the others, still baffled. "Where are we going now?"

Adam was watching Jean's stride, their expression still conflicted, but it was Elanor who answered. "To the Vault. Where all the secrets are kept." Her tone was leaden, as though with dread. "To the Vault of the Veil."

Chapter 16

The Vault of the Veil

The far end of the hall had but a single door at the head of a double staircase and it was, Barty could not help but notice, a rather forbidding looking thing. Where the Hall of the Oak was a place of warmth and light, this massive door was black, wrought entirely of iron. It was not featureless however—it was a grand and dramatic creation with a relief depiction of a knight in armour, driving a great spear through an enormous dragon. The door itself was a good twenty feet tall, a vast monstrosity on mighty hinges that did not look like it could be moved by any amount of effort. However, Barty was quite aware that this was not an obstacle to Adam, who was now approaching it.

Jean was at their elbow, reaching into his coat and pulling out a large, ancient set of heavy keys, jangling like the chains of the damned. Barty, Elanor, and Lily lingered in their wake. Barty happened to glance out the tall window to the right, and was surprised to see that they were both above and at the edge of the lake shore—this part of the Manor was built upon a great finger of rock that thrust out over the lake.

"I rather hoped that I was wrong, and we would not have to resort to this," Adam said, their tone unhappy.

Jean grunted as he turned one key, and then another, scowling. "Of course you did. And you should not have to." He turned the next lock, then a third after that, each keyhole cunningly hidden in the relief upon it. There was a series of loud, booming clanks behind the wall of iron, to which Jean nodded, then turned to Adam. The giant sighed and moved forward. Vast hands settled on the centre of the great portal, and pushed, dividing the door down the middle with an ear-splitting groan of rust and wretched, pitted iron.

Jean gave a grim sort of smile as the darkened abyss before them was broken open. He glanced back. "We would likely spend hours greasing the hinges to get in if Adam was not here." He reached up, patting the miserable Adam on the shoulder, and stepped inside, his attitude strangely energetic. Adam reluctantly followed, the two vanishing into the darkness, swallowed up by the gloom.

Barty held his ground a moment, and noted he was not alone in his hesitation. Elanor shuddered, but he halted himself from offering her support, not least because she would despise it. Lily, however, took a casual step forward into the dark, and he could not help but speak up. "Careful, Miss Braithwaite. We cannot see where we are going, after all."

The glowing gaze of her eyes turned on him then and tilted with a faint air of curiosity. "It is dark for you?" She glanced from Barty to Elanor, then lowered her head. "I keep forgetting. I am sorry." She sounded crestfallen, in such a way that Barty felt immediately ashamed. He tried to smile, to reassure her, as he summoned his courage and passed through the doorway.

The air beyond was stale, stagnant, with a metal tang to it

that tasted like blood on the tongue. And it was cold—very cold—with no windows. The light coming from the opening behind them seemed to be sucked into the stone beneath their feet, and he blinked as his eyes tried to adjust, but failed.

"Do not trouble yourself with our limitations, Miss Braithwaite. My lack of awareness is my curse." He tried to sound lighthearted about it, as Elanor brushed past him to stand resolute beside the shadowy figure.

As she did so, Lily looked back to Barty, her stare lingering in a way that made him feel awkward. She looked away again, her voice somehow more distant than usual as she spoke. "It was like this when I awoke. I suppose it must have been dark, but I could see quite clearly." She reached up to touch her painted brow. "There was so much happening. It was... very confusing." A pause, as she met his eyes with a quiet intensity. "I remember though. I saw Adam, and they were reaching for me, like they could... see me." She glanced into the darkness, likely at that very giant, then back to Barty, her eyes focusing once more. "I saw you. I *knew* you."

"Me?" Barty blinked at that, exchanging an equally mystified look with Elanor as Lily went on.

"You were on a table, with Jean. There was... there was blood on your face. It was like you were looking at me, but through me, at something else—and then... and then..." She stumbled to a halt in her words, her gaze turning dim. "I do not understand. But I *knew* you. I knew your name."

The gloom suddenly felt far more oppressive to Barty, as all eyes lingered for a while on Lily, unanswered questions looming large in thoughts. But they were banished by the hissing strike of a lit match.

Jean was some distance away and above them, the small flare illuminating his position on a raised staircase that had been invisible, and yet he had tread upon with full confidence. Staring down at them, he spoke.

"You are describing the moment that Adam entered his torpor." Without turning his head, he tossed the match to his side. Immediately, a far greater flame exploded into life, burning hot and bright and illuminating all that the fearsome dark had concealed.

Barty, Elanor, and Lily were at the base of an ascending stairwell. The architecture was exceedingly old, akin to what Barty had seen in classical cathedrals—massive stone, and seemingly far more ancient than the Manor itself to which it was attached. Jean stood with Adam beside the blazing brazier that he had lit, and behind him, the staircase ascended on after a short terrace. There were two doors; one at the level that Jean stood, and one further up at the top of the steps. It was an unusual bit of structure, but Barty was gathering this was an unusual place.

Jean turned to the door behind him, set into a recess in the staircase that continued up on each side of it. His voice echoed with a mausoleum timbre as he went on, "This implies that between you, however improbable, there is a connection."

"I barely remember it myself." Adam's voice was deep, their voice troubled. "It was like a dream—at least as they are described to me—but waking. I remember reaching out to touch... something." He looked back to Lily who, with Elanor and Barty, ascended the stairs. "I wish I had answers to what happened in that moment. But I can at least vouch that what you say is the truth."

"Answers are why we are here, Adam," Jean said with a frown. "Though be patient with me, this door will require more than strength." He approached the portal before him carefully.

Barty could see more clearly now with the light from the brazier. The door was black iron, pitted and worn, and seemingly of a single solid piece. Great hinges grasped each side, and there was, to his eye, no hole for a key. It was a rather forbidding doorway to say the least, but there was more to it than that. Something about it spoke to patient inevitability; as though it knew it had to do nothing but wait as a coiled serpent might do, assured that its prey would come to it.

"What is this place? What is the Vault of the Veil?" Barty asked finally, his voice subdued. Adam and Elanor exchanged a look, but it was Jean who spoke, as he ran a careful hand over the iron door.

"The Vault of the Veil is where the Society keeps all of the things it deems forbidden, Mister Bartleby," he said with a grim satisfaction. "Knowledge that can drive one mad. Magic that can damn you with its mere understanding. Weapons that have purposes so dark that they have a will of their own. And other horrors that need to be locked away." He glanced back, a gleam in his eye caught by the firelight that was far from pleasant. "Curses built of blackest night. Spirits bound and caged where they can do no harm to others, for there can never be enough suffering to satisfy them. Old Gods and Devils that forgot how to die. They all end up here, in one fashion or another." He grinned, showing far too many teeth, clearly enjoying the dread that Barty felt running down his spine at his words.

"Mary Shelley was someone who once had my role within the Society," Adam explained quietly, as Jean went back to work. "She was the genius, the scientist and, frankly, an incredibly accomplished magician as well."

Barty could not help but note the tone of Adam as they spoke. There was sorrow in their voice, the sort of sorrow that only grief could bring. A raw, open wound behind the words that bled afresh with every syllable. And yet the giant continued, "She held many other interests, and kept some very... dramatic company." They coughed.

Jean, tactful as ever, barked a laugh. "She found Lord Byron's hedonism *boring*, which is akin to saying Caligula, the Mad Emperor of Rome, was not all that interesting at parties." This earned them a glare from Adam.

"Yes, well—she had different tastes than her husband. Now, should you not be working on opening that?" Adam replied frostily. Jean gave a nasty chuckle, and continued to make odd gestures at the door—pressing at certain spots with a light touch, pausing at others, and muttering to himself.

"Regardless," Adam said stiffly, but some of the sadness was at least out of their voice. "She made many discoveries, and learned many things—breakthroughs in the understanding of alchemy and scientific application with esoterica that had been either lost or never learned, setting new standards and opening new pathways for the Society, though it was somewhat larger in those days." Adam frowned then, looking away. "At one point, however, she had all of her knowledge locked away, by her request. She made sure that it was only to be kept under the provision that it would be used for the right reasons."

Barty found this answer somewhat lacking, and thus with what tact he could muster, he asked, "What happened, that she felt that she had to hide all she had done?"

Adam remained silent, refusing to look at Barty, strangely vulnerable as they did so. The moment dragged on, until at last, Elanor sighed from behind Barty, and spoke quietly. "Adam is what happened, Barty."

The giant sighed softly, and met Barty's eyes with difficulty. Their corpse face, though mostly impassive, nevertheless had the look of a pain concealed, buried deep, even as Adam gave a sad smile. "Indeed so," they said with a heavy sigh. "Lady Shelley managed something that had never been done before; something sanctioned only to God, as the priests would tell it—she created life itself. She created me."

"She showed everyone what was possible, but it was too much for most," Elanor said grimly.

Adam nodded, their eyes on the fire of the brazier. "She crafted an abomination, in the eyes of any sane observer. An unholy blend of the unwilling dead, unable to protest her defilement and profane machinery, wrought together with a means that was forbidden, knowledge that no one dared to seek, and that she kept hidden. Even from me." Adam did not seem to even note their presence in that moment, the flames barely reflected in their eyes, their inhuman, frightful features brought into sharp and terrible relief, shadowed and dreadful. Barty could not help but shudder, even if it shamed him.

But it was Lily who stepped forward timidly, and reached out one delicate hand of wrought brass to rest on Adam's bicep.

She was looking up at Adam, and when she spoke, her voice was gentle, conveying an emotion her porcelain face could not.

"I have scarce known your company, Adam. But that does not make my words to you any less true." Her metal fingers shifted, squeezing what lay beneath with care. "You are none of those things you called yourself—you are no abomination."

Adam's head lowered, their long black hair falling to one side, their expression twisting but unyielding in its ability to conceal what emotion was being truly felt. "And what would you say that I am then, if none of those things? What would you call me, if not that?"

"The only thing that truly matters in this world," she answered firmly. "You are *kind.*"

Adam grimaced and was about to speak, perhaps to refute, but Jean cut through the moment, his mocking tone gone as his voice turned hard. "James used to say the same, or at least, to the same effect." Elanor and Adam froze at that, but Jean did not turn, standing with his hand pressed against the blackened iron. "You remember, do you not, Adam? And if I recall, you never thought the words of my son useless."

There was a pause, as though Adam was rearranging the tide of their thoughts, guiding the flow elsewhere as they straightened up. "No. They never were." They spoke with a finality of agreement, and they shifted back to Lily, who remained amidst her meek confusion, and carefully patted her hand as they bowed their head.

"Thank you, Miss Braithwaite. And forgive me, for doubting myself. I will remember this faith you have placed, should it come again—it shall ward such thoughts away in future." The warmth had returned to Adam's voice, and Lily gave a demure bob of her head. Jean, having glanced back, gave a nod. For a moment, Barty could have sworn he saw him smile.

As Jean worked, Barty looked ahead to the stairway that continued on past the recess. There was another door at the height of the stairs, set amidst white pillars. Barty glanced to Elanor and pointed. "What is up there?"

She shrugged. "The chapel. But we seldom venture into it."

Barty frowned, giving the place a wary look. "But why is that? I mean—" He stopped as Jean swore softly.

"May I be allowed to concentrate? This is much more difficult than it seems."

Barty was contrite, mumbling an apology. Jean grimaced, then turned back, shaking his head. With a deep breath he straightened his shoulders, and his fingers pressed down on the iron. He spoke something then—something Barty could not grasp, a word, or a series of words, that seemed to muffle in the air itself, as though they came from underwater or from behind a wall. It made his skin prickle, his spine twitching as he hunched in on himself as though to ward off a blow. He could not help but wonder that his mind had simply *rejected* the sound itself, and refused to hear it.

The iron twisted around Jean's hand. Warping like liquid, it wrenched into a new shape, the substance, for a moment, turning malleable. It was strangely painful to look at, as Jean turned his hand with an implacable movement and brought with it a screech of shifting metal that matched the sight all too well. It was impossible, and from the way Jean was braced, quite difficult. He pulled his hand back sharply as though burned, and the iron door slowly swung inwards.

Barty had known all kinds of darkness in his life; most were innocent, almost comforting in their quiet—the gentle shadow of oblivion before sleep when blankets and bedclothes gave one the soothing delusion of sanctuary, an armour against dreams and other terrors—but there were others, too. The kinds in alleyways where the stain of old nightmares blended with the mire of forgetting. The unforgiving absence where there was supposed to be light, but instead, there was only the stillness of shapes without form. There was the dark beyond the doorway in the orphanage, that bided its time before it slid inside, liquid and venomous, hungry and merciless.

There was a new darkness beyond that door; one that breathed, the kind that waited. It was a void that hungered, an abyss so great that it had a pull all of its own to drag you into its depths—and once you realised you had gone too far, it closed in on you, and then there was neither screaming nor God to save you.

Jean stood at the threshold, staring into the void, staring it down until it blinked. As he did so he spoke without turning his head. "Follow behind me. You will see doors as we descend. You may hear sounds, or see things. They cannot harm you. Fear is something you bring with you, if you come down here." He paused, then turned his head, frowning. "You do not have to, should you wish otherwise. All of you."

Barty opened his mouth, but held his tongue. Adam was the one who spoke instead, their voice firm. "I will come with you. My maker would have wished for it."

Elanor nodded. "I will follow also—but only if Miss Braithwaite wishes to accompany us."

The automaton shrugged her shoulders gently, her eyes dimming behind her mask. "I am unsure what there is left to be afraid of, at this point," she said with surprising clarity. "I will go with you."

That left only Barty. He sighed as all eyes turned towards him, and gave a helpless shrug. "You truly expect me to turn craven and run back now?" He could not keep a note of peevish irritability out of his voice, but it was a mask for his dread. "Let us be about this."

Jean gave a harsh chuckle, and nodded. Then without another word, he strode within. The group followed after, with Barty at the end of the line feeling rather exposed. But there was nothing for it now. They passed into darkness, each one vanishing into the void one by one. Barty closed his eyes as he stepped within—and when he opened them, he gasped.

The shadows retreated, replaced with a sort of soft, grey light, that came from no obvious source. Behind him the darkened veil remained, but he could make out the shape of the great iron door and the light beyond, muted as it was. Before him were steep descending stairs, which the others were wandering down. The walls were high, but not so high as to not feel somewhat claustrophobic. The strange twilight they were in was jarring, but Barty was able to travel by it as he plunged down the steps in pursuit.

"How did you do that?" he asked, his heart beating fast.

Jean grunted, but Adam sighed in faint annoyance as they answered, "Since Jean remains recalcitrant when it comes to actually teaching you at times, Bartholomew, I will explain. He made use of an old enchantment—one of the more common, the one of alteration. Alchemists refer to it as *transmutation*, but I prefer the more accurate term." They shrugged then, frowning at something, as Barty struggled to understand what that meant.

"That door has been around since the Society began," Jean growled. "The enchantment of alteration upon it is quite complex—to even make use of it, one must understand the nature of the spell, then know the unique sequence of contact at each point, and lastly know the keyword, all of which will change at each sealing. After that, you can command the property of its iron to respond." He paused in his step, looking back at Barty. "Congratulations, Mister Barty. You are learning of magic today."

Barty opened his mouth to protest. He thought of mocking such a concept, to defy it, and to call it nonsense. But then he saw Lily and Adam looking at him expectantly; being confronted with the truth of their impossible existence made the reality of magic itself a stark and terrible notion. "I rather thought you held society magicians in contempt, Jean," he said instead, a somewhat lame defence.

Jean gave that harsh laugh. "And so I do. They claw and crave for the real thing, and only gather dross. No one who seeks magic should ever be trusted to make use of it. If nothing else, history has taught us that over and over again—and you will learn it too, I am sure. Whether you wish it or not."

"I rather feel at times I am drowning under the weight of things I have no understanding of," Barty mumbled to himself, bitterly resentful even in the presence of such terrible wonder.

He had not expected anyone to hear his mutterings, but Lily was before him then, looking up at him in his path. Her head was slightly tilted, her face mask immutable, but there was once more something in the glow of her eyes that conveyed an emotion, hidden behind that concealment. "Then we have something in common in that regard, Mister Barty," she said with shy sympathy. "Let us learn of these new things together, shall we?"

It brought him up short, reminded him of the paleness of his own shadows compared to her own, and the bravery that she yet mustered to offer *him* comfort instead. She half reached for him then, as though to take his hand, but she pulled it back hastily. Before she could hurry away, he spoke. "You are entirely right, Miss Braithwaite." He inclined his head. "Would that you had been in our presence well before now. I think we could have used your wisdom in our household many times over, not to mention the pleasure of your company."

She covered her mouth with one hand as a faint, timid giggle came from behind the mask. She then straightened, and offered an arm out to him, crooked at the elbow. "Do be a gentleman and help me down these stairs, Mister Barty. I would rather avoid stumbling."

She waited expectantly. Barty, not quite understanding why but suddenly feeling flustered, carefully linked his arm with hers, the hard, strangely warm metal oddly comforting as he did so. Lily leaned into him somewhat, settling herself, and they moved down the stairs together. As they were navigating the steps, Barty caught Elanor staring at them. Her expression was neutral, difficult to read in the strange light, but something about it made Barty nervous.

The staircase ended, levelling out to a passageway lined with doors. Each of them was bound with chains of different metals in mixture—there was silver, and some Barty could have sworn were gold, but mostly it was blackened iron. The doors themselves were heavy, pitted and black, and they each were silent and still. But more remarkable was the structure of the walls—the place appeared carved out of stone, the black granite shot through with lines of quartz that glinted brightly with a light all of their own. This was the source of the strange grey light that permeated the place, but Barty could not understand how it did so.

"Walk in the middle of the corridor," Jean said suddenly, his voice hard, even tense, and kept low. "Do not stray. No matter what might happen."

"Whatever could you mean?" Barty could not help but ask, as Lily edged in nervously closer. "The doors are all well and truly locked, I do not see how—"

His voice, he realised, was somewhat louder than his guide, and this was likely due to his own nervousness. This then meant that he could be heard, and not only by present company.

The door to his right *boomed* with a sudden, shocking sound of a great weight striking against it. The chains shifted, but the pitted iron did not move. A sudden howling came from behind it, a hate filled screech of rage and helplessness. Barty and Lily sprang backwards, scrambling away from the horrible commotion, each one matching the others pace until the immovable steel arm of Adam reached out to stop their passage.

They firmly shook their head as they looked wordlessly down at the pair. Adam then turned their impassive gaze behind Lily and Barty's backs to another door. The chains were vibrating, ice forming at the corners of the doorway, spreading over the door with a faint crackling sound. They were close enough that Barty felt himself shiver uncontrollably from more than just the cold.

"Do not touch the doors," Adam said firmly.

In that moment, Barty would have bitten his own fingers off rather than do such a thing. "I thought you were jesting," Barty finally said as he and Lily moved back to the middle of the corridor, where Jean and Elanor were waiting. "When you spoke of what was down here."

"In part, to be fair," Jean said with a shrug, without specifying which part he meant. "But you are not ready to find out more. And what we want is two levels lower." He turned on his foot. "So come now. We do not have all day for this."

There was another staircase at the end of the hallway, narrow and open around a central shaft. It descended to a glittering, darkened depth and Barty shuddered, not wanting to peer too closely into that void. Lily was still by his side, and as they went deeper, she clung to him tighter. She did not shiver, but Barty felt that it was only because of her new form that this was the case. And yet, still she came. He had to wonder what drove her, at this point. What bravery allowed her to walk this path—to go from one prison to another, and yet be the one to steady *his* unwilling nerves. It stiffened his resolve. She deserved better behavior on his part, to feel safe. He had to do better for her.

The door they reached was much the same as the others—black iron, and black chains. A padlock was opened, a keyhole turned, and Adam's strength was once more put to bear to unveil what lay within.

Jean reached into his coat, there was a flare of a match being lit, and then he went about lighting a series of lamps along the walls that looked like they had been left ready for this very moment. A considerable chamber with cloth covered shapes, bulky and indistinct, was laid bare.

"Have you ever been down here?" Elanor asked quietly as she stood to one side, clenching her fists to quell her anxiety.

Adam shook their head. "Never. The reasons why should be obvious."

Jean grunted, as the room became more and more brightly lit, the flare of lamplight almost blinding after the strange, muted grey they had passed through to get there. He walked along, pulling off sheets and letting them fall to the ground. Hidden beneath them were sealed crates, chests, and other locked boxes—but that was not all. Other things were revealed, things that Barty felt a spine twinging sense of recognition when he saw them—glass and copper structures similar to what he had seen in Braithwaite's laboratory. But the last thing, found at the very back of the chamber, was something far more telling.

Tucked away in a corner with a space of its own, the sight made all of them stop in place. It was laying flat, too large to be kept upright. Adam was barely shorter than the ceiling, but this device did not quite manage to keep below that point—it was a cage, shaped like a man, of metal with various cables and wires coming from it. Each had been cut at one point, trailing like severed nerves yearning to feel life once more but long denied. It looked dead, and empty. And yet Barty knew what it was.

"Is that...?" Elanor asked, her voice hushed.

Adam, staring at it with their jaw clenched, nodded. "Yes. That is where I was made." They were rigid, locked in place, staring with their massive hands curling into fists. "I had hoped I would never see it again. Waking up in its embrace once was enough."

Jean turned, moving to a substantial metal framework against a wall that housed a series of cylinders, of brass and glass, all wired together. There were switches on it, and though when Barty had last seen such a device it had been fully en-cased in metal, he recognised it. And so had Jean, just as he had recognised the device of Adam's birth.

"So. Now we know something, at the very least," Jean said, running his hand over one of the exposed cylinders. "Someone has access to Shelley's research." There was no mistaking it. The design in the cellar that Barty and Jean had found was not similar—it was the same.

"Impossible," Adam stated bluntly. "She made sure all of it was here."

Jean turned on them, scrutinising Adam with his gaze. "And she never lied to you, did she?"

Adam looked away. "This should have all been destroyed," Adam said, their voice tight with anger.

"If it had, we would not know what we do now," Elanor said quietly. "And we would have nowhere to look to unravel *how* this came to be."

"So, Lord Braithwaite did not come to this conclusion naturally." Jean's voice was thoughtful, as he started to wander about. "Someone informed him. The *who* might be recorded in here somewhere—thus we had better get to work."

"And by 'work' you mean to ransack her research and life's endeavors?" Adam's voice was unhappy, bitterly so.

"Knowledge can only be accrued by study, Adam. All genius is sparked by something learned. You were the one who told me that," Jean replied firmly, as he began to rummage.

Adam looked helplessly at Jean's back before turning, moving to stand at the door and facing away from the contents of the room. Elanor went to help her father, opening up a chest and looking through it. Lily extricated herself from Barty's arm and followed after Adam—Barty joined her.

"I am sorry for all this, Adam," Lily said after a long hesitation. "You have been entirely considerate for my wellbeing in all of this..." She looked at one metal hand for a moment before recovering. "... situation. But this difficulty is my doing—I do not enjoy being a bother." Her glowing gaze lowered. "I have felt enough of one, for what feels like several lifetimes over."

Adam sighed at this, but their vast shoulders slumped. "Forgive me. I thought I would be quite able to manage this."

"You do not have to stay, if it is too much," Barty interjected. "Myself and Lily could come with you, if she so wishes, and keep you company while Elanor and Jean work."

Adam turned then, their eyes sad as they looked down at the pair, but there was a smile on those twisted lips. They lifted their gaze and swept it around the room. "Everything Mary wrote about me is here," they said finally. "In her twilight years, she pleaded with me to never read her personal diaries, that she regretted what she had written. I understand why. At first I was nothing but a disappointment to her."

A huge hand swept the crowded chamber. "Every doubt. Every hesitation. Her anger and sorrow and shame. All of it about me, and from the hand that made me come to be. She viewed me as a mistake and a burden at first." Adam sighed, and stepped into the room, placing a hand on a cabinet as though it was an old friend, long missed. "I remember all of it. But I also remember when her feelings towards me changed. I remember learning medicine, every tome I could consume, as she was overcome with illness. Seeing the light of life drip from her eyes as time devoured her with its relentless advance, and yet I remained unchanged, despite my wretched origins."

Barty listened as the giant went on, the music of Adam's beautiful voice a river of sorrow that filled that chamber with its grief. "I remember the day that, despite all I learned, I could not save her. How I begged then that she had not given my consciousness sensation, that she had not wrought life from the aether, that I might not feel. I felt as though I was trapped within myself. That I was turning to poison, black fire burning in my mind and what I might dare to call my soul." The massive fists closed with a grinding of bone and metal. "Searing at my heart and with no means to escape. It threatened to consume away all I ever was or could be."

For a moment, the air turned still, a charged potency as Barty remembered the incredible, terrible power of Adam, a strength that could by accident shatter anything it touched. Slowly, the hands unclenched, and Adam's shoulders eased. The sorrow returned, but gentler now. "But I remembered then, as I remember now, what it was that she told me; that we ultimately always choose our regrets. Always. The decision might be difficult, emotion might render it agonising—and it might well be made in ignorance. But it is what we *choose* and thus must bear responsibility for. I could make those choices, hastily, because of my pain—but then I would have to live with the shame of it forever." Adam's expression turned bitterly amused then, as they looked down to Barty. "I might well have been her shame. But I could choose not to make her death mine."

A quiet fell. Lily was staring at Adam, her visage a pale flame in the lamplight. Whatever words she might have wished to say were lost in that pause, as Barty struggled to find his own response. But the notion that Adam had put forward, of the nature of choice and regret, was one that Barty could not help but feel weighted down by; it was easy to tell oneself that there was no choice behind what they did. It was much harder to admit that there was always an opportunity to do something different.

Standing here now, the result of the choices he had made since coming into the company of Jean Reynard—and perhaps well before that—Barty had to wonder which ones he would eventually regret.

Someone who clearly had no time for such things was Jean, for in that moment he started swearing loudly. Lily visibly cringed from the harsh language, but Adam became exasperated. "Must you, Reynard? What possible cause do you have for being so upset?"

"Because there is no *order* to it!" Jean snapped back, coming into view, carrying a pile of leather-bound journals, slamming them down on a crate. "It is not simply formulae, or the scientific method—this is *all* of Mary Shelley's writings on these matters, and I have to inform you she wrote *prodigiously* about everything she could."

"My maker was very diligent in writing down all of her thoughts." Barty could not miss the note of pride in Adam's voice.

Jean was having none of it. He waved a hand disgustedly at the offending pile. "Be that as it may, I am rapidly learning that this is the case throughout all of this storage. I have not the slightest idea where to start the search, let alone what I am looking *for*."

Adam snorted, making their way over with heavy, slow steps. "Come now, Jean. You have not lost your wits recently by any stretch. Show me what you have, and we shall narrow things down somewhat." The giant walked away to join Jean and his daughter, and Lily and Barty were left alone.

The brass bodied girl stood awkwardly for a moment, interlacing her fingers with faint, soft clicking sounds, before she looked to Barty and asked with a timid tone, "Might we step outside for the time being, Mister Barty, while they work? I would hardly like to be underfoot."

He glanced into the depths of the chamber—the trio were bustling away in the opposite corner, and Barty could find no reason to deny Miss Braithwaite. There was something about the impassive, carven mask that was her face that made it hard to refuse her, but not nearly so much as the sound of her voice, which conveyed all the emotion that her features could not.

Back in the grey light of the corridor, she paused, looking down at her hands. Barty noticed it, and took the moment to speak to her privately—something that, until now, he had been unable to do. "I am sorry for all of this. It must be very bizarre to hear all these..." He waved a hand helplessly. "... strange things."

She turned her mask towards him, then sighed as she looked down at her hands. "Strangeness is all that I have, Mister Barty," she replied quietly. "I was just thinking that I wished to shiver at all the peculiar things in that room, but I cannot even do that. *Mentally* I wish to, but my... form does not allow it." She closed her hands. "I am not sure how much I can bear this."

"That is why we are here, Miss Braithwaite," he interjected, taking a tentative step towards her. "If there is a way to discover what has been done, we will discover it here."

She looked back to him, and nodded. "I truly do hope so. I very much would like to be returned to my body as soon as might be possible."

A sliver of ice scraped down his thoughts and his spine. "I am sorry—returned?" he could not help but ask with a growing sense of unease.

Lily nodded to him. "Though being ill was no joy, I would prefer it over this. But you seem quite sure that you can learn how this happened—and thus undo it as well, correct?" She did not sound hopeful. Instead, she sounded quite sure of herself. As though it was already understood and was a forgone conclusion.

Something clanged into Barty's thoughts like an iron bar falling onto cobblestones, rattling and banging, locking him in place. *Returned to her body.* He remembered her story then, of how she had fallen asleep, and woken in her new form. Lily did not know that she had died; that her new life was one created, that her old body was buried in a graveyard. *She did not know she was dead.* And she was already hanging on by a thread.

He was acutely aware that he was alone with her; there was no one else to answer this, to tell the lie that needed to be told. He had to take that fragile trust that had formed, that gentle inclination to turn to him, to take his hand and believe him true, and brutalise it. He had to lie. There was no one else who could make this betrayal. It had to be him.

"Yes, of course," he said with a nod, feeling the words blacken his soul. "One step at a time, but we will yet reach that goal." Seeing her eyes glow brighter with happiness as she nodded along to his reassurances made him hate himself; a self-loathing so fierce he wished the Devil that had given his tongue the silkiness to speak such lies would come for him and drag him to the hell he deserved. Deserved, for telling a girl who had gone through her own damnation something he knew could not come true, to give her false hope. He understood now what Adam had said. Barty had chosen his regrets.

He had to change the subject. He floundered and grasped for any lifeline, any topic of conversation where he could run far away from what they were currently discussing. He landed on the first notion that crossed in his mind—one that had been hovering at the back of his thoughts. "I was meaning to ask you, Miss Braithwaite—earlier today, it seems you were sent to wake me, but I do not recall such happening? Did you become lost?"

She stiffened up, going rigid and silent, though the glow of her eyes flickered considerably. Unsure, he pressed onwards, trying to console her. "I can understand entirely, the Manor is all together too large—one of the others should surely have taken the responsibility."

She shook her head, a small, hurried movement, but would not look at him. "N-no," she said with a hesitant stammer. "I volunteered t-to bring you your breakfast and tea. I was told which room was yours."

"Oh." Barty's confusion bloomed a touch greater as he puzzled at it for a moment. "But the—" He cut himself off from remarking about the state of the tea and toast, both of which were cold when he awoke, and that she had placed them so close *without* waking him in the after, but he would have imagined she would have just knocked instead, as was customary. "Apologies," he finished lamely. "It is not important."

She nodded, and he fell silent, but his mind was racing as he fled the earlier falsehood that still accursed him. *You just told a dead woman that you can fix things. You just betrayed a soul's last hope.*

"I was watching you sleep." She said it with her back to him. It caught him off guard, wrenching him out of his thoughts. He watched her metal, segmented shoulders drop—such a human gesture with her body so very strange—as she went on.

"I have not been able to sleep since I awoke in that... dark place." Her voice was soft, and distant. "I wish to—I *long* to. But I cannot do so. I cannot even close my eyes, but even if I could I never feel the pull of sleep." A note of despair then, amidst the metallic overtones. "So I watched you sleep. Hoping somehow it might remind me of it." She turned her head, her glowing eyes focusing on him intently. "You... do not sleep peacefully, Mister Barty," she said, cautiously. "Your shoulders shake."

What could he tell her? Of the nightmares that often plagued him, that he denied in the waking hours? Of the memories twisted by time and more besides to become entirely too consuming? No. No, he would not presume such a burden upon another, upon her, when he had just comforted her with a falsehood, and she had already suffered enough. He would not dare.

"I tend to be anxious, after travel," he offered instead. "It disturbs my sleep." It was a lie, but it had the benefit of being an obvious one that she could recognise as a shield against the truth. She accepted this and nodded, before looking away again and speaking once more, with awkward hesitation lacing its way through her words.

"I must apologise—it does not, of course, do for a young lady to, well... do such a thing." She sounded ashamed. "If you are betrothed, I should hope that your lady *never* finds out such an impertinence."

"Be-betrothed?" Barty stammered, for now it was his turn to be embarrassed. He shook his head, waving his hands defensively. "No, no. I fear I have nothing like that in my life. I am not promised to anyone."

"Oh?" There was a strange note of nonchalance in Lily's voice that Barty did not understand. Was it smug somehow? "Well. In any case, we should keep this a secret between us, don't you think?"

He nodded, not knowing what else to do. But before he

could puzzle out what any of this might have meant, he was forced to set aside his bafflement as Adam pushed themselves out into the corridor.

"Bartholomew." They spoke Barty's name with their usual congeniality but Barty nevertheless jumped as though caught in some guilty act, without truly knowing why. Adam raised a perplexed brow, and continued on, "Could you go help Elanor? She will need assistance." They themselves had, beneath one arm, a large, heavy chest that they were carrying with ease. "I shall escort Miss Braithwaite back to the library."

"But of course," Barty said hurriedly. Remembering his manners, he turned to give a slight, awkward bow to Lily, who returned it effortlessly with a graceful curtsey, her glittering brass frame moving with such fluidity that Barty had to wonder how at ease she was becoming with it. "Until our next conversation, Miss Braithwaite."

She nodded a genteel dismissal, and he bundled himself into the chamber, still troubled by the unnamed feeling. He soon found Elanor and Jean, crouched beside two open chests. A pile of books was beside both of them—leather-bound tomes, each with the look of a personal diary.

"This woman was *beyond* prolific," Jean grumbled. "She could put thoughts to page faster than some could draw breath, it seems." He glanced up to Barty. "We will leave much of this down here, but we need to start taking these upstairs so that we might read through them. It's too much to parse through with ease." Still crouched, he waved vaguely to Elanor. "Help her get these to the library"

Barty nodded, but remained where he was, awkward for a

moment. Elanor paused in her rummaging to look up at him with a mixture of suspicion and curiosity, a brow raised in a wordless question.

"She thinks we can return her back to her body," Barty finally said. "She does not know that she has—" He stopped himself from saying the truth. "She does not know what has happened to her."

Jean paused. "What did you tell her?" His tone was cold. Calculating. Barty felt pressure in that voice. A warning.

"I lied," he answered, miserably. "I told her we would."

"Good." Jean sounded relieved.

Elanor turned on him at that, sharply. "We should tell her the truth, Father." Her words were harshly accusing.

He scowled, turning on his haunches in a squat to face her. "And what would that solve? What would that grant us? Would you rather offer her false hope, or a truth made of despair?"

"She should know what happened to her," Elanor said stubbornly. "He should have told her the truth, we *all* should have." She looked away. "It is a cruel thing to lie to her about this."

"When have we ever been anything but cruel?" Jean replied with a bitter chuckle, straightening to his feet. "Right now, she has hope. She has something to cling to. She has something to strive towards. That, even if it is ignorance, is a blessing for the right now, and the only solace we can give her." He glanced at Barty. "If it is any help, Barty—yes, it was cruel, but it was the right thing to do. *She* is not the one suffering that knowledge right now. Would you rather be the one to bear it, or put it on her?"

It was not even remotely hard to answer. "Myself, if I could."

Jean nodded in approval, a flicker of pride in his gaze. "Good. She has been through enough. Until we know more, until we can offer more, we can stand to bear a little discomfort. While telling the truth might make *us* feel better, *we* are not the ones who need to." He spoke the last sentence to Elanor, his tone cold.

She did not look back at him, but gathered up her stack of books and stood to shove them into Barty's arms, before collecting her own with a grunt. "Fine. Come then." She stalked off, expecting Barty to follow—who, after seeing Jean open another chest to be searched, did precisely that.

He trudged after Elanor, who betrayed her obvious irritation, if not anger, with the set of her shoulders and refusal to look at him. But as they were ascending the stairs her anger was forced to vent, as she snapped over her shoulder, "It is unbecoming of you to play with her affections, Barty."

This made him stop. "I beg pardon?" He could not conceal his bafflement, even as the stack of books he carried made his arms burn.

Elanor turned to face him, her expression hard. "While I struggle to disagree with my father's logic, I still cannot help but judge you. You lied to Lily—even if it was the right thing to do, you should not play her false, particularly in your case with how she feels about you. It is cruel." Her anger was palpable, and he took a backwards step.

"What about my case? What do you mean?" he replied defensively.

Elanor bristled. "Are you so used to the affections of women that you have come to disregard them? Or are you just an imbecile?"

He took another backwards step but felt a swell of both panic and anger rise up. "Clearly the latter. I have no idea whatsoever of what you are speaking of."

Elanor glared at him, then turned to put her armful of books down on the step behind her before turning back to him, crossing her arms across her chest imperiously. "You are then unaware that she *very clearly* has some measure of feelings for you? She has made her expression of them quite plain."

Barty felt his stomach lurch with exquisite discomfort. "What? But she is—"

"She is a young woman, who has been housebound her entire adolescence and womanhood," Elanor snapped. "And you, regrettably, are the first man of her own age that she has had a chance to interact with." She narrowed her eyes at him dangerously. "Did you *truly* have no idea of her infatuation?"

Barty, stung to the quick, his cheeks turned hot, felt his temper rise. "How could I? I have never known such things!" He looked away in shame. "No one ever has before. I do not even know what it *looks* like." But even so he remembered; she had trusted him, had looked to take his hand out of all of those present. She had watched him sleep, she had tried to get closer to him. He had felt something was happening—he just had not understood what.

There was silence—perplexed silence—before Elanor spoke carefully and without anger, though suspicion remained. "You spoke of a girl you used to know. Charlotte. I thought she was..." She did not finish the thought.

Barty felt his anger flare again. "She was my friend," he

retorted. "Nothing more than that. She was the voice on the other side of a wall, a face I never saw." His memory crawled back into that black pit. "She was my friend in that place when I had naught. She was hope when none was allowed to me." He felt his thoughts harden, the shadows of that past once more rising up to choke the present. "When I never saw her again, she taught me that hope was false, just like it is for Lily." He faced Elanor now, whose expression was twisted with conflicting emotions as he went on, his voice turning harsh, "And in so doing I learned that hope, however false, is *still* better than none at all, even if both drive you mad." He set his jaw. "Even if you have nothing, you can still believe. And I will *not* take that from her."

Elanor said no more and Barty had nothing left to say. He stepped past her on the stairwell, and continued upstairs and out of the Vault. As he walked through the grey light, with Elanor's eyes on his back, he wished he had never come to this place.

But wishes were like hope, and something he had long known to be false, too.

Chapter 17

The Scars We Carve

The next day, Barty wandered.

The grand kitchen of the Manor was a foreboding sort of place designed to feed a battalion of inhabitants, and yet only a small part of it was now used. This was where Barty had decided to take his breakfast. There had been no one present when he arrived, having woken late after spending a long afternoon hauling piles of books out of the vault, before assisting in trying to parse through the scattered, seemingly disjointed, notes of Mary Shelley. He had not gotten far, and truth told, had not done much. Mostly he had watched Adam, who had been less and less able to hide their sorrow as they read the words of their creator, of her secret thoughts and scientific discoveries. They did not share what they found.

Eventually, he had given up amidst the cavernous silence and left them there, making his way back to his room and to his rest. Now he feared to go back to that room, knowing Adam would still be there, still working.

As Barty worked his way through his joyless porridge, there was a commotion behind him—the door leading to the outside opened, and there was a flash of green grass and of brick structures beyond before a woman bustled within. She was a grey-haired, ample bodied woman with red cheeks and bright eyes, and wore a dark servants outfit. She had a wicker basket under one well-rounded arm and a mighty leg of ham held with the other, which she carried without effort. Coming to a halt, she laid eyes on Barty, spoon sticking guiltily out of his mouth. She cocked a brow, and then spoke in a voice so motherly it made Barty feel warm inside. "And who are you then, dearie?"

Barty swallowed, tried not to choke, and, remembering his manners, leapt to his feet and delivered a stiff bow. "Bartholomew Bartleby, ma'am," he managed in a voice rusty to his own ears. "But you can call me Mister Barty if you wish."

She chuckled, mockingly inclined her head. "Mister Barty Bartholomew Bartleby then, is it?" She winked, grinning, her cheeks puffing and shining redder than ever. "Maybe I shall call you Mister Bee. Mrs Cosgrove, at your service!" She gave a warm laugh, heading to the stove. "And I know *all* about *you*." She gave him a warning look over one shoulder, still grinning.

God help me, Barty prayed. Mrs Cosgrove? Clearly her husband had told her everything. He winced inwardly and could not keep it off his face. Seeing this, the woman laughed.

"Oh, wisht boy—I have long learned to read between the lines of my husband's griping. What are you having for breakfast?" She put down the basket, then slammed the ham leg on a cutting board. Picking up a knife with a twirl, started to slice off strips of ham with practised ease.

"Uhm, porridge, ma'am." He gestured vaguely at the half empty and altogether meagre bowl.

Mrs Cosgrove took one look, and snorted. "*That* won't do.

Sit yourself down, I'll make you a proper breakfast." She shook her head, clucking her tongue. "Toast and tea one day, porridge the next, a proper scarecrow you are."

Barty, still off guard, mumbled a protest, but the woman turned, clapped a hand on his shoulders, spun him about with shocking ease, and marched him back to the seat at the kitchen table once more. "Sit," she commanded, and he did. "Shush," she ordered, and it was so. That tone was impossible to argue with.

He opened his mouth as she returned to the creation of a proper breakfast, but she waved her knife at him and cut him off. "And no apologising neither, young man. My husband decried you as all manner of unflattering things, but he said you apologised far too much as well. Fret you not." She went back to cutting and humming aimlessly, opening the basket to produce several eggs. Fishing about in a cupboard provided her with onions, and the loaf box some bread. She set a frying pan upon a sooty black stove, the fire already lit and burning low. She was industriousness itself, slicing bread, ham, onion, and more with equal efficiency. Some mushrooms came out of nowhere, along with enough butter to drown in, and she began to cook it all with the casual proficiency of a master of her craft. "So then," she finally said as she worked. "You do not say much, do you, Mister Bee?"

Barty had been lost in watching her work, but embarrassed by her words, he turned his eyes to the miserable grey mush of his porridge. "I would not want to interrupt," Barty mumbled in reply, and the woman laughed, a strong, clear laugh without rancour nor fear. Despite himself, Barty felt his lingering anxieties fade entirely.

"You and your manners, lad. Fie upon it, I can see why you irritate my darling husband." She glanced back at him, grinning with the corners of her mouth, eyes crinkling up in her mirth, and looked back to the stove. "Since you are so nervous, let *me* do some talking a while instead, for a breakfast is no time for silence."

And so Mrs Matilda Cosgrove, for that was her full name, spoke with the gusto, the openness, and the warmth that her husband entirely lacked. She talked about her two sons and daughters, who worked the grounds and the household, who lived in their own cottages attached to the Manor itself, and how they had *their* wives and husbands and children, all either working earnestly away here or at the nearby village on the other side of the lake. She was a font of information, of friendly chatter, and she served up Barty a breakfast that, by its very magnificent scent, made him hungry all over again, while she bitterly bemoaned the lack of a pair of kippers to really round it out. And Barty listened, and drank it in, and basked in the glow of her gossip.

That warmth turned to frost as, in the midst of describing the trials of granddaughter number three, the second, more terrible half of the lovely woman who had seen fit to fill his stomach to a wonderful state of fullness that Barty had never known before, made himself known. "You continue to make yourself at home, I see."

The butler, dressed as severely as ever, stood at the main entrance to the kitchen. Barty startled to his feet, but the loud laughter of Mrs Cosgrove was a weapon all of itself, the shield against wrath without compare.

"Oh hush now, Gerald," she chided, sipping her cup of tea cheerfully. "He's a wonderful lad. You gave the most *awful* impression of him, and here I am telling him of our Sadie and her little Susie, and wouldn't you know, he's been paying attention and listening and behaving himself *well* in hand." She grinned up at Barty, winking. "Gerald here painted a picture of you being a *rogue*, imagine that! Up to no good he said, 'a bad mannered street urchin.'"

"And I stand by it," Cosgrove muttered, a man whom the humble name of 'Gerald' fit as well as a crown on a pauper.

His wife, however, laughed uproariously. "Nonsense! He's been nothing but polite, used all his pleases and thank yous, and very kindly too! And an appetite on him, I'd almost say he's been starved up until this point." Her laughter died, and a keen, critical eye was cast on Barty then. "We're going to put a stop to that, however." Her voice was firm, determined. "You need some meat on your bones, Mister Barty, lest a chill bring you lowly. I'll see to that."

"It is something that will have to wait for the time being, my dear," Cosgrove said, his tone resigned. "The master of the house needs this one for something." He gestured vaguely towards Barty.

His wife nodded, putting down her teacup and pushing herself to her feet. "Then that settles that then. And don't you dare." She gently swatted Barty's hands away as he went to scoop up the dishes. "I will take care of these. Be off with you!"

Chastised, he stepped back, but he inclined his head. "That was wonderful, Mrs Cosgrove."

She grinned. "The breakfast or the conversation?"

"Both, without question," Barty replied, feeling a grin come to his own face. The woman chuckled and started to efficiently bustle about, as Barty followed her husband out of the room.

The atmosphere was frigid in the corridor, mostly because of Cosgrove's presence, but Barty nevertheless felt better than he had in days. Mrs Cosgrove was a wonderful cook; the food had been better than any he could remember having. Had he ever eaten so well before? Cosgrove said nothing as they marched along the corridor, until Barty could bear the silence no longer.

"Your wife is a wonderful woman, sir," he said hesitantly. Cosgrove halted midstep, and turned, his brow furrowing. He glared at Barty a moment, eyes hard and fixed upon him as the object of his ire quailed, before he took a deep, steadying breath.

"*Please* do not call me 'sir'," he said firmly. "You are to refer to me as Cosgrove. Are we clear? Mister Cosgrove if you must."

Barty nodded. "Yes, s—" He caught himself as those eyes narrowed. "Yes. I can do that."

"Good," Cosgrove responded icily, clearly noticing the near-slip. He turned again on his foot. "I have considered your proposal," he continued as they marched along. "I have decided I shall grant it."

Barty bit his tongue before asking what he knew would be a stupid question. Proposal? After a moment he recalled that he had asked for permission to enter the workshop, and his heart leapt. "Thank you, Cosgrove." He even remembered to use the name correctly. "I am sincerely grateful."

A warning finger was pointed upwards. "I *will* however insist on either myself or Adam being present, and only then may you enter. I will not have you wander about unattended, nor are you to touch anything without either of our permission, and supervision. Failure to do so will see you evicted forthwith and in perpetuity. Am I clear?" he snapped the last word with finality, glaring over his shoulder.

Barty swallowed and nodded hurriedly. "Perfectly clear, s—uh, Cosgrove."

The butler scowled, but seemed to accept this as he pushed the door to the library open. The sun was shining upon the scene—spread out couches and tables took up the space before the great, petrified tree and upon the available surfaces were the books and chests taken from the vault. In the middle of it all sat Adam, cross-legged and holding a comparatively tiny notebook in one huge hand. They did not look up as Barty and Cosgrove passed, heading towards a door that was directly opposite the workshop. Barty felt his greeting to Adam die on his lips. They did not look like they had even moved since the night before, save to turn just one more page with a vast thumb, delicate and precise, their corpse eyes unable to conceal an abiding pain.

Cosgrove paid Adam no heed—or more accurately, Barty felt, he respected their solitude. Instead he guided Barty to a door directly facing that which led to the workshop on the opposite side of the Hall. Pushing it wide with one hand, he stood to one side and gestured with a lift of his chin before striding away, his task completed. Barty knew a dismissal when he saw it. He stepped inside.

He was not sure what he expected, but it certainly was not what he found. The hall within was hugely spacious, the three other walls all set with high windows and a series of oversized doors on the far side, thrown ajar upon a broad, stone balcony that overlooked the lake. The contents of the hall however, were better suited to a battleground.

There were racks of weapons of all kinds, firearms, crossbows, longbows, swords and spears and axes, and a multitude Barty could not identify. Segmented dummies were spaced here and there, heavy and brutally marked by strikes and dents, the wood different shades in places where parts had been replaced. There were suits of decorative armour, some paintings on the walls of knights in poses or combat, but it was sparse in comparison to the rest of the Manor. This was a room for work, and someone was working in it now.

Elanor moved with the sort of fluidity one normally found only in observing water running down a stream, or dust dancing upon the breath of the wind. The sword she held in one hand was a basket hilted rapier, glittering silver steel that wove in tight, compact movements as she spun and slid—sharp jabs with a turned wrist, straightening and then moving into a lunging thrust which covered a shocking amount of ground with an astonishing amount of speed. Sweat streamed down her face, her white blouse stained with the effort. She wore tight trousers, cut off at the knee and no shoes. She did not even glance at Barty, her expression grimly intent as she moved, swaying and deflecting imagined blows, twisting and turning and relentlessly continuing her advance. Her blade *sang* through the air, cutting slices out of it, as she pursued her invisible foe.

"She's very good, I think," Lily said from behind him, her voice hushed and hesitant, just as Barty realised that he had been staring.

Barty spun to see the brass and porcelain girl, once more clad in clothes from Elanor's own closet, seated against the wall by the door rather timidly. She had found her cat once more, and the black and white feline sat with a gentle resignation on her lap as Lily gently stroked her fur. Daisy cast a green-eyed stare that said nothing to Barty, and yet he could not help but feel judgement. He nodded to Lily, however, and eased onto the wooden bench beside her, the glow of her eyes flaring a moment.

"I fear I am no sound judge," he confessed in a hushed tone, not wanting to break Elanor's concentration. "But she is certainly... impressive to observe." He meant it. But as he watched Elanor move, he was suddenly and painfully reminded that she was very much a woman—and a very attractive one at that. For fear of being a lecher, he tore his eyes towards Lily instead—and the continued judgemental stare of the cat she held, who seemed to know his thoughts all too well.

"I was expecting to see Jean here, is he nearby?"

Lily nodded, and pointed past the still twirling Elanor to the balcony beyond. "He went out there a short while ago—but stay a moment," she gently pleaded. "He will not have gotten far." She reached out to place a hand over his as though to persuade him, that strangely warm metal of her grip nevertheless unyielding in its strength.

He was reminded of Elanor's words regarding Lily's affections, and for a moment wondered if he should remove his hand. But he dismissed that rude thought immediately and nodded instead, settling back into his chair, and despite himself smiled. "You are probably correct, Miss Braithwaite. Besides, if I tried to cross the room right now, I would wager I could catch an errant sword thrust for my trouble."

"My sword *never* goes where it is not supposed to," Elanor snapped as she thrust sharply. "If I meant to stab you, it is because I wished it." A pause, before she continued, "Again, that is." She was looking at him now, squinting out of the corner of her eye in the midst of a lunge, before taking a defensive backstep and deflecting with a twist of the wrist. Admonished, he shrugged guiltily at Lily, who covered her mouth and laughed a dainty, girlish giggle.

"I see Daisy has adjusted well, in the meanwhile," he managed lamely.

Lily nodded, stroking the cat's fur between their ears gently. "She appears to quite like it here. Lots of places to wander about." She glanced to Barty then. "I would offer you to hold her, but she tends to be somewhat shy of strangers, I am afraid." A small sigh escaped her. "She has something of a sense for people, I find. She knows those who can be trusted."

Barty remembered how the cat had come to be Lily's companion, and could not help but chuckle. "I would agree with that, actually." He focused on the cat for a time, which blinked slowly at him. "I have never had a pet myself before. There was not much time for it."

"Well," Lily said with a little lift in her tone. "You may not have this one—*but* if she allows it, you may stroke her fur a moment." And with that, she lifted the black and white cat and placed it in Barty's lap. He froze, surprised.

Daisy settled, and the pinpricks of claws digging through his trousers came after—a singularly unpleasant sensation to say the least, but the cat soon let it pass and then simply sat there, looking up at him. Her feline expression let nothing slip, a poker face without peer, but yet it seemed entirely too knowing. Without any recourse available to him, he reached up with both hands, and with one holding the cat in place, carefully scratched the fur around her throat. This set the green eyes to closing, and a purr vibrated through her whole being.

Lily clapped her metal hands together—gently, but there was a faint metallic ringing nevertheless and laughed joyfully. "I *knew* she would like you," she said. If she could smile properly with her masked features, she would have been beaming. "I told you she was a good judge of character."

In light of his lie to Lily the previous evening, Barty did not feel such kind judgement was warranted. But the weight and warmth of the cat, combined with the wonderful, expansive breakfast, was soothing in a way that Barty did not quite know how to deal with. All these unusual feelings were disrupted by the presence of Elanor, striding towards them and slamming her sword back into her scabbard. Daisy leapt free of Barty's embrace and secured herself under Lily's chair where, with a reproachful look, she started to clean herself.

"If you are quite done," she said dryly to Barty, reaching up to pull clear her hair tie and shake her mane of dark hair loose, "my father is probably waiting on you still." She sounded stern, but there was a look of amusement in her eyes as she stood with hands on her hips, breathing hard and shining still with sweat from her endeavours. That amused look turned to confused curiosity after a moment, and Barty realised he was staring again. "Whatever is the matter?" Elanor asked.

Barty hopped to his feet and, making muttered apologies, hurried off, his cheeks flaming, Elanor's puzzled stare following. Murmurs and then laughter, high and clear, chased him out onto the balcony and into the sunlight.

He took a moment to gather himself once he arrived. Jean was nowhere to be seen, so he took in the balcony itself. It was broad, large enough to allow for a great number of gathered folk, or, as he could now see, a firing range, with targets placed at one far end towards the water of the lake. There was a stairway leading down on this end, towards the water, and to a pier that hugged the edge of the Manor before turning sharply out over the water. Dark, and still, the lake was a mirror on this near windless day and the Manor itself, jutting far out into the lake, acted as a break against the breeze, making the water on this side completely calm.

Now, Barty could see Jean, but was for the moment halted in place by what he saw. Jean was wearing his breeches and nothing more, his boots sat next to a tidy pile of folded clothes at the bottom of the stairway to the pier. Barty was shocked by the sight, by the fact that Jean seemed to have markings all over his back—Barty could not quite make them out as the man walked with a determined pace to the end of the pier, but he *could* see he was moving with a touch of difficulty, because held at his stomach with both arms, was a large, smooth, lakeside stone.

He did not understand what was happening until Jean, stopping at the edge of the pier, far out onto the water, stood for a moment to brace himself, then tensed. Barty, with a startled cry, scrambled forward—but it was too late. Still holding the heavy stone, Jean stepped off the end of the pier and vanished from sight, the splash of his entry muted as the water closed over his head with an outburst of froth and protest.

Barty ran blindly, nearly falling down the stairs as he went, but as he stumbled along the pier, pulling at his shirt in order to dive after Jean, he heard Elanor behind him. "Barty! Calm down. He knows what he's doing." She did not sound the least bit worried.

Barty was hopping up and down in place, about to yank one of his boots off, so in a rush to remove his clothes that he only managed to get about halfway with each article. She was at the top of the stairway, entirely unbothered, with Lily hovering a little awkwardly at her shoulder. Elanor had a smug sort of smile as she pointed to the end of the pier. "Go on. Wait for him there. He won't be long."

Her confidence brought his panic up short, even if doubt lingered. "... If you say so," Barty finally managed, trying to recover his dignity as he resettled his boot and made his way along, adjusting the rest of his clothing back to neatness. Behind him, Elanor and Lily returned inside, leaving Barty standing awkwardly at the end of the pier, the surface of the lake now still save for the occasional gently rising bubble.

It was an interminable amount of time later that the bubbles came faster and then, with them, Jean Reynard burst out of the depths, sucking in a great lungful of air. He tread water, sweeping his tangled hair back before he realised Barty was there, and squinted at him. "Well. There you are." The hunter swam over to a series of carved out lines in the stone that formed a crude ladder, and hauled himself upwards. "I was wondering what was keeping you."

Barty took the moment to inspect Jean—it was hard not to. He had never seen the man even partially undressed before, and now he was down to his drawers, revealing a powerfully built body of lean, compact muscle, wire, sinew, and bone. But it was the tattoos that drew his eye—and the scars.

Jean's back, arms, and chest were covered with a vast array of unfamiliar, eldritch symbols that Barty could not identify, interwoven with scar tissue. Some appeared Celtic, some Christian, but there were many, many others. Flowing words were etched with black ink in languages Barty did not know. The scars were even more remarkable. Some were faint and simple, mere blemishes on skin that barely hinted at the damage caused. Others were more savage—ragged and crude scars that could only have come from teeth and claws, and jagged rips in the skin that had been torn apart then pulled back together. But across that broad back were marks of the lash—whip wounds that had carved long furrows in the flesh, a mutilation of the body that looked like it still hurt, even now. Jean seemed to pay it no heed. Instead, as he went through a series of stretches, he gave Barty a puzzled look.

"You have some words to go with that stare, Barty?" His tone was dry, a little scathing, and it brought Barty out of his stupor. He shook his head to banish his horrified fascination.

"What were you *doing* down there?" he asked, turning his head to the black depths from which the hunter had arisen.

Jean laughed harshly and sat himself down on the stone, stretching one leg in front of him and hugging the other, both hands wrapped around his knee. "Why do *you* think I went down there?" he challenged instead, to Barty's irritation.

He scowled as he considered his answer. "At first, I thought you were trying to drown yourself. Made a proper fool of myself scrambling after you," he confessed, to which Jean laughed—a little mockingly, perhaps, but less so than Barty would have feared.

"The nominal answer was deep diving—a breath exercise, to train the capacity of the lungs." Jean sniffed, then blew his nose into his hand, shaking the excess away. "Been too long since I had practised. Time at the Lodge softened me somewhat." He sounded annoyed about it, as though he was disappointed in himself. "But there is rather more to it than that." He frowned, looking at the water. "Down there it is dark—excruciatingly so, and cold. So cold that it presses in on you, crushes you, even as red light starts to fill your vision." He rubbed his jaw. "I can never banish the memory of the first time I was sent down there. I was younger than you are now, quite substantially so. Locke had..." He trailed off, grimacing, and shaking his head, leaving the rest unspoken.

Locke? Barty wondered. *His old teacher?*

"I panicked and nearly drowned trying to get out," he continued. "Never wanted to go back." He took a deep breath. "There are ghosts in that dark, ghosts that watch you and remind you of things you never want to see again. And yet, I go down. It reminds me of things I must not forget." He gave a grim sort of smile, looking up at Barty. "Offers a peace and quiet too, if only briefly. You would not believe how silent it is."

"What does it remind you of?" Barty asked, following Jean's stare to likewise gaze at the mirror surface of the lake.

Jean shrugged. "Fear is a thing of pieces, Barty. A thing of different shapes and colours, and down there, in the dark, is one of my fears. Each time I face it, it becomes a little bit less. If it is a choice of beating it, or being beaten by it, I will choose the one where I fight." He nodded. "This, then, is how I do that."

Barty shivered, looking into the stilled abyss. "You tell me these things, and I cannot help but wonder if I am... not the right person for this."

Jean snorted. "Yes, you could wonder. But you are." His tone was flat, bluntly contradicting. But Barty was not dissuaded.

"I am right in this, surely?" he protested. "You've said it and seen it for yourself. I am useless in a fight. I cower, too afraid to do anything." He gestured vaguely back to the Manor. "Your daughter is a braver, far more capable individual than I."

"And yet you are here," Jean replied coldly. "But I would have you explain why you think *I* do things like dive into the darkness of a lake, before I tell you why I *know* you could."

This pulled Barty up. His thoughts raced, trying to force the answer that for the moment eluded him, but for once Jean did not rush him, even as he sat shivering, drying by the light of the sun. Barty took this chance to take his time, slowing his thinking before he remembered something he had once said about Jean.

"You stare down your fear," he said quietly. "You always have—I used to think nothing frightened you, Reynard. Now I know that things do, but you walk *towards* them rather than away." He frowned, turning back to his teacher. "I do not know if I could do that."

"Except that you have. More than once," Jean replied simply. "When you chased after Hyde in Bedlam. When you went after the truth like a dog with a bone to know what happened to Jack the Ripper. Hell's teeth, when you shook my hand after we killed that wretched ghoul in the graveyard—you were afraid every time. And just like me, you walked towards it."

Barty was unconvinced. "And yet, I do not think I am nearly strong enough for this... everything that has happened, with Lily, with Adam..." His tongue stuck in his mouth, but he forced through it. "I did not enjoy concealing the truth from her, Jean." He lowered his voice. "Even with all those reasons, I feel like a coward. I hate feeling like I need to run away every time there is danger."

Jean was wordless for a long moment. Silence spread outwards, a ripple from a stone into still water. A bird called from the forest skirting the lake, away from the Manor, and then its echoes died away. Quiet reigned over all.

"What do you think strength is, Bartholomew Bartleby?" Jean asked finally, his voice subdued, slicing through the silence with the grace of a blade through the wind. "Do you think that I am strong?" Jean was not looking at Barty, but was staring over the water.

"I do," Barty responded at last, and Jean shook his head, chuckling, but it was bitter, and darker than the deepest depths of the lake upon which they now sat.

"What then, is my strength? Is it my cruelty? My viciousness?" He looked up at Barty now, his dark eyes gleaming. "My rudeness, or my rage? Are any of those things what you would call strength?"

Barty hesitated, reminded once again of all the times he had seen it displayed to him. That hesitation was all the answer he needed to give.

"They are my weaknesses," Jean said, looking away. "They are the wounds I bear, the scars I carved in myself by my own deeds. They are what I use to hurt others, to pretend that a part of me is not yet bleeding." He grimaced, and though he was surely cold, he was no longer shivering. "James was strong. Not because he could fight, though he did so well enough. He was strong because he smiled. Strong because he gave a damn. Because he forgave and because he *cared*." The hunter sighed, rubbing his forehead in his shame. "And I cannot bring myself to. I cannot do those things. All I know how to do is hurt people—even if they deserve it, it does not change what it is."

Barty was silent, but he remembered what Adam had told him, when speaking of Shelley. *We choose our regrets*. Adam had been able to resist making their own. Jean had not.

"You *are* strong, Barty. Because of all those reasons and more. Because there is horror in your past, and yet you are no slave to it. You chose to turn from it, and you chose not to let it define you, either. It is far rarer than you think. What you are is *brave*. That simplest and truest of things."

"And yet I am afraid all the time," Barty objected.

Jean scowled at that. "And what is bravery, without fear to defy? Naught but foolishness. And you are no fool. Thus, you *are* brave. And with that bravery, comes your strength." Jean pushed himself to his feet. "However, it is strength that has not yet been tempered; it needs to know what it is to burn, and I do not think it does yet."

Barty was conflicted about this, his moment of pride dashed in the face of Jean's admittance that Barty remained insufficient. "I am sorry my character has not yet met your... standards, as it were." He couldn't keep the frosty edge to his words from his voice, but it made Jean snort, shaking his head.

"Fret not—there is no insult in such a thing. It is better by far than a father, too afraid to unlock the door to his son's room, for what he might find there." He sighed, stretching and rolling his shoulders. "One day, perhaps. Potentially even today."

Barty did not know what to say. He felt embarrassed, ashamed, and he could not grasp why. "I would still say you have strength, Jean," he finally stumbled, gazing down at his reflection in the lake. "You know yourself, at the very least." He grimaced. "I am still trying to figure out who I am. Let alone why I am here."

The crimson-lipped smile of a woman in red flickered in the faint ripples of the water, a shadowed stare of eyes he could not see looking up at him from the water. He blinked and it was gone as Jean snorted, not noticing.

"And yet, you have not *asked* why you are here. Right now, that is. I did summon you after all." His tone was sardonic.

Barty blinked, as he remembered. "Well—yes. I was wondering that."

Jean gave that sharp-toothed grin that always lingered on the edge of wickedness and, with an energetic stride, made for his clothes at the end of the pier. "Excellent. Now tell me Barty—have you ever ridden a horse before?"

Chapter 18

BARE HANDED, BLOODY MOUTHED

O n the matter of horse riding, as an orphan of the city,
Barty had not, until that point, ever partaken thus. And
when they finally arrived at their destination, he was wishing
that he still had not.

Jean had brought him to the Manor stables, where they had
both mounted a pair of steeds—thankfully a sedate, old mare
for Barty, which had patiently waited for his floundering efforts
to get into the saddle. It was this blessedly tolerant beast upon
whose back he had learned to bounce in the least comfortable
of ways as they had cantered along. Jean had ridden easily on
a steady, but grumpy, massive Clydesdale, a horse far too big
for Barty or, for that matter, Jean as well. Both horses were
normally used for other purposes around the Manor, but Jean
had put it on himself this day to take Barty somewhere, and
so it was he had been forced to learn as they rode to their
unspecified destination.

They had followed a road surrounded by old, shadowy forest, overgrown and wild, that led west for some miles. The
journey reminding Barty of just how secluded the Manor really
was, concealed from the world—and keeping the world from
it. As he was jostled about in the saddle, he was surprised to

see a train line cutting through the hills to the south, and roads upon which the occasional cart or carriage would travel. He had to wonder if any one of them knew about the presence of the Manor.

It was mid afternoon by the time they reached their destination; a cluster of buildings, some boats, with a single road leading out of it—a village, if one deigned to describe it as such, abridging the lake itself. It did not have a name, but if it did it would have been called 'Lakeside' or something else that was less a name and more a description. Barty did not question it. He was too busy worrying about how much his inner thighs hurt. Despite Jean instructing him for the entire ride, he had learned little and felt far too much.

He almost fell off the horse as they stopped outside a long, low stone building, with a thatched roof that had grass growing thick upon it in a green layer. It was old and weathered, ancient beyond Barty's ability to guess. Carefully sliding out of the saddle, he staggered immediately upon touching ground, his knees buckling. Already he was not looking forward to the ride home. Maybe someone would lend them a cart—but the dearth of carriages available was a forbidding reminder that a greater misery waited on the horizon. The countryside was, Barty was starting to learn, a most disagreeable thing to a Londoner.

"You have us here, but you have not told me what we are *doing* here," Barty complained.

Jean, with a far off look in his eye, gave a rasping chuckle. "We, Barty, are here to see a man about a drink." He marched down a set of steps that led to a battered door, the hinges creaking as they swung, and Jean slipped inside. There was a flare of golden light, and unexpectedly, an outcry of voices from within with tones of recognition. Barty, not knowing what else to do, followed afterwards. Before he even stepped past the door, he knew what awaited within from the smell.

The tavern was awash in light, lanterns scattered haphazardly on tables or hanging from the ceiling. A long coal firepit set in the floor burned bright, with openings in the ceiling that let the smoke drift upwards. The interior was hot enough to start a man sweating and awaken a thirst soon after. There was a bar at the far end and tables lined the sides around the firepit where hard bitten men, stained by their work and duties, were seated around drinking from fired clay mugs. They were raising mugs to Jean, who was warmer than Barty had ever seen him, moving from table to table to offer greetings and ask questions—questions about crop and harvest, about families and herds. Barty was bewildered. Having been born and grown in the city, he had never come across what country folk appeared like, nor their natures. Everyone seemed to know Jean. Barty however, was viewed with suspicion, if he was noticed at all. He hurried after Jean, and lurked at his shadow until the hunter moved to the bar.

"Afternoon, Henry," Jean greeted the man properly, holding out a hand. The man at the bar was a white-haired, withered old fellow, wearing a stained apron and smoking from a seething, terrible pipe, but his hanging jowls were turned in a smile at the sight of Jean. Taking the offered hand in his own, a mass of calluses and swollen knuckles, he shook it firmly.

"Afternoon, Mister Reynard. Be the usual?"

Jean shook his head. "Not this time. Bring out the special

reserve." He turned then, reached out, and took Barty by the shoulder. "Brought you a new one, Henry. He's here to learn today."

Henry looked Barty up and down, who stood blinking and wearing his fearful bafflement in his every hesitant movement. Henry tugged his wispy beard with thumb and forefinger. "He ready? Looks like he's more pup than war dog."

Barty wanted to respond, but Jean shook him fiercely by the shoulder and the words tumbled out his head before he could speak them. "Nonsense. He's ready as I was. And you remember that day fair well."

Henry rolled his eyes. "Were cleaning up for days afterwards, that one."

Jean snorted. "You have never cleaned this place a day in your life, Henry." There were a few raucous cries of amusement at that from behind Jean, and some agreement. Henry scowled and shook a dreadful dishcloth threateningly, to more laughter.

Henry paused then, and focused on Jean with a serious look on his face. "While I'm going about it, you should know. The old man is here, lad."

Barty watched Jean's expression turn, the well-natured look draining away. The seriousness he normally wore slid back, the lines of his face turning hard once more. "Where?" The cheer, too, left his voice, which was lowered as the tavern kept its rowdy commentary going.

Henry turned his head, jerking his chin to his left at an isolated corner to the rear of the bar where no light reached. There was a table there, and with their back to the wall, almost entirely hidden in darkness, was a figure. Barty watched a hand come out of the shadow—a hand wearing a leather, segmented gauntlet—that beckoned to Jean as he laid eyes upon them.

Barty had not seen Jean like this before. Not afraid, but hesitant. His jaw tightened, and then he finally exhaled. He nodded, then glanced to Henry, the publican giving him a sympathetic look. "Bring us the drink. We shall talk more in a moment. Come along, Barty." The barman departed towards a cellar, and Barty and Jean approached the figure in the corner, a patron that no one wanted to go near—let alone acknowledge.

In the darkened corner, Barty soon adjusted to the gloom to make out the fellow—and was surprised. Henry had not been wrong in his description. The seated man *was* old. He had white hair, wild and untamed, and a thick beard down to his chest. His clothes were rustic and crude, more akin to armour than simple garb—sturdy leathers, set with riveted pieces of iron. Across his back and shoulders was a tattered animal skin, and though it appeared to Barty to be a wolf's it seemed far too large. He leaned forward slowly, his eyes bright even in the darkness, and he grinned at Jean, a hard, fierce grin that seemed all too knowing.

"Been a while, Reynard. Was wondering if you had made it home." His voice was raspy, harsh from smoke and drink. "Knew you were back." He tapped his nose. "Never lies to me, this." He eased back, as though relenting from a challenge.

"You have not changed, McIntyre," Jean said dryly. "I admit, I didn't expect to see you here." His hackles were up. The seated man, McIntyre, seemed to sense it.

He sighed, then gestured. "And you haven't changed, neither. Find yourself a seat, lad. Who's the one you brought? You have another lamb and not tell me of it?"

Jean, in the midst of dragging a stool over when the offer had been made, froze in place at that. He remained locked for a heartbeat, before moving to slowly sit. "No." It was all he said, his tone cold. He gestured then to Barty, wordlessly—the lack of voice did not make it any less a command. He sat down as well.

McIntyre squinted at Barty, his face a lined mixture of scars and folds, weathered and bitter. He was large, bulky for his age, and clearly still terribly strong. "So. Going to introduce me to the boy?" He continued to eye Barty up and down. It was a distinctly uncomfortable feeling.

"This is Bartholomew Bartleby, my associate, and student." Jean grunted, his manner subdued. "Barty, this is Alastair McIntyre. An old friend of mine."

"And of Theodore Locke," McIntyre rasped. His gaze temporarily shifted to Jean as he spoke, he once more squinted at Barty, who nodded and despite himself, held out a hand to shake. It hung there, untouched, while McIntyre stared at it with such a ferocity that it should have scorched it until Barty retreated. "He's a timid sort. You raising this one soft too, I see."

"No, he is not." Barty was the one who spoke, surprising even himself. Jean cast a warning look, but the old man laughed harshly.

"Really now? I saw your hand, boy. Got the work marks, but not the battle scars. No calluses, no blood." He snorted, spat. "Locke made sure you bled every night and every day, Reynard. He taught you *right*. Taught you the old ways, like he and I both learned."

"And I have my scars to prove it," Jean growled. "Stick to your wolf killing, old man, and I will keep to my work." They glared at each other across the table while Barty shrank. There was a tight, painful tension to the air—but it was McIntyre who faded first, shaking his head.

"Aye. I suppose you earned it, well enough." He scooped up a bottle from the shadows, and pulled the cork. "Heard what you did in France, after all that went and happened." He grinned. "Fine work that. About time it was done." He took a swig.

Jean's expression was wooden, but it tightened around the edges in its shift to cold fury. "Do not speak to me of what I did, McIntyre." His tone was flat, but there was a threat in it that made the old man pause.

He lowered his drink, frowning. "There's no judging here, whatever you might think. I am just glad you finally saw reason. You *can't* trust 'em, boy. But I take no pleasure in telling you that." He took another swig, as Jean remained silent and terrible. "Seems you learned it well enough in any case."

"I was in a good mood, McIntyre. Trust your sorry arse to ruin it." Jean's tone was cold, his posture tight.

The old brute opposite him grinned. "That's the bite I was looking for. You need another thrashing to cool your temper?"

Jean snorted, snapping back. "I take no pleasure in beating an old man. I'll spare you the indignity."

McIntyre laughed at this, grinning toothily. "There's that Locke spirit in you, lad. I missed it." He seemed in better humour now, but Jean's mood remained dark. The old man turned to Barty then, watching him with a grin. "You need me to teach this one, like I taught you? Show him the tricks?"

"No need," Barty responded coldly. He did not like this man. "Jean teaches me plenty well enough." This was hardly correct, with Jean's haphazard teaching, but he would sooner bite his tongue off than admit it at that moment. The old hunter sneered, but Jean intervened.

"You know as well as I do it's true, McIntyre. Your quarry is not a problem on the isles any more. And there are none left in France, now."

"Don't remind me." The old man scowled, settling back into the gloom. "You're making me miss the old days. Can't even go on a holiday to Verdun and skin me another." He sounded disgusted, but Barty felt his skin crawl.

"Consider me an outsider to the conversation," Barty finally asked, looking from one to the other. "What are you talking about?" Both looked at him, but where McIntyre merely grinned, Jean spoke, even as he glared back at the old man across from him.

"Werewolves, Barty. Not the mixed bloods you have seen, but the full thing. McIntyre is a werewolf hunter."

The old man raised his bottle in a mock salute. "Retired now. Nothing but the mongrels left to kill." He gulped down a mouthful, gritting his yellowing teeth. "But I'll gut them too."

Barty remembered then, how James had tried to end the conflict between the hunters and the wolves. How he had managed to negotiate a peace, that, with his death, had been shattered and served as the catalyst of Jean's one man war of extermination. He remembered how ashamed he was of it, how the guilt for that bloodshed haunted him. Something that this man very clearly *approved* of. The thought made the hair on the back of his neck stand up, and he understood then, the sort of creature McIntyre was.

As if noting his stare, the old predator leered, and reached up to tug at the wolfskin around his shoulders. "Shame then I won't get another of these, unless I go far enough afield. Maybe into Germany—but that would mean going to bloody Germany." He scowled, but looked at Barty with a glint and that horrible smile returned as he explained. "You see, you can only get one of these off a werewolf. But not a dead one, no—when they die, they turn back into the human wretch that they once were. So"—he winked, his grin vile—"you've got to keep them alive as you peel it off. Takes some practise. Especially since they tend to *wriggle*." He tugged at the tattered fur thoughtfully. "Maybe I should anyway. This one is getting old."

Barty felt sick. He remembered Benji, anxious, helpful, and good-hearted back home. Suddenly, it became clear to Barty why Jean had made sure Benji stayed at the Lodge. Even the chance of crossing paths with this animal was a risk not worth taking.

There was another shadow then. The barkeep, Henry, had returned with a tray upon which stood two narrow glasses. An amber liquid sat in each, innocent and still, but the care with which Henry put them down made Barty cautious. Henry tapped Jean on the shoulder then, jabbing a thumb towards the bar. Without a word, Jean stood and both men walked towards the bar. This left Barty alone with the drinks. And Alastair McIntyre.

The old werewolf hunter watched him with a knowing sort of look, a sort of cruel smugness that seemed painfully familiar.

He chuckled then, setting his bottle down and leaning forward to rest both elbows on the crude table. "You're wondering where the animosity between me and him come from, don't you?" Barty shrugged, not trusting himself to speak, but the old hunter laughed softly. "Course you do. Written all over your face." He reached up, tapping his temple. "Not hard to figure out. And not hard to see, either. He does not like me much—but he does not need to." He gave a grim smile, but it eased into a pensive expression, the hard lines easing on his face.

"Do not mind us, lad." His voice was, surprisingly, much less harsh in that moment. "He and I are a mirror of each other. See too much of the same beast in another. Even if we're the same, we're too close to what we both hate."

"He's nothing like you." Barty finally found his voice. It was hushed but harsh, cutting over the chatter of the pub. McIntyre raised a brow, a knowing, loathsome sort of smile coming to his scarred face.

"Is that so? Never taught you the hard lessons has he? Always been *nice* to you, has he?" He gave an ugly chuckle, not needing an answer. Barty felt a twinge of doubt then. "No, boy," McIntyre went on, "he's the same as me. Maybe much, much worse. He doesn't *want* to be, but if wishes were horses, then beggars would ride—and he and I share the same muck in that regard." He snorted. "He tried to be softer once. Learned the sort of mistake that is, in this life."

"He learned from other mistakes, too," Barty retorted. "Ones he regrets far more."

"Like you?" McIntyre replied dryly. "You look like a mistake, to me. A comedy of errors, bumbling from one disaster to the next, never knowing the audience is laughing." He laughed then, nodding past Barty. "Here comes the next one now."

Jean's hand landed firmly on Barty's shoulder. "Barty? Get up. It's time." He hauled Barty to his feet, and reached down to pick up both glasses, one in each hand. He did not look at McIntyre, but the hunter did not seem to care, grinning in the dark as he watched.

"Time for us to leave?" Barty asked with a wary backwards glance at McIntyre, but Jean shook his head.

"Not at all. Follow me." And with that he marched on, even as Barty noticed the bar had, to a man, gotten to their feet, clutching their drinks. They were all looking at Barty now, sizing him up. He did not like it.

The back of the tavern opened up into a battered, run down backyard. There was a latrine off to one side, a stable and a chicken coop, but most of the space was dominated by dead grass flattened and worn down by many stamping feet. There was a wooden high fence surrounding the area, and as Barty watched, the crowd of tavern goers shuffled around to line the walls, creating an open square in the middle. Jean kept him to one side, watching, as Henry joined a group and started to speak to them animatedly.

"Jean. What *exactly* are we doing here?" Barty felt an inkling of suspicion, but one that had not quite formed fully yet.

Jean answered by holding out one of the glasses he still carried for Barty to take. "Drink this. You'll need it."

Barty took it, eyeing the man as he did so. He held the glass, and then sniffed, feeling his eyes water immediately as his sinuses cleared. The alcohol, whatever dreaded brew it might have been, was more fierce than any he had ever known. "What *is* this?" It felt like fire to breathe it in, he couldn't imagine drinking it.

Jean grinned. "Old, is what it is, Barty. Older maybe than the first stones placed here." He patted his shoulder. "You should feel proud. It is for special occasions, this."

Barty did not quite believe him. He did not know how he could possibly swallow the liquor either. "Are you going to drink yours?" he asked, trying to stave off the notion of drinking what he was holding.

Jean, however, shook his head. "No. They're both for you. One for now, and one for after."

"After what?" Barty felt his suspicions rising in a swell of growing panic.

Across the way, a rough looking man with a weathered face talking to Henry nodded, while staring across at Barty. He had a confident, determined expression. His compatriots all cheered, slapping the man on the back, as he started to pull his shirt off.

"After you fight him," Jean said cheerily.

Barty choked and nearly dropped his glass. The man across from him was no powerhouse, but nor was he a slouch either. His arms were browned from working in the sun, his knuckles worn, his face without fear. He watched Barty, who flinched from the stare and rounded on Jean, finally finding his voice after shock stunned him into silence.

"What? No!" This brought a lot of eyes towards him, even some jeering, but Jean spoke firmly, focused only on Barty.

"Look at me, Barty," he said firmly, any humour fading. "You and I spoke of this on the lake. You said you wanted to be stronger, didn't you?" He reached out, pushing the glass towards Barty's chest. "This is where it starts."

"Are you mad? He will beat me into the dirt!" Barty said, his voice strangled. "I've never fought anyone before!"

Jean snorted. "You tell me you grew up in an orphanage, and never had to throw a punch? You know what to do."

"That was just *children*," Barty hissed in desperation. His heart was pounding, his eyes darting about looking for an escape. There was none. The place was enclosed, and the crowd was watching him as Jean's hardened stare rooted him to the ground. He felt like a mouse in a cage. He felt like he was back in *that* place, where he grew up, unable to run, unable to flee, unable to do anything except hope it would not happen but even that was a lie, and—

Jean's hand caught him across the face. It was not brutal, but it was sharp and swift. It stung like ice on a burn, but it ripped Barty from his panic. "Look at me, Barty. Focus." Jean's tone was hard now. "If I knew another way to teach you, believe me—I would. But I know you. I know what you fear." He frowned. "You told me that you hated feeling afraid. You told me that you hated the idea of running away—something I know you could do, could have done, but haven't. What is different about this time?"

Barty swallowed, looking at his feet, the sting of the slap still ringing in his ears and across his face, spreading heat over his skin. But Jean was unrelenting.

"What did I tell you?" His voice was softer. "Out on the lake, what did I call you?"

Barty struggled, his hand trembling as he held the glass. "You said that I was brave."

"And so you are. You have *always* been brave, Barty, from the moment I met you." He gave his shoulder a squeeze, reassuring and firm, before letting go. "And because you are brave, I know what's going to happen now." A finger was jabbed into Barty's chest. "You are going to drink that. Then you are going to do what you have done, time and time again. You are going to walk towards the things that can hurt you, and through that crucible you will be forged a little bit stronger."

Barty stared at him, then at his apparent opponent, who was now standing on the opposite side of the impromptu ring, waiting patiently. The man had a look of acceptance on his heavy, crude features. Patience, without fear. But there was no mockery either. It was almost as though he understood Barty in that moment. Maybe he did.

He drank the entire contents of the glass. It was black fire going down his throat, smoke and cinders and the burning of the world. A great roar of approval went up as he did so. What was he thinking? He was still sore after riding the horse, but as that inferno hit his gut, it melted away. He was taking his own shirt off, walking forward. What was he doing? His mouth felt dry. His hands were shaking. Every nerve felt alive and electric. What madness was this? Was he just trying to prove Jean right? Did he need to believe it too?

Henry walked to the centre of the makeshift ring between the pair, and beckoned them both forward. Barty felt the liquor coursing through his veins as he stepped from the crowd, feeling gooseflesh rise all over his body. He felt scrawny, too skinny, too weak. Why was he doing this?

"Understand the rules then, yes?" Henry grunted at them both. "No biting, no gouging, no kicking them when they're down. And if one man quits, that's it."

"Can I quit now?" Barty heard himself say, and the crowd erupted into laughter. Even Barty's opponent grinned at that, a twinkle in his eye as he displayed broken teeth. Henry rolled his eyes however, giving Jean a sour look over Barty's shoulder.

"Fine, fine. First turn of the glass, lads." He pulled from his belt a small hourglass, and flipped it, the sand starting to fall immediately. "Let's see what you've got!" Henry stepped back, and with nothing between them, Barty realised how close the other man suddenly was. His opponent raised both fists, balling them up, as he gave Barty a nod. Without knowing what else to do, Barty returned the nod—and felt the world explode.

At first he did not know what had happened, as he felt himself reeling back. His legs were wobbly underneath him, not quite obeying his commands as his thoughts bounced around in his skull, careening off the inside of what felt like an empty space save for the ringing. There was pain, but it was far off, his cheek swollen already; but the sting of Jean's slap had been worse. The blow had been disorientating—but it did not hurt as much as he thought.

He had been punched, of course. He had seen it coming, a sharp straight right through an open guard on an unprepared opponent. Crisp and clean, it had smacked him in the face and wrenched his head back. He could taste metal in his mouth, and it was full of thick liquid. For a moment he wondered if the drink had come back up, but it did not nearly burn enough for that. No, this was blood, and he contemplated that as he saw the blur that was his adversary move in.

He put his arms up with fists half clenched, to ward against the hits he knew were coming, like one might protect their face from the rain of a storm rather than any sort of accurate defence. It proved worthless, as the weaving shape slipped through the cracks and picked at him with stinging, agonising strikes that hit the ribs, the face, one smacking against his ear and making him turn. He tried to move, to back away, but the crowd pushed him forward. There was a roaring in his ears, his heart a pounding drumbeat on the tides of fury and surge of blood. It hurt. He hurt all over. But less than he thought. There was laughter, mocking on the wind. Why was he doing this?

Because he had *chosen* to. Jean had pushed him, sure. Forced it maybe. But he could have hidden, couldn't he? He could have said no, surely? But he had not. He had chosen this. This was his.

Time slows down when you are fighting. Each lungful of air takes a million years, each steadying of the feet a million more. The sand falling through the hourglass, which Henry stared at obsessively with one eye while keeping another on the fight, felt like the end of time itself. Barty had no idea what he was doing, trying to block and strike back, but his blows had no real weight to them. His desperation made him reckless, and he threw a punch that was too wide, too big, and it put him off balance and into a left cross that turned the world off for a heartbeat before it came surging back. He was on his knees but could not remember falling. The crowd was roaring, but though he could not hear it, he *felt* it in the cavity of his lungs.

He looked up. Jean was there, and where everyone else around him was a blur of motion and empty, formless sound, he was still. He looked down at Barty, with a look that Barty had not seen on his face before. Confident. Knowing. He nodded then, jerking his chin in a wordless gesture. It pulled Barty to his feet, a hook through his nose yanking him upwards, as he stood, unsteady and wobbling a moment. He turned to face the other man whose name he did not know, but whose fists had etched onto Barty's skin, and the crowd howled once more. But the glass turned as the last grain fell, and Henry raised a hand to halt the proceedings. The crowd did not dissipate. Barty stumbled backwards, to be caught by Jean, who spun him around.

"One turn down. Two more to go," he said, his voice far away.

Barty was aghast. Two more? Of that? He tried to protest, but the words did not come as Jean grabbed him firmly by the back of the head.

"Look at me, Barty." His voice was harsh, but intense. "Why are we here? Do you know yet?" Barty shook his head, still lost, and the grip tightened. "Tell me. Are you as frightened as you were when you first started?"

That made Barty halt. He blinked. When this impromptu fight had begun, he had been shaking with terror. The fear of the pain to come had ripped through him, despite all his attempts to drown it. Now? Now it was there, but he shook for another reason. Adrenaline was coursing through him. Things hurt, but not as much as he thought. The fear he felt was less, even though he knew he was outmatched, even though he knew he could not win.

"You are learning something about yourself today, Bartholomew Bartleby," Jean said with a nod and a gleam in his eye. "Now get back out there, and learn some more." He spun Barty back around with one hand, gave him a shove as Henry raised his voice, and sent him headfirst into the sound and fury once more.

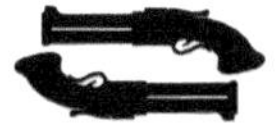

TWO MORE TURNS of the glass happened. And somehow, Barty remained on his feet for both of them, but collected all manner of bruises for his trouble, and blood besides. When the last call came, the man he was fighting had caught him as he had collapsed, and helped him to a battered stool as the watching crowd shouted congratulations, advice, good-hearted mockery and more.

Jean arrived, handing him the glass of liquor he had kept throughout. Barty did not even think as he downed it—it did not burn as much this time, for it was tempered by the blood in his mouth, and there was fire aplenty in his lungs. He had remained standing. He had even gotten a few punches in, and he almost felt like he had found a little of a rhythm in the chaos by the end. His blood was racing, his heart was pounding, and as that searing spirit spread its numbing from his stomach, he felt the pain that the lingering adrenaline could not keep away retreat a little further.

He had his eyes closed—despite it being a choice of his own, he had to admit in the case of one it was because he had to, the flesh around it swollen up so. His knuckles hurt from where he had struck, though he had not expected the ache in his wrists and elbows. But it was nothing compared to the agony in his face. He felt something cold pressed against it—a wet cloth, fresh with water from the lake. He opened one eye to see Jean holding it in place.

"How did I do?" His voice was rough. He'd been screaming his defiance at one point in the ring, hadn't he? He did not remember why. The scratch in his throat was a reminder.

Jean chuckled, glancing over his shoulder. "How did he do then, Mickey?"

The man called Mickey was pulling his shirt back on, his expression thoughtful. He had a few marks on his face, nothing serious save for a trickle of blood from his nose that he ignored. "He needs teachin', s'what." His voice had a melodious tint to it, a rural brogue that was at odds with his brutish features and his savage right hook. "But he's got the heart of it down." He walked over to Barty, who was too worn out to remember to flinch away, as the man who had just given him a thrashing held out a hand. "We'll do it again some time, yeah? Good fight, matey."

Barty blinked once, then reached out and took what had recently been a fist, now offered to him in respect instead of adversity. Mickey shook his hand with a grin, and with that firm grip Barty felt something warm in his heart blossom and flower. The fighter nodded to him in approval, and then sauntered off to the bar.

Barty watched him go. He had expected that he would hate the man, or at least feel fear, after the beating he'd just taken from him—he had suffered plenty in the past from people he had feared to the point of sleeplessness. But not this time.

It was not long before he and Jean were riding back. They went slow, even as the sun started to lower in the sky, with Barty clinging to the saddle, part blinded by the blazing ball of fire and the bloodied sweat in his eyes. Jean brought a bottle from the bar with them, and he applied it liberally to Barty as a tonic to keep the ache away. McIntyre had not been at his table when they went back in; he was nowhere to be found at all.

"So, how do you feel?" Jean asked, as they left the village behind, Barty's back still feeling the welts of the congratulatory smacks he'd received from the villagers, who had been far warmer to him in the aftermath of the brawl.

"Like a man who has been run over by a herd of horses," Barty replied, but he chuckled as he said it. Jean grinned, reaching out to steady Barty in his saddle from his own massive horse, nodding. But Barty went on, his tone still rueful, "I am remembering something Adam told me... that we choose our regrets." He winced, pressing a hand gingerly to his battered face. "I think I will regret this in the morning."

Jean rolled his eyes. "Adam would say that. And they are right, in the broader sense of things. But we choose what we overcome, as well." He handed Barty the bottle, who had a mouthful, reassured once more by the searing warmth. "We are defined by what we have overcome. And today, Barty, you fell—but you got back up. And you kept standing." He nodded, and Barty finally understood the tone of Jean's voice. He was *proud*. Not the muted, grudging pride he occasionally felt for him, this was fiercer than that—fiercer, and more true. It made Barty sit up taller in the saddle.

"Today cost you some blood. You can always get that back, though. But what today taught you was something no one can take from you, Bartholomew Bartleby. And you *will* remember it." Jean sighed then. "We are forged by our adversity, as much as our shame. It is inevitable that at some point, you are going to face a challenge you do not see coming. You need to learn how to react to that, and to know you cannot always run away. Today showed you that you do not have to."

Barty remembered the old, white-haired werewolf hunter, brooding in his scars and malice, a malice that he had seen in Jean more than once, but could not see now. "Is this how you learned too? Did Locke teach you this way?" Barty immediately regretted asking the question.

There was a touch of stillness, as though Jean was remembering, and a distance in the hunter's tone as he replied, "He taught me in a... similar fashion."

Barty had a flash of memory then, of the whip scars seared into Jean's back. He hurriedly buried it, and rearranged his thoughts, taking another sip of the bottle. "In the morning, I am probably going to complain about this," Barty said slowly. "I would like to complain about it *now*, but I will... try not to." He took a deep breath. "Right now though, I feel... I feel..." He was unable to put words to the sensation.

"Proud," Jean said, and Barty blinked, staring at Jean wordlessly, as he held his gaze. "You feel proud, Barty. Because you did not fall. Because you gave it your all, and faced what you were afraid of—not an enemy, but your own perceived weakness." He took the bottle off Barty, and drank a mouthful. "You were never weak, Barty. But you needed to be shown it was true. This was the only way I knew how."

Barty felt a lump in his throat. It swelled, and choked him, as he felt a stinging tear down his cheek. "Thank you, Reynard." He meant it. It was a silly thing, he knew. And yet it was everything.

Jean gave a chuckle, and passed back the bottle. "You won't thank me tomorrow. Tomorrow, you start training." He squared his shoulders, sitting up in the saddle. "Can't have you throwing that sort of nonsense in the future. But it was a good start." He touched his heels to the sides of the great Clydesdale he rode. "Now we better get back. Mrs Cosgrove will give us a far worse beating if we are late for dinner."

It hurt, but Barty grinned. He picked up the pace, noting this time he did not jostle so much in the saddle. They left the village behind, and whatever Barty had lost back there, right now, even with all the bruises and the pain—he knew he would not miss it.

Chapter 19

Unbound, Untethered

In the coming days, Barty would understand just how deeply he needed to appreciate the efforts of Adam in learning all that they could about treating injuries. The morning after the ride—the last of the journey being lost from memory thanks to the liquor masquerading as medicine that Jean had given him—Adam had concocted him something which, miraculously, stopped his skull exploding like a bomb. After applying cold cloths and more to get the swelling down, Barty learned that there were yet more tools at Adam's disposal, as he began settling into a new, and difficult routine.

Each morning, he would wake and partake of a hearty breakfast thanks to the marvellous efforts of Mrs Cosgrove. Afterwards, his time was spent in the sparring room until lunchtime. There, Jean would teach him how to fight. Barty was enlightened to the value of the jab, the necessity of kicking out a man's kneecap, how to brace his wrist and keep his hand loose until the apex of the punch, and much more. What he thought was mere brawling quickly became more and more complex. He had it demonstrated to him how the body was a series of balances and counter balances, how moving one part meant another had to move as well, how one movement made could force a response elsewhere. Jean showed him that a brawl had as much analysis as a crime scene, and every body part told its own story.

It did not take him long to understand why he had not informed him all this at first; it would have taken a lifetime, with no practical to fall back on. It had been a difficult task—but he was up to the challenge. The fear had faded. There was a joy in feeling strength, a joy he had never understood before now. And it was stronger than pain.

He studied how to use a sword, and for that he trained under Elanor. Though admittedly, this was a teaching that Barty struggled with in comparison. Elanor taught differently from Jean, and the lessons he learned in brawling at times conflicted with blade work—he would watch the wrong point, the wrong part of Elanor's body as she moved, and fail to see the strike coming. She often lost patience with that, and each time he took a sharp strike of punishment in a sensitive place he should have been defending. This was made all the worse by the faint air of awkwardness that remained between them, which lingered even in the most strenuous of engagements.

It did not help that she tended to wear the same terribly fetching outfit that had arrested his eye so thoroughly the first time he saw it. But he had nightmares of what might happen if he told her that while she had a sharp blade in hand or nearby, and so he had buried his thoughts deep—but never deep enough. Elanor remained stubbornly beautiful through-out, even when she lost her temper with him. He felt this was supremely unfair.

He was, by no account, good at these two things. It was

something that Barty freely admitted and that Jean and Elanor firmly reminded him of—though they did on occasion offer encouragement so that he might not become completely dejected as he sat on the floor in the midst of his own defeat, stinging shame, worse than any blow. But the third aspect of his martial training actually took him quite off guard—and everyone else.

Barty had fired a gun before; he had the necessity forced on him during his encounter with Hyde in the Bedlam asylum. But he had been desperate, and frightened, and those were hardly good circumstances to do so for the first time.

They had set targets out on the stone pier, so that any missed shots fired would splash harmlessly into the water, which at first was what Jean had expected—and Barty too, if he was honest. So it had been a complete surprise when Barty had fired his revolver—provided to him with reluctance by Cosgrove—and at a range of thirty yards, had nailed the target with each and every one of the six shots.

This was repeated, twice over. Barty did not miss.

True, his shots were not at all a tight cluster, but he was shocked. Not nearly as much as Jean, who had given but basic instruction; control his breathing as he fired, make sure the crosshair was level in the sight, and visualise the barrel as a pointed finger at the target as well. To keep both eyes open and not to squint too hard. And last of all, to squeeze, and not pull. Barty had listened, put it into action, and it had worked. Before long Barty was practising with somewhat more powerful weapons—a lever action rifle, a double barrel hunting shotgun. It was when he managed to shoot a flung clay plate out of the air, with the shotgun kicking hard into his shoulder, that he finally earned some grudging praise.

"You are many things, Bartholomew Bartleby," Jean had told him, "but a bad shot is *not* one of them."

And that seemed to be about all. But it was, for Barty, a mixture of pride and shame. He was good at something, true—but he was all too acquainted with what guns were used for, what they were capable of. Jean displayed a casual brutality in their use he did not want to become familiar with. But there was no time to be wasted, and he pressed on to more, day after day, as the week rolled on.

Throughout each session, Lily was present. Each of the household insisted on it, in truth—as much as possible, Lily was to be kept in company. Sometimes she would walk the grounds, in the presence of whomever was available—Elanor, Adam, and Barty all took turns to keep her accompanied at all times. Adam had explained why—she needed people to ground her.

Barty noticed that Lily often would reach out to touch those she spent time with, to take a hand, or an arm, to bring herself close. Not just to him, as time went on—it became obvious that she in some way *needed* it, to calm herself. No one objected. No one minded. Barty for his part tried to keep her spirits up—she tended to fuss over him, especially when he returned bruised and battered. This gentle trend continued as he worked himself into exhaustion each night, the strict training of Jean and Elanor such that what spare time he had was spent doing *something*, be it training or study. Her enduring kindness was something he never failed to find touching, her consideration for others despite her own desperate, terrible situation. But he was worried for her. She struggled in her new circumstances, torn between being glad of her freedom, but at the same time missing her family, and of course the torture of her existence. Sometimes she was well, speaking of things that she adored and longed to see, such as her dream to attend the ballet and the opera, things that she had been but able only to imagine and read about. At other times she was found alone, face in her hands, locked in silence that would have been weeping if tears could exist for her. Always she put on a brave face when she was found, and comforted, if any could be seen on her immobile features. Always, were her carers reminded that they were only delaying the inevitable.

The afternoons were also far from free, for that is when the research took place. The effort to learn more from the writings of Mary Shelley, the brilliant genius that had made Adam, was proving fruitless and frustrating. And not least because there was much to learn.

Shelley had been many things; a writer, a scientist, an engineer, a poet, a philosopher, an alchemist, a magician, and a political rebel—all that and more. As such, her writing covered numberless topics; much of her writing was in short hand, formulae, and numeration. Jean and Adam did the majority of the study, but they would occasionally read things out that Barty would write down—a reference to a book, a page to return to later, or a scratching of information that might prove relevant.

During such time, Lily was not present. Elanor would instead take her to one of the many rooms in the Manor to keep her both comforted or entertained, or out onto the grounds itself.

There was good reason for this. The notes of Shelley were, at times, difficult to get through, not because of their complexity, but because of the horrors they dwelled upon.

Aside from the intricacy of the magical elements and the engineering, there was the nature of the subjects covered. In the basement laboratory, Jean had touched on the dreadful circumstances of the unfortunate women, each of them pregnant at the time of their death, and how that unborn life could be used. Barty had not understood it then. He had not wanted to understand it at all. But it soon became crucially, unfortunately important.

They were in the armoury. This was the third aspect of Barty's studies and Cosgrove took what time he could deign to spare to instruct Barty on the nature of myriad weapons, the forges, and the laboratory that Adam kept. Barty spent his time performing maintenance on various mechanical devices when necessary, taking the work off of Cosgrove's hands. It was a talent he yet still had a knack for, to understand the construction of something and put it back together. He had missed it—the chance to lose himself in mechanical understanding, and to triumph in ingenuity and revelation. He had to admit it was simpler than dealing with people. A grandfather clock from the house had lost time, so Barty worked on finding the slipped gear while Cosgrove worked on the far more important things. Which were firearms.

The double barrelled rifle called Delilah was brought back into form under Cosgrove's careful eye. It took extraordinarily patient machining on the butler's part, as he worked himself into a sweat-drenched lather by the light of the forge. On occasion Adam would assist—being able to handle molten, red hot metal as easily as Barty might spin a finger in a glass of water, the giant made such tasks quite simple indeed.

Cosgrove had more than guns to work upon. As Barty gently adjusted the clock to keep proper time, the butler worked on refining the armour Barty had been caught examining on his first inspection of the room—the heavy steel plate designed to deflect a bullet. Cosgrove had, in fact, demonstrated this veracity when Barty had once entered and been forced to dive for cover as a ricochet bounced off the chest plate and over his head, where it had buried into the wall. Cosgrove had been upset about that—the wall, not the fact he had nearly killed Barty. In fact, he seemed quite resentful that Barty had not sacrificed himself to prevent such a calamity. Some men are difficult to please.

He was working on something else this day however. It was long, and very heavy, and brutally murderous. The Maxim model machine gun was a belt-fed, watercooled device of concentrated slaughter, capable of firing some six hundred rounds a minute. It was not, Jean had said, any sort of use whatsoever to a hunter, instead designed for warfare and to be wheeled around and set in a defensible position, to fire on oncoming forces, rather than hauled around by a lone person.

Cosgrove had taken this as a personal challenge. How he had gotten his hands on what was purely military hardware, a crime for which hanging was the *smallest* of punishments, he did not say, and no answer would have surprised in any case. And now he was reworking the mechanisms and materials, finding ways to make it lighter, to make the bulky ammunition feed more functional for a lone individual. He was making progress, and apparently had been for more than a year. Barty remained sceptical. The damn thing was entirely too menacing for his liking. If any of the weapons in the workshop suited Cosgrove's personality, it was this unforgiving monster—that, or a headsman's axe.

Adam was above them, on the upper platform where their modest, expansive laboratory was found. They had created a device that Barty recognised—one of the glass cylinder mechanisms, much like that had been found in both the terrible cellar and in the vault. As Barty watched, drawn from his work on the clock, Adam made use of various unknowable machinations to set an indefinable *something* spinning in its core that soon set the entire machine to humming—vibrating, much like the ones that had been in the cellar in the warehouse. They held out a hand towards it and, as Barty stared in fascination, arcs of energy leapt off and seemingly attached to Adam's fingers. They frowned as they beheld the reaction, moving their fingers slowly—each fingertip had its own dancing arc of blazing power, twisting and shifting with hypnotic beauty. The light itself was blinding, illuminating the look of contemplative sorrow on Adam's features.

Barty could bear it no longer. He left his workstation and clambered up the steps to the upper level, where Adam held out their free hand in a warning. Cosgrove barely glanced up as he continued etching symbols into the heavy, rifled barrel with a diamond tipped engraving tool.

"What *is* that, Adam?" Barty asked, his voice hushed.

Adam did not turn their head as they spoke. "You recognise

it? I created my own to understand the process." The hand with the flowing energy lifted upwards, the arc of raw, unfettered power holding even as it bent and twisted to follow. "And now that I do, I see it for what it is. This is, essentially, a binding tool."

"It does not look like any sort of rope to me," Barty managed awkwardly.

The giant actually gave a soft chuckle at that. "Nothing quite so crude. These devices—capacitors if you will—are able to hold and create a charge. They created a polarisation effect to draw energy from the storm that surged overhead, a sort of attraction charge. They captured that energy—however briefly—and then used it to create life, where before there was none." The fingers moved as though playing an instrument, the arcing energy shifting over each fingertip in a loving caress. "Take heed, Barty. You are witnessing the primal shape of galvanisation. Promethean fire, from which life might spring."

Barty could read it in Adam's face—the bitterness. "From where you came as well, isn't it?"

The giant looked over at him, then closed that mighty fist. The flaring energy blinked out, and was gone, as Adam sighed. "Yes, Barty." Their voice was soft, and sorrowful. "This is where I came from."

Barty moved in closer, to take a seat nearby. "Might you tell me what you can?" He gave a rueful smile as Adam looked at him doubtfully. "As simply as you can, at least. Much of this is beyond my understanding."

The giant considered a moment, then gave a timid shrug. "Very well." Adam gathered their thoughts before going on.

"The notes of my maker demonstrated an understanding of... utilisation of the neverborn," Adam said slowly. "Souls that were denied their chance at life, denied their potential—the life that might have existed becoming instead a future that never came to be." Adam shook their head, sighing. "Understand that this is not a judgement. It simply is what it is—not all lives are ones that get to live. The world is not so simple that it can be one or the other." The giant grimaced. "But such is what it is. The neverborn are... different. And they are vital to the act of resurrection—and galvanisation."

"What is that? Galvanisation?" Barty asked.

"It is the energy that powers the body. The two parts—the power to create the movement, and the mind to give that power purpose." Adam held up two fingers to indicate. "One cannot work without the partner to its synchronicity. Magic can work only in one; science in the other. You need both to make the process complete, and that is a frontier with little knowledge. Until Mary Shelley."

Barty nodded, frowning. He shuddered though, unsure. This was something he did not understand, and did not want to, but he still wanted to *listen*. There was much that he had gathered over the past few days during the note taking. He wanted clarification upon it. "Between that and your notes, I am gathering that this is at odds with how Lily was made."

"This is correct. Lily is entirely different from how I was created—Shelley bound a neverborn, a life that never was, to... this shell, this body." Adam grimaced, looking down distastefully at their hand. "They used the energy of galvanisation to bind that energy and create life—create *me*. But Lily... is not that. Lily is a life that already lived. A *specific* life. And instead of a new, unknown life, hers is one that lived before, in a body that was her own. This new form she bears is quite unlike that. And I do not yet understand what it might mean."

The giant contemplated the still humming glass cylinder before them, rubbing their massive jaw. "There were three unfortunates in that cellar. None of them were Lily herself. Were they all necessary? Was there a mistake leading up to the creation? And how did he manage it? How did he bind Lily to that form?" Adam sighed in frustration. "And *why?* Because of her illness? Why did he do such an awful, wretched thing to her? The strain of her new life is a constant, unending misery. She remembers too well the life she had before. I cannot imagine how awful it must be."

"You have no memory of a... previous life?" Barty asked curiously.

Adam shook their head firmly, dark hair spilling across their features. "None. While understanding and realisation may have come quickly, and consciousness formed swiftly on my awakening—I have no flashes, no hints at the life that might have come before. I was born fully formed and knowing to the world, but without the ability to convey myself. It took... time." They fell silent, frowning. "But I did learn. Lily had quite the opposite situation. She fell asleep, and awoke into a nightmare she could not rise from. I would not say that I cannot begin to explain it—but somewhere in these notes is the clue how."

Barty frowned then, crossing his arms over his chest. "And this is all of her notes, correct?" Adam hesitated to respond as Barty went on, "Because when we found the first of these"—he gestured vaguely to the cylinder—"capacitors, as you call them, Jean said that this made it clear someone had found a way to copy the research. That something must have been left behind. Do you still disagree with that?"

Adam shook their head, looking away. "Not any more, no." They frowned. "Not just for that—there are references to a volume that appear from time to time in the notes, in the margins. Mary refers to a collection of her research that... simply is not here. I am sure of it. I would undoubtedly have found it by this point if so."

"Instead of finding answers, we are finding more mysteries," Barty grumbled. "This is not how I expected this to go, in truth."

There was a harsh snort from below. Barty peered down, to see Jean had—somehow—appeared out of the aether, standing near Cosgrove, who was replacing part of the assembly of the evil-looking machine gun. "You should know by now that this is how these things tend to go. If you do not, you have not been paying attention," Jean growled as he glanced up. "You could perhaps *try* asking the young lady in question about these things. She is quite amenable to conversation, after all."

Adam frowned. "I am not sure about that. She has been under enormous pressure as of late, and some of her behaviour has been... concerning me, somewhat. Her moods vary to degrees that I struggle to properly gauge." They sounded doubtful, to which Jean scowled.

"Your heart continues to be far too kind for this line of work, Adam." His tone was scathing at first, but then it softened somewhat. "However, you are right in some regards. The girl is struggling, and more than I feel comfortable with. We shall need to do something about it, but I am at a loss as to what it might be."

Barty felt a compulsion to speak up. "I can go and look for her, if you would like. Perhaps she and I can talk."

Adam looked speculatively at Barty, but nodded. "She *does* quite like you, I have to admit," they said carefully. "She tends to be happier in your presence than mine, that much is certain."

Barty's cheeks flushed red, the hot sensation of guilt coiling in his soul. "I am not sure why that is," he lied, and he could not help but despise himself for it. He had come to understand why it was the case. Adam gave a sad smile, knowing, but sympathetic—and it made Barty feel all the more worse, because Adam did indeed know why too.

Barty was the hope, the representation of what could be—of the life she dreamed for but could never truly have. She longed for it even now, the life of a normal young woman, to perhaps have a suitor, a social circle of those her age. The tragedy of it was that she was closer to that experience now than she had been while living. Adam was a reminder of what was, and what had become—for all their kindness, their understanding, and the warmth of their being, Adam represented a terrible future. A lonely existence, where her dreams could never come true. Adam, better than anyone, understood—and yet, it was still something that none of them could fully grasp.

Barty departed the armoury in shame, as Jean was testing the weight of the Maxim. He did not like confronting that realisation, did not like seeing Adam as something other than the person they sought to be. Adam strove, continually, to be other than that which they inexorably *were*, and instead what and who they chose to *be*. It was something they had proudly told Barty during the days that they first met. Lily did not mean to hurt Adam with that pushing away—she probably was not even aware that she was doing it. And yet it was a painful reminder of what was not to be, and perhaps, never could be. It was not right. And it was not fair.

He went looking for Lily, and called out her name as he searched. She was not with Elanor, who was going over the piled notes in the library, which was admittedly unusual.

"She left for the west wing, I think." Elanor didn't look up, her expression intent as she peered through one of Shelley's journals, twirling a lock of her otherwise bound hair. She was still in her fencing gear, curled up on one of the couches. "She displayed a bit of interest in the music hall." She paused then, as though considering something, but realising Barty had not moved, she lowered the book to give him a suspicious look. "What is it?"

Barty was caught off guard. He had not been staring—in fact he had been looking anywhere else to avoid being taken for staring. But he had been concentrating on it so hard that he had forgotten to say anything, and so he desperately tried to cover this fact, fumbling as he did so. "How does she seem to you? Has there been much change in her condition?" He glanced at her, but would not turn to her.

Elanor squinted a moment, then she sighed. "I do not know, Barty," she confessed, subdued. "Unless she tells you her thoughts, there is no way to read them in her." She grimaced then, clearly unhappy. "She has lived much of her life trying to make sure people do not worry about her. A gentle and selfless thing, but it makes it terribly difficult to actually know how she feels." She pinched the bridge of her nose, and now Barty did look at her—and saw for the first time the shadows under her eyes. She had not been sleeping well—or more likely, she had been keeping herself awake as long as possible each night to keep Lily company, for her inability to sleep was such that inevitably, she was forced to spend hours alone in silence, or in the company of Adam. Though Barty had a feeling she had been back to watch him in his sleep. She had just become more skilled at concealing it.

"Go check the west wing, Barty. I would appreciate it," Elanor said then, her voice softer. He nodded, and made his way, hoping that Elanor would get some rest in his absence—but knowing to mention it would only bring resentment.

He ventured on. Calling out Lily's name, he heard no answer—but this did not concern him at first, the place was quite large after all. If she was occupied, she would not hear him. But as he entered the west wing, there was an undefinable sensation of discomfort in the air, wrought in deathly silence.

It was not that the place normally felt alive; it was actually something that made sleeping in the guest wing difficult. The eastern wing of the Manor had the kitchens, and the rooms of all the members of the Reynard family. Adam had a room there, and beyond the kitchens were the cottages where Cosgrove, his wife, and myriad offspring of their clan resided, where Mrs Cosgrove reigned as the supreme ruler and with an absolutism that far outdid any mere monarch. But Barty dwelled in the western wing alone, and there was no sound, no presence.

Compared to the bustle of London, the ringing of bells on the hour that came with it, the lack of background sound was painful to deal with. He would often wake in a startle from the sheer *absence* of sound. Of course, this ended once the horizon gave the slightest hint of dawn's presence, and the woods exploded into birdsong. It at least gave him some solace.

And yet, the quietest dead of night did not compare to the feeling he had now. This was different; there was a *wrongness* to the air. When his footsteps caused a creak in the floor beneath him, he jumped without knowing why. The hairs on the back of his neck stood up. He wished he had a gun with him, the revolver that he was becoming ever more familiar with, and hated himself for it. He did not like that it was the first thing that his mind went to.

He did not call out, not any more. Instead, he moved carefully, slowly, along the hallways, pushing open doors without knocking. The feeling, the *knowing*, would not go away. In fact, as he went from room to room, it became worse and worse.

On the second floor, he found her. She was facing the westernmost edge of the Manor, an open space with high windows that looked out over the forest and the lake. She stood at one of those windows, staring out as the sun was lowering. A shower of rain had put the landscape to glistening, the golden light of the day's end giving the scenery a lining of fire, fierce and warning, the clouds a blazing, burning orange. The light dimmed, as gloom and twilight swallowed the world.

And Lily stood there, silent, rigid. She faced the window, and she did not move, and she was still, so very still, that Barty did not call out to her. He felt his skin crawl, his heart beat faster, as sweat formed on his skin. *Something was wrong.* He did not know what, but instinct had kept him alive for much of his life, and at this moment it was screaming at him.

It took him a moment to understand it. Until now, despite everything and how she appeared, Lily had always seemed alive. And through her being alive, no matter how strange her appearance, she had felt *human*. For all the unnatural nature of her visage, her manner was such that it never strayed from thoughts that, yes, this was a person. A normal, ordinary person, under everything else. But right now, that was gone.

It was something Barty thought she had shared with Adam, this sense of living despite all else that spoke otherwise. But when Adam had been frozen in place in the cellar of the Lodge, there had never been the feeling that there was *nothing there*. Instead, it felt all along like that they were about to wake up. Any moment, they would have stirred and everything would be as it was. That potential, that energy, had lingered in the air around Adam at all times. Now, in Lily's presence, there was only a silence, a stillness that radiated out from her like ripples from a stone thrown into a pond. It was chilling.

He drew closer, holding his breath. She was wearing a long dress, and stood frozen like a mannequin upon which it was being displayed. He drew alongside her, and at last, he tried to speak her name. It died in his throat. Her porcelain mask stared out over the grounds, towards the forest, but something about it chilled Barty to the bone. And then the realisation came, and hit Barty like a hammer. There was no light in her eyes. The green burning light was gone. Just empty glass remained. He was alone. There was no one else here.

"Lily?" he asked in a choked, terrified whisper. A shaking hand reached out and touched her metal shoulder—it was cold. Terror gripped him, but a new kind of fear. "Lily, are you there?"

For a sickening heartbeat, then two, then three, there was nothing. And then, with a stutter and a flash, the green glow in Lily's eyes returned, almost as though she had blinked. In an instant, her posture changed, her bearing shifted. Life blazed through her all at once, an unnatural shift that was as startling as to be frightening. She turned towards him, her eyes flaring with surprise.

"Oh. Mister Barty? How lovely to see you again." Her tone was bright, and cheerful, just as it always was when she spoke to him. But her head tilted as she saw his startled countenance, flinching away from her. "Barty? Whatever is the matter?" A note of gentle bewilderment crept into her voice.

He fought the urge to scream. It had been so *sudden*. One moment she was naught but a statue of brass, porcelain, and glass. Now she was alive again—warm. He swallowed, forcing himself to smile. "I was just looking for you. Apologies. I think I was meant to be your guardian for this evening."

She shook her head, the green glow flaring in her eyes then muting. "Evening? But it is still just afternoon..." Her face shifted to the setting sun. "Isn't it?" That growing doubt intensified. The friendly tone turning worried.

"The sun sets early around here," Barty lied, stepping in and offering his arm. "Come. Let me take you to the library. I think Adam wished to talk to you as well?"

He had to distract her. Whatever it was that was wrong, he

had to stave off that fear, even as he wondered how he would tell Adam and Jean. So he lied again, and tried to comfort her. And again, she trusted him, nodding her head and taking his arm. Barty led her from the window and the setting of the sun, wearing a smile to hide his shame, even as the spectre of that memory lingered behind him.

A place where a body stood, but no soul lingered.

Chapter 20

The Manor Ball

"There you are!"

It was Elanor, more energised than usual, pointing an accusatory finger at Barty. She had foregone her training clothes, instead opting for a more ladylike attire of an ankle length skirt and blouse of dark blue. He sat in the kitchens, with a mouthful of egg and bacon, wearing a baffled expression. An embarrassing moment of chewing and swallowing followed thereafter, before the ability to respond was finally presented. "You need me for something?"

She lowered the finger, squinting at him. "Can you dance?" The question took him entirely off guard, and he shook his head. Elanor rolled her eyes and sighed. "Well, today you are learning. I have an idea."

Barty was not prepared for this. Mrs Cosgrove, however, looked excited. "Oh, dearie—what do you have planned?" She clapped her hands together. "Did you need me to bring my husband along? It's been *so* long since we both turned a jig."

Elanor grinned at that, mischievous and cheered. "Why not? Do let him know, we shall be starting at six of the clock. Now then, as for *you*." She turned serious again to Barty. "You are coming with me."

He knew better than to argue. He scooped up a couple of slices of buttered toast, mumbled his gratitude to Mrs Cosgrove with a bow even as she bade him to hurry, and followed after the young Miss Reynard. She barely slowed her determined march, hair flying behind her as she strode with a fierceness. "What exactly is this about, Elanor?" he asked through a mouthful of bread.

"Well I thought that was obvious, Barty. *Dancing*," she chided. "Specifically, ball dancing, like all young lords and ladies like to do." She paused in her steps, took a moment to get her bearings, then turned right down another corridor. "Haven't you ever wondered what it would be like?"

"Not particularly," Barty confessed. "I have had other things on my mind—but that is not what I meant." Having finished his toast, he tried again. "I *mean*, where did this come from?"

It had been two days since the incident with Lily, and her moment of unnatural stillness. Barty had explained to Jean and the others what had occurred—but there had been no answer forthcoming. Lily had not mentioned anything odd, and Adam's careful probing, not to mention their other questioning, had not borne fruit. Whatever had happened, it yet remained a mystery. But now that Elanor was full of energy about whatever *this* was, intuition told him there was a connection.

"If it is not obvious to you, then I hardly feel like telling you will help your understanding," Elanor grumbled as she pushed the doors to the Hall of the Oak. She stood with her hands on her hips for a moment before loudly decrying. "Right then. Let's clear this out of here." She turned to Barty and, with an imperious wave of her hand, summoned him forward.

As they were putting the scattered files, chests, and furniture to one side of the hall, Barty had to find out more, his curiosity demanding satisfaction. "So," he grunted under the weight of a dragged chest. "I understand *what* we are doing. But I am at a loss to understand *why*."

She was about to answer, when from behind them came the somewhat wrathful voice of Jean. "Yes, *do* explain why I am suddenly seeing all our research being hurled aside, daughter dearest." He strode in from the training hall, his expression perplexed and suspicious. "What are you up to?"

Elanor made an exasperated sound, but straightened up, folding her arms across her chest defensively. "This evening, I have decided to hold an evening of dance," she said firmly. "For Lily's sake."

Jean frowned, looking from one to the other. "This is hardly the time for such things, Elanor." He folded his own arms across his chest, a pugnacious stand off building between them. But Barty sensed there was a different current to the air. Elanor's temper however, flared.

"This is the only time for such things, Father! The girl has been cooped up here away from her family for more than a week. She has been patient, and tolerant of us whisking her away from her life—but we need to do more than that." She turned away. "She... she told me of how she used to dream of going to a ball. And how she used to read books on ballet and imagine practising the movements. But she could not even leave her bed. Now she can, Father. And I think we should take advantage of that." She hugged herself tighter, then turned and waved anxiously at Barty. "You agree, don't you Barty? We can put everything back where it was tomorrow. But surely one night...?" Her tone and expression were pleading. It was not an attempt at deception. This appeal was a genuine one.

He nodded, to both her and to Jean. "She is right, Jean," he heard himself saying. "This is an excellent idea." He stole a glance to Elanor, who had brightened considerably at his words, as he went on, "While I have no talent in either music, or dancing—I will help how I can." Jean said nothing, but watched Barty intently, who met that stare and did not back down from it. "This is the right thing to do. You know that."

For a moment, the tension twanged in the air. Then it snapped as Jean threw up his hands in defeat, letting out a chuckle. "Very well, very well." He sounded only faintly resigned, a slight smile playing about his lips—Barty was quite sure only he noticed it, and had to wonder how genuine his resistance to the idea actually was at the sight of it. "I shall see to the music. Elanor, do me a favour, and teach young Barty how to dance, would you?"

"Me?" Barty blinked, as Elanor drew up alongside him promptly. "Why me?"

"Because, Barty," Elanor said, sizing him up with a critical eye, "Lady Braithwaite was raised a lady, and despite her lack of practise, the ability to dance is likely ingrained in her very blood. *You*, however, are what we might call useless." She grinned then as he opened his mouth to object. "But we can set about changing that." Despite her teasing, for once, she actually looked pleased about the entire affair, her eyes sparkling somewhat more than usual. His customary protest died in his throat.

"I presume you have already spread word of this in any case." Jean glanced sidelong at Elanor, who shrugged innocently. "Very well. The piano will do for the most part. But I will see what else can be managed." And with that, he strode from the hall, leaving Barty and Elanor alone.

There was a moment of pause, before Elanor finally took a deep breath. "Thank you," she said. "Maybe I would have convinced him anyway but... you made it easier. So, thank you." She nodded, and he returned it, feeling awkward for a moment. This was a side of Elanor he did not get to see much, and it left him off kilter. But he felt a blush in his cheeks for a reason he could not understand. Not quite yet.

"Where is Lily at the moment?" he asked, not entirely out of curiosity but more to cover the silence.

"Going through my wardrobe—and some of the others. There are clothes enough here in rooms from generations ago. Someone must have liked balls once upon a time." She huffed, then rubbed her chin thoughtfully, in a manner not unlike her father. "I admit I have never been to one either. But Mother insisted on teaching me to dance for one. I am sure I remember enough to instruct you."

And with that, she strode to the middle of the space they had created, and held out one arm to him imperiously. "Now get over her and stand before me."

"Right now?" Barty asked stupidly, taken off guard. This earned an exasperated glare.

"Yes. Right now. Don't just stand there like a goose."

There was no arguing with her. He scrambled over and stood

awkwardly, fingers fidgeting by his sides a moment. Elanor gave him a withering look, then reached out and took his hands. Hers were cool and strong, her palms callused from holding a sword, even with the gloves she wore. And yet, he did not find it objectionable. She held his left to one side, with the elbow bent, and the other, she carefully set at her hip.

"Place your hand on my back," she instructed. She seemed to note the rising panic in his eyes as she quirked a smile. "I will not bite you, Barty. Relax." Her voice softened, the smile understanding. "Now come on. It won't be much, but we should do this right, don't you agree?"

He hesitated, then nodded. "You never really explained—why me?" Barty asked as she ran him through the basics—how he was supposed to be the lead, and how to both step, and turn, and guide all at the same time. It was a strange sensation. He was clumsy about it, but for all her claims of being without practise, Elanor moved like water, smooth and inexorable. She looked away, a sorrow on her features.

"Because Lily will want to dance with a boy her age. She has never had the chance before. But she has dreamed of it for years," she explained. "Adam will do their best, and Father will not dance at all—he has his reasons. But you are the one she is going to want to choose. You are the one who can make this special."

Barty felt it acutely; the recognition that Lily had affection for him. The importance of what he was doing suddenly became overwhelming. "Then you are correct. We had best do this properly," he said quietly, watching her face. Reminding himself yet again—a fact easily forgotten as he concentrated on remembering the steps—that she was very, very close to him. And unlike usual, without a sword or knife in hand. The difference it made was striking.

She smiled. A lock of her hair hid the scar on her face, but it did not need to. It was a pretty smile—no, a beautiful one, scar or no—and it froze him up a moment, and he tripped, stumbling into her awkwardly. She leaned back, only slightly, as she steadied herself to stop him from falling completely. He regained his balance, but for a split second, he was pressed against her, and her face was close to his—too close, and yet a wild part of him thought, sudden and sharp and from nowhere, that she was not close enough.

He pulled away, his cheeks flaming. There was colour in *her* cheeks too, quite unlike her, and perhaps a knowing sort of look too because she gave a smirk, shaking her head.

"Do mind your step, Barty. We cannot have you flinging yourself at Lily like some sort of uncouth brute." She winked. "Have to be careful with such things. A lady might get the wrong idea, after all."

"O-o-of course," Barty stuttered, blushing so hard he feared he would catch fire. She had the good grace not to laugh, but she *did* clearly know.

"That aside, you're not terrible at this. Hopeless, yes. Terrible, no," she mused speculatively. Her smile tinged with sadness as Barty resumed their pace. "James had two left feet. He never managed to get the hang of it." She took her hand off Barty's shoulder to wipe hastily at one eye. "But he never failed to make people laugh as he did so. It was worth watching him trip up for the grin he gave everyone afterwards." She sighed then, falling quiet.

Barty did not know what to say. But as they practised that dance in silence, the steps to the count that they had learned to time to their breath, he remembered that there was something he *should* have said. In fact, he should have said it days ago.

"I am sorry, Elanor," he said. She gave him a confused look then, frowning, but he was not finished. "When we went to see your mother—I was resentful, I was angry, I was..." He stopped making excuses. "I was a fool. I said things that were abominable. And I am sorry. I will never say anything like that again."

The steps slowed, then stopped, as she looked at him with an inscrutable expression. A flicker of a smile appeared at the corner of her mouth. "Well, it certainly took you long enough," she said, then she laughed, shaking her head in apparent disbelief, before gently tugging on his arm to make him resume once more. He hesitated, not quite sure how to respond to her words, before he did as she bid, after which she started to speak.

"All jests aside—I do appreciate you saying that, Barty. But let us please be clear about what happened." Her voice turned firm. "*You* said some terrible words. *I* nearly got you killed. Twice, in fact. Once with my mother, and after when I left you behind and those thugs took you." She grimaced. "In my defence, I did not mean either of those things to happen. But I can also admit I would have a hard time forgiving that happening to *me*, and so I cannot really hold much of a grudge." She exhaled, and looked up at him from under her lashes. "Though it is nice to hear you say that, either way. Apology accepted, Barty. And my own given."

"And likewise, accepted," Barty said, his voice wavering somewhat. It felt like a rock had been lifted off his heart, a weight he had not known was there. Even his breath felt light. Getting rid of that feeling was better than he imagined it would feel, and he could not help but notice that Elanor's mood towards him had improved somewhat.

Though there was little time for small talk after that. Barty instead concentrated on learning the steps. It was tiring, especially with his body so worn down by the daily efforts taken in the training hall, but determination nevertheless drove him onwards. So he pushed on, relentless, until it was time for him to go and get ready.

ELANOR HAD TOLD HIM what needed to happen. How things were to be done properly, and had made him practise *that* as well. And so it was, a little after six o'clock, that all was ready. The board was set. The time had come. The Manor of the Society of the Hound came alive, however gently. The sound of a piano playing—a patient, almost thoughtful refrain that carried down the corridors, danced out into the night, and to the right and listening ears, was heard all the way out in the surrounding forest.

Barty strode into the Hall of the Oak. Be confident, Elanor

had said. Be forthright. So he had set himself and pushed open the double doors, to stand for a moment and take things in.

The Hall had been altered, just enough. The great frozen tree still took up its heart, but now the couches and chairs had been banished to the sides to create an open stage. Candles were everywhere—casting a warm glow that turned the centre of the hall to golden light, the upper levels and the rear that led to the vault and beyond cast in shadow. A piano had been fetched from some corner of the Manor. That was where Mrs Cosgrove sat, beaming happily as she played. Even to Barty's untrained ear, her music was not the finest, nothing so great as for a concert hall or symphony. But she played with a restrained enthusiasm, a cheer that was deeply needed. She brought the energy of a lively tavern playing, in her demeanour, but Barty could tell she understood the significance of this night. Beside her stood her husband, severe and dour as ever, but nevertheless dutifully attendant, ramrod straight and staring ahead with that unfathomable discipline his position required in times of such formality. He was dressed in his black and white butler best.

Barty knew he did not measure up to Cosgrove's impeccable standards, but he had tried. It was not much compared to the more finely tailored fashions one might find in London or Paris—but it was finer than he was used to. His vest was done up tight, his coat trailing to his mid thigh, his boots well polished. He was not alone in his attempts; Adam, too, had made a clear effort—there was evidence of combed hair, and an ironing of that vast coat they wore. There was only so much that could be managed, it was true, but they had done all they could.

But there were two others that stood out the most—one, the very individual who had done their best to organise the event. Elanor wore dark blue satin, a dress perhaps pulled from a generation or two ago that she nevertheless wore effortlessly, her hair elaborately pinned behind her head. A silver necklace with a shining black jewel at the heart of it topped it all off. She arrested Barty's eye yet again, but it was impossible to miss the one for whom all this had been arranged.

Sat upon a chair, with Elanor at her side, was Lily. Her dress was an elegant and simple thing, of cream silk and lace. She wore gloves of the same material up to her elbows, and most of her metal body was covered, as though to hide what she was. Barty did not begrudge it of her. Last, but not least, her mask had been gently painted—the lips were pale pink, eyebrows had been darkened, and blush applied to the cheeks. It was tastefully done, and Barty thought he recognised Elanor's hand. It was a little gesture, but he hoped it had been a joyous one for them both.

It was a show, really. A little show, with a little crowd. Nothing more than that, a get together between friends. But for one girl, this was the most important night of her life, both before and after it.

It was time for Barty to do his part. He made his way over, and gave a little bow before Lily and Elanor—the latter of which watched him with a mixture of appreciation and amusement. He knew his bow was not very good—he wobbled a bit on the way down—but he pressed on. "Good evening, ladies. Lady Braithwaite?" He held out a hand to her, as she stared up at him with a luminous glow in her eyes, bright and wavering. "May I be so bold as to have this dance?"

Her mask remained as ever was, but her eyes flared and trembled, as though whatever light was within her that gave that fire blazed with joy. She nodded, as words failed her in her excitement.

Barty was again reminded of just how much this moment meant. To anyone else, it may not have seemed like much. Not nearly enough, in truth. This whole hall should have been full of light and song and laughter, with a dozen suitors lining up to take Lily's hand as she smiled to one and all. That could not be so. But the fact that just this little thing meant so much to her, and that it gave her such joy that even her immobile features could not conceal her excitement, gave him a strange feeling. Wistful, that he could not give her what she deserved. And proud, that he could do this for her.

The piano started up again. But it was accompanied now by something else; a soft, keening note of a violin, coming from behind him. He glanced back, caught with his hand in Lily's in this moment of surprise.

Jean walked across the floor, violin singing from his shoulder as he played. His expression was oddly distant, and he was dressed most unusually. Rather than his heavy coat, he wore a loose, flowing shirt, a red scarf looped around his waist. It startled Barty to see it and reminded him of the outfits he had seen worn amongst the Romanichal that had accompanied Esmerelda. There was a rustic tilt to the way he played now—something constrained but wild, a fire that could grow fierce and yet, for now, was subdued. It was much like how Mrs

Cosgrove played—not the finest, not the best. But the truth of it rang out in each sighing note. He looked back to Lily, as Jean approached the piano, taking up his place. Matilda nodded, and both began to play as though they had done so a hundred times before. And maybe they had.

"He always has to make an entrance," Elanor murmured, mourning dramatically, as she gave her father a despairing sort of look, before glancing back to Barty and Lily. "Go on, you two. This is your time."

She was speaking to them both—but Barty knew it was meant for Lily. And he agreed, wholeheartedly. He gave her hand in his a squeeze, feeling the metal and doll porcelain under his grip—warm but unyielding—as Lily nodded.

"But of course, Bartholomew," she replied formally, with only a hint of a tremor in her voice. "I would love to."

She pushed herself to her feet effortlessly. Barty, still holding her hand, walked with her to the middle of the floor, as the music rolled on. He took his place, and true to Elanor's word, she took hers. And so they began.

He did his best. She did not move like Elanor. There was a grace to her that was unlike anything Elanor could do, an unreality to her motion that took him off guard. She was... graceful, fluid, and effortless, but it was unreal, enough to make his hackles rise somewhat; the way her body danced was strange, the joints and shifting different from what a living body could do.

None of that was important now. So he stepped with her, and led her through the waltz, a silence settled between them as they went through the steps. She seemed afraid to say anything. He realised this just as he understood that right now, it was his responsibility. He was not the only one feeling awkward in this moment.

"It is strange, doing this with people watching," he confessed, and her mask lifted, her glowing eyes flaring a moment. There was a fraction of a pause in her steps before she recovered.

"Somewhat, Bartholomew," she said ruefully. "It is strange for me to do it at all."

"You are doing magnificent, Lily," he interjected, with honesty. Those glowing eyes brightened in what he knew now to be a smile. The stately pace continued, to the gentle twisting of the music, of piano and violin playing—clashing only a little. Elanor had moved over to Adam, who towered above all with a proud look on their face; a parent, glad to see a child act freely. Barty wondered if it was himself, Lily, or both of them.

"I know this is a silly little thing," Lily said then, her tone far away. "This is not how it normally works, I know. But I appreciate you all... trying to make me happy." There was a little catch in her voice then. Barty felt her fingers on his hold to him tighter. There was a twinge of pain in the pressure. But he paid it no heed.

"Lady Braithwaite. Lily." And there was something in the way he said it, some sincerity that gave it weight. She looked up at him, as the dance continued, but he spoke firmly. "No one is here because they do not wish to be. No one is doing this because of obligation. We *all* want to do this."

He turned the step, easing her along with him. "This is not a burden. These are people who have, in a very short time, come to care very much for you. And it is right, and good, that people should do a kindness for those they care about." She blinked, and he gave a grin, as a thought occurred to him. "One of the people here, after all, is Jean. No one has ever made that man do something he did not want to do—and look at him." He nodded his head to Jean, who had his eyes closed, away from it all, playing for someone he could not see. Lily watched him, then looked back to Barty, hesitant.

"You have earned, at the very least, this night, Lily Braithwaite," Barty said quietly. "Speaking for myself, at least. My only regret is that we never had the chance to do so sooner." He led her through the turn and spin, something he had only practised a couple of times. Lily moved flawlessly through it, and despite herself she laughed as she twirled. He pulled her back to him, and caught her easily. "You never need to apologise to any of us," he said. "We are, one and all, here for you."

The moment held, the glow of her eyes wavering. She finally nodded, and he knew then that if she could weep, she would. But being unable to do so seemed to rally her, and she straightened up. "Very well. Do you know any other dances, Mister Barty?" There was a quaver to her voice, but she drowned it out under the challenge.

He grinned. "Not quite. But I am ready to learn."

For the next half hour, she put him through his paces. He swore she was making it up as she went, as they moved together. There was awkwardness, for certain, as he tripped up time and again, but it was worth it. Lily found his earnest attempts hilarious, laughing throughout, and it was laughter unlike any he had heard from her; clear, and true, without any trace of it being forced. For that short while, Lily sounded like what she was and yet also should have been—a young woman, enjoying the life that she had, without fear or worry. It was an honest sound. It was a good sound. Barty could take some embarrassment for that. It was the least he could do.

When he finally fumbled his last misstep and barely escaped a fall, Elanor at last rescued him. She gracefully interjected herself, taking Barty's place in the dance, a thing that clearly surprised Lily at first, but she soon warmed to. They started talking earnestly as they danced together, and before long both were laughing. Barty guessed it was about himself; he did not mind.

He arrived at the side of Adam, who reached down to pat Barty on the shoulder with a gentle tap that nearly drove him to his knees. "Well done," they said simply with a smile.

Barty, wobbling on his feet a moment, shrugged. "It was my pleasure." He glanced up at the massive giant. "I am surprised you have not requested a dance of your own yet."

Adam looked awkward then, a most uncommon thing, seeming smaller just a moment. "I would like to. But it might not be fair of me to do so."

Barty snorted softly at that. "Nonsense, Adam," he chided. "There is no reason you can think of, that I cannot call foolish."

"That does not necessarily make it so," Adam responded in a sardonic tone, but they shrugged regardless. "But I appreciate the vociferousness of your response." They squinted thoughtfully a moment, then appeared to nod to themselves. "I will keep it in mind, Barty. Thank you."

A new sound came then—an unexpected one, drifting from

an unknown source. The soft sound of pipes being played grew in volume. Barty looked upwards, as the music shifted in tone—the pipe player, invisible and unknowable, was not like Jean and Mrs Cosgrove. No, this was a master, able to weave their music beyond the realm of mere notes and melodies. Adam and Jean frowned, Mrs Cosgrove blinked, but the dance went on, as the new sound flowed through windows, echoed out of cracks, and flittered along the bookshelves. There was a slyness to it, a feline mischief. Barty knew who it was, without knowing how.

"It would seem the Prince of Midsummer has invited himself," Adam said, their tone rueful, confirming Barty's suspicions.

Puck was there, and yet not. Present and yet absent. But a certain energy manifested; there was a tension in the air, for at least a moment. It eased down as time passed, and the dance proceeded ever onwards. Adam seemed to be gathering themselves, as Lily and Elanor continued to speak as they glided across the floor, as animated in their conversation as their movement. Elanor was nodding emphatically about something, as Lily listened. Neither seemed to notice the new instrument being played, nor where it came from. But they were too caught up to care.

At last, Adam took a deep breath, and stepped forward. They walked towards the dancing pair, towering over them both. "Might I... be so bold as to cut in?" Adam's beautiful voice was, for once, strangely timid. Shy, as though expecting rejection.

But Elanor smiled, banishing their fear, as Lily nodded, reaching up. Adam removed their glove, and revealed their own hand. Of a cruder nature than Lily's, wrought differently and yet, sharing much the same, Adam's hand dwarfed her own, and they loomed *enormous* over her, but Lily was in her element now. Confident, in a way Barty had not seen her. Sure, in a way that was both strange to see and lifted the heart. There was difficulty in their movement due to the sheer nature of their size being so different, but nevertheless they made it work, Lily taking long strides to Adam's careful, small steps. It would have been comical, were it not so touching. Barty did not need to ask, to know—that this was not just Lily's first dance.

Jean played down, as the pipes of the invisible Puck rose up. Mrs Cosgrove was focused, even fierce, as her fingers danced across the keys, as Jean drifted out of the lower key and into silence. He leaned against the piano, a drink brought to him by his servant in one hand. Elanor had whisked away from the room for a moment, so Barty made his way over to Jean.

"I never knew you played," Barty said quietly.

Jean raised a brow and shrugged. "I used to, far more often." The hunter turned grim for a moment, his eyes far away, watching the giant and the lady of brass dance awkwardly and sweetly in the middle of the hall. "My wife used to dance while I did so."

Barty felt awkward. But he pressed on. "In the Hall, here?"

Jean shook his head. "By the water, with the light of a fire, under the stars. It's where both our spirits reside—I think it is the only place either of us were ever truly happy." He made a face, shaking his head. His unusual outfit made more sense now. A tribute to a woman whom Jean could not see, and yet still loved.

"You declined to dance, yourself. I was wondering why that was?" Barty asked carefully, but he felt he already knew the answer.

"I dance for and with but one woman, Bartleby. Her, and her alone. Without her in my arms, my heart dare not sing—and my feet shall not move." Jean sighed, watching the dancing duo with regret. "She would have loved this evening. It is exactly the sort of thing she would suggest. She would be proud of Elanor for coming up with it."

Barty watched Jean for a long moment. The man looked older now, as opposed to when he had entered the hall with the violin, where there had been an energy about him that granted him the youth of years gone. A gentler air was about him now. Softer, quieter. There was regret in his eyes, the sort that took life out of someone, never to come back. The reminder of a life without Esmerelda weighed upon the hunter, despite his attempts to conceal it with his gruffness and wrath. The pipes of Puck, like a breath of wind that crafted music through cracks in stone, were pensive, and subdued.

"Then we shall have to make sure she comes to the next one, I suppose," Barty finally said.

Jean blinked then frowned darkly at Barty. "Do not speak such things," he said, with a faint growl.

"Should I not?" Barty replied boldly. "Would you not rather have some hope?" Jean went quiet, as Barty went on, touching his chest, "I know all about hope. I know how false it often proves to be, Jean. But it is the only counter to despair."

Jean took a sip of his drink. "No." His voice was forced,

subdued but there was note of unexpected passion to it. "No, I disagree. Hope and despair are counterpoints, Barty, both sides of one coin, and linked entirely because of it. Stray too deep into one, and the other becomes the stronger. It is a knife edge of existence, anxious and yearning. I would not call hope the only alternative."

Barty was interested by this, joining the man in leaning against the piano. Mrs Cosgrove continued to play, as Jean set down his glass and lifted the violin once more. "Explain then. What would you call the opposition to despair?"

Jean quirked a faint smile at that. "You may call it maudlin, and perhaps it is. But it is love, Barty, and always has been. Be it a love shining and bright, or dark and terrible, painted in the worst shades of ourselves." He gestured gently to Lily and Adam, who were both talking to each other, nodding as they carefully moved through the waltz. "We are meant to be loved, Barty. Either we place our love in a person, or a thing, or an ideal. If we do not, we are to know despair. Shadowed, and empty, and alone, without a star to guide us. Love, or despair. That is all the states of being there are, and whatever philosopher or priest may argue otherwise, I will not be persuaded from that truth."

He pushed himself off the piano, setting the violin he still held to his shoulder, turning to face Barty. "Love may yet save *her*, Barty. Maybe. But despair never saves any of us. It only kills us, one piece at a time, until there is nothing left but the longing for the last." He turned on his heel, and strode out to the dancing duo. He continued to play, with a sort of energy now that was greater than before, walking around them in a counterpoint to their own movements.

The piano rose louder, the pipes of Puck along with it, and Lily laughed, overjoyed as the music ascended ever higher. The crescendo came bounding, leaping, alive and soaring. And through it all, Barty stood still, and wondered what love might mean to him.

THE NIGHT CARRIED ONWARDS, and yet at no point did it feel dull. Barty and Lily danced once more, and then, he found himself paired with Elanor upon her return from whatever mysterious errand she had partaken of, while Lily once more danced with Adam. As he spun and turned with Elanor, who laughed as they both increased their pace, he realised he was enjoying himself far, far more than he had expected—and he had held high hopes regardless. It might well have been the fact that he got to dance with Elanor again—who remained a vision in her gown—but he tried to chide himself for thinking like that, no matter how difficult it was to do otherwise.

But now there was a pause, for Elanor and Lily had made hurried excuses and whisked away. Mrs Cosgrove was tittering with her husband, who stood stonily to one side but neverthe-less had a pinkish cast to his cheeks thanks to the wine. Barty and Adam were discussing the merits of further recitals, and whether Benji would enjoy learning the process as they had done. Jean was back where he seemed best suited, in shadows at the edge of the candlelight, which was starting to burn low, the glow of the Hall dying down.

The haunting that was Puck's melody continued in the background. On occasion, Barty would pause to listen to it, recalling stories as he did so, of souls who wandered into woods to follow mysterious music. He shivered as he remembered that none of them, according to the tales, were ever seen again. He felt he understood the why of it now—the why, in that they went after such a beautiful sound, and the second, if it was indeed Puck who called them, they were never found again. There was a teasing little turn to the pipes that reminded Barty of that high laughter, with its joyful cruelty, and he was glad that he was yet safely within the Hall.

The door to that Hall opened, and Elanor returned, without Lily. She strode in with purpose, determined, and with head held high as she did so. Taking a spot in the centre of the floor, she spoke loudly, her voice echoing throughout the hall.

"Ladies and gentlemen—apologies for making you wait." She paused until all eyes were turned to her in curiosity. "We have but one final surprise for you this evening. I present to you, the Lady Lily Braithwaite—with her own performance." She turned, and held out one arm in triumph.

Around the door, came Lily. She had changed her clothes, and now stood fidgeting awkwardly in a dress of chiffon and silk, short to the knee, and delicate pointe shoes that covered each foot, bound with silken ribbons at the ankles. Barty was confused, as Elanor went on, her grand tone dropping to something far more ordinary—and kind.

"Lily and I found a ballet dress amidst all that we were looking through," she explained, as Lily stepped forward hesitantly, her head bowed in embarrassment. "And it is something that she has very much wanted to do. So, amongst friends..." She looked to those gathered.

It was Adam who moved first. The giant moved around the room, wordlessly dousing the many candles. Barty joined them. In the end, four candelabras that made up each corner of the dance floor were all that remained. Jean took up the violin, and the woodwind sigh of Puck's distant pipes picked up once more, curious at first, then with a growing interest.

All was dark, save for that one square of light, and within, the girl of brass and porcelain in a chiffon dress, anxious and earnest, unable to take a breath to steady herself. But Elanor remained at her side, and reached out to take her hand, that gentle touch grounding the girl. Barty stepped forward, knowing that he needed to help—and that he should.

"Lady Braithwaite?" She looked over at him, the fire of her eyes flaring with hope. "We would dearly love for you to dance for us." He said it with the sincerity that defined him. He had lied to her this past week—to protect her, and he hated it nonetheless. But now? Now he could be honest to her. And so he was.

She seemed to relax at that, and he stepped back to the edge of the light with Adam, Elanor joining them. And then, Jean started to play. A single, high and potent note carried over the hall, reaching out with invisible fingers to lift Lily up, and give life to her steps.

She was awkward, at first, like a flower unsure to bloom. A

bird hesitant to fly, trying to leave the nest for the first time, to wield a body that was and was not, to spread her wings and take to the sky. But gradually, moment by moment, step by step she did. Rising up on her feet effortlessly, kept aloft on the points of her metal toes, Lily started to dance unlike any ballerina had ever done—or could ever do. Elanor stood at his side, and he barely noticed as she took his hand, seemingly without thinking. Like him, she was silent. Like him, she could only watch.

There was a grace to her that went beyond what a human body could manage. Though her form was brass, lined and cased with porcelain, it moved with a fluid strangeness that a body of mere flesh and bone could not. She suffered no weakness, no weariness; she was not limited by her strength, as any other dancer might be, nor her fitness. For all the terrible flaws and woes of her form, this, *this* was where she was free. She moved faster, more sure, more confident, and as Barty blinked back tears he did not realise he was weeping, did not understand the reason why, until he saw it.

For the first time in her life, Lily was *alive*. Alive and without fear. Alive and without reservation. She lifted one leg and stretched out her arms and spun on nothing more than one toe, her legs straight as arrows, keeping herself in that slow turn as she bowed her upper body forward, with her lifted leg extended and turning as she pivoted. She was free. She was beautiful. Everything he, and Elanor, Adam, and Jean had done to get to this moment for her, in that moment... it was all worthwhile. It mattered. It meant the world.

When she fell, it did not seem real. The movement had been

so pure, so fluid, that when her legs gave out from under her, Barty simply did not comprehend it at first. Nor as she tumbled down with a metal clatter and a shattering of fragile porcelain, the pieces scattering across the floor as she buckled, her body twitching so violently that it looked like she might fracture beyond repair. It was too sudden. Too awful to understand.

Barty was still, as the music stopped and Jean dove across the floor to her, as Elanor and Adam sprang into action. He was frozen. It could not be happening. Not now. Not like this.

He moved forward, slowed as though the air had the weight of worlds. As the last of candles burned out, and the light of Lily's eyes flickered and wavered in desperate, confused fear, he tried to tell himself it was not real, that the dance would go on forever.

But hope, he remembered, as he found himself knelt at her side, Elanor crying out Lily's name—hope was what he had always called it. What he had learned in the orphanage, each day and the day that he had left it most of all, when he found himself entirely alone. Here then, was the reminder of that truth.

Hope was a falsehood.

Chapter 21

Unexpected, Unwelcome

They took her to bed. The episode worsened, where Lily's body simply stopped properly responding to her. Throughout, she struggled, sometimes going limp, sometimes thrashing, until the spasms slowed and stopped, giving her back some measure of control. Adam stayed by her side throughout, their enormous strength the only thing that stopped the worst of the convulsions. And then it was over. But not without the lingering effects.

Barty entered Elanor's bedroom, where Lily was being kept. It was mid morning, but Elanor was still asleep, perched on a chair at Lily's side. Barty had a tray of belated breakfast which he quietly set to one side, and kneeled beside the bed. Lily lay curled up on her side, and she did not look at him. The black and white cat, Daisy, was a fluffy ball at her feet, seemingly untroubled by the changes of the world.

It had been hours into the night, into the black void of the time just before dawn, when the episode had ended. Only then, did the household go to sleep, but they did not go far. Adam stood watch in the corridor, Jean slept on a couch in the hall-way, and Barty had done the same; there was something about needing to remain close by. Unable to rest, unable to sleep and dream, Lily had lain there, forced to feel her body failing her, and then remained imprisoned in her terror, wondering if it would come again.

Barty did not know what to say. He and Elanor had tried to hold her hand, to ward her fear—the jagged shards of her broken body digging into them—but for the first time, that touch that had calmed her brought no comfort.

He kept his voice quiet, and tried the simplest, stupidest of questions. The question that all ask in times like this, the one that is born out of fool's hope that the answer will not be a terrible one. "How are you feeling?"

She did not move. For a moment Barty felt a spark of dread, but this was not like the time by the window. There was life here still, in the silence. But it was a fearful, fretful thing. Fragile, and cracking.

"My body is all wrong." Her voice was soft. "It doesn't... I cannot move properly any more. It does not..." She trailed off, curling in on herself, her movements hesitant—almost stuttering, with brief, abrupt pauses. She still wore the ballerina dress, though it was torn and frayed now. Much of the porcelain that had encased her limbs and torso, though segmented and reinforced, had been chipped or come free entirely. A cracked doll, a shattered dancer as one might find in a broken music box, a bird fallen from its nest before it learned to fly, and left in ruin.

"We will find a way to fix this, Lily. We will figure out an answer."

She shook her head and spoke in a harsh whisper. "Please stop lying to me, Bartholomew." She finally rolled over, and looked at him steadily, her mask splayed with spider cracking but yet whole. It gave her a terrible, far more frightening appearance as she stared at him, her burning gaze bright and for the first time, fearsome. "Do not. Not about this."

His tongue stuck to the roof of his mouth. She watched him for a moment longer, then looked away as she carefully sat up, hugging her knees with that same, faintly jerky motion. "You have been kind. All of you. But I am not a fool, Barty. Not about this, at least," she said sadly, looking down at her hands. "No matter what body I am in, I know when it is failing. I know what it feels like to fall apart."

He did not say anything else. There were no more lies to offer her any comfort, no matter the cost of his own self hatred. At a loss, he moved to the bed and sat by her side, reaching out to take her hand. Awkwardly, she shifted closer and rested her head on his shoulder, leaning against him. She was not as warm now; there was a coolness to the metal that was not there before. He wordlessly gathered up a blanket, to cast it over her shoulders. She should not be cold. It was not right that she was cold.

They sat in silence and he held her hand, gave her his shoulder. Looking past her, he saw Elanor was awake, and watching them. But she did not rise or stir. Meeting Barty's eyes, she gave a weak, tired smile with too much sadness in it to linger long. She understood. For what felt like forever, they remained there—no words spoken, no gestures made. But there was nevertheless something comforting in their shared presence.

But then there was a boom, distant and echoing, of a door

knocker being put to use on the Manor's front door. Elanor sat up sharply, blinking back surprise. Lily shifted away from Barty, also confused as she huddled in her blanket. Rising from the bed, Barty reached the door, opening it as Cosgrove marched towards the waking Jean, who stirred groggily on his couch.

"Sir. We have uninvited guests." Cosgrove's voice was frost itself.

Jean stiffened, looking up and rising to his feet slowly. "Can you identify them at all?"

The butler nodded, that sharp, military nod. "Yes, sir. Black-coats." Barty felt ice run down his spine.

"Barty, what is it?" Elanor asked.

He looked back, unable to keep the answer away. "It's Eidolon. They've found us." *Not now*, he thought. *Any time but now.*

Elanor swore and leapt to the window, looking at the court-yard below, and then swore again. Lily stayed where she was, hesitant and fearful, her eyes darting between Elanor and Barty, and he forced himself to smile. "It will be all right, Lily. I promise. I am just going to ask what will happen now." And with that lie still hanging in the air, he exited the room, shutting the door carefully.

Jean was pulling on his coat. "Bring me the Winchester, loaded. And get the Maxim out. Wheel it onto the eastern balcony, from my bedroom. I will give you some time," he ordered clinically, his voice cold. Cosgrove was already gone. "Adam, cover the hall, in case they storm inside." He spotted Barty and, reaching into his coat, pulled out a revolver, tossing it over. Barty caught it, and without thinking, checked the rotating cylinder like he'd been taught, before snapping it back into place.

"What do we do?" he asked simply.

"First, we make them wait. They want to talk, or they'd have already raided the place." Jean's voice was thoughtful, but his eyes were hard. The softer side of him, the warmer side that had been present in this place, was gone. The world had rushed back in on them all, harsh and violent and cruel, and the threat of what could go wrong hung heavy on the air. "Once we are ready to greet our guests, you and I will go and see what they want." He gave Barty a long look. "If you are willing, that is."

Barty considered it. Briefly, but he considered it. Cosgrove, with a speed that only a butler on a mission might possess, had reappeared at the staircase leading down to the armoury, and threw first a lever action rifle, polished, beautiful and deadly. The American rifle did not fire a round big enough for Jean's tastes when hunting monsters, but it did fire a bullet plenty large enough to put a man down, and put them down hard. He cocked the lever that also worked as the trigger guard, loading one of the heavy rounds into the chamber, before catching an ammunition belt, helpfully full of rounds, also tossed over by Cosgrove who had already disappeared again. He looped it around his waist, and then exhaled slowly, his jaw tightening into that familiar menace, his eyes once more full of that old venom.

"Now then. Let us see to our unexpected party."

There was another booming from downstairs, as the door knocker was struck once more. Jean grunted in annoyance, but he was already nearing the door with a wrathful step, Barty just behind him. The walnut grip of the revolver in his hand felt slick with sweat. But he did not falter.

Jean did not hesitate. He pushed the door open with one hand, and the barrel of the rifle he carried came out first. He strode out onto the high step, and surveyed all before him, as Barty lingered in his shadow. Looking down on the scene, Jean squinted. "Wyrmwood," he said with all the warmth of a glacier and the welcome of a bear trap. "You've slithered a long way from home."

There were about two dozen of them, all told. A couple in the black wagons that had pursued them in London, with some on horseback, and a few men with tall hats on the ground milling about. At the forefront was Wyrmwood, his lizard eyes dark and full of malice, his oily hair shining offensively as he reached up to smooth a bristling moustache. "A pleasure to see you too, Reynard."

"Something far from mutual," Jean growled. "What brings you and your miserable showing here to darken my door?" He waved the gun barrel idly to the cluster. Barty noted that several of them flinched away. Jean seemed to enjoy this.

Wyrmwood sighed, and rolled his eyes. He had a black, silver headed cane with him, and set it point down at the bottom stair leading to the door, in a manner designed to create maximum offense. "Let us not play this game, houndsman. We are here for the girl."

"No idea who you mean," Jean said blandly.

Wyrmwood bristled. "Don't play games with me, Reynard. *Not* when it comes to this," he snarled.

Jean grinned, showing his teeth. "And don't come to my door

making demands, *Wyrm*wood," he purred in reply, emphasising the first part of the surname deliberately. "You know as well as I, as well as all of *them*"—he gestured with contempt to the gathered cronies—"that you are not ready to walk these halls. Out here, you get to slither away. And I suggest you do so."

There was a moment of pause. The members of the crowd exchanged looks without speaking, as Wyrmwood glared at Reynard. Barty was surprised to see it—for whatever reason, here, in this place, the members of Eidolon were afraid. As though the Manor of the Society, the Rock of Gwyar as Adam had called it, was a place of dark import and danger. Barty remembered the nameless, locked terrors inside the magically sealed vault of the Veil, and realised that he had never asked if the things within had keys to escape—or be unleashed.

"Would that I could do so, Reynard," Wyrmwood said with a smile that in no way reached his dark eyes. "But I am afraid that this concerns the security of the Empire, and the Crown."

Jean snorted, the barrel of the rifle raising slightly. "And you spoke of this being about some girl, but a moment ago. Is that how you cope when every woman who rejects your advances and flees as far as they can from you?" He cocked his head. "I'd wager you would be terribly busy, in that case. I cannot imagine anyone being anything but repelled by you."

There was a voiceless snigger to one side, as Wyrmwood went white with fury, rounding on whichever of his men had fatally let slip their mirth, but another voice spoke then, clear and cold and strong.

"In point of fact, Jean Reynard, this is about a father, and their child." A man stepped forward, into view through the crowd. Barty's eyes widened in shock—he knew them, as they continued, "Something you should know very well."

Lord William Braithwaite looked haggard. Jean tensed, the set of his shoulders going rigid as his jaw tightened. Braithwaite approached, his footsteps crunching over gravel. He was dressed much as the other Eidolon officers, but his clothes were more ragged, more travel stained. His face was worn, tired, unshaven, yet he still had that stony, cold harshness to him that had been there when they first met. Barty wondered if the man had slept since then.

"I am here for my daughter, Reynard. You would do well not to deny us," Braithwaite said ominously.

Jean's head tilted. "The last time, you threatened me in your home, your lordship. This time"—the rifle whipped up to his shoulder, aimed down at Braithwaite whom, to his credit, did not blink—"you are on *my* doorstep. Do not forget that."

Braithwaite held his ground. "I need to get my daughter back to London." His voice was strained as he spoke. "It is *vital* that you let me take her there, and swiftly. If you do not, then—"

"Then what?" Jean cut him off. "You'll threaten me? You'll use harsh language?" He snorted and spat. "You do not have the skin for this game, your lordship."

Braithwaite was pale with anger, and something more. "You do not know what you are doing." His voice was grating with the strain. Jean looked away from him in contempt. The assembled had drawn their own weapons now, but Jean did not back down.

"So, that's one of you figured out, at least." He shifted his aim then to Wyrmwood, who shrank back just enough to show his own nerves. "But I am wondering about your stake in all this, Blake. You've never been one to have a spine, let alone morality, so you are certainly not here out of the goodness of your heart. What is your angle?"

The captain of the Blackcoats straightened, despite himself. "The only thing that matters, Reynard, that has *ever* mattered—Queen and country, and the Empire," he said haughtily. "Lord Braithwaite and I are on the cusp of heralding in a new age. A *righteous* age, and with us at the head." He smiled then, a greasy smile full of false courage. "You should not be standing against us, you know. This is something we should work together on."

For the first time, Braithwaite looked doubtful. "This is not what was agreed upon—"

"There are many things we do not agree upon, William," Wyrmwood interrupted, "but some calls are not yours to make." He looked back to Jean, his eyes glittering. "Come now, Reynard. You *live* with one of Shelley's creations. You are proof itself of the usefulness of such things."

Jean went very still, even as Barty felt his blood run cold, and the hair at the back of his neck bristle. "What are you speaking of, Wyrmwood?" His voice was quiet. The captain seemed to draw on this.

"That creature is *proof* that these things can be made useful. Imagine the soldiers we could create, the armies that could be assembled. Who or what could stand against us then?" He lifted one hand outwards. "Come then, put away the gun, let us reach an agreement—"

He never got to finish. Barty had already been raising the

pistol he held, but Jean moved in a blur. A tightening and ex-plosion of muscle so fast, so violent, that he seemed to simply be *gone*. Then, Wyrmwood was down, Jean standing over him, pressing the barrel of the rifle into his eye socket, growling with rage. His hand was shaking, trembling with the effort it took not to pull the trigger, his teeth bared in an expression so feral it did not seem human. The hound was unleashed and it wanted to *kill*.

"*Is that what you want?*" he snarled, grinding the end of the barrel down harder, making Wyrmwood yelp in agony. The assembled mob had their guns pointed at Jean now, but he did not move. "A world of monsters, for conquest, and never mind the cost? You know where they come from. *You know how they are made, you utter bastard.*"

Wyrmwood was breathing fast, but Jean would not relent. Without looking up, he spoke. "Gentlemen," he spat in that horrible tone, "if you would cast your eye to the right, and look up."

Barty, his revolver raised, did as the crowd did, and looked where directed. The barrel of the Maxim gun was set on the edge of the balcony, with Cosgrove behind it, his expression implacable. The realisation sank in, even as Jean made it clear. "That man has you all in view, and you have no cover. If any of you try anything, none will leave here alive." He pressed down spitefully on Wyrmwood, who hissed through gritted teeth as the gun barrel threatened to crush his eye. "And even if I go down with them, no matter what happens, *you*, you wretched bit of filth, will be first." He paused, holding steady until Wyrmwood finally stopped writhing and lay trembling.

Jean's voice turned to a deeper menace. "Now get the *hell* off my land."

The moment hung in the air, rage and terror turning the atmosphere electric. It was Braithwaite who broke it, asking a simple question in a hushed voice. "Is my daughter all right?"

Barty shot a look at him. The man had his hands raised—he was unarmed. For the first time, he sounded fearful. But not because of the threat of violence. There was a hopeless, desperate look on his face that his exhaustion would not let him hide. His tone wavered on the edge of grief. "Please. Just tell me that she is, and we will go."

Wyrmwood tried to protest, opening his mouth. Jean stamped on his stomach, forcing the air out of his lungs with a *whoosh*, his pockmarked face going purple. Jean did not look at Braithwaite, but spoke through clenched teeth. "She is not. And no thanks to you. I will keep her safe from the both of you. Now." He stepped off Wyrmwood, who scrambled away on all fours, undignified and spluttering with pain and rage. "Get out of here."

There was a milling of feet, which Jean met by firing into the ground three times. Each shot booming, vicious and loud, echoing out over the grounds and spraying gravel where bullets impacted. "Go!" he barked, as the crowd scattered under the merciless eye of Cosgrove, tracking the cluster with the barrel of the machine gun. Barty watched as Lord Braithwaite, his face a tortured mess of consternation and helplessness, was all but dragged away by the scowling Wyrmwood. As they retreated out the gate and down the road, voices raised in furious argument.

Jean came alongside Barty. "When they are out of sight, get everyone together. We need to be ready." He rested the barrel over his shoulder. "They will be back."

"How do you know?" Barty asked, hushed.

"Because we have his daughter," Jean replied simply. "There is nothing he won't do for his child."

Barty felt his hackles rise. Because of course, Jean would know all about that. All too well.

"WE ARE MISSING something," Barty muttered, rubbing his jaw.

They were once more in the Hall of the Oak. Around him, the household residents were gathered. The entirety of the Cosgrove clan—quite a few of them in fact—were assembled in the Hall. Cosgrove himself was, simply put, bristling with firearms and other weapons of war. His wife carried, of all things, a blunderbuss, which she held with a worrying sort of professionalism. Anyone coming against her would class death as the least of their problems—she had loaded her weapon with what appeared to be a bag of nails. Barty would normally have been concerned about this, but right now, he felt it appropriate.

"Elaborate on that, Bartholomew," Adam said shortly. "It does not do to leave us in suspense." The giant was tense. Jean had relayed the intentions of Wyrmwood—the idea of using beings such as Adam as a weapon of war. Adam had not taken it well. The restraint that they had shown not to go after the Eidolon soldiers was not simply commendable, it was inhuman.

"I took Braithwaite for a ruthless, cold-blooded creature," Barty went on, staring at the wall. "But that does not equate to his desire for his daughter's safety." Elanor was testing the edge of a sword nearby, while Barty considered his own armament. He had not relished having the revolver before. It had too much weight to it—mostly metaphorical, he knew, but he stuck with it for now.

"You have a point you are getting at, I am sure," Jean growled, as he appeared from one side, setting down a wooden box loaded with ammunition. "Do hurry up and get to it."

Barty flustered under the irritation. "Well," he tried awkwardly, "if he's as ruthless as he seems—and if he is responsible for her... condition, what does he need her for? He could create more if he needed, with or without her, surely?" There was a pause, as Jean inspected him. "If that is their goal—where does she figure into it?"

"No idea," Jean said bluntly, as he checked the breach of his rifle. "When I have him before me, I shall be sure to either ask, or beat it out of him." He spun. "Cosgrove. Get your family together. I'll designate them positions."

Adam stood immobile before the petrified oak tree, like a war machine waiting to be unleashed; they had no weapons, but did not need any. Elanor made her way over to Barty as Jean assigned positions and tasks to each of the Cosgrove clan, a cluster of groundskeepers, stablehands, maids, and more.

"We should go and see to Lily," she said as she carefully placed her sword onto a table. "Best leave that behind too," she murmured, nodding to Barty's revolver. "Let us not scare her, if we can help it."

He did not disagree. Setting his weapon down beside Elanor's sword, they made their way out of the hall and towards the stairs. "This was absolutely the worst time for this," Elanor said heavily. Barty grunted, as she went on, "Lily is having a difficult enough time of things, but this... this was the last thing she needed."

Barty felt a growing sense of unease. "What does she know already? Is she aware of her father?"

Elanor nodded, distracted. "Yes. She came to the window and peered down. She was shocked at first, but she seemed calm when I left."

Something about that made Barty pause. A sliver of doubt worked its way down his spine. He halted midstep, then pressed up the staircase past her, pushing the door open. He knew what he would find, as surely as he knew the sun would set. Or rather, what he would *not* find.

So it was when the door screeched on its hinges, and he saw Lily, wrapped in a bedsheet and standing at the window that overlooked the courtyard, he was both relieved and surprised. "Lily!" he exclaimed. "Are you all right?" The black and white cat, Daisy, was sitting poised upon the bed, watching Barty with her unblinking stare.

Lily did not turn. With a smile and spring in his step, he made his way over to her and reached out to touch her shoulder. Her hand moved so quickly that he simply could not see it, and she gripped him firmly—painfully—around the wrist, halting him in place.

"I am quite fine, thank you." Her reply was aloof, hard, and for a moment he was startled, if not frightened, before she let his hand go, hugging herself once more as she turned her cracked mask towards them, looking from Elanor to Barty. "My father has left then?" Her voice remained tight and careful. Wary. Barty and Elanor exchanged looks helplessly. His wrist hurt where she had held it, but he put it behind his back for now.

"He has left for the time being, yes," Elanor replied carefully at last.

Lily looked away, back out the window. "I see." There was a cold finality to the way she said it. For a long moment, an awkward silence hung thick in the air, before Lily broke it.

"I observed your father pointing a *gun* at my own, Elanor. Could either of you care to explain what that was about?" There was tension in her voice, a cold, harsh tone that Barty had never heard from her before.

He swallowed. "I am... not sure," he lied, for the third time to her. "But I am certain it was just a mistake."

She looked back at him, her glowing eyes watching him for a long moment. "I see," she finally said, and this time, he felt that she truly *did*. As though all his falsehoods were rendered unto ruin. A pit dropped into his stomach. *You should not have lied*, he told himself. She said the same, without saying a word.

"I would like to be left alone now," she said in that brittle, cold voice, but now it was near tears. "Please."

Barty did not have it in him to argue with her. From the way

Elanor was backing out of the room, neither did she. When they were once more in the hallway, they moved away before they started to quietly, but urgently, speak.

"What do we do now?" Elanor hissed softly, her expression one of consternation.

Barty shrugged helplessly. "If I knew, I would do it. For now, we do what Jean told us to do. We need to keep the Manor protected." He looked back to the room where Lily remained. "We keep *her* protected."

"I do not think she trusts us to do that," Elanor said ruefully. "I do not think she trusts us much at all right now."

Barty put a hand on Elanor's shoulder, which made her pause as if in surprise, but he paid it no heed. "We will talk to her. But for now, we need to focus on one thing at a time."

Elanor grimaced, but bereft of other options, she nodded and stalked off. Barty remained where he was. Part of him wanted to go back into Lily's room, to explain to her what had happened. To confess, to apologise, to find a way to make her feel better. Or himself. He was not sure which, and that doubt held him at bay.

He would regret it later.

WHEN THE MOMENT CAME, it happened all at once. Twilight was upon them, and Barty was on patrol of the halls. The house was quiet and empty, and he was alone. Much of his time had been spent thinking on the matter of Lily, of what to tell her. But it turned out, Lily had been doing some thinking of her own. While adjusting his coat, feeling the revolver sitting heavily against his chest, he happened to look out a window and see her outside. She was walking towards the rows of roses and short hedgerows that bordered the forest, her head bowed. She had surrendered her ballerina outfit and now wore a plain dress that hid much of her damage. While he was glad that she was up and about, he was concerned.

Elanor found him, staring outside the window as the sun was devoured by the horizon. She followed his line of sight and sighed, setting her sword point down on the floor in a moment of contemplation. "What are you thinking?"

"That we should tell her everything," Barty said. "Everything we know, and about what happened today." He glanced back to Elanor. "After everything that has happened, we don't know how much time she has, Elanor." He took a deep breath, turning his gaze to Lily, who trailed along the roses, towards the edge of the grounds. "The next time she falls, she might never get up again. She should know why."

Elanor grimaced, watching alongside him for a long moment. "She knows, doesn't she?" she said finally, catching Barty's eye. "That she does not have long. She said as much before."

Barty nodded, and sighed. "She does. What do you even say to something like that?"

"Whatever you have to, to make them feel better," Elanor said simply. "Whatever it takes to make them feel comforted. No matter what it costs you to say it. After all"—she gave a small shrug—"you are not the one who is dying."

Barty felt those words ring in the hollow space of his heart. "She does not deserve this. This is not fair." He heard his voice shake.

Elanor reached out to take his clenched fist. "Father used to tell me, there is no justice in the cruelty of the world, save for what we force from it." She gave his hand a squeeze then, sorrow etched on her face as he turned to her. "But you are right. This is not fair. And it is not right. And we will do what we can for her." She forced a smile. "And you have done a great deal, Bartholomew Bartleby. Between the ball and helping her through all of this, along with all the effort you made to make yourself useful, you have done more than enough to be proud of yourself." A touch of colour came to her cheeks then. "You've shown yourself to be a good man, Barty. Be proud of that."

She held his eyes then, and he felt his heart race in his chest. There was something in Elanor's face, in the way she looked at him, that said more but was inexplicable, an emotion he was not used to seeing. She did not move away, as his fingers slipped into hers, and she interlaced their shared grasp together. Her lips parted, but no words came out. Time seemed to stop.

Which is why when he heard himself say, "We should go and see to Lily. It might be dangerous out there," and Elanor blinked, blushed, and let his hand go, a part of him very strongly wished to strangle himself then and there. What was he *doing*? But Elanor was nodding sharply, her expression turning closed.

"Of course. Come on then."

They went out into the garden via a ground floor exit, passing no one on the way. Jean had most people on corners and watching corridors—this side was his and Elanor's, while Jean was with Adam keeping an eye on the front of the Manor. Cosgrove was probably in a dark corner somewhere, ready to cut the throat of anyone who walked past it. He was a worry to Barty.

But outside, the sky was overcast. There were more storms coming, pushing warm air ahead of them. Remembering how they made Adam anxious, Barty could not help but wonder if they did something similar to Lily, that perhaps this was not helping her mood. He put that thought aside for now.

Lily had walked into the deeper hedgerows, standing alone and pensive, as Barty and Elanor reached her. She turned, as the pair came into view, her glowing eyes flaring. "I believe I said I wished to be left alone." Her voice was sharp, and it caused both Elanor and Barty to halt.

"It is not safe for you to be out here, Lily," Elanor finally said. "If you have another episode, you should be somewhere we can take care of you."

"Take care of me?" Lily asked incredulously. "You cannot help me. You do not even know how to."

"We are trying, Lily, truly," Barty said quietly, stepping forward, but Lily rounded on him.

"You are *lying* to me, is what you are doing," she snapped. "About what happened today, and I do not know what else. Are you lying to me now?" Her voice broke. "I thought you were my friends."

"We are," Elanor said, her own voice cracking. "We *are* your friends, Lily." She took a step closer, but Lily turned away.

Elanor stopped where she was—but Barty did not.

"You are right, Lily," he said, approaching as her metal shoulders shook with trembling and helpless emotion. "We have not told you everything. Not because we wanted to. But because we were afraid."

"Of what? Of me? Of what I might do?" She hugged herself, her knees quivering.

Barty reached her, and put a hand on her shoulder. "No. Of hurting you." He struggled for a moment. "None of us want to hurt you, Lily. None of us could bear it." He took a deep breath. "We will tell you everything. Everything we know... I fear some of it will frighten you. But it will be the truth."

Elanor was there then, at his side. She reached up to Lily's mask to turn her face to both her and Barty. "We are your friends, Lily. We love you. Please don't think otherwise. *Nothing* can ever change that. We love you. And we are so, so sorry."

Lily looked from one to the other, the glow of her eyes wavering, and then with a stricken sob, she threw herself at them. Barty felt his spine compact from the weight, but he held on, hugging Lily to keep his balance. Elanor did the same. They held her as she sobbed, unable to shed tears. With a shaking voice, she finally spoke. "I... I am sorry. I did not mean to get angry." Elanor, side by side with Barty and locked into that impossibly strong hug alongside him, struggled to get a breath while shaking her head. Lily barely seemed to notice, her voice agonising with its desperation. "I want to see my father. I just... I just want to talk to him."

Barty was about to say such a thing might be difficult, when a new, unexpected voice spoke from nearby. "I am right here, my little flower."

Barty felt his heart turn to ice, as Lily, surprised, let go of both he and Elanor. Elanor immediately slipped to one side, her hand going to her sword, but she did not draw it. Her features had gone intent in the twilight, sharp and hawklike. Barty's hand strayed to the revolver he had, but he too, did not draw it; Lily was between him and the newcomer.

Lord Braithwaite stepped out from behind a hedgerow. He had one hand raised, the other at his back, his expression intent but undeniably relieved. "Finally. I have found you, Lily. I have been so, so very worried." He did not even look at Barty and Elanor. They were frozen in place, off kilter and unprepared, even as Lily dashed to her father to embrace him with that same intensity she had just held each of them.

They were in the depth of the garden, and bordered by trees. The Manor was not far, but there was no one in sight, and no way to signal in the failing light. Again, Barty thought he should draw his gun. Elanor was stepping carefully to one side, her hand on her sword hilt, and tense. But Lily clung to her father and sobbed, as he held to her.

"What are you going to do to her?" Barty asked at last. Maybe if he fired the shot into the air, it would get attention. His hand strayed into his coat. Would Lily understand? Lord Braithwaite slowly looked over at Barty, his expression inscrutable.

"I am going to make things right." His voice was cold, hard. "And you are not necessary towards that."

They came from the sides, from behind bushes and trees. Elanor sprang forward, her sword halfway out of the scabbard before they closed on her. She caved one's face in with the hilt, but two tackled her bodily with their full weight. She rammed her head into one of them but he was ready for it and they bore her down to the ground. She grunted, unable to cry out, as a gag was stuffed between her teeth and her arms were held. Barty drew the revolver, but before he could bring it to bear, an arm went around his throat and crushed inwards, blackening his vision, as a harsh breath and snigger was at his ear above the pounding of his blood. His hand clutching the gun was gripped hard and pinned in place by two more hands from another man. He could not breathe. Something cold, metal and sharp was pressed against his side, threatening to cut, to plunge, and to take his breath from him forever.

Dimly, he heard Lily gasp. "Father! Don't hurt them!"

There was a pause, and through the darkening around his vision, Barty saw Lord Braithwaite hold up a hand. Elanor kicked and struggled beneath two men wearing the black of the Eidolon soldiers, as Lord Braithwaite spoke coldly. "We can use that one—bring her with us. Him, leave behind. But alive."

Wyrmwood's voice growled at Barty's ear, letting him know who had a hold of him. "You do this and *he'll* be coming after us."

Braithwaite, his arm possessively around the frightened Lily's shoulders, shrugged. "It matters not. If by some miracle he finds us, he will be far too late." He made a commanding gesture. "Restrain her. We are leaving."

Barty struggled again as Lily met his gaze. Her glowing eyes spoke of shock, of fear, of doubt. He pleaded with her in that moment, silently begging her to act; to stop what was to come with his eyes as his words were stolen from him by that strangling grip. And yet she turned away, guided by her father. Elanor tried to scream as a sack went over her head. Wyrmwood snarled in his ear, "Lucky for you then, that she likes you."

Something hard and heavy struck him behind the ear. The world turned off, a candle blown out, and he fell into a void where nothing waited for him.

HE AWOKE TO WATER thrown in his face, on his back in the dirt. He could taste bile in his mouth, and smell it thick in the air. In his unconscious state, he'd thrown up. He coughed, and choked, and shivered through the ache and cold.

"Where is Elanor?"

Jean's voice stopped him dead. It was cold, cold in a way he had never heard before. He blinked away the water and pushed himself up shakily, feeling dizzy, sick, and foul.

"Answer me, Barty. Where is my daughter?"

He struggled to get the words out. It was dark, very dark. The overcast sky now the black of a deep night. How much time had passed? Hours? It had to be hours by this point. But kneeling next to him, his eyes glimmers of rage in the shadows, was Jean, looking down at him. Barty felt fear. He had to answer Jean. Something told him he would not get asked again.

"Braithwaite," he croaked. "Wyrmwood. They took her.

They... they took them both." He reached into his coat, patting himself down.

Something was shoved into his face. "Looking for this?" Jean's voice was flat as he held out the revolver. Without waiting, he dropped it onto Barty's stomach. There was no admonition—there did not need to be. He'd been armed, and he had done nothing. He had not been fast enough, and now Lily and Elanor were gone. Jean had said they would be back, and yet Barty had been overconfident, believing in the sanctity and safety of the Manor. He had been wrong.

A match hissed to life and Adam appeared, lighting a lantern. It burned bright in Barty's vision, painfully so, his head throbbing with the weight of the blow he'd taken. Holding the lantern aloft, they crouched beside Barty as Jean turned away, his eyes dark with that lingering fury. The massive hand of Adam reached out to gently touch Barty's cheek, and the back of his head. Barty winced. Even the faintest contact was agony.

"You've taken a serious blow to the skull. You're lucky you're breathing at all, Barty," the giant said quietly. There was something subdued in them now. Something that, Barty had to think, almost looked like fear.

"Adam." Barty's voice was rusty, acid burned. "I tried. I tried to—"

"Enough," Jean growled, and Barty was silenced, as though his words were ripped out of him. The air itself seemed to *bend* towards Jean, as though the rage that was resurfaced in him, as the fury of losing his child manifested, the world itself was tearing around him in that moment. Adam shook their head, their eyes a warning. Barty looked away, and saw laying next to him, Elanor's sword, half-drawn from its scabbard. He reached out and took it, and using it as leverage, pushed himself to his feet.

There were hoofbeats, riders approaching. Two appeared out of the darkness—Cosgrove, with whom Barty presumed was one of his sons. Both were armed, and both with looks of grave concern, rode over the grounds without care to the damage of the hooves on the gardens. "They took the train, two hours ago. They're long gone by now." Cosgrove grimaced, looking to Barty briefly, scowling before turning back to Jean. "They had Elanor restrained. Claimed to be putting her under arrest. She was still alive when they left—and furious, it has to be said."

"Still alive," Adam said with a sigh of relief.

Jean did not relax. "We know where they are going?" he grated.

Barty coughed. "London." Adam glanced back at him, frowning, as Barty went on, "Braithwaite talked about taking Lily back to London." He forced himself to remain steadfastly upright. His skull hurt, but he was not going to stop, even as the world spun unsteadily. "But they won't be going back to the laboratory, or his home. They cannot."

"Someone knows," Jean growled with malice. "I will get the where from them."

Barty took a step forward as Jean went to move. "I am coming with you."

Jean spun on him, with a sudden, explosive fury. "*Are* you now? You think you can demand that?" His rage was that of an animal, snapping at the air in bloody wrath.

Barty, for once, was undeterred. Whether it was the light-headedness, or something else, he could not tell. *They took Elanor. They took Lily.* And he had not stopped it. Shame was on him now, cutting through his spine with glass talons, but deeper than the shame was the anger. Righteous, indignant, and hot, a fire that would melt that regret away. They had come to their home and ripped it asunder. "Yes." He forced himself to speak. "I am coming with you."

Jean glowered, angry still but his eyes narrowed. "And will you hesitate again, Barty?" His voice coldly intent.

He shook his head. "I will not." His skull felt like it would fall off his shoulders as he shook it, but he held on. "Never again." He grit his teeth. "They took Elanor. They took Lily. I should have stopped them."

Jean Reynard glared at him. For a moment Barty wondered if he was about to be attacked, before the enraged huntsman seemed to get a grip on his anger, biting it down. "Fine. But if you do—"

"I will not." Barty's response left no room for doubt.

Jean snorted, unimpressed. "You remember that. Because now we are doing things *my way*, and they will not be hindered." His burning gaze swept across those gathered. Even Cosgrove, even *Adam*, flinched under that ferocious stare. "Not by *anyone*."

Barty swallowed, and nodded. Jean grunted, turning. "Cosgrove, come with me to the armoury. Barty, whistle for our woodland sprite coachman." He strode off down the path. "We are going back to London and I know *just* who to see."

He was off, stalking across the garden with the grinding,

inexorable step of death itself, Cosgrove hurrying after him. Barty went to follow, but Adam's vast hand came to a halt on his shoulder.

"Be careful, Barty." Adam's voice was stern, but laden with dread. "I have seen him like this only once before."

Barty blinked. He soon understood. "When James was killed?"

Adam nodded, without looking at him. "This is the one they all fear, Barty. You have not seen it yet. Not really. You must be careful."

Barty swallowed. "Is anyone going to tell them that?" he said, gesturing to what he thought was the direction of London.

The giant at his shoulder gave a grim, terrible smile. "It is far too late for that, Bartholomew Bartleby. They are already dead." The giant sighed, and started to trudge heavily away. "The hunter is coming for them."

Barty was left alone, holding himself up by the sword that Elanor had lost. He took a deep breath, then, with a full body shiver, he whistled for Puck. Three quick, one long and high. He heard the ghostly chuckle on the wind, the rising clop of thundering hooves and the grinding crunch of dreadful wheels, as the silver-haired coachman once more slithered into the world. For once, Barty was not concerned about that. He had agreed to something, now. He had seen the brighter side of the life the Society offered. Sad in many ways, yet warm in so many others. But the dark had come creeping back, clawing its way in through the edges.

Remembering that look in Jean's eye, Barty realised that for once, the dark would not like what it had found.

CHAPTER 22

HELL BECKONS

Tommy Two Bob was a complicated fellow.

By night, he was a criminal. Not just *any* criminal, but the master of the Wards. This was a special kind of criminal in London, and one that commanded far more than mere respect. But it *required* fear, the sort of fear that would remove not just the reality but even the mere contemplation of rebellion. Tommy Two Bob had that fear. He had it in spades, bought in butchery and paid for in terror. From a young age, he had learned that ruthlessness was its own reward, and that the one who hesitated had their throat cut by the one that did not. Tommy did not hesitate much. And his knife was very, very sharp, and the foul river Thames was very, very deep.

But by day, things were an entirely different matter. During the sunlit hours, he was Thomas Hampstead Brown. A respectable dealer in dried goods, a wholesale marketer and supplier. While he did not mingle in the circles of the upper crust, he was, as far as things went, vaguely known, vaguely respected, and kept a level head. Never too much attention drawn. Never too much notice. Never too much money and just enough of all three to make oneself invisible.

528

His wife had insisted upon it. For the sake of their three little ones, he was to maintain the veneer. Normally, Tommy Two Bob would sneer at such notions, would have—once upon a time—trampled such convention into dirt. But Mrs Hampstead Brown was a fierce woman. She *had* to be, to keep the ragged king in check. But in check he was kept, to keep that life in one hand and the other in hers, and their children grew up knowing nothing of it. When the time was right perhaps, but Tommy was no fool—his children were not as cruel, not as harsh, not as ruthless as he was. The woes of giving them a life that he had been denied was that they would never have the edge they needed to rule the Wards. He mourned that on occasion. A time would one day come when he would need to pick an heir, someone who was ambitious, but knew loyalty. It was a tricky thing to manage, a delicate tightrope to walk. Too much of one would mean not enough of the other, and that would never work. It was a difficult thing, to be a man with two legacies—the family he had raised, and the Empire he had built.

He had considered Pete at one point, but *that* had turned to sewage before he could act on it. Now the man was nothing but trouble, and it kept landing on his door and stinking. He would have to do something about it. Pete had outlived his usefulness. The next time he crawled out from under a rock, Tommy would pick it up and smash him to paste with it.

In any case, it was something to deal with another time. Now he was going home. His home was on the edge of the Wards, a well kept secret that no one but those he trusted most knew about. But because he was not a fool, he had a watch kept on the place. Tommy did not trust anyone much, but he made sure of the people who watched his family, mostly by making sure that each of them had a family of their own, and that if anything ever happened to *his*, they would lose *theirs*. It was effective enough. Who needed trust when you had fear? The men who kept an eye on his home, secluded away on a little private street, were smart men, hard men, who could take one look at a shrouded alleyway or broad avenue and know what was in it, could see a threat a mile away, and deal with it. And each of them had a vested interest in making sure that not only was Tommy's family safe, but that none but them knew that this was where they lived. It was a solid arrangement. Truth told, it paid very well too. Some things Tommy saw no point in being cheap about.

Because of all this, he was very confident that things would be well when he unlocked his front door and walked inside. It was just past midnight, after a long evening of skullduggery and thieving. Only a couple of deaths, just to keep the senses sharp, just to keep the toes on the edge. Tommy could not have anyone going slack on him, after all. It would not be long before he had to wake again and pretend to be a normal businessman, but Tommy was used to it. He could not remember having slept more than four hours in his entire life, seeing sleep as the enemy to the ready mind. He was smart. He was prepared. He was ready for anything, and knew no one would touch him here.

It was thus to his complete, heart-stopping surprise when, upon entering the kitchen, he heard the familiar click of a pistol hammer, but in a hand that was not his.

Jean had not bothered to aim the thing. He did not have to. He sat, a ghastly shadow in the gloom, his eyes pinpricks of murder. There was the hissing burst of a match as Barty lit a candle, setting it down on the table with a slightly shaking hand, avoiding Jean's eye. He had seen the man do things this night that he never hoped to see again.

They had stocked up and departed from the Manor in less than an hour, and then ridden across darkened laneways and roads. The coach had moved, and moved fast—but they could not catch up with the train. Puck had explained before they left, while pointing at the cloud dark sky, there was no walking the stars, without starlight. England's famously foul weather had worked against them at last. So they had done it the hard, relentless way, without halt and without pause, in breakneck pursuit.

Jean had not spoken. He had just concentrated on that hateful violence that drove him until he had been given a chance to let it out, and he had done so all at once. He was *different* now, like some sort of switch had been pressed, some primal fury found and reawakened. It was so terribly, frightfully focused that it became a lens. Like a bloodhound he had tracked to this place, and then arranged matters so that he and Tommy Two Bob could talk. In awful, bloody fashion.

He reached over, watching Tommy, and lit a cigarette on the candle flame. Doing so showed the blood on his hands, red and wet, splattered on his face in ghastly droplets. "Your family is alive. For now. Sit down, Tommy." He didn't raise his voice. He spoke quietly, and evenly, smoking with one hand and holding a gun with the other. The calm made it so much worse.

Barty had to give Tommy credit that he was due. The man did not shout, did not flinch. He did not move. "There are three men watching this place," he said flatly, his voice hushed.

"Four. They're all dead now," Jean corrected him, as Barty shuddered, feeling his gorge rise. "And the next four will not be along for another six hours. By which, I will have done all I need to do." He let the knowledge sink in. Without another word, he tipped the cigarette towards a chair at the other end of the table.

Tommy finally looked shaken. There was, for the first time since Barty had met him, a true measure of doubt, even fear on his face. He sat down slowly, carefully, watching Jean and only him.

Jean, for his part, did not hurry. He let the moment linger, allowing the helplessness to mature into dread, before he started to speak, his voice measured, quiet. "Right now, you're thinking about the knife in your boot. The other at your wrist. Not the one at your back in your belt—that would not be fast enough. Let me stop you there." His tone went darker. "None of them are fast enough, Thomas."

The ragged king looked thoroughly dethroned, staring at Jean as though seeing him for the first time. "What do you want?"

"Information," Jean said flatly. "And I do not have time to play the usual games." He took another drag from the cigarette, the length of it dark with the blood of dead men where he held it. "I need to know where Cripple Pete is. And by extension, where his new master is."

Tommy looked wary then, his eyes narrowing, hunching in

his seat. "I have no business with that lot. Crown business, that is. Once I learned it, t'was was enough to wash my hands of it." His voice was tense. "I'm not playing that game. I told you before."

"Don't," Jean said quietly, and Tommy froze in place. Jean stared him down for a long moment. "Your wife, Alice. Your daughters, Jane and Mary. Your son, little Thomas." He let the words hang in the air, as he ground the cigarette into the table. He named them each, one by one, his voice as lifeless as a gravestone.

"You wouldn't," Tommy said slowly. "You're not that sort, Reynard. You're on the side of the angels—you'd not go that far." Even as he spoke, it sounded like he was trying to convince himself most of all. Fear was a stranger to Tommy Two Bob. But it was not to Thomas Hampstead Brown, and that was whose kitchen they were in; that was who was sitting at his own table across from a demon covered in murdered men's blood.

"Wouldn't I?" Jean said softly. "They ever tell you what I got up to in France? After they took my boy from me, which you... so *enjoyed* making jests about?" He spoke the last part of the sentence through clenched teeth.

Tommy swallowed visibly. "I heard stories. I didn't believe them, they couldn't—"

"They are," Jean cut him off with a hiss. "All of them. Each and every one is true, and more you have never heard. I am everything they say I am, and right now I am *in your home*, Thomas." He went quiet, and settled back. "Now talk."

Tommy's hands clenched into fists on the table. Like a drowning animal looking for a way out, he turned his eye finally to the silent Barty, wordless in his sickened horror, standing behind Reynard in miserable observation. "The mouse hasn't yet found his squeak I see. You going to let him do this? Are you?" There was a subtle note of desperation in his voice.

"They have his daughter," Barty said, his voice leaden. Everything went still. Barty could see the gears falling into place in Tommy's eyes as his gaze went back slowly to Jean, who remained cast in shadow, the candlelight flinching away from him. The realisation that the man in front of him who had committed atrocities, the stories of which had crossed oceans, was once more on that same bloody path to damnation.

"You have one chance, Thomas." Jean's voice was a soft, razor-sharp drawl of purest menace. "Cross me now, and I'll sell your youngest to the Devil himself, and make you watch what happens next. You know I can. You know I would." He gestured with a slight flick of the barrel of his gun. "Now talk. Where can I find them?"

Tommy watched Jean with his one good eye, his expression twitching, a hunted rat cornered in a trap. Sweat beaded and ran down his forehead. "You'll let my family be? I don't care about the rest. But I'll tell you this and you'll leave. Deal?"

Jean, with the pistol still pointed, appeared to consider the thought for an uncomfortably long time. As though the possibility of murdering the sleeping family was one he did not want to let go of. Or maybe he just wanted Tommy to think that way. "Perhaps," he said. "Talk."

Tommy sagged, both hands clasped on the table, the fingers twisting together to keep them from shaking. "I wanted nothing to do with this, when I saw the Crown boys—that's the sort of smoke you don't cross, not if you're just a lad from the Wards. We know our place." He held up both hands as though to fend off a blow. "But I went. I had my lads find out where they were just... just in case."

"In case you needed to make a deal later," Jean growled, and Tommy flinched. "You speak as though I don't know what you are, Thomas. Get to the point."

Two Bob writhed, a worm on a hook. Barty wondered if he had even been in a position like this before—his vicious confidence, his smug cruelty, was all gone. Out there, he had been a king, the ruler who was obeyed without question. Trapped in a room with a nightmare promising damnation, he crumbled. His single eye looked this way and that as though seeking an escape. Jean allowed none.

"You actually mean it, don't you?" Tommy said slowly, the dawning realisation of horror as the terrible reality of Jean Reynard was shown to him. "I know liars, I know a man who is saying things just to sound tough, but... you mean it, don't you?" Jean said nothing. He did not have to. Tommy started to shake. "There's an old fortified manor, up near High Beech—past the old royal hunting lodge," he said, licking his lips. "Past the rangers road. S'atop a high hill, you can see it for miles around. Had them followed to there. S'where they took everything from that warehouse I sent you to. They've been there ever since. If you want to look anywhere—you look there." He shuddered. "That's all I've got. It's all I know."

Jean was silent. Thoughtfully drumming his fingers on the tabletop for a moment. "You understand what is at stake, correct, Thomas?" Continuing to deliberately use his proper name, instead of the cruder, street name that Tommy was known by—there was power in a moniker, and Jean mercilessly ripped it away.

The ragged king nodded, silent. "Good." Jean slowly pushed himself to his feet. "Then you understand that I cannot afford to make any mistakes. You understand I need to be sure. After all, it's what you would do, isn't it?" He stood up, and gestured with his pistol again. "Take me to your wife. We'll start with her."

"Reynard—" Barty tried to whisper in horror, but Tommy had tumbled out of his chair. He did not charge, he did not run, he fell to his knees and grovelled, hands clasped before him in a prayer.

"Please, no, no, don't—it's all I've got, all I have. They're there, I *know* they are, please, you have to believe me!" His voice was strangled, muffled in terror, as he begged and sobbed, his resistance shattered. His pride broken, the ragged king of the Wards begged for the life of his wife and children.

Jean said nothing. He did not even blink, the shadows that were his eyes in that darkened room reflecting nothing, giving no hope. Barty felt sick. When all this had started, he thought that the darkness had come back into their lives, found them and pulled them back into the world. He was wrong.

And then it became loud in that space, as a small voice spoke up. "Papa?"

The child was no more than four-years-old, if Barty had to guess. Perhaps they had heard voices and had awoken. Maybe they were just after a drink of milk to chase the nightmares away, but had instead walked into a living one. They were standing in the corridor, not far from Two Bob, rubbing at one eye, confused and in their night clothes. The grovelling crime lord of the Wards scrambled over and seized the child in his arms, huddling them to himself to shield them from Jean, who stood as the spectre of death, looking down, the gun still in his hand.

This was the same man who had taught him to stand up for himself, to protect himself. Who had inspired him by saying he was proud of him. Who had played music for a dying girl to make her smile, and shared his wisdom to give Barty warmth and colour to his world. This was that same man. And yet, he realised now he was wrong. The darkness had been with them all along; he had been standing at its side the entire time.

Jean stared down. Then sighed, the note tinged with disgust. "Very well then. This is how this will go, Tommy." He turned away, holstering his weapon. "I am going to go. If I do not find what I am seeking there..." He paused at the hallway, turning back. "You have an... active imagination when it comes to these things. I am sure I do not need to tell you what happens then, do I?" His eyes gleamed with hellfire in the candlelight. "I will come for you. I will find you. And you will be the last to go." He looked at the terrified, silent child that Tommy still held. Their eyes met, something that Barty wondered would haunt both of them for years afterwards before Jean turned away, speaking over his shoulder as he went. "Say hello to Alice for me."

Tommy dissolved into broken sobbing, breathing hysterically as this sliver of unexpected hope was flung his way. His frightened child, his son, stood frozen in numbed shock as Barty all but ran out of the place. He did not dare look back.

Jean was waiting for him outside. It was raining, and the hunter stood silent under the downpour, looking at one red, bloodied, hand, rubbing thumb and forefinger as the falling spray failed to wash the gore away. "We need to hurry. The storm is nearly here," he said quietly, his voice subdued.

"Would you?" Barty had to know. He had to know if Jean really had meant what he had threatened. The memory of that staring child pursued him still. It always would. "Truly, would you have actually done it?" He did not even try to keep the sickened disgust out of his voice.

Jean looked back at him for a moment, the gleam of those eyes in the darkness a terrible sight. Barty felt the ice down his spine grow thicker. Finally Jean shrugged, and looked away. "I do not know, Barty." The rage was muted, for the moment, the merciless cruelty dulled. "Probably," he finished simply.

The coach arrived, silent and cold. Puck was smiling, and around him the shadows were alive and writhing, their edges gleaming with teeth of silver. He winked at Barty, but he seemed different. Throughout the journey, he had not yet said a word; no laughter, no playful jokes, no malicious mischief. Just silence, and shadows, as he grew fat off the dread.

Adam was on the top again, the carriage sitting lower on the axles; even though they had packed less, they had taken much *heavier* things this time around. They looked at Barty with an unreadable expression, as Jean relayed to the wordless Puck of where they needed to go. Then, both Barty and Jean climbed into the interior of the wagon, taking what seats they could in the crowded space. They left that silent street, the nightmare of what was remaining behind. Barty felt like the very stones shuddered at their passing. Not for the last nor first time, did he wish he was somewhere else.

Jean lit another cigarette. He'd been smoking them constantly since the journey began, and Barty had to admit they seemed to quieten his mood. For that, despite the smell, he was grateful. Anything that would take the edge of Jean's rage away was welcome.

"Where to now? What do we do?" He felt he already knew the answer, but the silence was oppressive.

Jean exhaled a cloud of sweet smelling smoke that made Barty's eyes burn and his throat itch. "We go and get my daughter back. And we kill them all." There was no arguing with that tone; it was as simple and as absolute a statement of fact, as the rise and fall of the sun. Barty shivered.

"And... and we will save Lily too, correct?" There was silence, that grew. "Won't we, Jean?"

The shadows that were Jean's eyes looked away. "If it comes to it."

The pause hung heavy, the air laden with miasmatic fear, with the promise of horror yet to come. Barty felt it play over his heart and skin, felt it drag him back down into the dark. Except now Jean was the thing he was afraid of, the thing that was breathing down his neck while trapped with it, and—

And he remembered that he had faced it down before. He remembered how, and he remembered why. He felt his fists clench. That frightened child reminded him of something. It reminded him of himself, years and years ago.

"I won't accept this." He said it softly, but saying it was a strength of itself. "No. I will *not* accept this." His voice rose.

And Jean turned his head, those dark eyes blazing. Barty felt the fire now. He levelled a finger at Jean and brought that fire to his voice as he spoke. "You taught me not to hide from my fears, Jean. You had me bloody my fists to do so, you taught me to stand, and I am going to repay that now. Be better than this. You are more than *this*."

Jean, for his part, did not immediately shoot him, but he stared at the pointing finger for a long moment, then leaned forward. "What are you getting at, Barty? Explain yourself to me." There was that menace, that invitation to hoist himself upon his own petard. But Barty was well into doing just that. He had learned something about himself, after all.

"I am sorry I did not stop them taking Elanor," Barty went on furiously. "I am sorry I was not fast or good enough. But even if I could not have stopped that, what you threatened in that house, I will never let you do so long as I live. I *swear*, to God, to country, to *you*, if you ever try to hurt a family like you promised to do just now, I will stop you, Jean Reynard. No matter what, I *will* stop you."

Jean's eyes blazed. In an instant, he was across the wagon and forcing Barty against the seat with his forearm crushing into his chest. He was shockingly, horribly strong, as immovable as an iron bar. "Will you now?" he snarled. "How, exactly, do you plan on doing that?" The end of the cigarette he held between clenched teeth flared bright into flame.

Barty brought the revolver in his hand under Jean's chin, and pressed it there. "Any... way... I can, Jean," Barty growled, forcing the words out with what little breath he had. "Like *you* taught me."

A series of emotions played out over Jean's face. The pressure on his chest lessened, but Barty kept the revolver where it was as he sucked in a breath, forcing the words out. "You taught me to act in spite of my fear, Jean. You taught me to stand against the things that frighten me. You did so that I could fight back." He swallowed, as Jean eased off but remained close, his jaw tightened. "I know you are angry. I know you are scared. I know it makes you do horrible things, Jean." Barty's voice cracked as he fought to control it. "But I know you are better than this. And I won't have you do another thing that you will spend all your days regretting." He lowered the gun. "You have too many already."

Jean stared at Barty with a mixture of warring emotions in his eyes, too fleeting to be identified, before he relented. Without a word, he sat back, tossing the still burning cigarette out the window, as he covered his face with one slightly shaking hand. The coach rattled onwards. Barty kept his mouth shut for now, his jaw clenched tight, his chest aching, and his breath sharp out his nose. He dropped the revolver onto the seat, as though it burned him.

Finally, Jean seemed to get himself in check. He lowered his hand, his eyes no longer shadows, no longer pits into the depths of hell. He was Jean Reynard again, a tired, bitter man who was already too old for this sort of thing, worried for his only child, and not knowing how to express that terror. He was a person Barty recognised. Jean gave a bitter snort. "So. What are we going to do? Ask them to give Elanor back nicely?"

"No," Barty replied. "We're going to kick in their door and fight like hell, and save them both."

This made Jean blink a few times—and then he chuckled. It was a sad sound, a tired sound, but it was genuine. He nodded, sinking into his chair. "All right. That we can agree on then."

Barty took a deep breath. His chest hurt, but he would get over it. Jean, for his part, had made no complaints against the gun either. "We save them. Like I should have done from the start," Barty continued, his voice intent. "She is not my blood, but they are, both of them, my friends. And I don't have so many as to do any less for a single one." He clenched his fist, the hot rage returning. It made the lump on the back of his head hurt, but not nearly enough that he could not overcome the nausea it induced. "But we do not cross that line, Jean. No matter what happens, we do not cross that threshold. I will be there to stop you, if I must."

Jean grunted, but there was acceptance in it. "Very well, Bartholomew Bartleby." He settled back into the coach, laying his head back and staring at the roof where Adam sat above them, the ceiling sagging inwards. He spoke then, as though something was weighing on his mind. "You *do* understand I am going to kill every Blackcoat bastard that gets in my way, correct?" he asked curiously.

Barty shrugged, helplessly. "Well," he tried awkwardly, "it is not like they've covered themselves in noble glory in all of this—and I do not expect they'll give up quietly anyway, either." He did not like it—but he could not stop it either.

And besides, it was a bit late now. The four dead house guards around Two Bob's home made that very plain indeed.

"Good," Jean replied, satisfied. "We'll make a killer out of you yet, Barty."

He let the moment pass. But the thought of it followed long after, nipping at his heels, all the way to their destination. If he forgot the memory of that child, held by a frightened father, it would never be too soon.

Chapter 23

The Coming of the Storm

It was dark, with dawn not far away. The storm had eaten up the sky and pushed the wind and rain ahead of it. Thunder rolled on the horizon, drawing ever closer. The anticipation of its coming filled the senses with restless anticipation—Barty could feel the air around Adam buzzing with the repressed energy, the spark that leapt between their fingers brought to the surface by the storm. Something indescribable gleamed in their corpse eyes, but their face was troubled.

"That is more a fortress than anything else," they said doubtfully. They were amongst the trees of the forest, to the northeast of London itself, secluded off the road. There were distant lights of the greater city, but here in the depths of what was once a royal wood, a hunting ground no less, there was not much save for poorly tended unpaved roads, that wound here and there through the woods. The place they were looking for, however, was a stark, looming presence that was impossible to ignore.

It was as Two Bob had said. Amidst the woods, it stood out, thrust up atop a hill. Wrought of very old, grey stone, and tall—Adam was indeed correct in their observation. It was an ancient, fortified tower, surrounded by a high grey stone wall, with a single barred gate blocking entry.

There were glowing lamps situated haphazardly about, at the gate and on the walls, and shining through the windows. They were not of mere flame, but the strange white glows that had been seen in the Braithwaite house. Barty pointed this out as they sheltered out of sight among the trees and undergrowth of the woods, with Puck lounging idly on the coach. Of all of them, he seemed the least concerned. It would, in fact, be more accurate to say he was not concerned at all, to a degree that was quite disturbing.

"That is not all." Jean grimaced. He was using a looking glass, frowning as he stared down at the imposing structure. He took his eye from it and passed it to Barty. "Look at the roof. Recognise anything?"

Barty took it and, after a moment of struggle, managed to get the looking glass fixated on the crenelated rooftop of the tower. He didn't see it at first, but then what Jean had pointed out swam into focus. There were long poles, covered in a layer of copper. What appeared to be a crane had been installed upon the roof, with rigging apparatus leading upwards. The entire building and the walled grounds were also brightly lit, blazing with that clear light wrought by whatever knowledge of science Braithwaite had employed. Nothing had a chance of getting in without being seen, something further illustrated when guards on the wall became visible, shadows moving amongst the lights.

"How in God's name are we getting in there?" Barty asked. They were concealed for now, out of range of the lights and within the depths of shadow that would keep even Adam hidden, but not forever. The place was manned with armed men, who were no doubt confident in their fortifications, who would spy them out. But this was the place that they sought. This was what they were looking for, and Barty knew, emphatically, that who they were looking for was in there as well. Elanor and Lily were close. He felt an itching in his palms to do something about it.

Jean, however, *was* doing something about it. He had slipped back to the coach and was now pulling its contents out; heavy metal boxes, which he moved around with painful grunts under their weight. Barty felt a moment of fear as they were laid out. He had an idea by their shape of what was inside.

"I do not see how we are going to sneak into the place, with all this," Barty said doubtfully, looking back to the fortress. Nevertheless, he helped Jean as best he could, assisting in the unloading.

"We are not going to be sneaking anywhere," Jean said flatly, his voice grim. "Adam?"

The giant loomed close, the air still buzzing as the rain fell upon them. They were more menacing than Barty had ever seen them, shadowed and terrible. He realised he wasn't the only one there who was anxious. "Yes, Reynard?"

"I shall leave the gate to you. Do you think you can handle it?" He reached into a crate, pulling out a cloth belt, heavy and rolled, set with the brass casings of rifle rounds at regular intervals.

"You understand that you are taking a risk this way, correct?" they responded with a faint hint of concern.

Jean nodded, frowning as he kept working. "I have taken it into consideration. The problem is, I do not think we have time to contemplate any other method." He took a deep breath, pausing, and looked to Barty and Adam, noting the worry etched into each expression. Jean sighed, and spoke carefully. "I truly have thought about this." His tone was almost apologetic as he glanced to Barty. "I do not believe they were going to harm Lily. And from what Barty told me, they... require Elanor for something. If they did not, they would have just left her behind." He looped a holster over his back, slinging the lever action Winchester rifle into place. "So... I believe that not only are they both still alive, but that they are being kept alive, and their wellbeing is both necessary and important right now. I know it is a gamble, but we have no time to find out. If that laboratory has been replicated, then the coming storm will put whatever they have planned in motion." He grimaced, looking from one to the other. Neither Barty nor Adam were daring to argue at this point. "The police will not help us with this. They likely have orders to keep far away. There is just us. And therein lies our advantage."

"And how exactly do you figure that?" Barty asked.

Jean opened a large box. The Maxim gun gleamed, shining with the intent to wreak havoc and sing its mighty song of terrible destruction. It had been fully rebuilt by Cosgrove—the shrouding of the barrel removed, the casing replaced with new, lighter, and stronger metals of unknown making, pulled from secret knowledge that only the Society of the Hound knew. It was more portable, designed to be utilised by one man, with a new trigger system attached to a handle that the shooter could hold and fire from the hip. The barrel was etched with strange symbols, carved into the metal faintly with a practised hand.

Barty was not sure what they meant. He would have to find out, he thought.

Jean shoved the cloth belts of ammunition into Barty's unprepared arms, as he spoke firmly, a fell light in his eyes. "Because they are confident. They are prepared. They believe that they have strength of arms and numbers." He dragged out the final case. It thumped onto the wet ground with a faint splash as Jean stood over it and kicked it open, revealing what lay within. He gave a grim smile as he stared at it in appreciation for a long moment. "They have no idea," Jean said with grim satisfaction, "just how wrong they are."

A murderous chuckle came from the side. Puck was there now, having slid across from the wagon, hanging upside down by his legs from a tree branch, his eyes gleaming in the gloom as he chortled, swinging back and forth. "You've got a dark air about you, hunter," he crooned. "You all do, but you, oh, you *most* of all." He grinned, that sharp grin of too many teeth and too many secrets. "You will scar the earth this night, scratch your hatred into the cursed stone. So much terror. So much blood." He closed his glowing eyes and took a deep breath through his nose, as though scenting such things on the air itself. But when he opened his eyes, his expression was serious. "But do be a dear hearted one, and bring back the girl of gold. She is a shattered thing, but that shattering is a beauty all of its own, and precious despite all that. She deserves to finish her dance." He seemed to be looking at Barty in particular as he said it. There was a stern warning there, but something else. Something that Barty did not recognise, but he felt his spine straightening with a growing resolve, without understanding why.

Barty took a deep breath. "Well then," he said slowly, as Adam appeared alongside. "Shall we go get them back?"

All three exchanged looks, and nodded. It was time. There would not be a better one.

THE BLACKCOATS OF Eidolon were many things.

They were a mixture of soldiers, and lesser nobility; officers who never quite made it but also knew how to ingratiate themselves to higher rank. Wyrmwood's cadre was a particularly nasty bunch—they were trained, prepared, and ready for all manner of problems that the hidden world provided. They believed themselves capable of handling many different threats that lesser men would be broken by, that would flee from the sight of rather than confront.

Barty wondered if that was true as he watched Adam pick up an artillery shell.

How they had gotten a hold of such a thing, he did not dare to wonder; *how* was not important. The shell in question was, from all accounts, something generally fired from a long range cannon, designed to be used on battlefields. Barty had been wholly ignorant that he had been sitting next to such a thing during their journey. Why Adam had brought it in the first place, he had no idea. Except now, it was exactly what was needed. Adam hoisted the sixty pound artillery round with one hand, and shifted their grip until they held it with their forefinger placed precisely on the base.

"Where... where did you get that?" Barty asked. He was as armed as he felt he could manage in the situation—Elanor's sword at his belt, his revolver in one hand. Jean had set over each of Barty's shoulders the partly folded up stacks of cloth ammunition belts for the Maxim gun as well. But it all felt utterly worthless when confronted with the simple sight of Adam holding what was designed to destroy whole buildings—and everyone inside—with the nonchalance of a cricket ball.

"Stole it from Cosgrove," Adam confessed shyly, with a quirk of a smile. "I admit, I always wanted to use it. I think I was just looking for the excuse." The giant looked to the overcast sky, squinting, then peered back at Barty. "You think he's ready?"

Barty swallowed, and nodded. "As ready as he's going to be." He gave himself a final look over, adjusting the ammo belts one last time. "I better get moving." He started to half run, half scramble in a hunched over crouch, heading towards the lit up manor.

"I'll give you thirty seconds. Good luck, Barty," Adam murmured hoarsely behind him.

Barty started to count down. Twenty-five. He was lumbering towards the gate, giving it a wide berth; he knew full well what was coming. The trees surrounding the hill were giving him cover, but not nearly enough. He knew eventually those standing watch at the gate would see him.

Twenty. He was closer now. He could see the shapes walking the wall, which meant any moment now they would notice him.

He drew his eye from the guards; he was not looking for them, he was looking for Jean, who had needed to approach earlier, with far more care, taking his time. He'd had to. Burdened as he was, he had no chance of running. Barty was not surprised that no one had seen him. No one saw Jean Reynard if he did not wish to be seen.

Fifteen seconds. Barty hugged the shadows of the trees, the light from the manor over the grounds casting long stretching lines of darkness for him to hide in. It was Jean who had told him how to do that, in the brief instruction he had given—Barty recalled the lesson of the trainyard, keeping his movements controlled and smooth to not draw the eye. Closer. Closer now. The wall was drawing nigh.

Ten seconds. Someone saw him. A voice shouted from the wall above. A floodlight was turned on and began to search. Voices were raised. There was the sound of movement. *Keep the gate far enough away*, he remembered.

Five seconds. He stepped out from behind a tree, and the floodlight landed full on his face, blinding him. He stopped, raising his hands. Cries of halt, and the aiming of weapons sounded—the wall was lined with shadows above the gate, with barrels of rifles pointed his way. He felt his heart pounding in his chest.

Three seconds. Realisation sunk in. Decisions processed. Do they hold fire and find out more? What were their orders exactly?

Two. Looks were exchanged. Was it just one of them? Were there others?

One. Barty stopped counting as the world was ripped asunder.

The sheer force of the round being thrown tore the air apart. Barty had once seen Adam lightly flick an unstable device they had wrought with the force of a gunshot. This was not that. Adam had gotten their back into this one, and launched the shell with all the strength they possessed. It *screamed* like a demon through the air, too fast and too terrifying to imagine, in a straight, flat line from where Adam stood, to the gate. No mere human being could exert that much force. It was hard to imagine any earthly entity, scientific or otherwise, could create such. And thus it was entirely reasonable to think that no one could ever possibly expect it.

Barty had been ready for it—and he *still* proved unable. The shell was a contact fuse device, the latest in British artillery. When the head of the round impacted with the heavy, iron-bound gate, it ignited the shell, releasing that pent up force within. The night was torn apart by an explosion, a vast concussive blast as iron, oak, and stone was ripped apart, alongside mere mortal flesh and bone. Barty was blown off his feet, careening off a tree as he tumbled. The gate vanished in a fireball, along with much of the wall around it. His ears were ringing terribly as he got to his feet, vaguely hoping that people within twenty miles would, somehow, mistake the sound for thunder.

The floodlight was gone. There was a cloud of smoke where the gate had once been, wisping out in the rain. There were groans and screams, dim at the edge of hearing.

Barty staggered forward. No one was paying any attention to him anymore. Barty could not blame them—he had been far enough away from the blast, but to be standing on top of it was something else. And besides, there was something new, and terrible, standing before them. A ghastly apparition, dredged out of dark legend.

Jean Reynard marched into the breach.

The armour that Cosgrove made, inspired by the tale of the bank robber and revolutionary in Australia, Ned Kelly, was made with somewhat more artisanal knowledge. Kelly had built his armour from stolen ploughshares and brute effort. Cosgrove had proper tools, better metal, and far more expertise. He had ascertained the weaknesses of the heavy suit of iron that had been used, and improved on them. The result was more akin to something worn by the knights of old, of blackened steel, strapped into place. It remained thick, and painfully heavy. Enough that Barty was not sure how Jean, especially carrying the Maxim gun slung at his hip, was even able to move with it.

But inside that manor was Elanor, and she was in danger. Barty should have known there was nothing Jean would not do. The impossible faltered before the will of Jean Reynard.

The disorientated, scattered Blackcoats had not even gotten their feet under them when Jean marched through, bringing the barrel of the Maxim gun to bear. Some tried to run. Some opened fire. Others, too shocked, did not even realise what was going on. The gun opened up with a staccato bellow, and then it did not matter any more.

Barty poked his head around the corner as gunfire thundered in fury from within the hellscape that was the courtyard. Jean was striding forward, the machine gun belching forth a roar of rage as it was finally used for what it was meant for—ripping people apart with concentrated, shaped hatred forced out of the barrel at six hundred rounds per minute.

Dazed combatants fired back, some even managing to hit their intended target. But Jean did not stop, even as sparks flew off his form from the impacts, the layered plate protecting him. The helmeted head turned, the visor a black hole from which eyes gleamed with terrible focus. His searing breath emitted as steam amidst the smoke, and Jean strode onwards, inexorable, unstoppable, a dread shape without pity nor mercy. He was death itself.

Barty staggered forward. Still stunned, he stumbled into the courtyard, taking cover behind a wagon parked beside the gate—what was left of it, at least, the impact of the shell having turned it into a jumbled pile of matchwood. He vaguely recalled that he needed to get the ammunition he carried to Jean, but the blow to his head had still not fully faded, and he had taken enough of them at this point that it was starting to become a problem. He fumbled about and heard a shout, looking up to see a man standing over him, raising a rifle to one shoulder.

A giant hand materialised out of the gloom, and the Blackcoat was plucked up and made immediately thereafter to vanish. There was a distant shriek to go with it, as of something flying or falling far, far away. The giant form of Adam appeared then, with an apologetic expression. "Pardon me Barty—I must apprise myself of this a moment."

Barty leaned away as Adam reached over and lifted the shattered wagon with both hands. Shots were raining from the top of the manor now, from men shouting and pointing down as they fired. Barty watched, dumbstruck, as Adam gauged the angle, bullets striking them with absolutely no effect, before they slung the wagon wreckage in a sidelong hammer throw at the roof. The mass of wood became a missile, thrown as easily as one might toss a child's toy. It smashed into the battlements, turning the hanging crane to splinters and shattering broken stone in all directions. Predictably, all the gunfire ceased; it appeared the men firing immediately found something better to do.

Adam gently took the stunned Barty by the shoulder and turned him to face them, as they delicately lifted the belts of ammunition from his nerveless fingers. "I'll be taking those. Stay close to me now, Barty. There's a good man." With that, they turned, striding forward. Barty huddled into their shadow as they advanced forward.

Jean had reached the door of the manor. There were still shots being fired, but they were haphazard, aimed blindly from behind cover. It turned out being attacked by heavy artillery, a machine gun, and a several tonne wagon launched like a dart at a board was not good for morale. It was not good for Barty, and he was not even on the opposing side. His nerves were in full revolt and his heart was beating so hard as to flee his chest entirely.

Adam handed Jean one of the cloth belts—he was in the process of discarding the first, the barrel of the Maxim gun steaming and hissing amidst the falling rain. Taking the second, he set it into the loading breach and released the bolt. It took a moment, the mechanism awkward, and Barty moved forward to help how best he could.

"The mechanism is going to jam partway through that one, I think. Too wet," Adam said with a frown, as Jean tossed the excess end of the belt over his shoulder. The hunter grunted from behind his helmet, a mixture of irritation and exertion.

"We'll deal with that as it comes. Get that door open."

The giant sighed, and then turned to look at the great door that led into the depths of the manor. It was ancient, seared oak, riveted and reinforced by old iron; the sort of door that would withhold enemies, that forbade entrance to the stoutest of hearts.

Unfortunately for that door, it had never come across Adam before. The giant drew back one arm, closed the vast hand into a fist, and delivered a straight right that would have knocked a train off its tracks. The door disappeared, ripped off its hinges and smashed into the interior of the building.

Jean did not hesitate. In he stormed, gun roaring. Barty followed, feeling the air ripping around him as shots were fired in answer, ricocheting off Jean's armour as he forged ahead. They were in a large central chamber, with an ascending staircase—the entire structure was one great hall in fact, looking akin to a mess hall. Barty dove for cover, crawling along the ground. There were overturned tables, which may have been caused by the impact of Adam destroying the door. The giant was entering now, lumbering through the doorway and thrusting the stone aside to fit, shouldering it to pieces with an ease so casual that one had to wonder just how much they normally restrained themselves.

There were indistinct shapes in the room, firing on them

all, but they were scattered and broken already. The agents of Eidolon may indeed have imagined themselves ready, and prepared for Jean Reynard and his violence—but evidence proved emphatically otherwise. Barty, from his crawling position, watched as the hunter bashed in the skull of a cowering Blackcoat with the butt of the Maxim gun, before bringing it to bear once more, bracing himself as bullets fired at him sparked off his armour. A round bounced off the shaped and visored helmet, snapping Jean's head back, but he brought it back with a furious snarl, swinging the barrel around as it continued to bellow death with ear-shattering force.

The barrel was glowing cherry red at this point, the handle that Jean held nearly breaking off with the force required to carry it. He roared as he fired, hatred incarnate and wrath unleashed, and Barty knew it was purely rage that kept him moving—the weight of all he carried and wore was more than he could even begin to lift, and yet Jean continued everforward despite its weight, steaming with the sort of fury that would not be stopped.

Adam emerged from the mayhem then, and pulled Barty to his feet with one hand, as easily as one might lift a feather. The other arm reached out, picked up a broad, heavy oaken dining table, and flung it at someone lining up a shot against them. The table did not slow at all in its momentum, bringing the luckless target with it before it exploded into splinters against a distant wall. The Eidolon agent, caught between table, solid stone wall, and Adam's terrible power, was rendered unrecognisable—and very dead.

It was chaos. It was carnage. Barty was not sure what to

do, as he all but clung to Adam in a panic. What difference could he make in this mess? What could he even do? He could not unleash violence like these two could. He could not even conceive of it.

Elanor. Lily.

The abrupt reminder of what he was here for ripped into his thoughts, and he jerked his head up to the stairs. "We have to go! We cannot get trapped here!" he shouted to Adam above the bellowing cacophony of gunfire, screams, and shouts.

The giant looked down at him, frowning. A bullet bounced off their chest. "Quite correct," Adam agreed then, almost thoughtfully despite the shocking violence, their voice soft in direct contrast to the battle. They looked over to Jean, who was steadily progressing, firing short bursts of gunfire from the burning hot gun. "Reynard! We are going up!"

Jean spun, bringing the massive gun around in a heavy swing to smash a leaping Blackcoat driven to desperation to try and tackle the hunter. "Go!" he thundered, the sound muffled within the helmet, as he brought down his armoured boot in a brutal high stomp on the unfortunate he had just downed. The sickening *crack* of crushed bone within fragile flesh followed Barty as he scrambled up the ascent. The staircase rocked as Adam followed, but the ancient stone held.

Barty's heart was pounding as he raced upwards. There was a door, closed at the top, and he rushed for it—but as his hand landed, Adam shouted a warning. He half turned, and it saved his life. A gunshot blasted a six inch hole in the door itself, and Barty felt a hot pain on the side of his face as the bullet ricocheted off the wall behind him. He was stunned, but Adam came surging up the space, their vast form barely fitting past Barty and charging *through* the entire doorframe, smashing it outwards as if a battering ram. Barty reached into his coat, finally drawing his revolver as he charged after them, but halted in horror.

Wyrmwood was there. Loathsome, cretinous Wyrmwood, lowering his rifle with a look of annoyance. "Persistent bunch, aren't you?" He sounded more annoyed than angry. "But then I've become used to working with stubborn fools."

He was standing in a large open hall. Another staircase to a higher level was behind him, but this floor was devoted to all manner of machinery. Cables were roped across the floorboards and ceiling, all of them leading to rows and rows of the capacitors. There were dozens of them, each one buzzing with a potent charge, vibrating with energy. And that was not all; metal containers, standing upright, lined against the walls—four a side, eight all told. Each of them stood about seven feet tall, broad and imposing, vaguely shaped like a coffin but much larger. They had cables protruding from each of them, all leading to a series of levers and switches—and at that switchboard, Wyrmwood now stood. He grinned, a spiteful, malicious expression.

"Shelley's monster. After so, so long, we finally meet. She really was as good as they say she was—magnificent craftsmanship." His voice was one of admiration twisted by loathsome envy, which dripped with wanton greed as he looked Adam up and down in appreciation. "The first iteration of something is always special."

Adam thrust an arm out to the side to halt and shield Barty

as they glared down at Wyrmwood, even as Barty unthinkingly made to charge forward with his heart full of rage, the wretched captain's words setting him afire with hatred. "What have you done, Wyrmwood?" Adam asked slowly, their beautiful, melodious voice rendered dark with a suppressed fury.

The man smirked, an unpleasant expression on an already ugly face. "What progress demands, and nothing less. For the glory of the Empire, we have begun what will become the defining work of history. This"—he waved grandly around the room—"is but the start of it. The first soldiers in the greatest army ever seen." There was a manic edge to his voice, a hysterical, childish glee.

Barty stared around the room, at the black cables, at the coffins. A stark, ice cold realisation slid up his spine. This looked different, but there was a dread familiarity; something had been done here. As the whine of the capacitors built up higher, the screech of building energy grew louder.

"You probably imagine yourself the pinnacle of creation," Wyrmwood cackled. "And perhaps so, but not any more. We have *improved* upon you." He reached over, grasping a heavy lever, and yanked it down.

The entire room exploded into white light and black noise. Lightning blazed from the capacitors and across the cables, sparks exploding outwards in furious eruptions, turning the air alive. Barty could taste metal. Energy arced towards him, but it lanced to Adam as though drawn to them, the air filled with a roar. Not from Adam, who gritted their teeth as electricity danced over their form and set their hair to rising, but from the metal coffin-like containers—which burst open, one after another.

Wyrmwood was fleeing, waving as he went in a mocking fashion, pausing at the stairs to gloat. "They won't last long, but they do not need to. After all, mass production is the true herald of industry! And with this, England shall once more rule the world! For Britannia!" he crowed in manic cheer as he bolted away.

Barty paid him no heed. He was instead, far more focused on the dreadful reality before him. From each of the containers emerged a nightmarish figure; half wrought terrors of flesh and steel, twisted and misshapen. Each of them was clearly *once* a man, and each was wearing remnants of an Eidolon uniform. Whether they had volunteered, or had been dressed in them as some hideous parody, Barty could not tell but whatever men they had been before meant nothing. What had once been simple flesh was now distorted by burns and tearing where the skin failed and ripped apart, bolted machinery in its place in hideous replacement, grafted with crude implementation. And they were *screaming*. Each of them wore an expression wracked with wide-eyed horror and blind madness—utterly empty of thought, and devoid of reason.

With torn voices, they howled to a heaven that could not hear them, each a sacrifice on the altar of progress made by a man who sought to make tools from souls. They were abominations. They were everything Adam was not. Barty watched in frozen horror as one picked up their container and hurled it across the room. They were destroying everything in sight, ripping cables up and smashing their fists into the floor as they went into a frenzy, wild beasts tasting blood and going mad. In moments, they would notice Adam and Barty, and that insanity would focus on them.

Barty felt it, as Adam stiffened. They seemed to *congeal*, a tightening of steel and cable, of force and wrath. They straightened, standing without a stoop; their shoulders broadened out, their feet braced apart. Adam had always given an air of care, of absolute, utmost gentleness, of restraint in every single gesture. Afraid to move freely in case they might cause harm, acutely aware of their power, Adam moved through a world made of glass, taking caution not to shatter it by their passing. Every movement measured; every moment tempered.

Barty thought he had seen it all, thought that he had seen Adam at their most potent, their most powerful, as they had stormed this fortress together. But he could not have *possibly* been more wrong, as Adam readied themselves.

"Get upstairs, Barty. Save them," Adam commanded, as energy cascaded off their mighty, impossible form. "I will deal with these."

Barty opened his mouth to speak. But Adam was gone.

The ground buckled beneath him as Adam's spring shattered where they had just stood. The wrought stone and ancient wood that made the floor cracked. In less time than it took to blink, Adam was amongst them, and the hideous, warped monstrosities, made in Adam's image but only as an evil mockery, shrieked and gibbered with the voices of broken beasts and charged to meet their progenitor. The storm was rumbling outside, but Barty could see the reality; the true storm was Adam. And it was here.

Adam's choice was not to be a monster. Barty finally understood just what that meant, as he witnessed the terrible ramifications of what that *looked* like. Adam stood taller, stronger, their shoulders unburdened by the weight of their existence—and the violence of that magnitude was awful. A mechanical arm was torn off, too fast to see how, and Adam turned to hurl it across the room, shattering another charging enemy to pieces with their makeshift weapon. They *surged* with power and fury as they were attacked on all sides, the creatures that were once men and now an unholy combination of machine leaping onto Adam in a bestial attempt to bring them down. Adam buckled under the impact, blows powerful enough to make the building rock, but they did not fall. Barty, frozen in place, stared in horror as the nightmare unfolded, and through the dreadful pile of limbs and bodies, Adam locked eyes with him.

"GO!" Adam bellowed, the first time they had ever raised their voice, and it rumbled the foundation.

Barty was running before he could think, leaping over a layer of cabling as the capacitors continued to shriek—to his left, one detonated in a shower of glass. Fragments fell around him, slicing through his coat, but he could not stop. The stairwell was just ahead.

A massive shape sprang directly in front of him, broken teeth bared in a lipless mouth, a graveyard reek on their breath as they howled like a foghorn and raised an arm wrapped and built of blackened iron to smash him from the world. He was midstep and had nowhere to go and no time... and he knew it.

A looping of black cables lanced out of nowhere, slung around the figure, and yanked tight. Barty got the barest glimpse of Adam, who was half buried under the mound of figures raining blows on them, as they held the cluster off with one hand. For the briefest moment, it did not look to be enough to stop the attacker, and then Adam gave a roar, pulled, and spun. Crude, blackened spikes welded to the bones of a hand withdrew from within an inch of Barty's eye, as the attacking monster was pulled off their feet and flung across the room into a bank of capacitors. At same time, Adam yanked one vast fist free, raising one of the attackers clinging to it, and brought both down on the ground at their feet.

The floor exploded. Half the room fell away in an instant—Adam, the beasts, the machinery, all collapsed in a blazing hellfire of sparks and detonations. Every window blew outwards and Barty was blown back by the force of it, up the stairs, the wind knocked out of him.

His ears were ringing, and his head hurt again. There was blood in his mouth, his hands were wet with it. He could barely see for all the smoke. Adam and the machine creatures were gone, presumably down to where Jean was still fighting.

Have to keep going, he commanded himself, as he spat blood to the stones. *Have to reach them*.

He staggered, climbing on hands and knees to the next floor. The stairwell was wide, and he scrambled up it, feeling glass shards digging into his palms, but he ignored it. Now was not the time. Pain could come later. He could make it that far. He had to.

CHAPTER 24

SINS OF OUR FATHERS

The stairway climbed, and Barty rose with it. Through an open archway, he beheld one final hall, high and vaulted. This was the pinnacle of the tower, and where the final truths lay hidden.

The room was dominated by a raised platform taking up much of the room. Beneath it was an array of machinery and apparatus humming, grinding, and buzzing away with growing intensity—capacitors, pistons and gears, a great engine powered by an unknown source. The platform itself had yet more of the same, and between it and the many chains and cables leading up to the roof, they obscured much of what was going on up there—a matter not helped by Barty's angle of view, leaving whatever was transpiring on the platform a mystery for the moment. There was an opening in the side of the tower, far too large to be a window and more akin to a barn door, and from the looks of it the means by which the machinery that filled the place had been brought into it, explaining the crane on the roof.

There were shouted voices now too, arguing, though he could not see their source. No one seemed to have noticed him.

"You *sicken* me."

It was Braithwaite, his voice cold with absolute disgust. Barty froze, holding his breath even though it hurt. The answering, snide snigger to the voice was Wyrmwood, somewhere above him. He ducked into the machinery beneath the main platform to hide, looking up through the floorboards to see the now loathsomely familiar spectre of Wyrmwood.

"And yet, you're the one who set about making all of this *happen*, William," Wyrmwood said with an ugly, madness tinged laugh. "I am not the one who made these things—I gave you the means, nothing more."

"I never wanted this!" Braithwaite snarled, his voice now strained and agitated. "I did not want any of this!"

Wyrmwood gave a disgusted snort. "I am well aware. All *you* wanted was to save your child. You have what you wanted, don't you?"

Braithwaite made a strangled, wordless sound of despair. "The girl's father is here. I never would have expected him to find us this quickly."

A footstep stomped overhead. Barty, with his revolver in his hand, looked for an opening as he moved to follow them. He thought he heard a muffled, gagged voice protesting furiously. Wyrmwood ignored it as he went on, "He's the hunter, Lord Braithwaite. He was always going to find us. But even if he reaches us, it won't be enough. His two pets are doubtless undone, and he is but one man—even if he manages to get through all of my men, the best of your creations is waiting for him."

Barty paused at that. He had not heard another figure. Nor

had he seen one. What did Wyrmwood—

A slurring growl was heard, too close, and machine like—but not enough to hide that it originated from a creature's throat. It came from directly behind him; he had not been the only one to think the space beneath the platform had been a good hiding spot.

Barty did not even bother turning. He dove forward with a speed he did not know he had, feeling a monstrous *something* swipe over his head with a force that would have smashed the life from him. He scrambled on all fours out of the depths of the sublevel, out into the light, and swivelled onto his back, aiming the revolver as a figure lumbered out after him.

They were nearly as large as Adam, but far more twist- ed. A human body encased in pistons, machinery, and other parts, like the armoured skin of a crab, bolted on and through the flesh beneath. The face was distorted and deformed, the parts where the bare skull showed through wrapped in plated iron. But Barty knew them instantly. The rotted teeth, the slab-jawed visage... He had gone through some changes, but Cripple Pete was just a monster in a different kind of flesh.

He nearly did not get the shot off in time. A malformed hand reached for him as Pete charged, letting out a roar that made Barty's ears ache. Barty fired, the shot bouncing off the reinforced skull of the thing that had once been the monstrous street thug to seemingly no effect, as he rolled to one side to avoid the rush. He did not waste a second looking back to see the crash. He sprang to his feet and blindly ran up the stairs, into the depths of the laboratory.

"Barty!" The voice was familiar, but weakened.

Lily.

Barty reached the top of the stairs, and had but a heartbeat to take the scene in. Wyrmwood and Braithwaite stood in the centre, facing off against one another. Along the edges of the platform were various pieces of machinery, and humming glass capacitors that had a faint blue light emanating from them. Behind them were two figures that stopped him cold.

Elanor was bound onto a metal bed, held upright and suspended in the air, restrained by leather straps and medical cuffs, the frame surrounded further by a metal ring. A steel skull cap with wires coming out of it was attached to her head, with contacts placed at her temples. She was gagged, her eyes wild. She looked angry. She looked frightened. One of her eyes was swollen as though she had been struck.

To the left of her, on an operating table, was Lily. Like Elanor, she was restrained, sitting curled up and despondent on the table, hugging her knees while restraining belts on her wrists and ankles kept her nominally in place. As Barty looked at her, she reached for him with one arm, but it abruptly failed and fell as though a string had been cut. Her face mask was still cracked, still bearing the smudged remnants of the makeup that Elanor had painted. That night felt like an eternity ago now. The glow in her eyes was flickering. Whatever was happening to her was growing worse.

He raised the revolver, pointing it at Wyrmwood but the man did not even flinch. Lily spotted him, and gasped his name—but Elanor screamed through her gag in warning. The world tilted; a massive weight ripped Barty off his feet and bore him down. Cripple Pete had caught him in his moment of pause and brought him low, one massive, twisted, and augmented hand holding Barty face down with a crushing mass on his back. The revolver fell from his hands and skittered over the ground, leaving Barty futilely grasping for it desperately, unable to move or get air into his lungs.

Wyrmwood sauntered closer. Blinking back tears, Barty twisted his neck to look up at the hateful figure looming above him. He recognised them. Not simply the man, who he knew all too well. No, it was the *look*. He had seen it before, all his life, in the wretched pits of that hell that men called St Mary's, and where no saint could be found. The knowing look of someone who had others in their power and knew it. It was the look of a sadist, someone who took delight in the misery of others, of the power of their own cruelty. It was as hateful as it could be. Barty strained for the revolver, grinding his teeth so hard they felt like they might shatter. The air thrummed with energy; his skin felt alive with it.

"Now then, Mister Bartleby," Wyrmwood purred, squatting down next to him insolently while Cripple Pete made Barty's ribs creak and nearly crack under their monstrous burden. "You're going to hurt yourself, doing that." He reached down, brushing back Barty's hair with a skin crawling caress. "And if you do that, you might miss the show."

"What... are you... talking about?" Barty forced out the words.

Wyrmwood gave an ugly, high pitched cackle. "Soon as that lightning strikes, you'll know." He waved vaguely to a window. The rumble of thunder soon came after. "I would wager you've only a few seconds." He grinned. "So get ready to say goodbye to your sweetheart. Miss Braithwaite needs a new body, and we have just the thing on hand."

Barty's eyes shot to Lily, who stared back at him. He could not tell her emotions; he never fully could. Her eyes dimmed and brightened as though something flickered behind them, and her body twitched and spasmed as she continued to try and make her fingers work the buckles that fastened her to the table. Tried and failed. *She* was failing; she was falling apart. He saw the cabling, leading from her to the restrained Elanor. He saw Braithwaite, who was standing at the control panel between them—he was staring at Barty with an unseeing expression, tortured and unsure. Realisation struck like a lead weight.

"You... cannot," Barty grated, desperately. "You *cannot do this*." The horror of revelation only made it more enjoyable for Wyrmwood, who cackled.

"Of course I can. And once we put this machine in the right hands, and *prove* how it can work, well, the possibilities are endless."

Barty strained. His bones shrieked, his muscles convulsed until they nearly snapped. The storm was too close. If he did not prevent this, the next lightning strike would end everything. "I'll... stop... you!" he gasped, each word making black spots dance across his vision. He felt his fingernails tear on the floorboards. *He had to do something.*

"You? All alone?" Wyrmwood sneered. He stood, turning the cane he carried in one hand. "Don't make me—"

BOOM. In this confined space, the roar of the rifle was immense. The weight on Barty's back lessened. There was the crack and crank of a rifle being reloaded, and then again, the concussion of the blast. The monstrous brute Cripple Pete staggered, and Barty dragged himself free.

Jean's helmet was gone. His armour was ripped away in places, and there was smoke coming off him where he had been on fire, his remaining armour and coat burnt and singed. He had abandoned the massive Maxim gun, and was now firing the heavy bore lever action rifle. He continued to storm towards Cripple Pete, cranking the lever action to eject the spent, smoking cartridge, and fired again. He did not say a word. His expression was split with rage that no fire could quell, blood on his cheek and brow amidst the soot. The world buckled and broke at his approach. A father had come for his daughter. There was no force that could stop him.

Cripple Pete howled, a man lost to the monster, and charged blindly towards him. Jean snarled back and met Pete head on, as Barty scrambled away to get his revolver. Jean was dodging, reloading and firing, blasting away chunks of flesh and iron as he did so, but Pete was a berserker and would not die. The laboratory, this last house of abominations, was in chaos. But the storm was here. He had to act.

Barty watched as Braithwaite desperately turned dials and yanked on a lever. Lily was still pinned, trapped in a body that would not obey her. Barty could see and hear her pleading with her father to stop, but there was no time. He raised the revolver.

Wyrmwood's hand wrapped around Barty's neck and crushed his windpipe, as he hissed like a viper in Barty's ear. "Got you, *again*." He seized Barty's arm before he could turn the gun on him. Barty could feel the air being choked out of him. His knees were wobbling. But he still held the gun. He struggled, but the man holding him was stronger, and crueler. Wyrmwood forced his hand away, towards Elanor.

He could see Elanor thrashing in her restraints as Braithwaite returned to his work, desperate, rushed. There was no time. They were all out of time. He looked to Elanor, and their eyes met. A silent plea. A hopeless prayer. He could not breathe, but he could aim.

Holding his breath was the easy part. Getting the revolver steady was something else. Jean had taught him 'to aim small, so as to miss small', but that was not exactly helpful when he was *not* allowed to miss. Not this time. He just needed a second. Not even that. He set his feet, and rammed his free arm back, smashing the elbow into Wyrmwood's ribs. A momentary grunt and the grip on him loosened—just a fraction, for just a moment. He did not hesitate. He fired.

Wyrmwood pushed himself away, spun the dazed Barty around and punched him in the stomach. Barty bent over double, falling onto Wyrmwood, who punched him again, and then again, blasting the little air left in him from his body. Dimly, Barty could see Jean and Cripple Pete locked in combat, tumbling over the side of the upper level walkway and out of sight as Jean held the maddened creature away with his rifle between them. Wyrmwood bore Barty down now, pulling him further off balance to the ground as he brought his cane to bear, placing it on Barty's throat and pressing down with all his weight. Barty struggled. There was no way to breathe. That vile predator smile grinning down at him, the beady rat-like eyes alight with the thrill of slow murder.

"How I wish you could tell me what it is like," he gloated, "to die like a dog." He spat on Barty's face as Barty pulled one hand away, fumbling blindly in his pockets as his vision went dark. "When we have this, I will live *forever*, in a new, younger body every time." His grin split his face in his frenzy. "You've been an annoying little rodent in all this. So be a good boy and—" He choked suddenly as he was cut short, and his face went pale as his grip slackened.

The switchblade Adam had given Barty had been something he hated. For the most part, he had never bothered to carry it with him. The notion of having such an evil little thing had not sat well with him. It was a thing used for secrets, a weapon people did not see coming, a sneaking thing to slip under a rib or a sensitive spot, and drive it home. Like he had just done.

"Shut"—his voice was raw and rasping as he grabbed Wyrmwood by the collar, plastering the man's nose across his face as he smashed his forehead into it—"UP!" he roared, getting one boot under him, and pushing his attacker clear.

The switchblade spun away, leaving a bloody hole in Wyrmwood's stomach where the knife had torn free. Barty dragged himself to his feet as Wyrmwood did, who was white-faced now with shock and fury. He gripped his walking cane, twisted the handle and pulled out a sword—long, thin, but terribly effective. Barty, staggering, drew his own.

With one hand, Wyrmwood wrenched his broken nose back into place. The Blackcoat captain grinned spitefully through the blood. "Going to show me what you can do then, are you?"

Barty paused, taking a breath. His throat felt like fire. His body hurt all over. But he was elated. He grinned, and with a rasp, he spoke. "No. She's much better, after all."

When Barty had fired his revolver, he had lived up to Jean's words. He was many things, but a bad shot, he was not. He was, in that moment, a very, very good shot. The bullet had caught Elanor's right restraint that had been keeping her arm from moving, and snapped it. As Barty and Wyrmwood had grappled, she had undone her remaining bindings, one by one, and once free, she was unleashed with the pent up rage of her incarceration unravelling all at once.

Hair flying behind her, eyes blazing with rage, revenge in her heart, and a snarl on her lips, she kicked Wyrmwood in the chest so hard with both feet he nearly flew out of his boots. The wretch rolled backwards, sprawling in an undignified heap. She spun, hand outstretched, catching the sword Barty had already thrown for her, and turned on Wyrmwood, who staggered to his feet. He defended with increasing desperation as Elanor showed what Barty and Jean already knew—that despite her imprisonment, her exhaustion and mistreatment, she was the finest with a blade any of them had ever seen.

But Barty could not watch the deadly duel as it raged. He lurched around to Lily, even as the glow of the capacitors intensified. The cables leading to the ceiling were coming alive, a charge passing up them towards the roof. But Braithwaite was crying out in panic, trying to adjust things still. Barty paid him no heed. He reached for Lily, as she did likewise with one trembling hand.

"I'm sorry! I'm so sorry!" she wailed, and her shame, her terror, was an agony Barty could not bear. "I was...

I'm..." She trailed off, trying to make her arms work. "Barty... Bartholomew, I'm..." Her eyes flickered again, and she spasmed. "I'm frightened."

Barty had lived a life in fear; had seen what fear could look like, feel like, and he knew what it sounded like. But never had it sounded so terrible in its awful, heartbreaking purity. He had to save her. He had to get her out of here, and take her home.

"I know," he said, holding her face gently in both hands. "But it is going to be all right." He hurriedly undid the straps holding her down, prying off the device that was attached to her head. "We are getting you out of here. We are getting you home." He held out a hand to her, trying to help her off the operating table. He turned—

Click. The gun that Lord Braithwaite held was similar to a sort Jean liked to use—a twin barrelled, ornate looking thing with a heavy calibre, and it was pointed right at his face with the hammer pulled. Lord Braithwaite was staring at him, a look of desperation and iron determination on his face. "You will *not* take my daughter."

Around them, all was chaos. Elanor and Wyrmwood were duelling still, all but brawling as their swords clashed against each other. Elanor was the more skilled, but she was exhausted, her hours and hours of straining against restraints slowing her down now. She side-stepped a thrust and was thrown into the heavy door by Wyrmwood's free arm. The bulky barn door opened slightly as she bounced off it and back into the room, barely spared from a tumble into the void. Jean was somewhere grappling with Cripple Pete, somewhere full of sound and roars and things breaking. The machinery of the lab was alive with energy, and the sort of power that broke the barriers of what was and was not possible.

"Why are you doing this?" Barty had to buy time. *Something.* Braithwaite's face twitched, as Barty went on, "This is madness—look at this! Look at the things you have done! What did you do to your daughter?" He knew it was folly to accuse him, but the anger was too much. Lily deserved better than this.

The man snapped. "I am fulfilling a father's *duty*, their *only* duty!" he spat, his face spasming in his fury into a snarl. "I was supposed to save her! I was supposed to *protect her*!"The snarl twisted, and a tear fell down Braithwaite's cheek. He looked on the edge of breaking down, but the gun did not waver—if his finger moved, Barty would be dead before he knew it.

Lily clutched his arm tighter. She was crying as she begged, "Father, please—you have to stop! He's my friend!"

Barty took a step closer as Braithwaite wavered, but the gun was thrust towards him once more. With no other options, with the sounds of blade striking blade, of rage battling with insanity, drowning out all thought, Barty pressed on. "Your daughter spoke of you to us, Lord Braithwaite. The man she described *loved* her. That man dedicated his life to caring for his daughter. This is not how that should look."

Braithwaite's jaw twisted, as the gun wobbled in his hand. "If you care for her, then help me save her." His tone was imploring as he twitched the gun to his left, towards Elanor. "Help me restrain her, get her back into the machine. Let me transfer Lily's consciousness into her body. It is the *only way*. The bindings of her spirit are breaking down—we only have moments left. Your friend has to die, for Lily to live. *Please.*"

Barty felt his heart turn to ice in his chest. Lily, too, went quiet, lifting a hand to her mask in shock. "Father... no... I won't... I can't do..." She stumbled into silence. Braithwaite's hand tightened around the gun. His desperate, last ditch plea made, the hand showed and the cards laid bare. Barty had to choose.

"No." He said it thickly, his voice leaden. He knew what that answer meant, what would happen. He met the mad Lord's eyes and held his ground, prepared for the end. He held Lily's shoulder a moment—it was yet still warm. "I cannot do that. I will not."

Braithwaite's face fell—then turned to that cold, hard expression, like a switch had been thrown, a decision made. "Then I shall do it myself." His finger tightened on the trigger.

As he fired, Lily moved.

Barty saw it in slow motion as she pushed him aside, lit by the arcing energy leaping across the room, the shadows cast by the ongoing fights creating a nightmare tableau.

But none of it was as awful as the bullet striking Lily's face.

Half her mask exploded in shards of porcelain as the round ripped half her head away, a burst of delicate brass instruments flowering out behind her head. It lifted her off her feet, turning her in a half spin through the air, a dancer performing her swan song before she fell, limp and broken. The strings were cut.

Braithwaite dropped his gun with an anguished cry as he fell to his knees, but Barty was already there, scrambling for the falling girl and catching her. One of her beautiful green eyes was gone, the unforgiving piece of cruel lead having gone clean through her metal skull. He could see the many gears, wires, and mechanisms that made up the interior of her head, as well as the strange metal casing that seemingly replaced her brain. It was brass and etched with strange symbols, which glowed green—but that glow was fitful and weak now, flickering and dying in time with the light in Lily's last eye. She looked up at Barty, and her voice, distorted and broken, slurred out.

"Are... you... all right?"

He was crying, and could barely see through the tears, as he struggled to say something, anything, that could take every-thing back. To undo what was in his arms and bring back what could have been. "I'm sorry," he pleaded, her own apology cast back at her, but his own felt so utterly, completely insufficient.

The glow in her eye brightened. "Don't be," she responded with her faltering voice. "This was my choice."

Braithwaite crawled over to them, but there was no more fight in him. He took Lily's hand, holding it in both of his as he wept, broken at last. Barty wanted to say something, an accusation, a helpless begging for a way to reverse this, an apology; but a shape flew overhead and crashed into the operating table, where they lay groaning.

Jean was battered, trying to push himself up with both hands, before his arms gave out and he collapsed to the ground again. There was stomping of enormous feet; Cripple Pete was com-ing, ignoring all else as they focused on their prey. They were bleeding, blood and black ichor both, their metal frame broken in many places, one arm severed just below the shoulder, but they did not stop.

Jean was without a weapon, the broken hilt of a sword in his hand. He reached blindly, picking up Barty's fallen revolver where it had fallen. As he aimed the barrel at the approaching beast, there was a cry. Elanor had fallen to her knees, struck down by a treacherous blow in the midst of her duel. Wyrmwood, cackling like a madman, raised his blade in triumph. They stood at the doorway, thrown open by their struggle and leading to the open air beyond. Outside, rain fell and lightning flashed. The charge rods on the roof shrieked, the capacitors whining in a frenzy.

Jean did not even hesitate. He fired the revolver across the room. Two fingers were ripped off as the sword descended and the Blackcoat captain shrieked, flinching as he dropped the blade, stumbling backwards towards the opening as he clutched his maimed hand. Elanor saw the opportunity, and rage gave her strength.

The sword came up in a savage upwards slash, and with it she carved off Wyrmwood's nose along with much of the left side of his face, the chunk of flesh and nose flying away as the man howled in an explosion of agony. Elanor was not done, for as the slash was completed, she turned and delivered a spinning straight side kick, a full extension of the leg with herself properly braced. It was perfect form, and it caught Wyrmwood in the gut so hard that he was lifted clean off his feet. With a falling scream of despair he flew out the opening amidst a flash of thunder and vanished into the stormlit void and the long drop beyond.

But there was no time for celebrations. With their remaining arm, Cripple Pete seized Jean and lifted him up, smashing him back down like a ragdoll. Blood flew from Jean's mouth as the armour held, but only barely. Once again, he was lifted. He fired a shot, but it merely bounced off Cripple Pete's armoured skull. Barty could only watch, Lily still holding on in his arms. He had no weapons left. There was nothing he could do.

A vast figure rushed over him. Adam's new coat was a ruin, and they were smoking all over, but they were, of all of them there, the only one that was not slowed. A mechanised hand seized Cripple Pete by the head and the other ripped Jean out of their grasp, lifting the monstrosity with tremendous force, and slamming them down once, twice, a third time into the operating table apparatus that Lily had been strapped to. It exploded into fragments, but the creature kept kicking. It thrust Adam aside, raising its metal arm and starting to beat at Adam as they struggled to hold the monster at bay. The two titans strove at each other, and though Barty felt Adam would prevail, he was frightened for the grounded Jean, for the wounded Elanor, and the shattered Lily he held. He had to do something.

"How do we stop it?" Barty asked. "Lord Braithwaite!" he implored, desperate. If that thing got loose, it could kill any of them in its flailing.

Braithwaite seemed to realise this at the same time. For a moment, his vision cleared, and he stared at Barty, at Lily, as sanity poured its cold water in his face to give him clarity. He spun, and called out to Adam. "The transfer device! Put it on his head!" He pointed, as Adam looked over, holding the frenzied Cripple Pete in place—and they understood.

Following Braithwaite's guiding hand, Adam seized the strange apparatus that had been attached to Lily's cranium, and forced it onto the frothing, roaring Cripple Pete. Braithwaite was already moving, reaching the sparking, damaged control panel he had been working so frantically as he bellowed a warning. "GET DOWN!"

Adam remained where they were, holding Cripple Pete with one hand. Jean, just as he had done in the basement when all this had begun, desperately sheltered both Barty and Lily. Barty saw Elanor dive for cover out the corner of his eye as Braithwaite threw the switch.

The surge was deafening. It roared as the air ripped apart, arcing electricity pouring down the cables, along the capacitors, into the air and at Adam, who seemed to attract each and every stray bolt, sparing those around them from destruction. Cripple Pete screamed then, an entirely human scream, drawn out and agonising as an indefinable *something* was pulled out of them, dragged out by whatever it was Adam was holding onto their metal plated skull. It was a shriek that turned to despair as it seemed to find nowhere to go, nothing to travel to, before it winked out into abrupt silence. The misshapen, twisted monstrosity finally went limp.

The room was still seething with energy, the air thick with the scent of ozone and burning metal. Jean slumped, exhausted, to one side, rolling over onto his back. Adam stepped away from the smoking, broken corpse that had once been Cripple Pete. Barty for a moment felt sorry for him—but then he remembered that awful cellar, and the things he had seen there. The moment faded.

"I'm sorry to have been such a bother," Lily said, sounding crestfallen. She was still in Barty's arms, as he held her off the floor. Elanor crossed the room and came alongside, kneeling next to Barty as he tried desperately to dismiss Lily's apologies.

"You have not. You never have been, Lily," he said, feeling the tears well up again. This was not right. It was not *fair*. He turned to Lord Braithwaite, who was slumped nearby, dejected and shattered. He, like everyone else there, was clustered in this small space, exhausted and broken.

"There has... there has to be something we can *do*," Barty implored.

But Braithwaite shook his head, his voice sorrowful as he replied, "There is not. I bound my daughter to that form, thrice over—but it was never supposed to be permanent. Just... just temporary until..." He broke down into sobbing. "Lily, I'm sorry. All I wanted was to save you."

She turned her broken head towards him. Even this was difficult for her now, the rest of her body no longer responding. The glow in her eye was starting to fade. But her voice was clear, and it was warm with her love. "I know, Father." She looked up to Barty, to Adam, who stood forlornly above them all, and Elanor, who was weeping. "But this... is what... I chose."

Elanor gently reached out to brush Lily's hair from the remnants of her face. "You should have seen her dance, your lordship," she said, smiling through her tears. "You never saw anything so beautiful."

The glow in Lily's eye was nearly gone. Her voice came, but it was faint, falling, as her father crawled on his hands and knees towards them. "I would have... liked to... stay a little... longer." Her voice softened. "I would liked to have... danced with you all... again..."

As her father took her hand with his own, his fingers shaking, the light went out. Lily's body all at once went utterly still, as though whatever was holding that vital force in her was gone. The life in her vanished. Barty knew that this time, there was no bringing it back. Lily was gone.

The place was falling apart, energy bursting as capacitors shattered, but none of them could have cared. In that awful moment, no one seemed to know what to do.

"What happened?" It was Jean, who still lay on his back, sprawled out amidst the wreckage.

Braithwaite did not turn to look at him, still holding his daughter's hand, gently squeezing it as though to feel one moment of that lingering warmth leaving her metal frame. He spoke dully. "It was her mother."

"What?" Elanor asked, her voice soft.

Braithwaite sighed, and in blank, empty misery, he explained, reaching up to carefully cover the ruin of Lily's broken, empty face with the hair of her still attached wig. "I searched in futility for a disease, but I was looking in the wrong place. Medical journals, patient charts, records... But I should have been looking in my home. All those years, it was her mother, poisoning her in secret. My wife is... mad." He shook his head, in brokenhearted defeat. "I never saw it, until after, when I could..." He swallowed. "During the autopsy, it became clear at last. When I confronted her about it, she was... confused. And then seemed to forget I had asked her. All that time, and I just... I just never knew."

Jean slowly sat up. "I've seen it, once before," he said quietly. "It is very, very rare. But it happens." He shook his head. "Do not blame yourself. No one expects to see a monster in the ones they love."

"If not me, then who?" came the bitter response. A capacitor nearby exploded, energy arcing across the room. Braithwaite did not even notice. "She said you would come, and that when you did I was to give you this. I did not believe her, fool that I was."

"Who?" Adam asked, as they reached over to gently lift Jean to his feet. Their power, once again restrained, their movements gentle, careful. Once more, Adam had made their choice.

Braithwaite looked directly at Jean. "Carmilla. The woman in red." Lord Braithwaite reached into his coat, and Barty held his breath, as he pulled out a leather-bound book. "She gave me this. The key to everything. Shelley's final research; the guide to immortality itself." He shook his head, holding it out to Jean, who took it silently. "All of what I have done, I merely copied from her. She had figured out every facet before anyone else even thought to ask the question. An incredible woman." He turned his head towards Adam, who stood in silent confusion. "And yet, in her own words, you were her greatest achievement." He gave a sad smile. "Her writings taught me the truth and value in loving what is. That this mortal shell is but a temporary thing." He caressed Lily's face gently. "Please. Can I hold her?"

Barty could not refuse him. There was smoke in the room now. Things were burning. Braithwaite took Lily's lifeless body from him and cradled her in his arms. She was still wearing her dress, one that Elanor had given her. She looked so small now.

"This place will collapse soon," Jean said flatly, holding the journal in one hand. He lifted Elanor to her weary feet. Adam did the same to Barty, effortlessly plucking him up with one hand. "We need to get out of here, Lord Braithwaite."

The kneeling lord, cradling his daughter, gave them a smile that held not the slightest semblance of joy, and Barty felt a sudden sharp understanding, before Braithwaite confirmed it. "Not I... I am staying here." He looked back to the broken, shattered doll in his arms. "I am right where I need to be."

Jean stared him down. Something exploded beneath them, a booming sound combined with the thump of a piston firing through the floor and embedding in the roof. The shriek of the capacitors had grown louder. The floor was starting to shake. Braithwaite stared lifelessly. "The charge has nowhere to go. There's too much damage." He sighed, and hugged Lily closer. "You must run, while you can."

Jean grimaced, and then pulled Elanor along. She protested, but there was no stopping him. He was hurt, but not so much that he could not do this. Adam followed, but Barty paused. He looked back to Braithwaite, as sparks from the damaged machinery cascaded off his kneeling form, holding the broken ballerina that had been his daughter in his arms. "I'm sorry." His voice shook as he spoke. "I'm sorry for all of it."

Lord Braithwaite, as shattered a man as there ever was, gave him a sad smile. "Would that such words mattered, Bartholomew Bartleby," he said in a fading voice. "But I would ask that you remember her." He closed his eyes, and turned away. "Go."

The roof was starting to come apart as Barty ran. He collided with the others in the room where the floor had partly collapsed, and as they reached it, the remainder fell away as well with a crash.

Adam gave no one any time to think or object, as they wrapped their arms around Jean, Elanor, and Barty, and jumped into the room below, smashing a table underneath and protecting all of them from the fall. Barty would have screamed on the way down if he had been able to breathe—Adam's grip was something incredible, like industrial machinery. But they were down, and then they were out, as the tower rumbled, shuddered, and collapsed. They fled together into the night as the storm roared its thunder, merging with the shattering of stone and the imploding fall of the structure.

The world felt like it was ending. And as he remembered a girl of gold, dancing in candlelight for the sheer joy of it, in some ways, Barty felt that it had.

CHAPTER 25

UNDER THE EYES OF RAVENS

B etween the storm, the explosions, the destruction of the tower, and everything else, they had managed to get away with quite a lot—but by the time London's finest had been roused, the Society of the Hound members had long vacated the battlefield. Barty wondered if Creek had once again been woken from his well earned rest, to hand out merry hell to all and sundry.

Barty was exhausted, and with the adrenaline wearing off, he hurt all over. They sat around Puck's coach, watching between the trees amidst the clanging of warning bells and distant, shouting voices. For the moment, the night and forest sheltered them. Enough for Barty to take time, and reflect.

Adam, unhindered by darkness, was carefully tending to Elanor—she had taken some blows in her captivity that had done her no favours. This left Barty and Jean, slumped against a wheel of the coach, staring out into the night.

"We should have been able to save them," Barty said at last, the aching weight of it on his mind demanding he speak. "Both of them." He still remembered how she apologised for causing trouble. He would never forget how it felt for the life of Lily to leave her while she was in his arms. It burned him.

"You cannot save everyone, Bartholomew," Jean said slowly. "It is a... trite thing to say, but it is the truth. There is no justice nor fairness in it. It just is." He sighed, shutting his eyes. "She did deserve better though. Even I cannot argue that."

"And her father? Should we have left him there?" Barty asked, staring at the still smoking ruin in the distance, with lanterns crawling over it like ants.

Jean shrugged. "He had lost his daughter—not once, but twice," he answered at last. "There are no words that can bring a man back from that. He truly had nothing else."

Barty felt uncomfortable at that realisation, glancing to Jean. The man's face was still covered in ashes and bloodied, but his eyes were clear. The painful parallel was there of course, but Barty would not give voice to it. Nevertheless, he was compelled to confess something. "If it had been you, I would not have allowed you to stay."

Jean snorted, then surprisingly, he chuckled softly. "Honestly, I appreciate you saying that. It is... oddly reassuring." He seemed to settle after that, relaxing his shoulders. "You are right. He did some terrible things—but not for the reasons I thought. The man deserved a better fate, perhaps. I am not one to judge—I may in fact be the last man alive who could."

With that he sighed, and reached into his now tattered coat, pulling out the leather-bound journal that had been given to him. "But here we have it, the last piece of the puzzle." He tapped it. "Shelley's last journal." He shook his head in disbelief. "I would wager he had this for some time. There was simply too much preparation. But how did she *know*, is what I wish to understand." He scowled at the book. "Continually many steps ahead of us all."

Jean continued to regard the journal with blatant suspicion as he went on, "There are many terrible secrets in this. We can look at what Braithwaite made and realise that what he said was true—the secrets of consciousness transfer, reanimation, and more. This is a dangerous book, Barty." He weighed it in his hand again.

Barty stared at it with the same suspicion he had given the artillery shell when Adam had been handling it. "What do you plan to do with it?"

Jean considered a moment, then a smile formed. Wordlessly, he held it out to Barty.

"What are you doing?" Barty asked worriedly, recoiling, but Jean chuckled and pressed it against Barty's chest, forcing him to take it.

"What I am doing," he said as he did so, "is giving it to you, for you to make the decision yourself. I am sure you will not disappoint me, however."

Barty was taken aback, holding the book in his hand, staring at it. Carmilla, the woman in red, had held this book. She had placed it in the hands of a man she knew would use it, and then simply waited to see what would happen. How she had known, *what* she had known, was inexplicable. But as he held it, he remembered all the things that he had not yet spoken of. All the moments when things had not made sense. Vague memories of a red-lipped smile, and bright eyes. A beautiful face that knew too much and told too little. Of three months missing that he could not recall. He shivered. This had gone on long enough, and he had said nothing of it. The notion of not confessing further was not something he could endure in that moment. Fear almost held his tongue—but it was having less and less power over him.

"You say that, but I think that..." His voice shook, even as Jean remained silent. "Jean—I think I have met this woman. I believe that she was involved in me finding you, somehow."

He waited for anger. For an outburst. For *something*. He closed his eyes tight, perhaps expecting a blow. When none came, he opened his eyes to see Jean looking at him with an eyebrow raised in perplexity.

"You only just now realised that?" Jean asked slightly incredulously, which, in no uncertain terms, threw Barty sideways somewhat.

"I beg your pardon?" He stuttered as he said it, and he must have looked so utterly taken aback that Jean could not help but laugh, reaching out to gently thump the younger man on the shoulder as he continued to chuckle.

"Oh, Bartleby." His tone was sympathetic through his mirth. "I realised that in the first days when we met. The pieces were there, especially the ones that were not. I have learned to recognise how she works, though I admit this affair with Braithwaite is one I should have seen coming."

"Are you not worried? Concerned?" Barty asked in shock, appalled at this response amidst the surprised gratitude. "We do not know her intentions after all—they are almost certainly nefarious, are they not?"

Jean snorted, shaking his head. "She may well be my enemy, and the enemy of the Society since time immemorial—but I know Carmilla enough to know but one truth. Her motives for anything are entirely inscrutable. I do not know why she sent you to me, any less than I know why she spent years teaching me, either." He watched Barty's face carefully after that confession. "You did not know that, did you?"

Barty slowly shook his head.

Jean nodded, satisfied. "It is a long story. A complicated one, that ended in much being lost. When time allows, I will tell you of it." He winced, then slowly started pushing to his feet. "Not tonight, however. For now, do not let this revelation trouble you, Barty."

"But... but surely...?" Barty could not help but argue, while wondering why the hell he was. The man had just thrown him an utterly unexpected lifeline, after all, but here Barty was determined to hang himself with it.

Jean sighed, reached down, and offered a hand to the stunned young man. Not knowing what else to do, Barty took it and allowed himself to be helped to his feet.

"Right now, it does not matter, Bartholomew Bartleby. Right now all that matters is what I know—you and I work well together. That is enough. It is *more* than enough. At least for now."

Amidst the swirl of thoughts at this, Barty saw Elanor, seated on a log with Adam bandaging their arm, turn her face away. An idea came to him, lancing through his confusion and giving him new purpose as he remembered conversations from ages past.

"Jean, do you remember Lady Beauchamp? From when all this started?"

Jean looked perplexed, but he nodded. "Despite my very

best efforts to forget her toad of a father, I do." He sounded puzzled. "What of it?"

Barty took a deep breath. "Do you think you could find the changeling, Misha? Perhaps... perhaps you might be able to bring the Lady Beauchamp and her beloved some measure of peace. Bring them back together?" He looked from him to Elanor. "You can perhaps make them forgive each other."

Jean looked even more confused, but he followed Barty's gaze. He frowned, turning back. A long pause lingered before he spoke quietly. "We did shatter a father and daughter tonight, Barty. Are you so eager as to ruin another?"

Barty shook his head. "No. Lord Beauchamp did that all on his own. But there is yet a chance for his daughter, Catherine, and that young man." He then nodded to Elanor. "You could both make something wrong, a right. Together."

Elanor was looking over now, her expression indecipherable. Jean was giving Barty a long, thoughtful stare. From the flicker of the smile on his face, Barty knew he understood. The relationship between a noblewoman and her changeling was not the one Barty was making sure would be repaired. Finally Jean nodded. "A little clumsy, Barty. But nevertheless, well played."

He patted Barty on the shoulder and strode away towards Adam and his daughter. Barty let him go, leaning against the carriage with an exhausted sigh. A sound from above made him open his eyes. The grinning visage of Puck was laying on the top of the coach, hands to their cheeks and elbows resting on the edge of the roof in childish wonder. He winked.

Barty tried not to scowl in reply. "Where were you, while

everything was happening? You just... watched?"

"In my defense, I did not do so in solitude," Puck replied with a shrug, the black raven feather that Barty had given for his life in the alleyway appearing out of nowhere in one hand, that now pointed to a nearby tree. "Behold, the heralds of the watchful eye, ever in darkness." There was a sardonic tilt to Puck's words.

Barty peered into the night, to the tree where one branch seemed strangely shaped. As his vision adjusted, he discerned that there were four bird shapes, shifting on the branch, and all of them looked towards him. There was an angry, screeching caw—an accusation if Barty had ever heard one—and all four great ravens flew off in different directions in unison, as though affronted. Esmerelda, apparently, had been present—or at least her agents. He should have guessed as much, but the notion of such a thing being unsurprising was a worry all of itself. He was becoming too used to strange things.

That understanding abruptly reminded him of a girl of brass and porcelain, buried now under the rubble. It made him re-alise that the acceptance was not, in fact, a hindrance at all. But it brought the crushing sorrow back. His eyes still hurt from the tears.

"I am sorry I did not bring her back, Puck," he said quietly, afraid to look at the silver-haired coachman. He wanted to give more explanations, to give reasons. To tell how they had no chance of doing so. It all tasted like ash on his tongue. Puck sighed, and slithered off the roof, landing light as a puff of air beside Barty as he put a spindly arm around his shoulders.

"You are a creature of many truths and many unknowing

falsehoods, Mister Barty," he said, not unkindly. "The truth of your care for that golden-hearted blessing is something I shall remember, when all the other dreams are dust." He sighed, looking up to the clearing sky a moment. His impish features were now muted into softened sorrow, something that, in all the time that Barty had known him, he had never seen upon the Prince of Midsummer.

"She was a precious shattering. The pieces of her were more beautiful than the whole, perhaps—but they deserved to be seen, to be heard. She deserved to finish her dance." The silver eyes narrowed. "I believe that I shall see it done. She was a dream to be remembered."

Barty did not know what that meant. A thrill of something that was not fear passed up his spine. This unexpected moment of sincerity warranted questions, but Barty did not think answers would be forthcoming. He settled on what he felt was, in that moment, the correct response. "... Thank you, Puck."

The silver-haired being turned his head to Barty in surprise as he went on, "I would appreciate that. So would she, I am sure." A slow, astonished blink, and then Puck closed those luminous eyes, extracted himself with delicate care, and bowed low with the grace of an angel. "You continue to astound me, Bartholomew. And I continue to be grateful for it." He straightened, with a genuinely warm expression on his face. "If you will excuse me. I should prepare for us to leave."

It was an excuse, Barty soon saw, for as Puck slipped out of sight behind the coach, he was replaced with Elanor. Her bruised eye already looked better after Adam's care, and she was watching Barty now with a mysteriously speculative expression.

"Adam said you should come over and get tidied up. We'll be going to the Lodge—well, Father and I will be. He said you and Adam are going to the Manor for now?"

This was news to Barty but he nodded. It was easier to go along with the story than try to argue. Awkwardly, he rubbed the back of his head, looking away as Elanor continued to stare at him intently. "Yes. There are a few things to take care of there, so we thought it best." He paused, finally looking at her and meeting her stare. "Will you be all right?"

Her gaze dropped. "I will miss her," she said simply. She absently wiped at her eyes with one bandaged hand. Barty had a sudden, stark, and painful realisation; Lily was not the only one who had been deprived of friends throughout her life. Elanor and her had bonded nearly instantly. He had never stopped to consider why.

"I will as well," he finally responded. "She was a good friend to us both, wasn't she?"

Elanor nodded, taking a deep breath as she looked back to the distant ruin. She sighed then, and without a word stepped close to Barty, wrapped her arms around him, and hugged him so fiercely that he thought his ribs would crack. Before he knew what to make of that, she pushed herself up by the toes and kissed him on the cheek.

He felt a bit dazed. "What... what was that for?"

She gave a soft, sorrowful chuckle, letting him go from her embrace, but taking one of his hands in both of her own. "You earned it, is why." She smiled, and despite her sadness it was warm, the sort of warmth that made his heart skip a beat.

"Thank you, Barty. For everything."

He swallowed to stop the wild fluttering in his chest, and inclined his head. "You are... quite welcome, Elanor Reynard." His voice was thick with an emotion he did not understand. He squeezed her hands, and she did the same before letting him go, climbing into the coach. Barty, still dazed, wandered over to Adam. Both he and Jean were watching him silently.

"Are you all right, Barty?" Adam asked, and all Barty could reply with was a nod.

The battle had mangled Adam's features somewhat, but they had already carried out rudimentary repairs. In hours, they had explained, they would be back to normal. But their expression bore their feelings upon it, and it was a sorrowful one. Jean said nothing though there may have been a faint, rueful smile. He simply nodded, as he made his way to the coach.

Barty became acutely aware of the journal he still held. He tucked it away inside his vest, as Adam began to remove glass shards and splinters from Barty's arms, and delicately made sure none of his injuries were serious.

"What do we do now?" Barty asked as his arm was wrapped in a bandage.

Adam sighed, and shrugged those vast, mighty shoulders, pistons and casings moving with an almost disturbing grace within the exposed flesh and machinery, but by now Barty was well used to it. He would trust Adam with his medical care just as fully as he would trust them with his life. How they looked meant nothing in the face of that.

"We remember her, Barty. From now until the last. We remember her, and what she meant. It is not much. But it will have to be enough."

Barty swallowed. There was such pain in Adam's voice that he felt his throat catch and his eyes start to burn once more. He nodded.

It would be enough. It had to be.

THEY HAD LEFT JEAN and Elanor at the Lodge. The reunion with Benji had been brief but heartfelt. In his spare time, Benji had been working on a new coat for Adam to replace the ruin of the one lost—it was surprisingly well made, the interior lining made from a curtain of all things, woven with patterns of songbirds. Adam's sorrow lifted momentarily at the sight of it.

Barty was tired, worn down, and his already healing cuts and scrapes were itching in a miserable symphony along with the aches of the bruises—but he did not want to stay. As dawn approached, he and Adam made their way to Puck and the coach. The massive form of Adam once more took their spot on the roof, and Barty fell asleep inside. Puck, to their credit, seemed to be considerate enough of their shared grief, and Barty's exhaustion. The stars raced by and the world turned on its heel, as time spun to Puck's impossible will. The velvet black sky turned to grey as they rolled into the driveway of the Manor.

Barty did not remember falling asleep in his bed. He wondered if Adam had carried him there—it would not have surprised him. When he awoke, it was to the cat Daisy nudging at his toes. It was growing dark once again; the day had passed him by, but he was grateful for it. Waking into the Manor had been harder than he expected—an emptiness now hung where there had once been a presence, a voice that had filled the space for a few short weeks, and then gone. The echoes of their words lingered in corners, sang in shadows, and danced amongst the hanging dust.

Somehow, those echoes were worse than the silence. They served as a reminder of all that had been, but could never be again. But Barty remembered well how memories could cut sharper than blades.

He had wandered aimless throughout the Manor. It was quiet. He found Mr and Mrs Cosgrove in the kitchens, both of them subdued. Barty could have sworn he had seen Matilda comforting her husband as he had entered, and he recalled that Cosgrove had immediately seen to Lily's every need when they first met and continued on after. He did not press the matter. He did not speak much at all to them, in fact, feeling uncomfortable about remaining. Mrs Cosgrove's look had been sympathetic towards him, and something about that hurt more than he could bring himself to admit—enough that he had been unable to finish his simple meal before leaving.

It was not long after that he found Adam. They had repaired all the damage done to them and was now standing by one of the fireplaces at the Hall of the Oak. They were patiently and methodically casting each and every book that they had taken from the vault into the flames. It was hard in that moment to tell what they were thinking, as they watched each book burn, one by one, staring at each and making sure it was cinders and ash before moving to the next.

Barty observed but said nothing. At long last, he reached into his coat and pulled out the journal Jean had given him. He had been tempted all the while to read it, but had resisted. However, something now prompted him to check this terrible book.

He found what he was looking for on the inside of the cover. The caligraphy was immaculate, closer to artistry than mere penwork, an immortal's handwriting perfected over a length of time unknowable. He shivered as he read to himself.

To my fated and fondest foe, Barty began, continuing in his private silence.

You have found this, as I knew you would. I commend you for your diligence, but you ever play as I expect you to, and as I taught you. Perform the parts I set for you, my dearest. Through your torment I shall ever forge you, until you are moulded into something suitable for my purposes. Know that I am proud of you, but will be prouder still when you at last see the pattern. At least I know you are drawing closer. Your destiny is yet within your reach.

Lord Braithwaite is a man you should see enough of yourself in, if not at this point then as his story and yours converges. I would advise that you could consider him a warning, but I would wager you have already figured that by now. He is walking the same road you have already tread, after all.

By now, you should be well acquainted with one

Bartholomew Bartleby. Adorable little thing, is he not? Barty felt mildly offended at this, yet he persevered. *However, he is someone you can trust, and count upon. He is like you more than you know, except more insightful. He lacks experience, but that will change. He is the chance for you to rectify your mistakes, the one opportunity you have to walk a different road. It is the only help I shall give you, moving forward—I felt it necessary to rebalance the field. There is no sport in our contest, unless you are at your best.*

We shall meet again soon. When you have failed to kill me again, we shall talk, I am sure. I do like to hear your stories.

Carmilla.

That was not all. Beneath the exquisite signature was an addendum.

In addition, while this journal describes abominations that are without question, there is a note at the finale which you may well find fruitful. As for the rest, do with it as you will. I wonder what you will choose. Take care, my darling. We shall be together again soon.

Barty shuddered. The message was oddly intimate, as though between friends—or lovers. There was something familiar in the cadence as well, the manner of speaking—it was strange that he could imagine her voice aloud in his ear as he read it. The implication made his stomach churn. Shivering, he turned pages rapidly, flicking through the notes and understanding none of it. He did not want to. He knew what the many equations, words, designs, and other arcane symbols were for. He wanted no part of them.

He found what he was looking for in the last pages.

A little while later he came alongside Adam, who had by this point little left to burn. Barty touched them gently on the arm, but it took the giant a moment to respond—they were seemingly lost in thought. Eventually they turned, looking with a blank expression at the book that Barty held. They frowned then, staring down at it.

"Jean gave it to you?" they finally asked, and Barty nodded, holding it out to Adam.

"He did. And I am giving it to you."

Adam was very still, then quietly reached down to take the journal, holding it in one vast hand. Their frown deepened. "You know what is in here, do you not, Barty?" Half obscured by their falling hair, Adam's face turned back to Barty, their eyes frightening for a moment. "With this, I could transfer my consciousness from this form of mine to another body—a human body."

"And all it would cost is the life and mind of the one whom you supplanted," Barty replied as he gave a shrug. They exchanged a long look, but it was Adam who looked away first. "Before you make any decision on the matter, I would ask that you read the last page." Barty's voice was quiet, and kind. "And if it is not too much to ask, I would have you read it aloud."

Adam frowned, searching Barty's face for an answer. But they finally relented, and nodded. With those enormous, mechanised fingers, they turned to the last page. Their eyes scanned the words, and then closed as a sigh escaped them. After a long, tenuous pause, Adam began to speak.

"'In these pages, I have created all my regrets,'" Adam recited slowly. "'I have crafted things that should not be, the means for life to exist beyond what life begets us. It is a terrible mistake, and it is my final test.

"'But the first mistake was one I never intended; the beautiful, blessed mistake. Adam, my darling Adam, was never supposed to come to pass—not as they did, not as I intended. I crafted them from my own flesh, my own unborn, and created a new and impossible life. The perfect mistake, as all life is at its origin—my perfect mistake. My child.

"'Shame for the life that I have inflicted upon Adam has stayed my tongue, and now that shame is compounded upon itself, halting me from my confession, and thus I cast it here. I am so very proud of them. They were my unintended child, the result of science wrought in grief and numbed to its cost to both myself and them. But I hope they understand. I hope they realise that they are loved, that they are blessed with a life as real as that of any other, regardless of how it came to pass. I hope they come to forgive me, for how I failed them. I do not deserve it, as I do not deserve their gentle affections.

"'I am the proudest mother that ever was. If ever you read this, Adam, know this. I love you. I always will. And you shall be loved as you deserved—with all the heart to be given to you, and with all the heart you have to give.

"'Mary W. Shelley.'"

Adam's voice was ragged as they finished. Barty remained silent throughout, watching as the giant gently touched the page, then carefully closed the journal. A moment passed, and then with a gentle toss, that last journal was cast into the flames. The edges blackened, ignited, and it, too, was consumed.

"You knew that I would," Adam said heavily.

"Not entirely. But I had hope. Or faith. Whatever you want to call it, Adam. If it is a choice to believe in you—I always shall." Barty glanced up at Adam, as the journal and all its secret, terrible knowledge was burned away forever. "How do you feel?"

Adam considered, rubbing their jaw as they frowned. Finally they nodded, as though reaching a final conclusion. "Better than I would have expected. It is as I told you, Bartholomew Bartleby—we are the ones who choose our regrets." They stared down at the burning journal. "This shall not be one of them."

Barty said nothing. It was one of those occasions when there were no words to say. Just the silence between friends, and in that moment, there was acceptance amidst the regret, recognition in all that sorrow.

Though the Manor was more empty than it had been, there were more than memories that remained, more than mere echoes; there was a family found, with all its flaws and strangeness, all of its oddities and differing means of expression. But above all else there was acceptance, and that was what made it a family at all.

◆━◇━◆

It did not take many days for Jean and Elanor to return. They had not said much of what happened, but they did not need to. Elanor had been beaming, her eyes lined with silver tears as she walked into the Manor, giving Adam a fierce and joyful hug. Jean looked in a better mood as well. Catherine and Misha had found each other again, and with Jean and Elanor's help, were now in a place her wretched father would never find them. It was a healed wound for not just them, but the attitude around the Manor remained subdued.

Barty was in his room when he heard the scratching at his door. The moon was full outside his window, the night one of those comfortable evenings, sharp and clear, the cold a refreshing sort. Midnight was closing in with each solemn tick of the clock, but Barty was not asleep. He was working by candlelight on a broken music box to keep himself occupied—at least, until the scratching came.

The black and white spectre of Daisy sat on her haunches, looking up at him with her head tilted, her tail swishing against the ground. She had taken to coming to his room to sleep, something he had found curious—she had chosen him out of everyone present in the household. But this time she was not entering. She simply swished her tail as though waiting.

At first, he engaged in the ever futile effort of persuading a cat of doing anything, especially what is in their best interests, an activity that went on for an interminable length of time before he relented. The cat turned and walked down the hall. Barty stepped out of the room—he was not sure why, but it soon became clear she was trying to get him to follow her, by the way she would stop and wait for him each time he halted.

It was a wild and strange thing. But this was the Manor, under a full moon, and between all the silent echoes in the corners it was a night of strangeness and muted wonder. He gave in.

They were waiting for him outside. Daisy led him to the lakeshore, hopped into Adam's lap, and curled up. They simply nodded to Barty, as Elanor and Jean sat to one side. They did not say anything. Words did not seem necessary, as the full moon waxed overhead, setting the lake to white fire, the constellations still and yearning across that silent surface. There was no wind. There seemed an absence of sound. Barty opened his mouth to speak though it seemed a blasphemy, but Elanor, her eyes gleaming and wet, caught his eye and shook her head. Silently, she pointed across the lake.

Puck stood in majesty upon the water. It barely rippled under his feet, which were bare, as was his chest, his silver hair streaming down to near his ankles, flying and wild and free. He had a set of pan pipes at his lips, and he spun upon the surface of the water as he began to play. The water remained perfectly unblemished as he pirouetted across its surface, the song growing louder. Other instruments joined in, from out of stillness and shadows. The forest came alive with a symphony of the unknown, its eyes no longer watchful. Now, they were here, amongst them, with them. And ever, Puck continued to dance, and sing.

But this was not for Puck. No, this was an introduction. The air turned to glass and silver, moonbeams shone and flickered, alive and blazing, as she appeared. No longer wrought of metal, no longer that sculpted form, but as she had been—and though none had ever seen her living, they all knew her instantly. She was but smoke and light, shining bright and alive, distant and yet near. Her hair was unbound, her dress woven from stars. Her eyes were open, and warm, her smile full of the tears only truest joy could bring. She walked across the surface of the lake as Puck spun and bowed, introducing her as a queen to the world that she had left behind.

Lily curtseyed to Jean, in respect and deference. To Elanor, she gave a phantom embrace as her friend wept and laughed in silence. For Adam, there was apology, acceptance, and love that would last until there was nothing else in the world. And then it was his turn; she touched Barty's cheek. He could feel it like one could feel a memory, a moment in a dream, and it had the warmth of remembered sunlight. She smiled, and her endless gaze, her shining eyes held him for a heartbeat—there was no more mystery in them now, and the love she bore was laid bare with nothing to hide it. She kissed his brow, as though to seal those memories forever. Her thanks to him lingered in the silence of his soul, as she turned back to the water and as he blinked away tears. Under star and moon she began to dance.

It was wild, and free; there was a beauty in its passion, a power that was life itself. She danced as her heart bade, her love driving her, and the stars themselves bent towards her. The world rose up from its endless slumber to gaze upon her. This moment was all there ever was. It was everything. In this moment, all eyes through time observed Lily perform. She was the dancer, the stage, and the universe, all at once. Barty watched, understanding that this event would live on long after he was gone.

The dance continued. Barty knew that it could not last. That the sun would rise and gently bring this music to its conclusion. He knew that morning would end it, and that the world would spin once more, and he, alongside this new family he had made, would turn with it.

But that morning was an eternity away. And this moment was forever.

Acknowledgements

This was a difficult one to write in many respects. I wouldn't have managed it without the team I got to work with throughout – starting of course with Renee, who gave me the opportunity, and the advice, as well as giving me one of the better twists of the story – not to mention the staggering amount of work, organisation, planning, funding, and more besides to make this happen. She's incredible, even if she's terrible at taking praise that doesn't make it any less true. This is, as ever, as much her book as it is mine. It wouldn't exist without her.

For Paris, my editor, who is nothing short of a powerhouse at this sort of thing. Under her careful eye, my lingering word repetitions were banished to the world beyond. Believe me, you have no idea how lucky we are to have her. If you had to read as many uses of 'upon' as I had the misfortune to make, you would want to strangle me. She works harder than you can imagine. The work is all the better for her diligence.

Dayna once more created an absolutely perfect cover for this one, with Lily taking the centre stage just as she should – Dayna knocked this one out of the park, in my opinion. And not just her, but also Reordan, our artist, once more came through with his creations for the tarot cards and more besides. Seeing these characters come to life is something deeply, overwhelmingly satisfying to see. I am chomping at the bit to see where else this goes.

Beyond the team, we have a lot of names to go through. Jess and Nova, for the Celestial Events Ball and their amazing encouragement. Glenn and Chris, Daniel and Ronald, for being the friends I need to get in my ear, and when I cannot do it alone, they're able to give me the support I need. Jay and Dale, for keeping me laughing and groaning in equal measure. There are a *lot* more of you I know only from your online handles; you know who you are, but some in particular truly stand out. I borrowed eyes from you on more than one occasion to see things differently – I am forever grateful that you gave me that opportunity. I needed it.

To my family; my uncle Peter, for giving me the stability I need to get this work done, to get these words down, and his family, whose support I will never feel I deserve and I will never be able to repay. To my mother, who does her best even when it is harder than it should be. But above all to my grandfather. Ronald 'Blue' Belsham. I know you cannot read this anymore. But everyone who reads this will know your name, as well they should – you are a legend that should never go untold.

And to you, those who have shown your support, who have bought this book and are reading these words; I see you. I hope this made you feel something. I hope it made you smile. If it made you cry, forgive me; but if such sorrow is the price of meaning, then understand it was, to me at least, well spent. And I am grateful for it.

Onwards and upwards. We'll see you at the next one.

www.ingramcontent.com/pod-product-compliance
Lightning Source LLC
Chambersburg PA
CBHW050944210726
48287CB00004B/1123